Book of Conspiracies

by
Kamalakar Gulukota

To: *My darling wife and
Our beloved son.*

*Without loving encouragement
from both of you,
Writing this book would not have been
A hundredth as much fun.*

Story of the Story - 1

The most vexing project of my life began fifteen years ago with a very relaxing vacation.

It was the Spring of 2007. My wife, our then eight year old son and I, were driving back to our home in Hamilton, New Jersey after a week of fresh air and fun in Acadia National Park, Maine.

A major thunderstorm forced us to get off the highway and seek refuge for the night at a delightful little sea-side hotel in Southern Maine. We did avoid the adventure of driving through a thunderstorm but little did we know that we were signing up for an entirely different kind of adventure.

Having no other plans on this unscheduled stop, we sauntered over to the atrium of the hotel where we picked up a brochure stating that an auction of "the Badrawi art collection" was happening in the conference room.

One item mentioned in the brochure caught our eye. It was a suitcase-sized box made of "hardwood from Deodar cedar" with "the most intricate designs carved into it". The brochure described the artistic style as one "known to have been prevalent thousands of years ago around present day city of Peshawar in Pakistan". Almost as an after-thought, the description also contained one throw-away sentence that the box contained some "ancient leaves with writing in an unknown script".

Our interest was piqued but we had no idea how to participate. An African American woman rolled over to us in a wheelchair.

"May I help you?" she asked while handing over a business card which said Vanessa "DubDee" Williamson, Auction Manager.

"Ms. Williamson" I began pointing to the item on the brochure.

"Please call me DubDee" she said.

"OK, DubDee", I said hesitantly. "What is this about these leaves in this box?"

"Oh those" she replied. "Yeah, it is very neat. The box has dried leaves, or little planks of bark, tied into

bundles like volumes of a book. Each leaf has markings on it and Mr Badrawi says it is actual writing in some ancient script".

"Really?", my wife said. "It is an actual manuscript? A book, but in a script that no one can read?!".

"Sure is!" DubDee replied. "Mr. Jay Badrawi – that is that one in the blue blazer over there – he is selling this whole collection to raise money for his ancestral community in Afghanistan. The details are in the brochure. Jay hopes the box will fetch several thousand dollars".

Well, there was no way we could spend even a single thousand on this – let alone multiple thousands. Yet, I persisted:

"Wait. The box will fetch? But what about the book?"

"You mean those leaves? I am not sure – we don't expect those to fetch much".

"So, can we bid on just the book?"

"Gee! I don't know. I don't think so".

"DubDee!" someone called out from the other end of the atrium and she raised her hand to acknowledge. As she rolled away, she told us:

"If you are at all interested, you better go in the conference room now. That item will be coming up shortly".

Ж

Just like in the brochure, the auctioneer's description was all about the box. He described its artistic style and mentioned that it was made of hardwood from deodar cedar, an evergreen coniferous tree native to the Himalayas which provides a particularly durable kind of timber. He mentioned the book, took it out of the box and carefully set it to one side of the box.

We joined other auction goers examining the item from up close. We were thrilled to see ancient leaves tied into neat bundles. On these leaves writing was done by tearing the letters into the leaf with a sharp writing tool. Before paper came into common use, this was how writing was done in India and the rest of South Asia.

The writing itself was in a script I could not recognize. It did bear some vague similarity to the writings on ancient

6

tablets from the Indus Valley Civilization. But, even if it was that script, it would be undecipherable; that script is still a mystery for scholars after decades of research.

My wife is a sucker for books of all kinds. And this being an ancient, never-been-printed book, she wanted it badly. I was hooked too. So, we decided to bid up to three hundred dollars as we walked back our seats.

Our pitiful plan was blown away within minutes. We managed to timidly start the bidding at thirty dollars. But within a minute, before we could even understand what was going on, it had gone beyond a thousand. We were left dumb-founded and watched open-mouthed as the price kept climbing. When it went over three thousand, we gave up and quietly left the conference room, disappointed.

Ж

Next morning, the weather had cleared. We loaded up our car and were ready to leave, when my cell phone rang. It was DubDee. She asked, if we could stop by her office. We were in a rush to leave, but since she mentioned it was about the book, we went up to her office.

"I have some good News", she announced. "The box was purchased by Scythe Furniture. It is a local company that wants to make a line of jewelry boxes based on the ancient design. They bid $7,350 for it".

"Wow!" I said, "Good for you!"

"Thanks. Well, I asked Scythe's purchasing manager what they plan to do with the book and he said they would probably just toss it. Jay, er.. Mr Badrawi, was so incensed by that disrespectful attitude, he almost canceled the sale. I remembered your interest in the book and thought perhaps I could salvage the deal if I could get you to buy the book and I can still sell the box to Scythe".

"Great", I said, "We would be delighted to buy just the book".

"After the Scythe experience, Mr Badrawi wants me to ask: What do you intend to do with it?"

"For sure, we would never toss it!" my wife said. "It would have a place of respect among our most prized possessions".

"Good to hear. I am authorized to offer it to you for

7

three thousand".

"What?" I sputtered. "Three thousand?! I am sorry, that is way out of our league".

"But you started bidding – even though I mentioned we expected it to go for multiple thousands".

"Yeah" my wife replied with naive honesty. "But, we decided to bid up to three hundred – no more".

"Hmm", DubDee replied. "See, for this sale to work, we have to convince Mr Badrawi of what you said: that you will treat this book with respect. And the only way he can think of is by how much you pay".

"Come on!" I protested. "Price is the only way to measure respect? Really?!"

"Mr Badrawi's great grandfather emigrated to the United States in 1903" DubDee explained. She was clearly stalling for time, trying to figure out how to proceed. "Back in Afghanistan, their community were the keepers of this sacred old book which tells the story of how that region came to be a nation five thousand years ago. The community converted to Shia Islam long ago, but still consider this pre-islamic book to be sacred".

"So, why doesn't Mr Badrawi just keep the book? Why sell it?"

"Because, last month he revealed that he has advanced stage lung cancer. He does not have much longer to live".

"Oh. We are sorry to hear that" my wife and I said almost in unison.

"Yeah", DubDee continued. "Mr Badrawi has been a pillar of our community here in Maine. He is a great lawyer and most everyone in town has sought his help at one time or another. He lost his wife nearly thirty years ago in a traffic accident. He never remarried and has no heirs. He is worried about this art collection but most especially this book. He wants to ensure it lives past him".

"I can understand that", I replied. "But still, there is no way we could spend three thousand dollars on it".

I could sense that my wife, ever a sucker for books, was almost ready to cave in and suggest that we somehow scrape the three thousand together. I wanted to forestall that and also was really peeved at the principle that money was the best way to measure respect. By that token, the rich would always be more respectful because they buy expensive stuff. I stood firm on the price, and so it was a standoff.

"I even called a prominent museum this morning", DubDee was still casting about for a resolution. "I thought I could donate it to them, but they declined. The director dismissed it saying there was no way to establish the authenticity of non-European artifacts that are in private collections. And he asked me, since it couldn't possibly have anything to do with Negro history, why I was so interested in it?".

"Sheesh! What a jerk!"

"Yeah well, screw him!" DubDee dismissively waved her arm. "He soured me on all museums".

DubDee probably saw that three thousand dollars was simply too much for us even though the interest in our eyes was clear. So, she caved-in by offering us a steal of a bargain.

"You are nice folks. Especially this cutie pie!", she squeezed my son's cheeks. "And you look like you are from that region of the world".

"No", I said, "We are originally from India, not Afghanistan".

"Close enough", she waved dismissively again. "Tell you what. If you promise that you will make an effort to translate the book, you can have it for what you bid: thirty dollars".

I was shocked into silence.

"Do you want it?" she asked in a tantalizing voice.

"There is no way I can promise to translate it. I don't know how to even ... ".

"No, No", DubDee interrupted. "I just want you to promise that you will try. You said price is not the only way to prove respect and I agree. Your promise to try, would prove to Mr Badrawi that you will treat the book with respect".

Ж

That is how I got an ancient book in exchange for the bargain basement price of thirty dollars and a promise to make a good-faith attempt at translating it.

I did not realize it then, but that promise was so extravagant that it would turn the steal of a bargain into a great swindle. Because in the end, fulfilling that promise to DubDee and Badrawi would end up costing me my spare time through fifteen years, three job changes and six address changes. And the job is still not done.

Ж

I got myself a giant magnifying glass and tried to pour over every leaf. I read up about how scholars go about deciphering scripts and tried to apply the usual strategies. I made a list of all glyphs on all the pages and tried to identify repetitive words. I noticed one recurring glyph that looked vaguely Chinese. Upon further checking, it looked like a combination of the characters in the Mandarin word Laoshi or "teacher". But this didn't help with anything on the rest.

I tried to see if the most common glyphs looked similar to any known language. They were not in any script of the ancient world I could look up. I specifically tried to compare it to symbols of the ancient, undecipherable script of Indus Valley Civilization; despite some similarities, this was substantially different.

All these were fun exercises in identifying some patterns but did not provide any meaningful progress toward translating the book.

I was stuck. After about two years of this lack of progress, I was ready to give up.

Ж

Spring cleaning time! My wife found the brochure of the Badrawi auction from years ago and suggested that perhaps that community in Afghanistan might have someone who knew the script. The brochure contained the contact details for the patriarch of their community in Herat, one Haji Pir-Basha. Fearing another dead-end but hoping for the best, I placed a phone call.

On a scratchy line the Haji spoke to me in surprisingly good, if heavily accented, English. He vaguely knew the story and summarized it: in the first book, three large, failed conspiracies awakened the people and resulted in a fourth conspiracy that steered them toward a better future. In the second book, a large empire grew from the nation in multiple waves of consolidation.

He knew some of the details but not the whole story and definitely could not help me with reading the symbols on the leaves; they were nothing more than meaningless scratches, even to him.

"Haji sahab", I asked desperately. "Is there anything else you can tell me?"

"Well, I don't know if it is really true" the Haji said "but my grandfather told me that when the Badrawis left for America, a hundred years ago, he was the one that helped them pack the book into a Deodar box".

"OK", I was not sure how this would help.

"It seems during the packing, the top leaf fell out and was left behind."

Great! Now the book was not even complete!

"I don't have that leaf", the Haji added hastily. "It is lost. But I know what it said, because my grandfather told me".

"Wait!" I was instantly skeptical. "You mean your grandfather could read this ancient script?"

"No", the Haji laughed. "Not anything in the rest of the book. But that first leaf was written in Devanagari script and the language was Farsi, or what we today call Dari in Afghanistan. I remember my grandfather joking that this may be the only instance of Farsi being written in Devanagari. Actually, I think he was wrong. There might be other ...".

"So", I interrupted because the Haji was rambling. "What did that lost leaf say? Did it give clues to the unknown script".

"Well, may be", the Haji replied. "It told the story of Bada Ravi, who was a poet and a scholar a thousand years ago. It is said that he was the court poet of king Mihira Bhoja. He is considered one of the fore-fathers of our community and, to this day, we reverently invoke his name as a great and witty poet. His writings have mostly not

survived but he was such a polyglot that he wrote nearly a hundred books – each in a different language. These included plays, poems and philosophical treatises. He was the best ... ".

"So", I interrupted the rambling again. "Did Bada Ravi write something on the lost leaf that could help translate this book".

"Yes. He claimed that he was the one that transcribed this copy from an older version. And he mentioned that he included clues: translations of passages of the book into a newer language. He told his reader: 'Every script is a puzzle. But if you solve my clues thou shalt unravel this whole book'. Now, before you ask: I don't know where he wrote those clues, what they are and how to find them. But they are there!"

"So, it said that this book is written in some sort of a code. Not in any known script".

"No. That's not it. The saying 'Every script is a puzzle' is an aphorism ascribed to Bada Ravi. I think he was saying that even if the reader is unfamiliar with this script, the clues will help unravel the book".

After I thanked the Haji and hung up, I was feeling encouraged that perhaps there was a way. If Bada Ravi left clues in some other script perhaps they can be identified by simply being different. It was like trying to play 'pick the one that is unlike others'.

The first real breakthrough came a few weeks after that phone call on a visit to India. My son planned an expedition to the Kalinga Edicts in Dhauli in the state of Odisha. We saw the rock edicts of Mauryan Emperor Asoka who ruled much of South Asia in the 3rd century BC. The edicts were written in Brahmi script. When I saw them, I got excited because I remembered some rare glyphs in the book which looked similar to the Brahmi symbols in the edicts.

I bought a book on the Brahmi script and started pouring through the leaves again with my magnifying glass.

Most of the book was definitely not in Brahmi script but some scattered passages were. Thinking back to what the Haji said, I wondered if these were Bada Ravi's clues in a modern language. If so, this was huge!

When I painstakingly deciphered the first Brahmi passage, you can imagine my excitement when I realized that the language was actually Telugu, my mother tongue!

I called the Haji back and explained to him what I found. He told me what that remarkable coincidence meant.

"You are the one! Bada Ravi is speaking to you through the centuries in you own mother tongue. You are meant to translate this".

Religious people have strange ways of jumping to conclusions.

Telugu language was formalized in about the eleventh century by which time, Brahmi script was more than a thousand years out of vogue. So, this may be the only instance of Telugu being written in Brahmi script.

Mihira Bhoja, Bada Ravi's patron, belonged to the Gurjara-Pratihara lineage and ruled a large territory in North India extending as far west as the Sutlej river and as far east as Bengal. If Bada Ravi was in fact associated with this lineage, that would place him somewhere from ninth to eleventh century. By then, Brahmi script was ancient and long forgotten. So, it was plausible that a scholar and polyglot like Bada Ravi might have designed the clue in Telugu using the ancient Brahmi script – which was dead and therefore stable - to help his readers decipher the book.

"Thank you Bada Ravi!!" I triumphantly said to Bada Ravi in my mind.

Not only did Bada Ravi's Telugu verse make sense, but it also fit into proper poetic meters of Classical Telugu. I admit that I had to relearn my high school lessons in Telugu Poetics but they did fit into meters called Seesam, Aata Veladi and Theta Geeti.

While such clues from Bada Ravi were scattered through the book they formed only a small portion of the text. So, the job was hardly done.

With a jittery faith, I compared Bada Ravi's first clue to the passage just above it. True to the promise, there was a character key in Brahmi, explaining the main script of the book. That character key clicked into the rest of the book and allowed me to unlock how to sound out the words. But *the language was still unknown to me.*

It appeared that the dominant language of the book was Persian but it was mixed in with another language. Further investigation indicated that the other language might be Brahui – the only language in present day Pakistan that is in the Dravidian class of languages. I knew neither Brahui nor Persian, but these languages were alive today and I could pursue a translation.

Ж

I painstakingly started going through the leaves, with Bada Ravi's character map and dictionaries of Brahui and Persian.

What follows is my translation of this ancient book to English. In honor of the huge debt I owe to Bada Ravi's clues, I have included his original Telugu verse (but using modern Telugu script) at the appropriate places in the story. For those of you who cannot read Telugu, I have also included a phonetic rendition of the same using the English alphabet, along with the meaning of the verses.

Would my translation be accurate? Who knows? Per the Haji's story, Bada Ravi wrote these poems. And just as he promised, they did in fact provide a key to translate the rest of the book. With a great deal more faith than was justified by that thin reed of tenuous rationalization, I started translating.

14

The First Conspiracy

Summer of 3658 BC

Somewhere near present day
Herat Province of Afghanistan

1. Sadanil Suthil

"Sadanil suthil" Jenon chuckled.

"What?" blurted Vika.

"It's an old Ivchean saying," explained Jenon, with a smile on his face. "'Sadanil suthil' means 'Every time, it's the rope'".

"What does that even mean?" Vika hissed, confused beyond measure, "I am saying that we cannot successfully execute our plan without a rope. And all you can say is", doing his best to mockingly imitate Jenon's voice, he repeated, "It's always the rope'"

Jenon and Vika were waiting in the maid's alcove adjacent to the bedchamber of King Yuda of Kunduj. Yuda was due to come into his chamber within the next hour. Their job was to kidnap Yuda and take him back to their own King Mayun.

Vika, in his mid thirties, called himself simply a message carrier. But he was the greatest message carrier there ever was. Legend had it that he could carry a message sixty kos within one day. Asked how he does it, he would just smile and mumble something about the secrets of his trade.

Jenon was in his early twenties - more than ten years junior to Vika. He was a cunning warrior and sneaky as a snake.

Both had undying devotion to King Mayun of Khet. When it was learned that Yuda was about to invade their tiny kingdom, King Mayun had approved a mission to kidnap Yuda and asked Jenon to lead it. Jenon had not selected any fellow warriors to accompany him. Instead he chose Vika, the Great Message Carrier.

Jenon and Vika planned the mission together and thought they had everything needed. Including notably, a long coil of rope. But getting into the palace and near Yuda's bedchamber was much more difficult than anticipated. In the process of entering the castle unseen by guards, they had to lose their accoutrements. When they finally made it to Yuda's bedchamber they were completely empty handed.

Vika wondered if all their hard work in getting here was in vain because they didn't have the rope. Nor were they able to smuggle a weapon into the castle. Without a weapon, even both of them together were probably not strong enough to subdue the vigorous Yuda. And even if they did somehow manage to subdue him, they would make enough noise to wake everyone but the dead.

"And then, it would then be our turn", Vika thought with humorless bitterness, "to get subdued by the guards".

The only point in their favor was Osilla, the muskroot drug, of which Jenon carried three doses in a tiny pouch. If they could get Yuda to drink it, he would be rendered somnolent. But every possible way of carrying Yuda out of the castle needed a rope. If only they could find some other way to tie up Yuda.

If only they didn't have to throw away the rope.

If only the passage-way was less guarded.

If only the guards slept more soundly.

If only.

Vika mused about the rope. Such a mundane thing and yet such a critical part of the plan. How in Ag's name were they now going to complete the mission? Jenon's nonchalance in the face of this insurmountable problem was irking Vika tremendously.

"What does that saying even mean?"

"Well," Jenon explained in an irritatingly pedantic voice, "it comes from old ship builders. When they want to build a big ship, they never forget the big things: the master ship builder, the lumber or the elephants to move the lumber. It's always the "small" things they forget. 'Sadanil suthil' - 'Its always the rope'. If you don't have the rope to tie the planks together, you have no ship - even if you have the best lumber, the kindest elephants and the most skilled shipbuilder. The proverb cautions you that small, mundane things are just as important as the big ones."

"Nice explanation, my master" Vika retorted sarcastically "So, now we are not just screwed. We are proverbially screwed! What are we going to do? How are we going to drag Yuda out of here?" After a little pause, watching Jenon's smile, he added angrily, "It's not funny!"

Enjoying getting Vika riled up, Jenon replied with an

imperturbable smile "Come on! You have to admit, it's a little funny. The proverb speaks about the rope metaphorically - to represent the small things that people tend to forget. And in our case, it's an actual rope."

"Yes. It's very funny." Vika said, rolling his eyes, "When we go back to King Mayun without Yuda - if we ever go back in one piece - why don't you tell him your ship-building story. I am sure he will find it very funny and give us ten sheep each for creativity. He probably won't even care that Yuda is going to crush his army and occupy his kingdom. I've known him a while - he has a great sense of humor".

"I agree that he has a great sense of humor" said Jenon, playfully adding annoyance to aggravation, "That's why, he sent along an old worry wart like you on this mission. Though he put the younger and more accomplished one - me - in charge of it".

"Why in Ag's name am I paired up with an infantile ruffian?" Vika gesticulated skyward. Then he took a couple of deep breaths and asked in a more calm voice "Can't you be serious for just a few minutes? What do we do?"

"Vika, my friend" Jenon said placatingly, "don't be cross. Our situation is not as dire as you fear. In fact, funnily enough, we are saved by the counter-proverb: Sadaril suthil: 'every place there is a rope'"

"What's a counter-proverb?" asked Vika, the non-linguist.

"A counter proverb is one that ...".

"Never mind! Just tell me how it's relevant"

"... states the opposite of another well-known proverb" Jenon ignored the interruption. "For example, they say *Heed the wisdom of the old* but they also say *God speaks through babes' mouths*. Those two are counter proverbs to each other."

"So, how does this counter-proverb 'sudurril suthil' save us?" asked Vika, his strong Khet accent mangling it.

"'Sadaril suthil' means everyplace there is a rope", elaborated Jenon "Therefore if you forget the rope, don't fret. Just use the one that's handy."

Jenon dramatically pulled the sheepskin cover off the

maid's bed revealing a network of ropes tied tightly against the posts of the bed. Yuda's maid slept on a small four post bed made comfortably springy by a network of ropes held taut by the posts. "We will use the ropes from here", Jenon added unnecessarily.

"Why couldn't you just say that in the first place?" pouted Vika.

"What would be the fun of that?"

Both men got to work cutting the net to form a long enough strings of rope. Vika's confidence in their plan was returning.

It was almost easy now. King Yuda should be arriving soon. They would add Osilla to Yuda's night drink of Soma. After he slips into slumber - made deeper by the drug - they would roll him up in the deerskin mattress on his bed. Then they would tie it up with the rope and simply carry him out of the castle as if they are taking laundry out for cleaning. By the time the guards find Yuda missing, it would be morning. They would have long left the borders of Kunduj and with any luck be almost at Khet. Their King Mayun would be well on his way to crushing the arrogant Kunduj.

"My only regret" Vika said cheerfully "is that in taking Yuda to Khet, I would have to reveal to you - the king of adolescent morons - some of my trade secrets, like how I carry messages so fast".

"Hey, watch your tongue! My people prefer to be called blockhead babies!"

They both burst out laughing but quickly suppressed it to maintain silence.

Vika was quite confident now. Based on information they had collected during their surveillance, he knew Yuda would come in accompanied by a couple of his Ministers or Generals. He would have a brief meeting and dismiss them. Then he would ring his bell for his nightly Soma, drink it and go to sleep.

Vika also knew that the maid was expected to keep quiet through the serving of Som. That silence suited their nefarious plan perfectly; if they had to speak for the maid, Vika was sure they would be caught.

The anticipation of success gave Vika a delicious thrill.

It will be wonderful, if they successfully pulled off the kidnapping. It would avoid a bloody war. It would ensure that King Mayun would remain safe and independent on his throne. And it would prove once and for all that size of the army was not the sole determinant of victory in a conflict.

So what if Yuda had an army ten times bigger than Mayun's? He would still lose. Poets of future generations would sing about how a small kingdom called Khet defeated the much more powerful Kunduj without shooting a single arrow. About how they used just the proverbial rope. It would be marvelous indeed!

"This is going to be wonderful!", he exulted to Jenon, "King Mayun would be pleased with us. Khet has as good as won this war before the first war cry is uttered. It will be a historic ..."

Jenon smiled and interrupted, "Not yet, my friend. We will share that sentiment and celebrate once we get to Khet. I am glad you feel the confidence. But remember: battle plans become irrelevant as soon as you need to execute them".

"Is that another Ivchean proverb?" Vika asked repeating in an imitation of Jenon's voice "battle plans become irrelevant as soon as you need to execute them."

"No, it's a saying in your own language. In Crit. I learned it from King Mayun's Minister Byram. We will have to think on our feet and improvise constantly against all the unforeseen contingencies."

"What contingencies?" demanded Vika, "I don't see any holes in the rest of our plan."

Jenon smiled. "If we saw them they wouldn't be unforeseen, would they? But let me try to enumerate: What if our information is false? What if today Yuda brings a woman here to sleep with? What if our Osilla has no effect on him? What if he is too heavy for us to carry? What if we are blocked on our way out? What if ..."

"Are you trying to scare me?"

"No. Just trying to ensure that you don't name your son before you get a wife".

"Lovely - your Ivchean sayings are ..." muttered Vika and instantly fell silent. The muffled voices of Yuda talking to two of his senior Generals wafted up the stairs.

It was a crisp New Moon night - dark as mascara. The gentle breeze flowing in through the open window was like a cool balm after a hot day. Yuda's bed chamber was at the top of the castle. Five fully grown men could stand - one on top of another - and just barely reach the window sill. The height strengthened the breeze making it more pleasant than at the ground level. The window also overlooked the narrow lanes of Kunduj. Vika and Jenon could see flickering oil lamps in front of most houses and could hear the muffled voices of people getting ready to retire for the night. An occasional firefly added luster to the gloom of the pitch dark night.

Ever the contingency planner, Jenon wondered if they would need to use the window as their exit. How would they descend from this height carrying a heavy load like Yuda's unconscious body? And Kunduj was colossal compared to Khet. Fully ten thousand people lived here in houses built right next to each other. The paths between the houses were so narrow, a grown man could not lie across on them without folding his feet. So, would it look suspicious in these narrow lanes to see two men carrying a heavy load of what looks like laundry? Jenon just hoped that, at this hour of the night, most people would be too asleep to notice.

Maid's alcove was directly abutting off of Yuda's bedchamber. Jenon quickly peeped to take a look and ensure that everything was in order for Yuda's arrival. He did not want the king getting angry at his maid as soon as he came in. It would not do at all for them to have to face the generals. Everything appeared to be in order. He quickly ducked back just in time for Yuda to burst into the room and sit on his bed. Two generals followed into the chamber but remained standing.

They were talking loudly enough for Jenon and Vika to hear them clearly. However, they could not really follow the conversation since the conversation was in too refined a form of Crit, even for Vika. They could only make out the general gist: Yuda ordered that something should be done before the coming full moon day. And seemed to be planning to attack Khet in two weeks. Bubbling with confidence, Vika thought "We'll stop you!".

The meeting did not last long. Yuda dismissed his generals just before the famous Gong of Kunduj rang, announcing two hours to midnight. Vika wondered how people in this village slept with that crazy gong sounding four times every night. Jenon covered himself with the maid's shroud, preparing to take Soma out to Yuda. Vika would have mocked him for donning a female shroud - but that would have to wait for later; till they were away, alone and on their way to Khet. Jenon quietly poured out Soma into an earthenware chalice and added the full three doses of Osilla to it. The drug dissolved into the Soma even before any of it hit the bottom of the chalice.

The next test was at hand. Jenon needed to pass off as the maid even though his build was much larger than hers. Vika prayed that Jenon's deliberate slouch, the maid's sheepskin shroud and the general cloak of nightly darkness would all provide sufficient cover and deflect suspicions. Yuda's lamp was lit but its small flickering flame was hardly enough to be considered even "dim". Both Jenon and Vika knew that this was the most dangerous part of the mission - the part which could unravel the whole plan.

Yuda rang the bell for his drink of Soma, walked up to his window and stood staring out on to his village and into the night sky. Jenon took the Osilla-laden Soma out to the king, passed the chalice into his impatient hand, stretched to one side. Jenon then bowed low and waited. Yuda transferred the chalice to his other hand and made a dismissive gesture.

Not a single word was spoken. Yuda had not even turned fully to look at "her". Jenon returned to the alcove and Vika smiled at him conspiratorially. 'That worked perfectly', they seemed to say to each other. The dangerous phase seemed to have passed without a hitch.

Ж

Yuda was pleased with himself. It had been an arduous day but a lot was accomplished. He had finally maneuvered his father into going on a long pilgrimage. The priests accompanying him would keep him busy in other-worldly thoughts. Yuda would not have to suffer any more nettlesome outbursts of fatherly advice about how to run the state. There could only be one king at any given time; and at this time it had to be Yuda. His father had been a great man in his day but now it was time for the next generation. It was good for the older generation to quietly slink away into their religious meditations and not meddle in affairs of the state.

Yuda was convinced that he was a much better ruler than his father. To take just one example, he remembered nights from his childhood which always found the castle in extreme chaos. It was noisy with all kinds of people coming and going at all hours. If his father wanted a nightcap of Soma, he would have had to yell out for someone and probably would have had to wait at least fifteen minutes before he would have it in his hand.

All Yuda had to do was ring the bell; the chalice of soma was placed in his hand. "This is much more efficient and peaceful" he mentally patted himself on the back for having trained his maid so well.

He sipped his drink while listening to the healthy cry of a baby from the village. Listening to the distant croon of the mother comforting the baby, he was amazed at how well sound traveled to this height above the village.

He then pondered his other accomplishment for the day. The invasion of Khet was almost ready; his generals had just said the final details could be ironed out within the next few days. He had ordered the invasion to take place the next Full Moon Day. If his father had been here, he would have gotten an earful about the need to maintain good friendship with neighbors. He would have quoted some earthy aphorism about how invaders were never invited as friends.

"Be content with the extent of your kingdom", he would have said, "Khet has always been friendly to us. What would you gain by invading them?"

What would he do without such priceless advice, Yuda thought bemused. What a silly question to even contemplate? What would I gain? Territory, of course.

He could not imagine ever being content with the size of his kingdom. His ambition was to expand it to span the world. He would build an empire bigger than any in history. He certainly could not brook resistance from Khet, right on his doorstep. On the other hand, perhaps it was just as well that Khet would resist. It would serve as a good warning to all other resistors: surrender or suffer Khet's fate.

Yuda finished his drink and turned to the flickering flame of his house lamp. He bowed and recited the Atheist

Prayer to Ag, the God of Fire:

This prayer, two verses in Theta Geeti meter, is the first clue left by Bada Ravi. Below are his original Telugu, transliteration to English and the meaning.

తే. గీ.

మిగిత దేవులు దాగుడు మూతలాడ
       సర్వ జనుల విశ్వాసము సన్న గిల్ల
నీవు గనిపింతు వత్యంత సుళువు గాను
       నాస్తికులు గూడ ముదముగ నమ్ము నటుల.
వాస దీపమందు పెను దావాగ్ని యందు
       యజ్ఞ గుండము నందున్న యగ్ని యందు
కానపడు దేవ, నేటి నా కర్మ లెల్ల
       నీకె యర్పింతు నమ్రత నగ్ని దేవ

Theta Geeti:

Migita devulu daagudu moota laada
       Sarva janula visvasamu sanna gilla
Neevu kanipintu vatyanta suluvu gaanu
       Nastikulu gooda mudamuga nammu natula.

Vaasa Deepamandu, penu daavaagni yandu,
       Yajna gundamu nandunna yagni yandu
Kaanapadu Deva neti naa karma lella
       Neeke yarpintu namratan Agni deva!

Meaning:

While other Gods play hide and seek
       Causing people's faith to crumble
You are visible most easily (to everyone so that)
       Even atheists happily accept your existence.

In the house lamp, in the large forest fire,
       In the sacred fire of the sacrificial pit,

25

You appear, Oh God! All of my work today
I humbly dedicate to you, Oh Fire God!

Suddenly Yuda felt awfully sleepy. He dismissed it as the result of a long and tiring day. He came near his bed and fell on to it heavily. As he was slipping into slumber, he felt his maid pulling the deerskin to cover him. He fell into a deep stupor congratulating himself once again for having instilled such devotion in his maid.

Ж

Vika and Jenon moved fast. They wrapped Yuda in the soft deerskin on his bed and then used the sheepskin from the maid's bed to cover over that. They tied the whole thing with rope they had cut out from the netting in the maid's bed. With every step, Vika's confidence was rising.

"What is the fastest way to Khet?" whispered Jenon, "Which way do we leave the village after we exit the castle?"

Vika, the message carrier, replied, "I know the perfect way. Let's carry him to the Chelivas" referring to the Southwest corner of the village where the royal servants lived.

They lifted the wrapped up Yuda and tied him in more rope. They knew there was a guard posted right outside the bedchamber - they could not possibly just walk out of the King's chamber with a big bundle of laundry at this time of the night. But, the maid's alcove opened into the main atrium of the castle one floor down. So, they used more rope to tie the wrapped up king and quietly lowered the bundle from the maid's alcove. This was the second most dangerous part of their plan: anyone walking by in the main atrium would have seen them lowering it. But luck favored them; no one walked by as they painstakingly lowered Vika as well as themselves down the rope.

They knew from their surveillance, that apart from the guard right outside the King's bedchamber, all other guards were concentrated near the castle's entrance. Two of those guards were playing a board game of Elephants and Camels and the others were watching it, while also keeping an eye on the entrance. Jenon just hoped that these guards were concentrating more on what enemy might come in from outside rather than on who might be going out from inside.

26

As they approached the entrance, Vika's tension grew along with the tightness of his grip on the bundle. Jenon walked along with studied nonchalance. Vika remembered Jenon's exhortation from the day before: "Don't even acknowledge the guards" Jenon had said "Just pretend as if it is the most ordinary thing for you to be carrying the bundle out". That was easier said than done for Vika, not used to this much tension. He could not stop from thinking that he was walking within six feet of heavily armed guards who had sworn an oath to protect the person they were seizing.

Ж

The youngest of the guards was Balu. Barely 15 years old, he was new to the job and also to the game of Elephants and Camels. He had learned the rules of the game just a few weeks ago. He could not understand the fascination so many people had for the game. Most of the time, the next move to make seemed obvious to him.

"Move the horse," he hissed excitedly, "you can threaten to capture his King!".

The other guards laughed derisively at his suggestion. The player just snorted and said, "If I move my horse the game is over! I just threaten. He will actually capture my king and walk away!"

Balu could not see how his move was so bad until he examined the board and thought ahead to just one more move. Investigating the possible next moves was so exhilarating that, for a brief moment, he understood the allure of the game.

Another of the spectating guards, who had been mercilessly taunting Balu for weeks, imitated his hiss and suggested a patently ridiculous move. "Capture the elephant" leading to raucous laughter from the others.

"Quiet! The king is sleeping" came the stern voice of a bearded old man who was clearly the leader of the guards. They all fell silent. Balu walked away from the game, sulking.

The commotion provided perfect cover for Vika and Jenon to quietly walk past all the guards. They were about ten steps beyond the outer threshold when Balu decided to take his humiliation out on someone else. A launderer who was trembling while carrying the clothes was too perfect an

27

opportunity to pass up.

"If you are too old to even carry the laundry, how can His Majesty expect you to wash it properly?" he needled Vika.

Vika was paralyzed with terror and could not even think of a grunt, let alone a response. When the moment of non-response became suspiciously too long, Jenon jumped in defensively:

"Leave him alone! He is on a vow of silence for tonight. Hasn't eaten all day and feels weak. But the king's orders for cleaning are not to be disobeyed!" and then added in a more light hearted tone, "Besides, he always makes me work harder than a donkey. I am the stupid donkey to his lazy master". The well worn Crit idiom dispelled doubts for just a brief moment. And that was all they needed to get past.

Jenon threw the entire bundle, on his shoulder and walked away while Vika followed him with trembling foot steps. Balu watched them uneasily till they turned the corner. He could not put his finger on it, but these characters seemed suspicious. May be he was just angry about being laughed out of watching the game.

But no! Didn't the bundle look too heavy to be just clothes? Since he was guarding the outer perimeter of the castle, wasn't it his job to suspect everyone egressing the castle of thievery. But, if they had any jewelry in the sheepskins, he would have heard a tinkling. Which he did not.

It never occurred to Balu that a person, let along the King himself, could be brazenly abducted. He did not know the new servant with an Ivchean accent doing laundry duty. But then he was himself new and did not know every one of the servants. Besides, he reasoned, wouldn't the other guards have checked them for valuable items?

That last question did it for him and he consciously raised his suspicion ten-fold; he knew for a fact that these men were not checked. His young mind fancied himself rescuing the King's jewelry from thieves while the so-called more experienced guards were too busy playing Elephants and Camels.

Wouldn't that be delicious? It would teach these idiots that Elephants and Camels didn't really help you serve your king.

He glanced again at the others and saw how immersed in the game they were. Yes indeed! He would catch these thieves and teach his fellow guards a lesson. The look on their faces when the youngest lad catches these thieves single-handedly would be priceless!

Nevertheless, it all felt to him like fanciful musings. He felt like he lacked the authority to stop these thieves. He certainly lacked the confidence to instantly demand and inspect their cargo. Still unwilling to give up, he quietly followed them, hiding in the shadows.

Story of the Story - 2

That. Was. Brutal!

Nearly six years after my breakthrough and almost nine years after I bought the book, all I had was one chapter. Roughly twenty-fold as much was still left. The story was thrilling enough to have me hooked but my resolve was flagging. I'd have to live to be two hundred to complete this translation. I was ready to give up but kept thinking about my promise.

My wife tried to console me. "Look", she said. The main reason you are trying to translate the book is to prove you will respect the manuscript. Well, we obviously will. So, it is OK to give this up".

"I know" I conceded. "I might have no choice – but still ..."

"Think of it as accepting defeat gracefully. Not as betraying a solemn oath".

With that rationalization, I gave up.

Three days later I got a phone call.

"Hello! This is Jalal Badrawi".

"Hello", I replied cautiously. I was immediately on edge. As if the late Mr Badrawi found out that I had given up and had somehow caused his estate to send someone to take the book back. When the silence prolonged a bit too long, I continued. "Are you related to Mr Jay Badrawi of Maine?"

"Phew! For a moment there I thought you had forgotten me. I am not related to Jay Badrawi – I am him!"

"But you said your name was Jalal ..."

"Yes. Now I go by my full name of Jalal instead of shortening it to Jay".

I was still confused. "DubDee mentioned that you had terminal lung cancer. That was almost ten years ago."

"Ha", he laughed. "I am presumed dead, huh?"

"No no." I tried to correct my gaffe. "That's not what I meant. I was just ... ".

"Don't worry, my friend!" he replied soothingly. "I am not offended. I was in fact supposed to die within months.

But I had what my doctors have called a miraculous remission. I am still here."

"I am glad to hear it".

"Yeah, I get occasional fits of cough. But other than that I am fine physically. But spiritually, I have felt hollow for a while".

I fervently hoped he was not calling to take the book back in order to heal spiritually. I would not have the heart to fight him for it.

"How did you get my number Jay?"

"Please call me Jalal" he started. "I got your number from DubDee's old notes. Hope you don't mind".

"No. Not at all. I am glad you called".

"You know", he said, "after they told me about my remission, I cast about like a vagabond traveling to places and doing silly things that I thought were on my bucket list. A second chance at life and all that. But nothing brought me any satisfaction. Then four months ago I went to Herat to find some peace".

"Did you? Find peace, I mean".

"Not really. What I found was that Haji Pir-Basha was very ill. He was dying".

"Oh no. I am sorry to hear that".

"He was nearly ninety. Had led a life filled with warlords, occupations, revolts, sundry violence and financial difficulties. Nevertheless, he was full of serene acceptance and equanimity. I spent several weeks talking with him to understand the source of such strength".

"You know, I also spoke to him on the phone a couple of times".

"Yeah. He remembered your calls very well. Anyway, when I told him that I no longer go by Jay but insist on being called Jalal – he laughed. He told me 'Jay or Jalal does not matter. Until you realize that you are Badrawi, you will not find peace'. I did not understand what he meant. He told me to seek you out. He explained that, as a Badrawi, preserving that story was my duty. That was the only thing that could bring me peace".

This guy was good. What a negotiator! He had not

even raised the topic and he already had me rooting for him. I would have a tough time saying no to him. Anyway, it was time to bring the cat out of the bag. I asked him directly: "So, are you calling to ask me to send the book back?"

"Well", Jalal replied after a brief pause. "I can't demand it. You bought it fair and square. And based on your calls to the Haji, you have been keeping your end of the bargain by trying hard to translate it. Fact that you did not make any progress is not your fault ..."

"But I have!", I protested. "I have made some progress on translating the book."

"Really?!" he sounded skeptical but pleased. "How did you manage that? I can call at another time, if you are busy right now".

"No, this is OK" I told him. Then I explained to him my trials and tribulations over the past six years. About the discovery of Brahmi script and the Telugu verse which enabled me to translate the first chapter.

"Wow. It was in Telugu? As if Bada Ravi was talking to you personally".

"That is how it felt to me".

"When do you think you will have it completed? Perhaps a couple more years?"

"Ha!" I laughed bitterly. "More like couple more centuries".

"What?!"

"Yeah. To be honest, I have given up. The progress is excruciatingly slow. It consumes too much time. With a full time job and a family, working on a document in two languages that I have no familiarity with. It is just too hard".

He was quiet for almost a minute after that.

"Jalal", I asked. "Are you still there?"

"Yes, I am here" he replied. "You know, I called to see if I could make you send the book back to me. But from what you told me thus far, I don't think I can do the translation by myself. Plus, I am fine now but who knows how much longer I have to live. I think you should keep the book. I would like to offer my help. Please don't give up.

Let's work together and complete the translation".

It was my turn to be silent.

"I can help you!" he persisted. "I am fluent in Persian and also vaguely acquainted with Brahui. If we work together, we will be able to finish it".

"A very tempting offer, Jalal", I said. "I would like that very much. It will reduce my dictionary look-ups ten fold. But are you sure you are healthy enough to try this? I mean it is very painstaking. What would your doctor say?"

"Ah" Jalal grunted dismissively. "She always pulls me back. Asks me to rest rather than exert. But I need to do this. This is good for my soul – even if it is deleterious to my body".

I accepted his offer. As the first order of business, I started taking careful high-resolution digital scans of each leaf and shared them with him on Dropbox. He started with the first chapter I had already translated and corrected some errors. I was gratified that what he pointed out were minor changes and that I had caught the overall story quite accurately so far. I quickly incorporated his changes.

Then we went on with the rest of the book. Progress was now swift enough that I could actually hope to complete it in the next few years.

2. Sika Ye Neecham

With every step Balu took in following the thieves, his confidence was flagging because of the nonchalant way they were walking. They were not even attempting to run or elude any possible pursuers. Even in his fevered craving for glory, he did not imagine that the load of the laundry could be slowing them down.

After about ten minutes of this quiet pursuit, he saw them turn toward the Chelivas section. People stealing from the castle would not go to the Royal servants section, would they?

This was the quieter part of town where the houses were bigger and the thoroughfares wider. At that late hour, the peaceful neighborhood was grave-yard quiet. Balu decided that there was no reason to pursue these laundry men any further and started falling back.

Suddenly, he heard them talk to each other and stopped, very alert. Wasn't one of them on a vow of silence? How can they be talking? He turned around and, still sticking to the dark corners, quietly moved closer to the thieves to listen in on their conversation.

Just like Yuda earlier that night, Balu was amazed at how clearly sound traveled on clear, quiet nights. As he started listening, all his suspicions were proven right and his fancies of glory from apprehending these thieves returned.

"What is Sika Ye Neecham?" one thief was saying. "Another one of your wonderful Ivchean sayings?

"My friend," the Ivchean replied "indeed it is another one of my Ivchean proverbs. It means, you fall hard only when you are at the peak. It's a cautionary against hubris. Let's not celebrate before our success is in hand".

"Well, I don't know about you", Vika hissed, "but I am enjoying the hubris. I mean, we pretty much have success already in hand. What can go wrong now? We are out of the castle. About five minutes that way is a simple climb up a wall and then a merry down-slide into the woods. Once there, we are home free! If this is the peak, I am enjoying the view. So, let me ask again: did you ever imagine we'd accomplish it?"

"Yes I did. And no, we have not accomplished it yet".

Accomplish what? Balu wondered. Clearly these men were thieves and must be stopped. He knew about the down slide the thief was talking about; he had gone down it several times himself on festival days when all boys in the town were allowed into Chelivas to slide down and into the river. He knew that at this time of night, under the veil of New Moon darkness, if they actually went down the slide they would be impossible to catch.

They could escape into the woods or even into the river itself. Balu knew that King Yuda was a direct descendant of Mother Amu, the holy river. But he had not yet learned enough religion to believe that Mother Amu would never let people get away with stealing from the king.

Balu's mind was fixated on the glory that comes from catching these scoundrels. He did not stop to consider the fact that he was just one very green soldier - just a boy really - against two grown men. He did not stop to make a concrete plan of how to stop them. Instinctively, he held his spear in an attacking posture, jumped into the dim light of the lamp in front of a house and yelled out for them to stop.

"Stop, you thieves! How dare you steal from the King!"

Jenon and Vika were stunned at this sudden turn of events. Jenon, all his contingency plans swimming through his head, recovered first and took the luxury of a few seconds for analysis. He recognized from the voice that this guard was the same young, inexperienced one that almost stopped them at the castle. Also, Jenon noted that the guard did not seem to know the full extent of their crime - he was only accusing them of stealing. Putting on his most obsequious voice, Jenon replied

"No sir! We are not stealing anything. These are simply the king's linens. We are to wash and bring them back in the morning". Jenon prayed that the guard would not ask them why they were moving into Chelivas and away from the washermans' quarters. To keep the guard from thinking of it, he diffidently added, "Would you like to check the load?"

As Balu approached them, he made his first mistake: he set his javelin back into the rest position on his back. When he reached them, he made his second mistake: he pushed Jenon and Vika away with a shove and officiously declared: "Yes. We will check and determine if you are telling the truth".

And then he made his third, almost fatal, mistake when he unrolled the bundle. Shocked to find the king lying unconscious within the bundle he took his eyes off the thieves for a few seconds.

Jenon, anticipating the moment of shock, took full advantage of Balu's roving eye. He leapt on to Balu at lightning speed, snatched the spear from his back and tried to strike him. Balu rolled away at the last moment causing Jenon to miss his mark. Balu was scraped deep in the left shoulder but escaped being stabbed through the chest. Jenon admired the young man's sense of duty enough to not be too disappointed that he had failed to kill him. He ignored Balu who was clutching his shoulder and screaming in agony and jumped forward. He dropped the spear thinking it was more important to put some distance between himself and the town than to be armed.

"Vika", he hissed to his accomplice "lead the way quickly to the chute".

Jenon loaded King Yuda's still unconscious body on to his left shoulder and since there was no more use of pretending nonchalance, started running as fast as he could. His feet kicked up some dirt and also a small pebble. In a freak accident, the pebble flew briefly in the air and hit Balu hard on the shin.

The added pain from the shin quickened Balu to the danger. Screaming "Ow", Balu drew upon his last ounce of strength and tried to pick up the lance stained with his own blood. But he was too weak from pain to hold it firmly, let alone throw it. So he dropped it again to the ground and picked up the pebble instead. He hurled it as hard as he could at Jenon before falling down bleary eyed from pain. The pebble missed the target.

After a few seconds rest, which allowed Jenon to get even closer to the down slide, Balu realized that it was now or never. If he did not stop them now, the King himself would be abducted. That shocked realization helped him find enough strength deep within to stumble up. He again picked up the dropped spear and charged at Jenon, shouting fiercely.

"Stop them! Parahush! Parahush!!"

Jenon was still at least a minute away from the Chute. Once Balu started yelling Parahush, Jenon knew their game was over. That was the signal for utmost emergency. All the King's servants within earshot were supposed to rush to assistance. Of course, there was no dearth of the King's servants in the Chelivas section. Finally, there was no way in which he, loaded with Yuda's body on his shoulder, could run faster than the young guard behind him, wounded in the shoulder but loaded with only a spear.

At that point he saw the Vika's silhouette at the mouth of the down slide making wild gestures for him to run faster. Jenon realized he had to drop King Yuda and run. His only other option was to die carrying Yuda's unconscious body on his shoulder. Better to lose today but live to fight another day. The guard would reach him in a matter of seconds. Perhaps I should have killed him when I had a chance he regretted, but only fleetingly. Gallant soldiers like that deserved their day in battle; they shouldn't be killed in a sneak attack.

Balu picked up another pebble and hurled it with solid aim to hit Jenon very hard on his right shoulder. Jenon realized he had no choice; he let King Yuda's body slip down to the ground and ran faster. Balu behind him slowed down to attend the king.

With the bump he received from being dropped to the hard ground, King Yuda briefly awoke from his Osilla-induced stupor and shouted out in a slurred voice "Quiet there"! Balu stopped where the king fell and felt furious "How dare this thief throw my King down to the ground!" was his first thought, before he consciously discerned that abducting the king was likely a far bigger crime.

In the meantime, his Parahush alert was working. Several men and women were slowly stepping out of doors with lamps in their hands and concerned puzzlement on their faces. Leaving his king on the ground for the moment, Balu ignored the searing pain in his left shoulder picked up the spear with his right hand and started running toward Jenon. Vika was watching all this, mouth agape, from his position at the mouth of the slide. As Jenon was climbing up, Vika jumped into the chute and slid down rapidly. Balu aimed as well as he could and launched his spear at Jenon. Just as

Jenon was about to step on to the chute, the spear lodged in the back of his thigh. Jenon let out an agonized scream, determinedly pulled the spear out of his thigh and tumbled into the chute, almost unconscious with pain.

The chute delivered Jenon with a thud right behind Vika. Vika picked him up and dragged him along the ground nearly fifty yards to the edge of the river. He quickly found what he was looking for: the trunk of a Deodar cedar that he had felled and moved to the banks of the river, in preparation for the getaway.

With great effort he pushed the log into the river and draped Jenon on it. He waded in after, and with one last heave-ho, launched it into deeper water. He held onto the log with one hand and to Jenon with the other and allowed the current to carry them away from danger. His bitter disappointment at losing Yuda was tempered by the relief that they had at least made it out alive.

Ж

Balu heard Jenon's agonized scream but could not see clearly enough in the dark to know how badly he had hit the thief. He quickly ran back to get the King to a safe place; he saw three men, Chelivas residents, approaching hesitantly and others observing from their doors. He picked the stronger looking among them and ordered:

"You! Parahush!! Run to the castle and come back here with at least ten guards. If you are not back within fifteen minutes, I will report you to the king for negligence. This is a supreme emergency! The king is dying!". The man dropped his lamp and took off like an arrow toward the castle repeatedly shouting "Parahush!" at the top of his lungs.

Then Balu asked the other two, "Do either of you know Minister Vaid's home?". They replied "Yes". But before Balu could say anything else, a guard came running.

"I am Minister Vaid's son and servant Suvaid, The Fortunate", he said breathlessly. "We heard your Parahush. The minister is on his way and will be here in minutes. What is the matter?"

"Two men tried to abduct the King", replied Balu, nestling Yuda's unconscious head in his elbow. "They ran that way and went over the slide. Please go and try to apprehend

38

them. I have sent for guards from the castle. I will send them also, as soon as they come."

Suvaid hesitated only for a moment to note that Balu's wounded shoulder was dripping blood. That gave him the answer for why Balu could not run after the culprits himself. Satisfied that this young child was not ordering him around, he ran to the slide and disappeared over its hump.

If anyone could find the culprits, it was Suvaid. Ever since his childhood, when he had helped his team to an extremely improbable victory in a game of Monkeys in Branches, he was famous as Kaidbar – the one who wards away misfortune. His fortune was as unstoppable as Mother Amu in a flood. Balu felt confident of that.

A few minutes later a venerable looking old man, Minister Vaid, approached the scene accompanied by two other guards. Vaid saw that the King was on the ground in the hands of a seriously wounded soldier. "Speak, soldier! Quick and brief." he demanded.

"Sire", Balu summarized the situation "two men abducted the king from the castle. I don't know what they did but the king is unconscious. I stopped the abductors and got injured during the confrontation. They jumped into the down slide and ran. I was not able to pursue them. Your son Suvaid, The Kaidbar, is in pursuit right now. I promised him that I will send others to help him. I also sent someone to get help from the castle."

"You have done well, soldier", Vaid commended Balu. He quickly took charge of the situation, much to Balu's relief who was very content to slide back into his pain with Yuda's unconscious head in his lap.

Soon after, twelve guards from the castle came running and Vaid started issuing orders. He ordered ten of them to take torches from the street, join Suvaid and arrest the abductors. He then commandeered a bed from a nearby home, ordered the guards to lay the king down on it. Then he bade them carry the bed back to the castle. Finally, he smiled at Balu and said: "You've earned it! Walk alongside the king's bed back to the castle."

Pleased beyond measure, Balu disregarded the pain in his shoulder and started walking on the right side of the bed.

Thus it happened that in the middle of a dark New Moon night, King Yuda of Kunduj was transported by only four guards on a make-shift curricle back to his castle in a drug-induced oblivion. He was accompanied on the left by the sombre Minister Vaid - dressed in a simple white tunic and stroking his equally white beard, contemplating the next move. On his right was the young and inexperienced Balu who appeared that night to be destined for greatness.

For anyone viewing that scene it was hard to tell if the King himself was destined for much of anything after this close brush with humiliation. Indeed many onlookers despaired that he might not even survive the night.

Future historians however would view that night as one of the crucial turning points in making King Yuda a pivotal historical figure.

Suvaid and the other guards that went over the slide to arrest the abductors had lost the game even before it began. Suvaid may be Kaidbar but this was not a matter of luck any more.

Jenon and Vika had floated away on the river by the time Suvaid thudded to a halt from the slide. By the time he oriented himself, the Deodar log was nearly fifty yards away on the river and hard to see. When the other guards came over the slide with their torches, Suvaid lost precious minutes obeying his first impulse to hide, because he was unsure whether they were friend or foe. After he saw their faces, and by the time they organized themselves enough to quiet down and start to listen for the thieves, Jenon and Vika were nearly hundred yards downstream of them and quietly floating further away.

From that distance, even in broad daylight, noticing the Deodar log with two men draped on it would have required the guards to know precisely where to look. In the cover of New Moon darkness, it was nearly impossible. The torches they carried were worse than useless; getting their eyes used to light at close quarters, and completely incapacitating them from making out anything in the dark distance. Their attempt to stay quiet and listen was also fruitless because in flowing seamlessly with the river current, the culprits made less noise than the river herself.

In any case, an unspoken assumption made the guards look through the woods rather than on the river. At the end of a futile hour of searching Suvaid ordered the guards to get back to the castle and report on the lack of progress to Minister Vaid.

Ж

Vaid settled the king back in his chamber and left him snoring softly. He ordered Balu to rest in the guards section. He summoned the Royal apotheker and ordered him to dress the wound on Balu's shoulder. Then he sent for the Praesha - the Commander of the Royal Guard.

The Praesha was as old as Vaid though he dressed like a younger man - a man of action. Both the Praesha and Vaid had joined the service of Yuda's father almost together. Long years of service together gave them an easy camaraderie with each other. After the Praesha arrived, he had a heated discussion with Vaid about how someone could just walk into the castle and abduct the king. The Praesha suggested that the apotheker should treat the king as well. But Vaid adamantly refused.

"If they really wanted to kill the king", Vaid hypothesized "they could have left him poisoned right here. Why did they have to carry him out?" Then he added with bitterness in his voice, "They could even have slit his throat for all the good your guards were doing!"

"That is water under the bridge" the Praesha protested. "We will discover how this happened. But the immediate duty is to treat the King and ..."

"No", roared Vaid "they could have killed the King easily enough. Since they did not, it stands to reason that they only wanted to put him to sleep. Now that he is back to safety, we should simply let the king sleep and awake normally. He will be back to his normal self in a couple of days."

Before the Praesha could protest, a guard came and bowed:

"Victory to the Praesha!", the guard reported. "We found the chalice from which His Majesty drank his nightly Soma. Some of the drink is still left in here. And it smells of osilla".

The Praesha snatched the chalice from the guard and

41

sniffed it and passed it on to Vaid. It was well known that while it induces deep sleep, osilla was not life threatening. Instinctively the Praesha steeled himself for an I-told-you-so lecture from Vaid and was surprised at the conciliatory tone in his next remarks.

"I apologize, Praesha", said Vaid right in front of the guard "for my earlier outburst. Chalk it up to the excitement tonight." Vaid gave the Praesha an embarrassed grin and continued "Anyway, this is not a good time for a senior minister to squabble with the king's Praesha. We should simply do our best to protect the king and his kingdom during this crisis. Once he awakens, the king will decide whether anyone deserves punishment, reprimand or reward. For now, would you please further increase castle security?"

Amazed at Vaid's humility, the Praesha bowed and left. He called in additional guards and rearranged the duties for maximal security. By the time Suvaid came back from the woods with the report that there was no sign of the abductors, the castle was bustling with quiet activity. Vaid received the report stoically and then, along with the Praesha, went to question Balu.

After detailed questioning, the most prominent thing they could discern about the abductors was that one of them, apparently the one in command, was Ivchean as judged from his pronounced Ivchean accent and dark complexion. The other one spoke Crit and did not have an accent but he was clearly there only in a helper role as he always deferred to the Ivchean.

Nevertheless, the very fact that he was there, meant that the Ivchean had some local support. Deeper questioning helped Balu recall the name "Vika" for the helper. Vaid asked the Praesha to send his guards all through the town to investigate for anyone who might have disappeared during the night. If this Vika was a local, it was important to apprehend him.

Vaid thought that an external threat, even if it was from Ivchea, could be handled. But if there were traitors within town, then the problem became much more difficult.

The Praesha dispatched men to investigate the goings on in town - looking especially for anyone who might be missing from home that night. Then he came back to Vaid with a worried expression. Vaid was sitting cross-legged, leaning against the wall. His eyes were closed but there was no sleep in his expression; he appeared to be in intense thought.

"Do you really think" the Praesha said with a grimace "that Ivchea is behind this? I mean we are armed and equipped well enough to repel any attack from Khet and other neighboring kingdoms. Hell, we can even go occupy them in less time than it takes to swim across the Amu. But Ivchea! If they attacked us, we would not stand a chance!"

Vaid looked at him thoughtfully. The Praesha did not interrupt his thoughts with any more talk. He also made himself comfortable, sitting down cross-legged and leaning against the opposite wall. At length, Vaid replied.

"I cannot think of a single reason for Ivchea to attack us. We are simply not important enough. Due to the planned attack on Khet that the king set in motion today, we probably will become important soon. But that is after we have occupied Khet. And Khiwani. And, perhaps even Koka and Gandar. Then perhaps we would be big enough to be interesting to some Ivchean city state. As it stands now - absolutely not. We would not be of interest to any Ivchean city. There is no reason for them to even look at us."

Vaid's voice trailed off giving the distinct impression that he had more to say. The Praesha did not interrupt. There was no more brilliant minister anywhere in the world than Vaid. The Praesha was keen to hear his analysis.

"However", continued Vaid "that is just analysis. We cannot ignore the facts right in front of us. The man had a strong Ivchean accent. He was spouting Ivchean sayings. And he was dark skinned. So, he was clearly Ivchean. And equally clearly, he was in command. But was any Ivchean city behind this? If so, why? I can't imagine what they would want from us".

Another long pause.

"I am going home", Vaid finally concluded standing up, "to get some sleep. Please stay at the castle and ensure safety till morning. In the morning, send for Commander Dron and have him relieve you. Don't let anyone disturb the King's sleep

43

till at least mid-day tomorrow. We will all meet here at that time and take the King's orders on the best way to proceed. If the king is still sleeping, then we will use the apotheker's services".

The Praesha nodded his head quietly to acknowledge Vaid's directions. As soon as Vaid and Suvaid left together, the Praesha went out to join the guards. Sitting in quiet thought like Vaid was not his forte; he was a man of action.

3. Sadiya baara

Daybreak found Minister Vaid returning to the castle where King Yuda was still sleeping. All the guards were on high alert and bowed to him as he entered. There was no sign that their embarrassed minds were entertaining any thoughts of Elephants and Camels. Vaid washed his feet and went straight to the Ag Myra, the room of Eternal Flame in the Southwest corner of the castle. The flame in the middle of Ag Myra had been burning ceaselessly for nearly sixty years.

Vaid remembered the history of the Ag Myra he was told in his childhood. Long before Vaid was born, when Yuda's grand father was building the castle he wanted a Myra, a prayer room, in the castle. Upon the priest's advice, he put it in the Southwest corner of the castle, and ensured that no living room was built above this chamber - "other than God's", the priest had reverently proclaimed. The old king ordained that a flame be kindled in the middle of the room and stoked multiple times every day to ensure that it never went out. Thus, Ag, the fire God, would have an eternal abode in the castle.

Vaid added more kindling to the fire and circumambulated it three times in silent prayer. When he stepped out, he saw the Praesha waiting to get in. As tradition dictated, they desisted from acknowledging each other with so much as a nod; in God's presence, mere mortals were not worth acknowledging. Vaid went into his office room and started pacing. He had to put the pieces of the puzzle together. The Praesha joined him a few minutes later and announced without a preamble:

"I want to investigate to find out exactly what happened last night. How could someone abduct the king right from the castle without a fight from any of my guards? I am so ashamed!"

"Praesha," Vaid asked with some concern "don't you think the investigation will go better if you have had some sleep first?"

"I took a small nap last night", the Praesha said dismissively. "I can't sleep before I find out."

"Alright, let us investigate together", Vaid acquiesced, "but please have Commander Dron take charge of securing the castle while we investigate."

As the Praesha nodded and was about to leave the room, Vaid added: "And please tell all the night guards to stay. Before they go home, we must question each one to get the story from as many different angles as possible." The Praesha nodded once more and left the room.

The twenty five night guards were assembled in the refectory and the Praesha addressed them.

"You shamed us last night", he declared severely, "You let the king be drugged and taken from his castle. If not for the actions of the youngest guard in the outermost periphery, the abduction would have succeeded. Through all this, none of you lifted so much as a stone to protect the king." He paused and slowly swept his penetrating gaze over all the assembled. If he was startled to find that Vaid himself had joined the guards, he gave no indication of it.

"We let the king down last night", he continued in a lower and more earnest tone, "and we will make amends for it this day. We will find out precisely what happened. How did the abductors gain entrance to the castle? And then to the king's night chamber? How many were there? Did they have any accomplices in our town? How did the abductors walk out of the castle carrying the unconscious king through twenty five of you who have sworn your honor to defend him? How did they simply disappear into the woods? Finally, where are they now? These are questions we must have answers to, so that we may make a full and proper report to the king.

"Some of you may be wondering what the king will do to you when he hears the full report. If you have any honor, stop wondering. You have broken your pledge to protect him. Honor dictates that you accept whatever punishment comes your way for yesterday's monumental failure. But that is for when the king wakes. He will decide what punishment to dole out to each of you.

"And to me as well. I don't, by any means, exempt myself from the dereliction of duty last night. But to dwell on possible punishment is to compound our dishonor. The only way to ameliorate that dishonor, is to remember that we still have a pledge to keep. As punishment, His Majesty may disown us but till he does so, we will keep our pledge. He may choose to permanently relieve us of our dishonor by dropping us onto a trident in which case, we shall keep our pledge till our last breath.

"And that pledge requires us to piece the puzzle of last night together. I expect all of you to cooperate willingly in this endeavor. Elite Minister Vaid will conduct the investigation."

Vaid moved to stand beside the Praesha.

"The Praesha's eloquent words shame and inspire us at once. They point out our shame and at the same time reveal a way to ease that shame. The fundamental thing now is for you to report truthfully all the happenings of last night. Do not worry about how it might look to His Majesty. Do not tell lies in the hopes of defending your own reputation. If you tell a falsehood now about even a minute detail, it will simply block us from finding out what happened. And that will take us farther away from reclaiming our honor. There will be plenty of blame to distribute from last night's debacle. Let's not add some more to it by telling lies and confounding this investigation."

He paused a moment and asked "Do you understand?"

"Yes, your eminence" they replied in unison.

"And do you agree?" he demanded.

"Yes, your eminence" again with vigorous nodding of heads.

"Good. The Praesha and I will interview each of you individually. Do not to consult each other just yet. The time for that may come later. We will compare our stories and add to each others' details later. For now I want to get first hand accounts from as many independent observers as possible."

Ж

In the next four hours, as the Praesha and Vaid questioned every guard, several revealing facts came to light.

First, one of the day guards, discovered a rope hanging from the night maid's alcove to the atrium as he was dousing the lamps. This suggested the route the abductors took for getting out of the bed chamber without the knowledge of the guard posted outside the door.

Second, several guards confirmed that the laundry men were taking out a big bundle last night. Each also sheepishly admitted that he did not pay much attention since he was focused on an intense game of Elephants and Camels.

Third, the guards searching the woods sent a report that a deodar cedar seemed to have been axed. They also reported that a trail from the felled tree seemed to lead to the river.

All that explained how the abductors got out. However it was still unclear how they got in and who they were. Then, the Peace Officer of Kunduj brought in Talu, the old maid who was to have served the king last night. Her story revealed further details of the conspiracy and indicated that the crime was in the works for at least a week. Vaid and Praesha listened in astounded silence as she recounted her story:

"Two men came to visit me a week ago. One of them named Kanavata was a tall young man with dark skin. He spoke Crit with a strong Ivchean accent. The other, named Vrajavoora, was the shorter and older of the two; he had fair skin. They said that they were related to me and that my uncle had just died in Gandar a month ago. They wanted me to go to Gandar to propitiate the Gods. I refused since I cannot leave the King.

"But I am as afraid of the Gods as any old woman. So, when they suggested the Raha Daur as a good way to conciliate the Gods, I agreed. So, all three of us have been secretly praying from sunup to midday at my home for the past week. They seemed like such nice young men, always courteous and very helpful around the house; I trusted them. The Ivchean asked a lot of questions about my duties in the castle. And I answered them".

The Raha Daur is a form of prayer where secrecy is of paramount importance. It is a prayer which is supposed to be entirely between the devotee and God. It is speculated that Raha Daurs might have gained popularity in response to the extravagantly vulgar displays at some prayers performed by kings and chieftains.

"Why?" interrupted Vaid. "Why would you tell a foreigner the inner workings of our castle?".

"Because he expressed a deep admiration for our King", Talu replied, "He said he is a servant of the Ivchean ambassador to the king of Gandar. He had traveled a lot but had never seen a castle run this well. He said he wanted to take some of the Kundujan efficiency back to Ivchea. My pride in Kunduj and our King Yuda did not allow me to be skeptical of his claim that we had something to teach even Ivchea."

"Alright. Go on. What happened next?"

"I have been keeping to my duty throughout the week in order to maintain the secrecy of my Raha Daur. Yesterday was the culmination and we had a feast well before sunset. I fully intended to attend the king at night for my duty. But, after the long prayer and the very big meal, I really don't know what happened. Because I seem to have fallen into deep sleep and was just woken by the Peace Officer".

"Is that really the whole truth?" Vaid asked severely. "Are you hiding anything?"

She looked at him with genuine fear in her eyes and pleaded "That is truly all I know, sire. Except for their names. The Ivchean said his name was Kanavata. The Crit one said his name was Vrajavoora. But during their conversations among themselves, I once overheard him being called Vika. So, I don't know what his real name was".

"Will you be able to recognize these men if you see them again?"

"Yes, your eminence. I have become quite familiar with their appearance during this week. I can definitely recognize them".

"Did anyone else meet them when they were at your house?"

"No Sire. They took the secrecy of Raha Daur very seriously. They rarely left the house during the day, and they would hide in the house if anyone visited me. They did leave the house at night, but they never let anyone suspect that they were associated with me. No one I know ever asked me about them and of course I never mentioned them to anyone till now. Besides I don't get too many visitors at home – just my foster son Balu. But even he has been busy training to be a palace guard these past two months".

Vaid dismissed her with final instructions "We may have more questions for you. And we will need your help to recognize them after we apprehend these men. Don't leave the castle till we tell you".

"Sire", Talu asked timidly. "Is it true that my Balu stopped these criminals single handedly?"

"Yes, he played a role", replied Vaid, his jealousy not letting him give Balu whole-hearted credit. "He did have help from a number of folks in Chelivas, and most importantly my son Suvaid".

That was to be the line about Balu's role in rescuing the king. But the official strength of that line was no match for the allure of the story line that the youngest guard – still in training – had rescued the king while the more experienced guards were playing board games. Thus the legend of Balu was born.

After Talu bowed and left, Vaid and Praesha nodded at each other in comprehension. The Praesha let a satisfied smile light up his face.

"So, that is how it happened! Now we know everything: how it happened and how it was foiled. I can make a full report to the King. My men and I will gladly submit to any punishment his majesty metes out, now that we know how this happened".

But Vaid stayed quiet for a long moment and replied softly "Sadiya Baara"

"What?"

"It's an Ivchean saying" Vaid said with a wan smile, "I am getting into the mood, old friend, by spouting Ivchean sayings. Sadiya Baara means except the important. It implies that one knows everything except the important things".

"But what important things don't we know?"

"Who. And why", replied Vaid succinctly, counting it off on two fingers. "We don't really know who they were and where they were from. Was he really Ivchean? Is Ivchea really behind this? Without knowing this, we cannot plan for what 'they' will do now that this attempt has failed.

"Second, why was the abduction was attempted? What would anyone want with a captured king? Why not simply kill him when they had the opportunity?"

"Sadiya Baara, indeed", the Praesha stood up and mumbled in a deflated tone. Then he asked, changing the subject: "Shall I send the night guards home?"

Vaid nodded.

It was mid-day. Just as the last of the night guards left the castle, word came that King Yuda was up and was demanding to know why he was not awoken at day break as was customary.

Ж

Jenon and Vika quietly drifted downstream on the Amu, on their slapdash raft made of a single log of Deodar Cedar. By daybreak, they had been coasting for nearly six hours. With their legs dangling into the river, Jenon's wound was thoroughly wet and still seeping blood. His condition deteriorated as he developed a significant fever. Worried about this, Vika started looking for a way to get to dry land and hopefully put some herbs on the wound.

The river was quite broad and flowing swiftly. Vika held on to the log with one hand and swam toward shore with the other hand. Jenon also tried to contribute effort, but he was too weak to make a difference; most of his energy was needed for just clinging to the log. It took nearly half an hour for them to get close enough to the bank to feel safe letting go of the log. As it slipped away, they both swam toward shore. When they reached shore, Jenon glanced at the log, still coasting away, and said a silent prayer: "Thank you Deodar! We cut you down and you saved our lives. May I get to be a hundredth as noble as you!".

Overcome with exhaustion, Vika and Jenon staggered across a stretch of sandy riverbed and slept under the shade of a Himalayan Fir.

At midday, the Fir's shadow shifted away and stinging heat from the sun awakened Vika. He roused Jenon. Without exchanging any words, they both went down to the river to complete their morning ablutions. Jenon was walking with a significant limp and gritting his teeth in pain. He washed his wound in the river which cleaned it but that left the gash still quite open and painful.

Returning to the Fir, Jenon sat down resting his back against the trunk. When Vika returned, Jenon took on the customary role of the warrior.

"Vika, my friend" he said attempting to get up and flinching in pain. "I will hunt up some food. Please build a fire

51

so we can cook it".

"No, the feast in Talu's house yesterday was very filling. I don't need to eat till nightfall at the earliest. And you also probably need rest more than you need food." Then he added musingly, "I certainly hope she will not be punished for our actions. She was a nice old lady." He paused a while and changed the topic, "Let me take a look at your wound".

After doing a brief inspection, Vika announced "It looks like a clean cut. It should heal well unless the bone was nicked. I'll get some honey and Pajam grass to bind it".

"Did the apotheker die and appoint you his successor?" Jenon asked with a smile on his face.

"I apprenticed in an apothecary a long time ago" Vika explained seriously without rising to the bait. "Pajam grass should do the trick for a wound like this. Pajam leaves get stronger when they dry up. So, tying up a wound with the Pajam holds the gash together even as the grass dries".

"Let us go!" Jenon made a move to get up.

Vika peremptorily gestured him to stay sitting. "I will go get them. Walking around on that foot will aggravate the wound. Until I bind it, just stay still and rest that foot".

"Thank you my friend" Jenon replied in worn out acquiescence.

It took Vika nearly an hour to come back with a handful of herbal supplies including a broad leaf that he had fashioned into a shallow bowl and had filled with honey. He made Jenon lie face down and tended the wound. He cleaned it once more with water from the Amu and let it dry fully in the mid day sun. Then he applied honey on both sides of the wound, pulled the gash together and stuck reeds of Pajam grass across the gash to hold it together. Then he tore off a piece of Jenon's tunic and used it to further support the dressing.

While they were waiting for the honey to dry and make a strong bond, Jenon glanced at Vika with admiration and said "I clearly chose wisely when I picked you to be my partner on this mission. I take back all the playful insults I sent your way. And again, thank you!"

Vika just smiled, knowing full well that the needling and taunting would return shortly. With some bitterness in his voice, Vika mused:

"We have our lives, our freedom and still have the ability to return to King Mayun and report on what happened. We have everything except Yuda - the thing we came for".

"It is what we Ivcheans call Sadiya Baara" replied Jenon, "It means we have except the important thing".

"Sadiya Baara, indeed".

Both men walked a few steps to the sandy river bed and lay down to sleep again for a few more hours.

Ж

Thus by mid-day, all the human actors in the story had reached a state of sanctuary and would look forward to planning their future actions. The Deodar cedar which carried Jenon and Vika however, would not reach such a restful place till nightfall. She quietly coasted along until the sluices just upstream of the city of Koka nudged her into one of their filter trickles. These trickles were strategically designed to keep large debris like tree trunks out of the free flow of the river near Koka's great river port.

As she lay lodged in the rocky bottom of the filter trickle, a sudden blast of wind dispersed her remaining seeds over a long distance. One, in particular, fell into muddy soil atop a nearby hillock. Nestled between two significant sized boulders, the seed was relatively safe till it germinated and grew.

If a latter day naturalist had witnessed the whole journey, he might have remarked that this was the longest distance any cedar had ever traveled to personally plant one of her seeds. And that she had also chosen a most perfect spot. As befitted the effort, that seed would grow in the future into a mighty deodar which survived many a flood and would be revered by everyone in Koka and beyond.

The Cedar seemed to know that she had accomplished the most important goal of her journey: planting and dispersing her seeds. So, perhaps of all the players that day, she was the only one who did not sigh "Sadiya Baara" even as she lay down in the mud to wilt and decay.

Such are the vagaries of fate however, that the only ones to study this deodar's momentous journey would not be naturalists but Minister Vaid's men. And their sole purpose would be to determine where Jenon and Vika had escaped to.

53

They would have no interest in her historic journey or in her
seedling growing nearby.

04 Soong dho Ovloo

Jenon and Vika woke up mid-afternoon and had a lucky break in hunting a wild boar. Vika set up a fire and roasted the pig. Their hunger satisfied with a big meal, they sat around the dying embers of the fire watching the sunset over the river winding to the West.

"So", Vika opened conversationally, "How did you get roped into this Soong dho Ovloo?"

"My Crit is a not too good. Soong dho Ovloo?"

"It means, literally, hunting after a rabbit with horns. Meaning you engaged in a hopeless cause".

"Well", said Jenon with a mischievous twinkle in his eye, "that had horns but it was a boar. Not a rabbit. And it certainly was not a hopeless cause - it was actually a delicious meal".

Vika gave him a look of friendly condescension and mumbled "Come on".

"Sorry, you meant the mission and you are not in a mood for jokes".

"No jokes are fine", Vika corrected. "But I just want to know why you agreed to a mission of just two men trying to abduct the enemy king right from his castle guarded by fifty men. We were outnumbered more twenty five to one. Preposterous! Who talked you into it?"

"Believe it or not", Jenon said with an embarrassed chuckle, "it was my idea".

"Now I have to know. How did this happen?"

Jenon began his narration:

Ж

Vika, my friend, I was brought up and trained in the grand Ivchean tradition of fighting. It's the tradition that holds cunning strategy to be far more powerful than brute strength. And information to be far more valuable than weaponry. So, I was never deterred simply by superior strength in an adversary.

I guess you could say Soong dho Ovloos are my specialty. Anyway, remember I was almost right. We did come very close to success. You were yourself eager to celebrate prematurely. So, no. Even now, I think this was no Soong dho Ovloo, even if it did eventually fail.

This all started about three months ago, when I had an absolutely frightening dream. In the dream, my wife Mali goes into labor in the dead of night and Queen Nuri also goes into labor the same night. And, as if two pieces of good News is too many, that same night, Khet comes under a vicious attack from Gandar and I am in the middle of a fight, defending our fort.

An angel comes down with two baby souls for the two women about to deliver. She leaves the Prince's soul with my wife and is taking my son's soul to the castle for the Queen. I shouted to the angel to please swap the souls and make it right. So, I lose concentration on the fight and get stabbed in the heart.

Funny that my main concern when I awoke in a cold sweat, was not that I was stabbed in the heart but rather that my son was being taken to the queen. Mali comforted me from the nightmare but after hearing details of the dream, she too was gripped with the fear that someone would stab me. However, neither Mali nor Queen Nuri was pregnant at the time. So, I managed to convince Mali to ignore it as just a silly dream.

Three days later, King Mayun announced that Queen Nuri was pregnant; Mali's fears rose. Soon after, Mali herself missed her period and her fears grew further. She thought we were watching the vision in my dream coming true because Mali and Queen Nuri could deliver on the same day. Today, Mali is 3 months pregnant and is still genuinely fearful that I will die the day that she delivers.

Anyway, she took me to Seeress Groot in the woods outside Khet. Groot analyzed my dream and told us to do a Pacifying Prayer and request God's protection. She said as long as we were humble, we had nothing to fear; an angel who took the trouble to appear in my dream would not let me come to harm in this way. So, Mali started doing the Pacifying Prayer every day. Since it required significant participation from me, I was tardy to my duties a few times. My fellow soldiers taunted me as the man whose wife would not let him go to work. I ignored it as just good-natured ribbing but word of it somehow reached Minister Byram.

He summoned me and, in front of King Mayun, censured me gravely. I had never heard of the Minister, let alone the King himself, getting personally involved in a trivial matter like disciplining a soldier. Anyway, Minister Byram demanded an explanation for my dereliction of duty and I told him the whole story.

King Mayun was stunned by my dream. Minister Byram interrogated me about the dream and one thing he kept focusing on was that I really had no basis to say it was Gandar that attacked us - it could be Kunduj. Or really any kingdom. He kept insisting that since I had never been to Gandar, there was no way for me to recognize it in my dream.

I pointed out to him, somewhat acidly, that I had no basis for knowing anything in my dream. How did I know that the angel had made a mistake and switched souls between the Prince and my son? "In dreams, you just know these things!" I insisted.

You know how pious King Mayun is. He took my dream as divine warning to him to be prepared. Two days later he summoned me to a private meeting of his inner circle and made me repeat my dream.

I remember the meeting like it was yesterday. There was the King, his Praesha and Minister Byram. This was the first time that the Praesha had heard the story and there was hot argument between him and Minister Byram.

The argument brought a touch of impatience to King Mayun's face. I gathered up enough courage to diffidently interrupt.

"Pardon the interruption from me sire. But, if you could make me aware of the danger we face, I might be able to remember more relevant facts from my dream".

"Are you now telling His Majesty" roared the Praesha "that you have not told us everything?"

"No sire. I just meant ..."

"Enough!" interjected the king. "This kind of quibbling is worthless. Praesha, Tell him what we know".

The Praesha first pledged me to secrecy.

"Do you swear that you will not reveal what you are about to learn to any enemies of His Majesty?"

"Yes sire. I swear on my honor, my wife and on Ag himself that I will not reveal" I replied in the usual way.

The Praesha then explained that secret observers had just reported some dire News to King Mayun: Yuda was planning to attack Khet soon after maneuvering his father, the old king, to go on a pilgrimage.

It seems King Mayun suspected trouble when he attended the Yuda's coronation ceremony a month before. Yuda's father, the old king of Kunduj, announced that he was looking forward to pursuing religious endeavors after transferring all state affairs to Yuda. When King Mayun with his natural sagacity inquired whether Kunduj would maintain its friendly posture toward Khet, Yuda publicly gave profuse reassurances of friendship. But, Yuda struck King Mayun as a brash and ambitious young man and his professions of friendship sounded too righteous to be sincere.

Since he was not fully satisfied, King Mayun ordered secret observers to Kunduj to determine if in fact Yuda was going to remain faithful to the political alliance carefully cultivated over two generations. This drastic News of Yuda's plans had proved the King's suspicions true. The secret observers and the surreptitious News had enough of a cloak-and-dagger appeal that my loud mouth did not allow me to be quiet.

"Sire, do they know" I inquired of the Praesha "that His Majesty now knows their plans?"

"You Fool!" the Praesha sneered at me, "Do you have any notion of what 'secret' means? Of course they do not know! And that is why I swore you to secrecy just now". Then he added menacingly, "And I will not hesitate to push you on to a trident if you reveal it to anyone!"

"So, why don't we take advantage of the secrecy?" I replied, ignoring the menace.

The Praesha just rolled his eyes and said sarcastically, "What do you mean, Your Brilliance?"

"What I mean sir", I replied "is that we know that they intend to attack. But they don't know that we know".

"So what?" the Praesha thundered. "Even in the old days Kunduj had a standing army as big as ours is at its biggest. For nearly a year now, they have been aggressively adding to their ranks. It is now twenty times the size of ours. Even if we make our army to the biggest size it can be, they will still be ten times bigger. So, I hope your brilliance sees we are hardly in a position to take advantage of this information. Now, get out before I decide you need more disciplining. And report back to me early tomorrow morning."

"But sir, ..." I started.

"Hoooo" interrupted the Praesha and pointed me to the door.

As I turned to walk out of the door, King Mayun said "Wait!" I turned around, bowed and waited to be addressed. The King turned to the Praesha and said: "Can you check on the guards at our castle gates. We will send for you shortly".

Praesha looked at the King as if he had been slapped. This sort of dismissal for the Praesha, especially in front of a soldier, was unheard of. The Praesha, his face red in embarrassment, self-consciously left the chamber.

King Mayun, still ignoring me, turned to Minister Byram and said "I want to hear his ideas about how to turn this into an advantage."

Byram began to argue "Your Majesty, you were right to ask your Praesha out. He was getting too abusive and was not suggesting anything productive. But he was right about this. How does it matter that we secretly know? We should not spend time on idle speculation. We must right away ...".

"Nevertheless", interrupted King Mayun loudly and raised his palm, a clear signal for Byram to stop talking. Minister Byram sat back quietly, half sulking and half enjoying the prospect that I will make a fool of myself. The King turned to me and commanded "Proceed! How would you turn this to our advantage?"

My respect for King Mayun grew ten times in that instant. I have never known a King to dismiss his own Praesha and shut up his Minister to listen to a lowly soldier like me. Also, his implicit admission that a strategy to deal with the situation was out of his reach showed breathtaking humility and wisdom. I bowed a little lower in my new found respect and started

"Your Majesty, you know that my life is dedicated to bringing you greater glory. You know that I will ..."

"Jenon!" interrupted the king impatiently, "How would you have us use this information?"

"You could order a surreptitious raid, Your Majesty", I replied as succinctly as I could, "I agree that our chances in a head-to-head combat are low because they have a bigger army. So, you could order a small group, of two or three capable men, to encamp in Kunduj. You could order them to wait for an opportune moment and then surreptitiously attack their castle and capture the cowardly King Yuda".

"Even if this small group is able to do it", Minister Byram countered "then what? Their army will still crush ours. Do you know that Gandar occupied Koka fifteen years ago. Even though the Gandaran king was killed in the battle, Koka remained under their domain until five years ago".

"Yes sire. But Yuda would not be killed. Kundujan army will know their new king is still alive and in our captivity. Their old king would be gone on pilgrimage. Even if they did seek his direction, the old king would probably chastise them for the crazy plan to occupy Khet and pull them back. Regardless. Whatever action they take, the army would be headless. We can easily sow further chaos and defeat them!"

King Mayun snickered in nervous laughter. "Are you on Osilla? In what world does an army of a hundred defeat one of two thousand?"

"Chief!" I responded, "this is the best opportunity for you to expand your domain".

King Mayun was irked that I addressed him as Chief rather than Majesty. But I did it deliberately. My calculation was that he was wise enough to know that his five village domain was hardly a kingdom. That he was in reality a Chief and only aspiring to kinghood. If he was irked, I hoped he was irked in the right way with a slight flare-up of his ambition.

"What do you mean opportunity?" he asked, barely concealing his irritation. "This is the gravest threat our kingdom has ever faced".

"I understand your irritation at being addressed as Chief, Your Highness. But your five village domain can be expanded dramatically on this occasion. What you called a threat is in fact the best opportunity for you to truly become a king. And then, Chief, it would be my unfettered pleasure to salute you as Your Majesty".

Minister Byram looked at me with grudging respect and said to King Mayun:

"Your Majesty, allow me to confess that this plan from Jenon is better than anything I or the Praesha have proposed. Our proposals have amounted to little more than 'Lets panic'."

"Indeed!", agreed King Mayun. "We cannot ignore any plan if it has even a remote possibility of success. I want you to analyze this plan. And Jenon! Convince Minister Byram of the details of your plan. We will try every way to mitigate this existential threat to our kingdom. We will meet again tomorrow to decide a final plan of action".

"As you order, Sire", I bowed. Minister Byram also bowed as the King regally left the chamber.

That, my friend, was the beginning of this unlikely military maneuver. Byram is a brilliant military historian. He told me that in the history of organized combat, smaller armies get defeated when they attempt even defense against a much bigger invasion force. And never do they seriously attempt counter-attack. I countered playing for defense could be the reason that most of those historical attempts were failures. The only way for a smaller army to survive was to attack back.

He told me he was willing to try my plan even though it was a fool's errand - though he did not use your colorful term, Soong dho Ovloo. He told me that it might be doomed to failure but that we had few other options.

I, on the other hand, never lost faith in the mission; my Ivchean training always insisted that this was possible.

Minister Byram spent that whole day with me, going over the details of how to capture Yuda. In the beginning, he was quite skeptical.

"You know Yuda is a vigorous and strong young man. You are not going to catch him like a goat in a meadow".

But, point by point, we expanded on the plan. I told him that we should pry open the weakest links in Yuda's security. It did not matter if he has a hundred guards on his castle, we should target the lowly maid who walks in and out everyday. We should find out from the lowliest servants how things actually happen in the castle and plan accordingly.

Once we get to Yuda, we should drug him and tie him up in a bundle. Then drop him through a window and carry him away on a pre-planned escape route. If the window is too high, we tie him up in a rope and then slowly lower him. Then once he is in our control, we force him to order his army to stand down, occupy Kunduj and get control of their entire army.

Byram was unconvinced: "Hold it! Really? We occupy Kunduj? and control their army?".

"Sir, but the element of surprise, ..."

"Is on his side" Byram thundered. "You seem to forget. They will decide when to attack".

"No Sir, it WAS on his side", I argued, not backing down one bit. "He does not know that we know. He thinks we are blissfully unaware of his perfidious plans. But YOUR sage plan to gather this information ahead of time allows us to turn the surprise on him. He could not possibly imagine that we would counter plot just as he is readying his forces. It will certainly be a big surprise for him when we try to nab him".

Byram took a deep breath and examined me with a smile: "You are serious, aren't you? Here I am, at a loss to think of a plan to defend ourselves. And you really think we can occupy them".

I took a deep breath, looked him straight in the eyes and replied with carefully chosen words.

"Sir. If this plan only defends our fort, I will consider it a failure. I think we have a chance of occupying all of Kunduj. At the very least, we will get half their villages".

That was it! He was convinced. From then on, it was "our" plan and not just my plan. He gave me valuable training about surreptitious attacks. He told me details about Kunduj and its layout. He taught me to have contingency plans on top of contingency plans. "Never just hope for success, make it happen" he exhorted.

Next day, he recommended to the king that the mission was worth pursuing. The king ordered me to lead the mission "I will never find someone who believes in it more than you", he said.

You know the rest. We left Khet, befriended Talu in Kunduj, got enough information out of her to finalize the plan.

And we tried to kidnap Yuda. And we failed at the last moment.

I was true to what Byram taught me. I had contingency plans on top of contingency plans. Most of them were never needed but some were indispensable during the mission. But you know, I never had a contingency plan for total failure.

Actually, it is quite funny that we were felled by the same sword we wielded. We befriended the maid instead of any of the higher ups and it paid richly for our mission. However, we ignored the junior-most guard of the castle. We implicitly assumed him to be unimportant and in the end it was he that foiled us.

Ж

Vika listened to the whole story with mouth agape. He did not know that there was so much riding on this mission. He said:

"That is quite a story, Jenon. It would have been so much better if it succeeded. What do we do now? How do we protect our beloved Khet?"

"We wait till tomorrow for me to be able to walk", replied Jenon. "Then we go back to Khet, bare our failure to the King and Minister and then take orders on next steps. If I know Minister Byram, he has a contingency plan for my failure. He thinks of many different things".

And then he added soothingly, looking out at the shimmering river: "Don't worry. Jenon's plan might be defeated, but Khet is not. We will occupy Kunduj yet".

Vika, in an effort to break up the somber mood, hurled a playful insult at Jenon: "You know, not only are you a lousy at missions but you are also no good at reading visions"

"Huh?"

"You completely misread the vision in your dream. It was not Gandar but Kunduj. It's not them attacking us but rather us attacking them. And you don't get stabbed in the heart but rather in your butt".

The two friends roared in laughter and went to sleep under the stars.

Ж

Back in Kunduj at midday, Minister Vaid and the

Praesha stood in front of Yuda.

"And that is how it happened, Your Majesty", the Praesha concluded his report. "I am ashamed for this lapse in security. I am ready to accept punishment for it. As are the men that you put in my charge".

He knelt down on one knee and bent his head down.

"Praesha, Praesha! Please arise" said Yuda, a bit embarrassed, and standing up himself. "You were my Father's Praesha and are now mine. You are as old as my Father. It was not so long ago that you punished me for youthful indiscretions. It does not do for you to kneel in front of me like this. I commend you for your service and for the investigation."

"I may be older in age, your majesty", replied the Praesha standing up "but am still your Praesha. My life is .. "

Yuda raised his palm. When the Praesha fell quiet, Yuda sat back down and said:

"The apotheker says I must rest one more day. I intend to follow his advice and go back to bed. I do still feel quite sleepy. However, before I do that, there are some things I want done, Praesha.

"First, send some men downriver on a boat. Ask them to find the deodar cedar these criminals used last night. Wherever they got off the river, they are unlikely to have taken the tree with them. So, if we find the deodar, we might know where they got off and will know where to look for them.

"Yes, Your Majesty. It will be done" replied the Praesha.

"Second, this young man - Balu - who foiled the attempt yesterday seems capable. I want you to put him under observation and give him The Test. We might need to use him again. One thing I pride myself on is recognizing talent and this young man just might have it."

"Yes, Your Majesty. It will be done".

"Next, I don't want to talk to all the guards right now. But tell them that they are to be alert! I am disappointed in them for last night and will let them know what changes I will make when I talk to them tomorrow."

"Yes, Your Majesty. It will be done".

"Finally, please send in my night maid Talu, and then

Balu. I would like to see them now."

"Yes, Your Majesty. It will be done".

"That will be all"

As the Praesha and Vaid bowed and turned to leave, Yuda called out to Vaid "Laushu! Please stay a while longer".

Yuda got up and touched Vaid's feet.

"This day, I missed my morning prayers. Allow me to pray to you, my Laushu".

Vaid touched Yuda's head and replied: "It has been a long time since I taught you any real lessons, my disciple. But I am proud of you for your bearing today".

"Is there anything else I must do?"

"Yes. Order the army to suspend preparations for invading Khet. We need the whole army to focus on apprehending these two men and bringing them back here. Alive. We must question them and find out the details of this attempt. We may still invade Khet, but first we must punish the kingdom that did this".

"Yes, my Laushu. I will do this" said Yuda "unless of course Khet is the one behind this".

Vaid joined Yuda in a chuckle at that sarcastic witticism.

"One more thing. I will craft a message to reassure all your subjects. And to invite them all to partake a big feast tomorrow night. You should personally host this feast for your subjects. Order your crier to go through all of Kunduj reading that message. If we say nothing, rumor mongers will spread unsavory messages."

"Yes, my Laushu. I will do this."

"Finally. Send messengers to your father on his pilgrimage. Let him know that you are alive, well and eager to rule. If he hears an exaggerated version of last night, he is likely to believe that he is needed back in his kingdom. It is not good for one to break one's pilgrimage so early."

"By Ag, my Laushu! You are absolutely correct. It would not do at all for father to return quickly. I will certainly do this".

A servant entered and announced "Victory to you, my

King. Young guard Balu has arrived as ordered".

Vaid rose, touched Yuda's head once more and said. "You are a wise conqueror, my disciple. I will leave now to promulgate your orders".

Yuda nodded to the servant, pointed to a decorative arrow hung on his wall and said: "Hand me that arrow and then send in the young guard". The servant took the arrow off the wall and reverently handed it to Yuda before leaving.

Yuda examined the decorative arrow. It was made of wood with beautiful designs on it. The arrow head had intricate carving of a leaping lion on one side and leaping flames on the other. Peacock feathers were used to streak its tail. The shaft was decorated with hexagonal tessellations along its length. Due to the art work, the tip was so blunt, that the arrow was useless as a weapon. But as a piece of art, it was priceless. Balu entered, knelt on one knee and greeted Yuda.

"Victory to you, my king!"

"I am pleased with your performance last night. When others might have panicked or neglected their duty, you held firm in your resolve. And did your duty well".

"I am honored by your praise, Your Majesty".

"Arise and come here". When Balu did so, Yuda continued "I was wondering what gratuity I should bestow on you".

"Being in your presence and hearing your praise is large gratuity for a humble boy like me, Your Majesty".

"For warriors like you, my boy, there is only one honor that fits. I had this arrow made for presenting to soldiers that show valor in battle. As I conquer the world, and become the First Emperor in human history, there will be many more such arrows to be bestowed on remarkable soldiers. For now, this is the first and only one. And for your service last night, I give this to you".

Balu was beside himself with pride and had tears of joy streaming down his face.

"Your Majesty! I am boundlessly grateful. I will consider it my highest honor if you allow me to play a small part in those future battles. I will consider my life well spent if I lay it down in the effort to establish you as the First Emperor".

"That will be all".

Balu bowed deep again and left with an extra bounce in his step.

When Talu, the night maid arrived later, Yuda's criticism was as severe as his praise of Balu was generous.

"You kept a Raha Daur, without telling me?" he asked accusingly. "You knew you are not to have any secrets from me. If you did not want the Praesha or the other guards to know, that is fine. But you have nightly access to me. You could have told me face-to-face. Did you think I was incapable of keeping a secret?"

"No, Your Majesty! I was simply trying to propitiate the Gods. I did not know these men were so evil. It was a mistake to not tell you. I bitterly regret it and will never repeat it. I stand ready for any punishment from you, sire. I deserve it"

"Yes you do! Only your long service gives us pause from sending you to the trident without delay. I don't want you back here tonight. May be not ever again; I don't know how I could ever completely trust you again. Now leave and do not come back to the castle unless we send for you".

"Yes, your majesty" Talu bowed and left.

Finally, Yuda summoned Commander Dron and asked him to suspend all preparations for invading Khet. "Make the entire army available to the Praesha to apprehend these criminals. We will meet again tomorrow to go over the details"

"Yes, your majesty!" Dron bowed and left.

As Yuda lay back down on the bed, he felt very tired. As he was slipping into sleep, his thoughts lingered on his day.

This was not a great beginning to my rule. The first day, in fact the first few hours, of freedom from father were marked by a kidnapping attempt. On me! Perhaps this was the last day of Father's rule. After all, he was here till almost mid-day yesterday. And though my coronation was a few months ago, his constant interference meant that he never stopped being king. So let's just say that he had a poor end to his tenure.

My tenure begins today. And with what I've done today, I have laid a solid foundation for glorious conquests. I should take advantage of this crisis to significantly rearrange the workings of the castle. All of the old guard can be removed; I need to bring in new blood. If he passes The Test, perhaps this boy Balu will make a good Praesha for me. I can let the old Praesha go. He might like to join father on his pilgrimage. They were old friends after all!

With that, Yuda dozed off into deep sleep.

Story of the Story - 3

We got into a routine. Everyday in the evening, Jalal and I would have phone call to work on the next leaf or two as we analyzed the scans. My contribution was in using the character map to convert the glyphs on the leaf into sound. From that approximate sound, Jalal would figure the correct Persian or Brahuic sound and explain its meaning. Then we would painstakingly put together the whole sentence and synthesize its meaning.

It was fun because we were making progress. Jalal would always complain that he wanted me to put in more time. But I had a full time job and a family. Anyway, I could not put in more than an hour on weekdays and about four hours on holidays.

One day just as we were finishing up our phone call, Jalal asked:

"Can I show you something unrelated to the project? I want your help in translating it".

"Sure!"

He emailed me a scan of a page of hand written notes. "I found this in the Haji's notes after he died. It looks to be written in Hindi but I can't parse it. Haji's notes, annotated it with a smiley and said these were words supposedly spoken at Bada Ravi's funeral".

I saw the following two couplets in my email and chuckled.

Shata bhaasha kovidam cha   Srestha kavim jyestha ravim
Kaala sarpa dashtam drushtva   Kaalidaso vadachchhoka.

Kaalee prasadopi mama   Kavitve bhavati doshaha
Kimiti vichitram tade   Ka bhaashaaya seemitam

"What? You understand it?" Jalal asked.

"Took me a couple of minutes but yeah, I think so. It is actually Sanskrit, not Hindi. It says: Upon seeing Bada Ravi, the expert in a hundred languages and great poet, on his death bed (literally being bitten by the snake of time) Kalidasa sadly exclaimed:– Though my poetry is a boon from

Goddess Kali herself, it still has the flaw of being limited to only one language. How strange this is!".

"This is Kalidas, the ancient Sanskrit poet?"

"Yes. For many, the greatest poet ever".

"Yeah, yeah. Didn't he write Shakuntala. And Cloud Messenger? They were wonderful; I read English translations of them".

"Yes. Those and several other works have survived. Legend says that Goddess Kali herself gifted him his prowess at poetry. So, at Bada Ravi's funeral, an attendee said that even Kalidas with the divine gift was restricted to just one language. But Bada Ravi has excelled in a hundred languages. So Kalidas himself concedes Bada Ravi's greatness".

"What a guy, this Bada Ravi!" Jalal replied. "I am beginning to understand what the Haji meant. I should realize that I am a Badrawi".

I was confused. "What are you taking about?"

"Bada Ravi. He was amazing. When the Haji said I was a Badrawi he meant that I should realize I am a direct descendant of Bada Ravi. My ancestor transcribed this book a thousand years ago. Now I must help translate it into a modern language. This story cannot be lost."

I was about reply with a witty barb like asking him to get off of whatever he was smoking. But I bit my tongue. He sounded very sincere. Many strange things motivate people. If this was his thing – who was I to object?

With that heart-felt phone call, the pace of translation hastened further. We came up with a newer schedule where Jalal would work on the translation by himself and I would check and ask questions after he was done. My questions often led to corrections on his work to more accurately reflect the original text.

This worked well because he clearly had more time to spend on this than I did. And doing the original translation is more time-consuming than just tweaking it. Even so, his enthusiasm was so great that I started to fall further and further behind.

70

5. Edhir mael Pakdhir

Jenon and Vika awoke at sunup and quickly finished their morning ablutions in the river. They sat down on the ground and briefly finished their prayers.

"How much farther to Khet?" Jenon asked.

"One more day of walking", Vika explained. "We need to walk right along the Amu for one Kos, up to the fern forest. Then, we turn west and walk about one more Kos to reach Khet. I have carried so many messages to and from Khet. There was not one time that I didn't wish we were closer to the river. That would have made my job so much easier".

"Shameful! Can you ever forgive the founders of Khet? Instead of thinking of you, they thought about silly things like keeping a safe distance from the Amu and her infamous floods."

Vika gamely hurled a twig at Jenon in mock anger which Jenon ducked and continued

"But listen. why would it take a whole day for just two kos? I know I am injured but I won't be that much ..."

"There is no path through these woods", Vika interrupted to explain. "These woods are thick and very difficult to walk through. And they grow right up to the river without leaving any sandy river bed to walk on. In fact, we would be lucky to cover that distance in one day".

"I am sure many people travel between Kunduj and Koka. What do they do?".

"Very few ever walk. Most people just use the river. It is so much easier to punt a boat even upstream, than to walk. No king has ever controlled this land, so no one ever thought to build a walking path. Even small distances are difficult to travel here unless you use the river. Perhaps that is why, Koka is such a significant river port. And that, in turn, is why Ivchea and Gandar are perpetually fighting over it".

"Koka is such an amazing city; comes right up to the river banks. I sometimes wonder how they escape Amu's floods."

"Well", explained Vika, "the city is some height above the river. On almost a plateau. But you are correct. If the floods are particularly bad and the Amu rises high enough, she will wash them away. Some day it is bound to happen, mark my words."

"Vika, the most high seer in the highest heavens,", Jenon mocked in sombre notes. "has come down to earth to proclaim that the River port of Koka will be submerged under Mother Amu. Take shelter, you fools. Tread not to Koka!".

"Shut up!" Vika laughed.

"Let's start walking", Jenon replied standing up with a slight grimace. "I am eager to reach Khet and report. I would love to see how Byram will get us out of this".

Their progress was excruciatingly slow because of obstruction from fallen trees and branches. Also, Jenon's thigh wound denied him much needed agility. It took them nearly till mid-day to travel just half a Kos, still well short of the fern forest. Jenon was very fatigued from the pain in his leg and both were ravenously hungry. They stopped for a rest and Jenon tumbled down to sit on the ground leaning against a birch tree. Vika left saying he would try to find some food but returned within a very short time, empty handed.

"No easy hunt today?" Jenon asked wanly.

"There is a camp of Kundujan soldiers over there" Vika replied curtly pointing with his thumb.

"What are they ..."

"They are searching for us! I overheard them. They know that we were going downstream on a Deodar Cedar. They even know that my name is Vika. If they find us, we will experience extreme unkindness. I want to get as far away from here as possible. And as quickly as possible. To hell with food! Can you walk some more? If we move fast we can probably evade ..."

"Wait!" Jenon whispered, "What were they doing till mid-day? Why did they not leave camp at day break?"

"I don't know. And I don't care to find out. They looked very somber, serious and scary. We should leave now. Right now".

Jenon nodded his head in agreement, but it was a half-hearted gesture and he stayed sitting. Vika took a few steps and when Jenon did not move, he wheezed, "Jenon!" in an exasperated voice. Jenon held up his index finger to ask for quiet as he thought. After several moments Jenon looked up at Vika with a smile on his face and said in a hushed tone: "Edhir Mael Pakdhir."

"What?"

"It is one of the first principles of combat tactics." Jenon explained. "It means literally, deflection (Pakdhir) is better than repulsing (Edhir). If a sword is going to rain a blow on you, you don't necessarily push it back but rather push it sideways. Same goes for a strong wrestler running at you. You don't try to stop him but rather to push him to one side and get him off balance. It is always easier to deflect a blow than to face it head-on."

"Again", asked a confused Vika, "what?"

"These soldiers are from Kunduj. If we do nothing, the entire Kundujan army will be bearing down on our beloved Khet. And we can't really repel them head-on. Why don't we use these soldiers to misdirect Kundujan fury? Perhaps we can do something so these soldiers think that yesterday's kidnapping effort was from somewhere else. Then Khet would not face a devastating invasion. We may have a chance here to stop the invasion before it starts".

"How?" asked Vika "By fighting six armed soldiers with our bare hands?"

"No." replied Jenon seriously, without acknowledging the sarcasm. "That would not be desirable even if it was possible. But if we can make them believe the attack came from somewhere else, they will report that back to Kunduj".

"How do we make them believe that?"

"I can talk to them and tell them that I met the real kidnappers in these woods. And I will supply them misinformation".

"You are mad! What if they recognize us?"

"How can they? No one saw us in Kunduj other than Talu, the old maid. And I doubt she is camping with these soldiers."

"What about the young guard? The one who stopped us. Or the guards playing Elephants and Camels as we walked out of the castle? They all saw us."

"Really? Are any of them at this camp?"

"I don't know!" said Vika in an exasperated voice. "I didn't carefully notice everyone's face during yesterday's dark night!"

"Exactly! So, what makes you think they noticed our faces? The only one who paid any attention to us was the young guard who stopped us. But I would be surprised if he is among the campers because I injured him. Even he, saw us only in the very dim light of a lamp. Surely, he can't identify us. And I will be disguised".

"What disguise? We have nothing to make a disguise with!"

"Since these fellows barely know us, disguise is best done with nothing", explained Jenon liberally rubbing brown dirt on himself. "The most important thing to fool a person is that the presentation should be different. For example, if we met King Yuda in the woods acting as a poor traveler carrying his own meager belongings, I guarantee you, we will not recognize him. Contrariwise, if an impostor is presented riding on an adorned elephant with an entourage announcing Yuda's arrival, we are certain to be fooled into thinking it is the real Yuda".

As Jenon continued to sprinkle dirt on himself, Vika said incredulously:

"So, you think this dirt will disguise you!"

"Not just the dirt. I will go alone and claim to be a Chadan Shaman. Since they are looking for two men, that itself will misdirect their attention. Also, they will be expecting us to run away from them. I will instead go to them voluntarily. So you see, the context will be totally different. They won't even consider that I may be one of the kidnappers".

"That is an elaborate theory Jenon. But let's be realistic. What do you plan to do if you get recognized? Do you realize, that you may get a spear in your stomach?"

Jenon applied some of the blood from his wound to his forehead to look like a shaman. Then he looked thoughtfully at Vika and nodded.

"Yes I realize. But if someone does recognize me, they are unlikely to kill me right here. They'll probably take me back to Kunduj. And then Yuda might put me to death after making me spill my beans. Even there, you have to agree. If I get caught, that might be my best chance to plant misinformation and convince them that I am from somewhere other than Khet".

Vika was taken aback by this dispassionate attitude. But Jenon stopped him even before he said a word.

"Don't worry, my friend. I don't want to be caught. I have no desire to be tortured or killed. I would much rather go back home and be with Mali as she delivers our baby. So, I will try my best to stay in disguise. But I am prepared to get caught. That is a cost I, as a soldier, am ready to pay".

"Hold on! Why don't I go? I may not be a soldier but I am as willing to sacrifice for the King as you may be ..."

"I know. I never doubted it", interrupted Jenon. "But your role as messenger is far more valuable now than any amount of soldiering either one of us can do. If I get caught, I will try to misdirect Kundujan wrath. You need to take the News back to Khet so that King Mayun and Minister Byram can make alternate plans. So, you stay behind in the shadows to watch what happens. If something goes wrong, go to Khet as fast as you can and relay the News. If nothing goes wrong and I am successful, let us go together back to Khet and report. Understood and agreed?"

Vika acquiesced, nodding reluctantly.

"So, where should we misdirect? Whom should we blame for yesterday's kidnapping?"

"Koka, perhaps?" Vika ventured. "It is half a Kos downstream of here. Koka is certainly strong enough to want to challenge Kunduj and pull the kidnapping shenanigan. Perhaps, King Pascheega of Koka wants to occupy Kunduj so they can be finally be free of the fear of Gandaran invasions. Besides, we did tell the old maid we were from Gandar. And Koka was under Gandaran control in the past, so it all fits."

"Flawless!" Jenon exclaimed nodding appreciatively. "Vika, my friend, we will make a master strategist of you yet. However, I won't provide any analysis - we'll leave that up to Vaid and his men. We'll simply plant the idea that the kidnappers were from Koka".

Jenon finished applying dirt all over himself and blood to the forehead and asked, "How do I look? Final touch is speaking Chada. Mask, it will do, my Ivchean accent to hide."

Chada language was prevalent among tribes near the southern coast. This far north, there were very few people who spoke it natively. The language shared enough similarities to Crit that, with some effort, Vika could comprehend it. Shamans from Chada were legendary travelers and were recognizable due to the bizarre grammatical structure they used in trying to communicate with Crit speakers.

"I did not know that you spoke Chada!" said Vika surprised.

"I don't. But I doubt that any of them knows Chada either. I do know some Chadan words. I'll talk like a typical Chadan Shaman attempting to communicate with Crit speakers".

"Jenon, I salute your audacity!", Vika laughed. "Alright fearless leader, I'll hide and watch you. I will take the News back to Khet, with or without you. And I'll run to the rescue, in case you have trouble".

"Remember, we don't want to hurt these men. We want them to go back to Kunduj with the untruth we supply them. So, don't rush to the rescue; hold back for the most part."

"Right. These armed Kundujan soldiers will be helpless in front of my prowess. I should restrain my strength in order to not hurt them".

Jenon joined in the chuckle as they walked toward the Kundujan camp and reached it in about five minutes. The camp was on a flat patch which was relatively clear of trees. They overheard hushed conversation among the soldiers and tried to listen for a few minutes.

Jenon took a deep breath. Vika approvingly nodded to Jenon and then, pointing to a tall, thick sagebrush went to hide behind it. He picked up a few rocks along the way with a self-deprecating smile on his face. Jenon waited until Vika was fully settled in and walked straight into the enemy camp loudly proclaiming a doggerel in a self-important poetic voice.

Another one of Bada Ravi' poems in the Kanda meter.

కంద:

భూపతి నిదురింప నతడు

    భీతిలు నటులనొక౦ బాము స్వప్నము నందున్

బుస్సున రెండేసి తలలు
భీభత్సముగ ఝళిపించి విషముం గ్రక్కెన్

Kanda Meter:

Bhoopati nidurimpa natadu
bheetilu natula noka bamu svapnamu nandun
Bussuna rendesi talalu
bheebhatsamuga jhalipinchi vishamun grakken

Meaning:

> While the king slept, to frighten him,
> A two headed serpent appeared in his dream.
> It shook both its heads and angrily
> Spit poison in his face.

Then Jenon looked pointedly at the soldiers and continued more prosaically, "Ah. Recognition you me give soldierly. Than yesterday's bastards, better are you looksy".

There were six Kundujan soldiers, each armed with a spear. In addition, three of them also had bamboo bows and a quiver of sharp wooden arrows. There was no way Jenon could have fought these men; no possibility of Vika mounting a meaningful rescue. He had to be careful. No misjudgments now, Jenon exhorted himself.

"Shaman!" one of the soldiers asked. "Won't you please help us?"

"Foolish the question is! To help others, a tree gives fruits. To help others, a Shaman lives".

"Shaman, we are soldiers of King Yuda from Kunduj. My name is Suvaid; I am the son and personal servant to Supreme Minister Vaid. I am leading these soldiers in pursuit of two evil men".

"King yours, angry will he be. Sit here you do, while searching there is to do".

"We stayed because one of our friends is very ill. We don't know what is wrong but he appears to be dying. Won't you help us?".

"Up to ill-hood person, take me".

They took him into the woods a good thirty yards away. A soldier lay unconscious on the ground. His legs were swollen and he had large purple spots all over his body. He was breathing in short shallow gasps. While everyone stood back for fear that this was some contagious disease, Jenon walked forward. Without too much effort, he was relieved to find marks of snake bite on the soldier's left ankle.

"Fools!" Jenon beckoned to the other soldiers "Closer come. Death nears your friend. This is the bite of a Koopor snake. Unless snake be still around, it is not contagious!"

The other soldiers came close and Jenon pointed to the snake bite marks on the victim's ankle. The soldier was beyond any earthly help. The other soldiers all stood around him comfortingly holding his hand. Within minutes, the soldier stopped gasping and breathed his last. They emitted a loud despondent cry almost in unison. As befits his new status as Shaman, Jenon sermonized to the little group.

"If snake no bite him, bit YOU it would have. Gave his life, your friend did, so rest of you may live. Help can't reach him anymore - unless it be from Amu herself. Grieve, but in pride. Tear not in sorrow, but in celebration of his courageous sacrifice".

"Thank you, Shaman" they mumbled.

"Why you do here? Too many civilized dies in these woods. Two evil men you say. Meet such fate they will too, have no doubt".

"Shaman, we want to catch them before they die. They tried to abduct our king last night. We foiled their plot and our king is safe but the criminals escaped by floating down river on a log of Deodar".

"Ah. Yes, the two-headed serpent in my dream - these two men it be. But, poetic the irony is. Evil as the devil they were. Yet they rode the immaculate Devadharu down the river". The irony struck a chord with the soldiers. Jenon was quiet for a moment, then suddenly jerked his head up as if struck.

"Could they be they?"

"What, Shaman?" Suvaid demanded "Who? Could who be who?".

Suvaid, the fortunate, thought if this shaman had seen the kidnappers that was proof of his luck. For he was Kaidbar. It was easier to separate hot water from cold water after mixing them than it was to separate him from his fortune.

"A dark Ivchean and a short Critan, were they not? Powerful narcotics, did they not have?"

"Why, yes! Did you meet them?"

Even Suvaid was amazed by his own fortune. Could his luck be so strong that, in this vast jungle, he would run into the one shaman that had met the kidnappers?

"Stole my food and beat me up, they did. Give me this, they did, as I tried to run away", Jenon pointed to the wound on the back of his thigh. He was amazed at how easily this was going. He wondered if his luck would hold. Will he really be able to plant the misinformation this easily?

"How dare they hurt a Shaman?!" Suvaid roared, "Tell us, oh Shaman. Where did they go? We will find them and avenge your insult".

Jenon noticed that Suvaid was play acting a little in order to pump for information. But he had to be careful. He should make them work a little to get the information. The harder it is for them to get it, the more likely they were to believe it.

"Your thanks. But small mind, a shaman keeps. No room for grudges in it. No need to avenge me, leave them be. Fall prey, they surely will, to some natural catastrophe. Without doubt punish them, Amu or Ag will".

"But, shaman! They are truly evil. They were about to destroy our whole kingdom by kidnapping our king. And they hurt an innocent holy man, a shaman, like you".

"Humans! Their nature compels evility. Floated away on the Amu they did. Clean away their sins she did, just as a mother cleans her baby. No need to punish them anymore, unless it be by Mother Amu herself".

With that Jenon attempted to walk away. "Wait!" Suvaid signaled a couple of soldiers and they caught him roughly, accidentally pushing him down to the ground.

"No different are you. Evility pervades you too! Hurt a shaman, you will!"

Suvaid gestured to his soldiers and they helped him stand up and bowed slightly. All six soldiers were standing facing Jenon. They were at the ready to prevent him from running away.

"How can I convince you" asked Suvaid "to do the right thing? Teaching these evil men a lesson is not only a matter of vengeance. It stops them from committing more evil. Wouldn't you want to stop the spread of evility? Wouldn't you want to help the world avoid further evility from them?"

"Ah yes" Jenon replied, still playing hard to get. "But kill evil men does not kill evility. Hearts of theirs must be changed".

"Either way, we must first catch them. They sullied all soldiers by acting so cravenly and all Shamans by hurting you viciously. They sullied Mother Amu by escaping from a crime on her. And they sullied all Deodars by cutting one down and riding away on its log".

Jenon detected a note of desperation in Suvaid's voice. He was listing everything he could, hoping that something would move this shaman. Perhaps it was time to give in.

"What say you!? They did not cut down a living Devadharu. The tree, already felled was she. Told me they did, that she was down".

"No, Shaman!" one of Suvaid's companions chimed in, happy to play his part. "They heartlessly cut down a living, breathing tree. She was the oldest and most sacred Deodar in our town. All of Kunduj worshipped at her feet every full moon night. Because it was New Moon, she was not attended last night. And these cowards cut her down heartlessly and used her for despicable ends".

"Outrageous!" Jenon roared. "Sully they did, the immaculacy of a Devadharu. Stopped, they must be. Tell you, I will. Koka, they wished to go. King's men they be from Koka".

"Are you sure? How do you know?".

"Talk, they did, as they ate my food. In Crit, not very fluent myself is. But comprehend them, I did. Planning, for journey to Koka, they were".

"What were their names?"

"Kanavata and Vrajavoora, they told me their names

were. But then they snickered evilly and told me their real names were Yuda and Vaid. Knew I, from that snicker, that they was lying. True names was neither of those names. As they left again on the Pure Devadharu, the dark Ivchean called the other one Beeka. His real name that was, says myself. The dark Ivchean's real name, myself has no knowledge on it".

By the expressions on their faces, Jenon knew that they believed his story. So, it was time to hasten them along and make himself scarce before something could go wrong. Jenon looked up at the Sun and announced:

"Behold! Set-ward journey, the Sun has begun. Time runs tardy for my afternoon prayer. And for your friend, time wants to set him salvation-bound".

"Oh Shaman, won't you please tell us how to ensure his salvation?"

"Snake-bitten was he. Strings, he must be decorated with. Lucky he is that Mother Amu is right here to look after his soul. If he becomes one with water, soul of his will reach to Togasvita expeditiously. Twenty three birch twigs get. Twenty three stones get. Pair one twig to one stone. Strong-tie to his arms and legs, twenty of them. The other three, make a crown of them and, to his head tie. Take along, thus tied body, with you. Drop it into a deep part of the Amu.

"Deliver, Mother Amu will, his soul to Rock Boha. Rock Boha will personally deliver him to Togasvita. Rapid movement on you! Help your friend for salvation. Then reach Koka and look for your enemies. May Mother Amu deliver your friend to Togasvita. And you to success with capturing the evil Devadharu cutters".

It was getting really strenuous for Jenon to keep up with the charade. He made haste to leave from there singing an old devotional song he had once heard from a Chadan Shaman

Rock Boha some call you,

Others call you Mother Amu.

Ag, the Fire, some call you,

While others praise you as ...

King of Togasvita

King of Togasvita

As Jenon limped from there, Vika stayed in his hiding place for a few minutes to ensure no one was following. When the soldiers quietly got to preparing their friend's snake-bitten body, he slinked away from the sagebrush. He stayed away from Jenon till they were out of earshot of the soldiers. Then he caught up with Jenon and said,

"Jenon, that was fabulous! I started believing your story myself!"

"Thank you my friend", Jenon said but kept walking speedily.

"Slow down. Can we take a rest and eat? I am very hungry!"

"Not now, Vika. We have to keep moving as rapidly as we can. We cannot risk those soldiers getting anywhere near us now. I too am very hungry. But we just have to keep running. I want get the message to King Mayun as soon as we can. Let's go!"

"Why? Khet is still going to be there tomorrow. As will King Mayun. What is the big rush?"

"You saw Kundujan efficiency back there! What if Yuda sent emissaries to his neighboring kingdoms? What if he sends a messenger with crafty questions designed to reveal if any of these kingdoms was behind the kidnapping attempt?"

Jenon's voice slurred as he spoke because he was shivering. Vika felt Jenon's forehead which was very hot and said firmly.

"You are in no position to run. Let's take rest and we will go tomorrow. Your fever can be life threatening".

"No" Jenon put his foot down equally firmly. "We must get the message to the king so he has all the information he needs".

Vika protested. "Even healthy, it will be hard. Don't do this ..."

Jenon ignored the entreaty and plowed forward. Vika had no choice but to follow.

Ж

After the shaman left, Suvaid ordered his men to prepare a water burial for their friend. Within the half an hour, they decorated the body of their snake-bitten comrade as the Shaman directed and started rowing toward Koka. When, they reached a deep part of the river, they said a prayer and, with a wailing lament, reverently pushed the body into the river.

As the boat continued to float downstream, the six surviving soldiers, watched the body sink to the river bed, weighted down by the stones. No one expected to witness Mother Amu delivering his soul to Rock Boha, even if they stayed. Each, lost in his own thoughts, quietly looked on to the river as the boat coasted smoothly along with the current. There was hardly any need for rowing.

About an hour later, one of the soldiers looked up at Suvaid and said

"Sir! I apologize for not having brought this up earlier, but I was too distraught. Should we not have apprehended the shaman? Probably Minister Vaid would have wanted to talk to the shaman himself?"

"You are correct." Suvaid conceded, "At leisure in Kunduj, we could have extracted more information out of him than was possible in the woods. Further, it probably is helpful to hold him as one more person that has seen the faces of these criminals. I should have thought of it too but I was also deeply troubled."

But he was Kaidbar. The Sun might miss hitting the mountain top on a cloudless day but his luck would never miss. Suvaid was sure of that.

"We were only asked", Suvaid continued "to look for the Deodar tree. We might return as failures if we don't find the tree, but if we took him back at least we would not have returned empty-handed ..."

"Koka!" one of the soldiers pointed out the city. Koka was sprawled along the East bank of the river. Right at the Westward turn of the river, and at a height, stood a majestic temple with a large archway to welcome visitors. At this distance, it looked very small. The boats milling around in front of the temple looked like flower petals floating on the river.

"However, now that we are here," continued Suvaid "perhaps we should conduct a quick search here for the Deodar before we head back. My luck might help us find the log. If so, the shaman might be secondary. But if we don't, we can return to the same area and look for him. He can't have traveled too far."

"A deodar! Is that the log we are looking for?"

Everyone jerked up as Suvaid mumbled: "I knew my luck would never fail me". As a swift current dragged their boat downstream, the men rowed hard to bring it close to the log.

"Yes indeed. I believe you are right." Suvaid said, "We might not need the shaman anymore".

After a quick discussion, Suvaid gave his orders.

"Men! We have accomplished more than what was asked of us. We were only told to bring, if we could, the deodar log. Our friend gave his life to delay us at the correct moment so that we met the shaman and gathered much more information than we could have hoped for. Let us return to Kunduj with the log as well as with the additional information. Ag knows, we have paid for it with the blood of our friend".

They were pleased to note that the deodar log had all the marks of being axed down rather than falling down naturally. They tied the log to the stern of their boat and started punting back to Kunduj. Punting upstream was more strenuous than coasting downstream. But they pushed hard with strength borne out of the enthusiasm that they had accomplished their goal. King Yuda would be pleased with finding the deodar log. Minister Vaid would be eager to hear about Koka's designs.

By nightfall they were near the periphery of Kunduj. Suvaid ordered his men to secure the boat. He disembarked and instructed them to stay there till they were relieved and then went to report to Vaid about the mission.

Ж

Thus the Deodar completed a long journey and came back to her home at the end of her life. She was near the end of her natural life and might not have survived the next winter even if she wasn't cut down.

Nevertheless, her posture was inscrutable; her feelings

84

were difficult to discern. Was she furious at the people who cut her down? Was she happy with those that brought her back home for her final rest? Was she happy with the thrilling journey she undertook at the end of her life - a journey far surpassing that by any other tree? Did she feel gratified that the journey had added meaning for having planted her seed so far away?

These questions were hard to answer. She just stayed on the ground to wilt down to death at the place of her birth.

Җ

About an hour into their walk, which turned out to be anything but brisk, it was clear that Jenon's resolve was stronger than his flesh. He was taking support with his hand around Vika's shoulder and dragging along. But, Jenon suddenly quickened and exclaimed: "There! I hear Mali!"

"That's right! Let's go to Mali". Vika thought he was telling a harmless lie to encourage Jenon but a few minutes later he also heard a voice singing something. Supporting Jenon by the shoulder, Vika hurried toward the singing and about fifteen minutes later reached a clearance in the forest where Mali was chanting the obstacle prayer to Bohamir.

This verse from Bada Ravi is in seesam *meter followed by one in* theta geeti.

సీసం:

టగడ మెక్కుట లేక టోగస్య మందదు

ఎండ మందు పిదప ముసురు వాన

పురుటి నొప్పులు లేక పుత్రుల పొందరు

మరణము పిదపనే మొక్క సిద్ధి

సంద్రమ్ము దాటక సురదీవి జేరము

చేదైన మందుచే చిక్కు నయము

అని నీవు సామ చోర అతులిత దయ ధామ

గురుతర విఘ్నాలు గురియ వద్దు

తేట గీతి:

మాకు గలిగిన శక్తితో మట్టు పెట్టు

గల విఘ్నాలు మాత్రమే గలుగ పెట్టు

85

దారి నిర్విఘ్ను సుగమమౌ దట్లు మాకు
తతిమ విఘ్నము లెల్లను తట్టి కొట్టు.

Seesam:

Tagadamekkuta leka Togasva mandadu
Enda mandu pidapa musuru vana
Puruti noppulu leka putrula pondaru
Maranamu pidapane moksha siddhi
Sandrammu dataka suradeevi jeramu
Chedaina manduche chikku nayamu
Ani neevu soma chora atulita daya dhama
Gurutara vighnalu guriya vaddu.

Theta Geeti:

Maku galigina shaktito mattu petta
Gala vighnalu matrame galuga pettu
Daari nirvighna sugamamou datlu maku
Tatima vighnamu lellanu tatti kottu.

Meaning:

Can't reach Togasvita without climbing the Tagada.
Only after scorching sun comes the rain.
Without labor pains one cannot beget children.
Only after death comes salvation.
Without crossing the sea, can't reach Gods' island.
Only with bitter medicine does one get cured. With those thoughts, Oh Bohamir!
O' thief of Soma!
O reservoir of immeasurable kindness!
Please don't drop great obstacles on us.
With our limited ability what we can destroy,
Allow only those obstacles in our way.
Make our path obstacle-free and smooth
By bashing and removing all other obstacles.

(Tagada is a mythic mountain on the way to heaven. Bohamir is a mischievous god who steals soma from people to preach

Mali was wearing a simple yellow wrap-around tunic which covered her up to her shoulders. She was facing a small pond, swaying back and forth with eyes closed, and was repeatedly chanting the prayer in an earnest monotone. Vika worried that this young woman had come this far out of the village so late at night. But when they got closer, he noticed that Seeress Groot, was sitting nearby to keep Mali company.

Jenon's heart melted for Mali. Even in his exhausted state, his first thought was about this proud girl who grew up in luxurious comfort in the great city of Urlapi was reduced to sitting unarmed and attended by only one companion by a lake at the edge of a tiny barbarian village. He was amazed at how she was always there when he needed her.

"Mali! Help!" he croaked out as loudly as he could. Mali jerked her eyes open and, seeing her husband took a sudden in-drawn breath followed by a short squeal which may have been "Je!". She fluidly rose up and ran toward them with powerful strides. Then she helped Vika pull Jenon safely into the clearance.

"Je! What happened? Are you well?" Mali cried in a worried voice.

"Yes, I am well", Jenon hoarsely replied with a smile. "And now that I am with you, I am even better." With that macho announcement, he slipped into unconsciousness.

"Mother!", Mali cried out to Seeress Groot. As the seeress approached, she asked in an almost accusing voice. "I have been doing the Obstacle Prayer you taught me. And yet this is in my path!?"

"Stop it!", the Seeress replied somewhat sternly. "The power of your prayers brought him back. Now it is our job to remove this obstacle". Then she turned to Vika and asked, "What happened?"

"It is not bad, just a small gash", Vika said diffidently because he was not sure how much to reveal. "Jenon was injured with a spear in the back of his thigh a couple of days ago. I tied it up with Pajam grass. But we have been walking through the forest and dirt without rest. He now has a fever – for the past few hours".

"Help me turn him over and see his wound" Groot

ordered Vika. Groot examined the wound and told Vika: "Pajam was a wise choice but did the wound also get soaked in water?"

"Yes" Vika replied. "For several hours – almost through the night. But that was in cleansing waters of holy Mother Amu. Surely, there were no evil spirits in there".

"Hmm."

When Groot poked her finger on the side of the wound, Jenon awoke and howled in severe pain. Groot put a comforting hand away from the tender spot.

"Pajam was a wise choice" Groot repeated unnecessarily. "It probably saved his life. However, we need to wash and dress it again". Then she turned to Mali and said "Do not be anguished, my child. We will heal him back to normal in a few days. Fetch my balm satchel, hanging from the hook on the third pillar".

Groot made Vika move Jenon to a bed of soft leaves and bade him lie face down. After Mali got back with the satchel, Groot prepared a yellow lotion of haridra and stirred it with a clean neem twig, which she then sharpened. Then she thoroughly cleaned the outside of the wound with the yellow lotion. Then, she poked through the tender spot on the wound with the sharp tip of her haridra-coated neem stick. This made pus ooze out from the wound and caused Jenon to awaken again and howl. Groot squeezed all around the wound draining out a dirty reddish yellow fluid as Mali and Vika looked on in shocked silence.

"There are evil spirits lurking all through the jungle", Groot explained. "Even if Mother Amu washed some of it away, these others have grabbed on. But now that we have washed it out, he will heal back to normal".

After a few minutes, Groot let up her pressure and tied up the leg with a cloth soaked in more haridra lotion and Jenon went limp in sweaty exhaustion.

"Tell the king", Groot said to Vika "that Jenon is wounded and will see the king after a few days". Then she turned to Mali and explained, "Let him rest tonight. He should be up and about by tomorrow and should heal fully in a few days. You both will stay here in my cloister and you will take care of him. Understand?"

Mali nodded her head, suppressing tears. Groot reassuringly patted Mali's cheek which helped let out a torrent of sobs. Groot let her cry for a while.

"Be brave, my daughter. He will be back on his feet by tomorrow, I promise. Wounds always look bad at first but God has filled us with miraculous healing powers. The evil spirits are now exorcised; so, those magical powers can work unchecked."

Ж

"Sadarril suthil: every place there is a rope".

Jenon, who was tying a cord of firewood with a rope, was startled. He stood up in a flash, wincing in pain, and picking up his club. It was a hammer like device fashioned by tying a heavy rock to the end of a sturdy stick.

"Hey, hey. Calm down! It's just me. Vika".

"Don't ever startle me in the woods!", Jenon's exclamation quickly morphed into a broad grin as he said "Vika!! It is so great to see you. Have you been well?"

Without giving Vika a chance to respond, Jenon dropped his club and hugged his friend.

"I am sorry that I did not come back to visit you" Vika said. "I really wanted to. But after I gave my report Minister Byram ordered me not to socialize with you. Something about us being easier to identify if we were together.

But I am so delighted to have run into you though. Are you well? I am glad to see your wound seems to be healing well".

"Yes", replied Jenon. "They sent instructions to me also to not seek you out".

"But as I was walking and saw you tying up all that firewood, I didn't care. I just had to check on you".

"Glad you did. My wound is healing fine. Seeress Groot told me repeatedly that your Pajam grass saved my life. Our antics with getting soaked in water probably didn't help any. But I am on the mend".

"So, how is Mali's health?"

"She is fine. I did not appreciate it the day we came in but I now realize that while we were away, she became very close to Seeress Groot. They now have almost a surrogate

89

mother-daughter relationship!"

"Yes, Groot is a very gifted Seeress. Our family have sought her blessing several times for pregnancies, injuries and animal bites. Every time she has helped unfailingly".

"I know. So, what brings you, the great messenger, back here?"

"Not messenger. I now have a second occupation".

"Oh no!" Jenon said fearfully.

"What? I was just going to say that I am going to go on a long pilgrimage".

Jenon sighed in relief.

"What did you think I was going to say?"

"I was afraid" Jenon replied " that you would say you defected to Yuda. Or something".

"For once." Vika burst out laughing, "I, the worry wart, got you, the blockhead baby, worried".

The friends both laughed, thinking back to their misadventure in Kunduj.

"What brought on the pilgrimage desire?"

"I have been thinking about it for a long time. My children are all married and have followed their Ivchean Dreams. They live in Ivchea, more than 100 kos away. So, other than my loyalty to King Mayun nothing else holds me here.

"Even in that, I am getting old and creaky; I am not as useful to the King as I used to be. So, when we heard about Yuda's father going on a pilgrimage during our mission, that re-kindled my desire. My wife, she also wants to do this except she wants to travel long and slow; and see as many temples as possible. As a Chadan shaman, know you must, that pleasurable this will be".

"Well, this decision has made you happy!" Jenon replied. "You seem a lot more relaxed and carefree".

"Yes, indeed" Vika replied. "I have come to ask the Seeress to guide us on when to start".

"What about the King?"

"Yes, I asked him the day after I reported on our mission. He gave his assent", Vika's face fell as he replied in a worried voice. "I am not sure about Byram, though. He said that in recognition of my long service, the King will permit me to seek Seeress Groot's guidance on it. Then he exhorted me to remember that I still work for the King and it is my duty to provide assistance to the King and his men, as long as I live."

"That stands to reason. I am surprised he even felt the need to say it".

"I know. That is what worries me".

"No. What makes you worried, my friend, is the inescapable fact that you are a worry wart."

"No no. Really. I worry that sending me to Groot is a ruse to prevent me from going: the King permits but Byram instructs Groot to intervene."

"Oh come on! Do you actively search out for things to worry about?".

"Why? Do you think such beguilement is beyond the King's Strategist?"

"No. It is not beyond the Minister. But we are not worth so much of his thought, my friend. I love you dearly. You have become like an older brother to me and I shall miss you very much while you are gone. But you are not, neither one of us is, worthy of such beguilement, as you so delicately put it. If he wanted you to stay, he would have simply ordered you to stay. He doesn't need these niceties. He wouldn't care that much about your feelings".

"No. Not my feelings. But he would care about the fact that the King said yes. He would want to appear to not contradict the King".

"No, it would not happen that way. Khet is a well managed kingdom. The King would have discussed it with the Minister before he agreed. If they hadn't discussed it, the King would have sent you to Byram rather than impulsively say yes. I am completely sure that the King and Minister are in agreement about approving your request".

"I suppose you are right."

"Of course I am right. And moreover, do you think for a moment that Groot will heed advice from anyone other than God? You think she will listen to Byram, even if he approached her with such a scheme?"

"I assume not".

"You assume correctly. Don't worry so much. Just ask the Seeress. I am sure she will give you the correct advice about when to leave".

After a moment, Jenon added more quietly: "You know, I really will miss you dreadfully. But I am happy for you. This will be very joyful for you".

"I'll miss you too but you are correct. This will be very enjoyable. You know, I have been employed as a messenger, for nearly twenty years and this village has been my home for my whole life. Now, this pilgrimage will be very nomadic. I can't wait for it to begin."

"No" Jenon said. "You've been a messenger and have been traveling all your life; this is simply an extension".

"You are right. These travels will be enjoyable because they will be more pious and less hurried. And with fewer blockhead babies for company".

Ж

Seeress Groot returned to the cloister after an absence of three days. As the Seeress took her medicine sack off, Jenon and Mali rushed to her.

"Welcome back, mother", Mali took the sack off her hand and hung it from a hook on the pillar.

"I have some good News for you two" Groot said. "Vika is going on a long pilgrimage along with his wife. They will be gone almost five years and their home will lie vacant since they have no children here. I advised him to obtain the king's permission to let you two occupy his home while they are away. This is an old tree which has provided many years of happiness to their nice family. She will look after your family too".

"Mother!", squealed Mali in excitement. "The past week of non-nomadism in your cloister have begun to give me the urge to settle down too. This is very timely ...".

"You are just having the nesting urge, my child. It is quite natural as pregnancy progresses".

"Yes Mother", Mali continued. "This is very good News. But are you sure these people won't mind. Vika's wife, Baegan, is very nice lady. But they may want to preserve the

92

home ..."

"Of course", Groot interrupted again. "And you will preserve it for them. They are very happy to give it to you. Vika seemed especially thrilled at the prospect. And they will be back after about five years to a well preserved home".

Jenon smiled. The man he had called his older brother only three days ago would actually share his home like an actual older brother.

"Strangely benevolent, Mother Amu's ways are" Jenon said. "Just as Mali is getting the nesting urges, She provides you with a way to fulfill it. Seeress Groot, you are Mother Amu incarnate for us. If the King grants permission for this, I shall be very happy. This will make Mali very comfortable and also we will be close enough to visit you very often".

Mali looked curiously at her usually mischievous husband. Groot responded, genuinely touched.

"Yes, my son-in-law. I shall miss having you right here in my cloister but this place is very close. And I will not be forgiving if you neglect to visit me".

Six days later Groot conducted a simple Karda Bool ceremony where Vika formally adopted Jenon as his younger brother. Mali and Jenon moved into the house right away

The pilgrimage was to begin in two months. Perhaps Baegan was getting cold feet or perhaps she was just anticipating the magic of a baby at home. She began suggesting that perhaps it would be better to wait until after Mali delivered to start the journey.

The suggestion was very appealing to Jenon and Mali who were thrilled at the prospect of having elders to help during pregnancy.

But no one imagined that this delay would prove be a life saver.

Story of the Story - 4

"Hello, this is DubDee". I was not expecting a call from her. I had not spoken to her at all since Jalal and I started our collaboration.

"Hello DubDee. How are you?"

"I am good", she replied. "How are you? And how is your son the cutie pie?"

"We are fine, thanks".

"I have some News. Mr Jalal Badrawi slipped on the snow last night and broke his hip".

"Oh no. Is he going to be alright?"

"Yeah. The doctor said, they want to move a bit more carefully because of his history of cancer. So, he will be out of circulation for a couple of weeks. But they think he will make a full recovery".

"That is good to hear. Please give him my best".

"It seems like he is really attached to the translation project you are collaborating on. He wanted to make sure you continue without him".

"Indeed! Actually, I have fallen far behind. This will give me a chance to catch-up".

"I know. He told me you were working as hard as you could but just did not have the time due to your other commitments".

"Tell him to get well soon or I will overtake him in the project".

"Will do" she chuckled. "That is actually what he was afraid of".

"Ha ha. No kidding!"

"Nope. He wanted you to have my contact information. In case you get ahead of where he is in the story, send me the work. I'll take print outs to him so he can work on it from the hospital".

"I did not realize you two were close".

"Yeah. He is like a father to me".

"Don't worry", I tried to reassure her. "I am sure he will be back in a few weeks".

"Yeah", she said simply. "You know he is the reason I go by the name DubDee?"

"Really? How did that happen?"

"When I was growing up – this was in San Diego – I had a friend called Lashonda Benning. In high school she used to torment me about my name: Vanessa Williamson. She would say I didn't look like anybody's son. So, I should be William Daughter. It annoyed me and I told her to cut it out. So, naturally, she kept up with it, often shortening it to WD and then DubDee.

"I went on two tours of the Iraq war. In the second one, I lost my legs to a road-side bomb. When I came back home, Lashonda was my room-mate. And she was of immense help in nursing me back to health.

"Even after I recovered physically, emotionally I was distraught. I would snap at people for no reason. I would yell at Lashonda all the time. One day she snapped back and told me to take my victim complex at losing my legs and shove it. She told me I better start acting nice or I might lose my friends, in addition to my legs.

"And she called me DubDee. I angrily told her to cut it out and she angrily doubled down on it. She taunted me by singing DubDee in different rhythms. I punched her in the face. She fell down with a bloody nose. But, I just rolled away on my wheelchair and left the house without even asking if she was OK.

When I came back a few hours later – still angry at Lashonda – I found her dead. Stabbed in her chest with a knife".

DubDee stopped at this point. I could hear her choking back tears.

"Oh DubDee. I am so sorry". Even as I said it, it felt hollow but it was all I could say. DubDee recovered and continued.

"But the worst was yet to come. The police pinned the murder on me. Our neighbors testified that Lashonda and I fought a lot. That I was an angry woman with nary a kind word for anyone. I myself admitted to punching her. And I was shell-shocked enough that I did not mount much of a defense.

"Jay Badrawi, I mean Jalal – of course he used to go by Jay those days – was in town then for some lawyers conference. My case made it into the local papers and he took an interest in me. He essentially adopted me. Nearly three months, he spent away from his work here, to get me acquitted.

"It turned out the real murderer was Lashonda's former boy friend. He had stabbed her, apparently just to prove his toughness to his gang and as revenge for the break-up".

"Wow" I had no other words to say.

"After my acquittal" DubDee continued, "Jalal encouraged me to move cross-country to Maine. He helped me with establishing my business as an event manager. And to get some peace of mind, he advised me to use DubDee as my official name – for honoring Lashonda and to get some peace. So that is what I did.

It took me a few years but, away from the hustle of San Diego and with help from this community – most especially Jalal Badrawi – I was able to reclaim my life".

"And now", I tried light-hearted banter, "he wants to take it away by pulling you into his obsession with this book".

"Ha. Yeah. But I don't mind. Please do keep me posted on your progress and I will let him know".

That is how DubDee got dragged into the project. During the time Jalal was laid up, I was able to catch up to him and also progress further. The doctor had not allowed him his computer so DubDee was our conduit in this exercise the whole period that he was in the hospital.

More importantly, I noticed that with the experience of the past few years, I was now able to proceed with the complete translation process: from the initial deciphering of the sound all the way down to getting the full meaning of the sentence.

But doing it alone was very inefficient and not as much fun.

The Second Conspiracy

Winter of 3658 BC

07 Taleyi Chachali

"Taleyi chachali" Commander Dron intoned.

"What? Fate is fickle?" Minister Vaid asked.

They were sitting cross legged on the floor in the middle of the secret chamber. King Yuda was on his throne set close by to them. Maintenance of secrecy required that they talk in low voices. There was about a fifty feet distance between them and the wall in any direction. No one could be close enough to eavesdrop.

At other times, this chamber was used as the hall where king held court. It was filled with carpets and chairs for the dignitaries. Converting it to secret chamber involved removal of all furniture except for the king's throne, so no one could be hiding in the shadows. Other than the king, only two men were present and all three were huddled in the middle of the hall. The guards at the entrance covered their ears with cotton plugs and barred entry to any one until the Minister came out and signaled the end of the secret conference.

"Yeah" Dron explained. "Only recently we were in this very room and planning a big attack on Khet. We said that made the most sense as our first foray because it is the smallest of our neighbors with the weakest defense and making them an example would encourage others to fall in line. And now here we are planning to attack Koka – our biggest neighbor with the strongest defense. And that too with a tiny force. Fate is indeed fickle to make us turn this much. Taleyi chachali".

Yuda was impressed. A soldier would never challenge the soundness of a king's decision. This was the closest Dron could come to expressing concern. Yuda received the message loud and clear.

"Commander Dron. Are you suggesting this is a bad idea?" Yuda asked him directly.

"Your majesty", Dron replied. "I'm but a lowly soldier. It is not for me to question the strategy designed by you and Elite Minister".

More red flags. He was actually the commander of his army, not a lowly soldier. What he was actually saying was that he cannot voice his criticism. So, Yuda gave him a direct order.

"Enough dithering! Explain your concerns about this plan. Imagine that it was suggested by one of your students".

"But remember" Vaid interceded, "you may not be privy to all the information that his majesty and I have".

Yuda threw an irritated glance at Vaid, Dron ignored that look and simply tilted his head at Vaid to concede his point.

"Well, your majesty", Dron responded to Yuda. "The first concern I have is the assumption behind the plan that King Pashcheega of Koka was behind the abduction attempt against you. As Minister Vaid said, perhaps there is evidence I have not seen. But from what I have seen it does not add up.

All we have is circumstantial evidence that must be balanced against Pashcheega's legendary reputation as Justice Incarnate. He would not resort to such chicanery. But even if we reject the notion that he is honorable, it still does not make sense. Koka has an army three times our size. It would be far easier for them to declare outright war and invade us than to do this. It does not match with what we know about Pashcheega".

"But it does match with what we know about Suvaid, the Fortunate" Vaid defended his son. "His fortune led him directly to all this evidence. It would be hard to square his legendary good fortune with the notion that it led him astray".

Faith in Suvaid and his fortune was a blind spot for the otherwise brilliant Vaid. While Yuda sensed this, he was still not confident enough to call it out. "Anything else?" he asked Dron.

"Yes, your majesty!" Dron replied. "It is our tactics. We are planning to build a boat – the Tunga – ride it downriver to Koka dressed as pilgrims. Upcoming New Moon night, when Pashcheega is known to take a dip in the Amu, grab him. Then we are to tie his mouth so he cannot shout and simply sail downstream until we meet up with another abduction force. There, we arrest him and bring him to Kunduj in a carriage".

"Yeah. What's wrong with the tactics?" Vaid demanded.

"This secret conspiracy" Dron started "does not befit His Majesty's honor. But even if we set that aside, it will not work.

The river is too filled with pilgrims, especially when the king takes his dip. It may be New Moon but there are plenty of lamps on the banks and the king is usually attended by several priests as well as his defenders. We won't be able to just drag him away".

"Do you have a better idea?" Yuda asked.

"Your Majesty, Minister Vaid", Dron replied. "If strategy calls for attacking Koka I would recommend just attacking them – not head-on but surreptitiously. Let us build up a bigger invasion force and storm the gates in the middle of the New Moon Night. Especially if we can hatch some plan for lulling the Kokan security into complacency, we can succeed".

"Hmm" Yuda was non-committal.

"Your Majesty, you ordered me to evaluate this as a proposal from one of my students. I would advise that student to reconsider his strategy. I would tell him that he may be focusing on the wrong enemy".

"So, you think we should abandon this plan" Yuda looked piercingly at Dron.

"I and the troops will follow your order and implement whatever strategy you decide".

"No doubt", granted Yuda smiling. "But that does not answer my question".

Dron paused, as if searching for words and finally said: "Apologies your majesty. Yes, I believe this, er.. this conspiracy is flawed. Since a head-on attack is not feasible, the best approach here will be a full-blown attack at night. It would be more honorable and also more likely to succeed."

"Alright", Vaid said somewhat dismissively. "We will take your thoughts under advisement. For now make preparations for the abduction plan, as outlined today".

Yuda was annoyed at his minister for closing the discussion, but the minister was also his Laushu. He did not have the confidence or the moral authority to show his annoyance. Dron stood up, bowed to the king and minister and left.

Ж

Balu stared blankly at the wall of his cell. "Prison!? How had it come to this?", he wondered.

It was only a month ago, the previous New Moon night, that he had saved the king himself from a kidnapping attempt. King Yuda was pleased enough to bestow the Arrow Honor on him. The king had permitted him to stay in the castle for a week until his shoulder wound healed. The king had even visited him and wished him good health on four different occasions.

Then last night, he had gotten drunk with a couple of friends. It was his first time to drink so much that he felt physically uneasy. As he was shuffling back home, five strong men jumped on him and arrested him on some bizarre charge.

Though wasted from drinking, Balu protested that he did not understand the charges. That he did nothing wrong. But the men were implacable, claimed to be following Royal orders. Then, none too kindly, they shoved him into this prison cell.

When he awoke, the bright sunlight outside indicated that it was mid-morning. Possibly almost noon. And, for the first time in his life, he had a splitting headache. He wondered why people ever romanticize drinking.   If he hadn't been drunk, he might have put up a better defense for himself. "I should never again drink like that", he admonished himself.

A month ago, he had a great Royal Honor. Today he was in prison. Balu finally understood the street play he saw a few months ago. The hero had poignantly and repeatedly sighed in Ivchean: Taleyi Chachali. Fate is fickle!

He looked around his cell and noticed that it was relatively large with two impalement devices in the middle and five shackles along the wall for stringing up prisoners. Clearly, there was room for other prisoners, but at the moment he was alone. He was also not tied up. Nor being tortured. Yet.

Someone opened a small rift at the bottom of the cell door and pushed a bowl knitted out of Shala leaves. Into the bowl was heaped some gray goop. Balu looked at the flavorless food with little appetite.

"Eat up, young Balu", a voice from outside said. "We wouldn't want you to die of hunger before His Majesty puts you to death".

"Wait!" shouted Balu hoarsely. "Why would His Majesty

give me the death penalty? I haven't done anything wrong!"

"That is what they all say" The guard laughed heartlessly as he started to move away. Balu peeked through the food slit and noticed that the guard was limping on a weak left leg. He held a tall bow which doubled as a walking stick and he carried a quiver of arrows on his back.

Balu smelled the food and felt violently sick. He pushed it away and, gathering whatever energy he had left, he cried through the slit.

"Sir! Help, please help!"

He repeated it once more as he noticed through the slit that the guard was still limping away. And then was about to repeat it a third time when the guard turned and asked brusquely.

"What is it?"

"I am feeling ill. I might vomit and I urgently need to do my ablutions."

"I need to do my ablutions", the guard mimicked scornfully. "You are the King's 'guest' but where do you think you are? In his castle?"

"Please sir" Balu pleaded, desperately controlling his vomiting reflex. "I don't want to dirty this place by vomiting here"

"Hah, Alright", the guard snorted reluctantly giving in.

He opened the door which led into an open courtyard. Hot sun was beating down from almost directly overhead. The walls as well as the floor of the courtyard appeared to be entirely made of stone. Into the walls were carved four different prison cells almost like caves - each with its own door, bolted on the outside.

The guard pushed him wordlessly toward a wall on which was hanging a rope ladder and gestured him to climb up. The ladder led up to the ground level, which actually was the top of a small hill. Balu realized that whole the prison was a bowl-shaped hole in stony hill. He must have climbed down that ladder last night when they brought him in, but he just didn't remember. The prison was ingenious! If the guard pulled out the ladder, a prisoner might break out of his room but would find it impossible to scale the smooth, stony walls;

they would be stuck in the courtyard. Balu saw that the river was flowing right next to the hill.

"We are on the banks of Mother Amu!", he observed somewhat pointlessly.

"Aren't you wiser than Minister Vaid himself?", the guard mocked. "We are next to the river since she provides an easy way to clean the prison when needed. Sometimes prisoners do worse than vomit, you know".

Balu felt ill again when the full import of his words hit him. He closed his mouth with his hand and pleadingly gestured toward a mound of dirt, asking permission to leave. The guard impatiently waved him off. Balu ran about twenty steps into the bushes before he violently vomited. As he emptied his guts out, he felt weak but relieved.

Balu shuffled back out of bushes and noticed the guard was sitting on a boulder next to the prison ladder. His bow was loaded with a sharp arrow and aimed straight at Balu.

"You may as well finish your ablutions. And then clean yourself up in the river. But don't think about escaping", the guard said with his arrow pointed unwaveringly at Balu. "You may run faster than I limp, but my arrows can easily reach you. Besides, the King will be very unhappy if you defy his punishment".

"Yes, sir" Balu said and meant it.

At least for the moment, he did not intend to run. He wanted to find out what was happening before planning his next steps. He finished his ablutions, stripped off his clothes under a tree to walked into the clear waters of the Amu for an invigorating bath. He briefly toyed with the idea of simply slipping away with the river. But, he really wanted to find out more about this strange turn of events. What had happened for the King to get angry with him?

He stepped out the river, feeling much better.

"There are some clothes on that tree", the guard yelled out.

When Balu looked up, he saw a sharp arrow unhesitatingly plant itself into the trunk of a tree, less than five feet from him. The guard was at least fifty paces away and by the time Balu turned to him, he had already loaded another arrow into his bow. "Granted, sir! You are a great marksman",

Balu mumbled to himself.

"You can wear those and wash your old clothes", the guard shouted.

"Thank you sir!" Balu bowed to the guard to acknowledge. He changed, washed his old clothes. He went up to to the guard and asked if he could dry his wet clothes on a tree.

"No", the guard replied. "Dry them in your cell. I am not letting you out again today".

Balu nodded. As the guard made him scale down the ladder, Balu tried to start a conversation.

"Sir, what is your name? I mean what should I call you? If I need something".

"God".

"Huh?"

"You may as well call me God", the guard laughed "because I am as unlikely as God to answer any of your calls."

"But why sir? I don't feel bad if you mistreat me because I know you are just doing your job. But, can't we just.... I mean, we both serve the same king."

"Don't you dare!" the guard thundered. "Don't equate your so-called service to mine. You don't serve the king; you steal from him."

"No sir, I do not" Balu interrupted vociferously, surprised at his own courage. "I have not stolen anything from anyone and certainly never from the king".

"Heh", the guard's grunt eloquently announced his disbelief. He quietly opened the cell door, pushed Balu in and locked it from outside.

"You better not bother me for the rest of the day" he intoned brusquely and left.

Feeling clean but exhausted, Balu lay down on the hard prison floor and slept.

Ж

Minister Vaid was fuming. He had just learned that the king had summoned Commander Dron for a secret conference. And yet, Vaid himself had not been asked to come. What could they be talking about?

105

It was bad enough that Dron threw cold water on his perfect plan. He would have asked his son Suvaid play a pivotal role in abducting King Pascheega of Koka. With that, he had no doubt that he could convince King Yuda that Suvaid ought to be his next Elite Minister.

Dron, with his tactical question of whether it would work and strategic question of whether it should be done, had ruined the whole plan. Dron had even had the audacity to implicitly question whether Suvaid's reputation as the Fortunate One was well deserved.

That was bad enough but manageable. He would have convinced the king, who was after all his disciple, to ignore those questions. But if Dron and the king were in secret conference, they were going around him? He was out of the loop. How could he fight that?

Just then, to his relief, word came that the king wanted to see him. When Vaid joined, Dron seemed to be summarizing something.

"That is everything, your majesty, Except Balu's test. I am leaving in three days and the test will be completed in eight days. Whom should I ask to release him from jail and evaluate his behavior? Assuming he passes the test, of course".

"Welcome, my Laushu" King Yuda bowed and acknowledged Vaid.

"Victory always to you, my disciple".

"Yes, commander. Don't worry about Balu – I'll deal with it. For now, please summarize the plan for Laushu".

"Oh? A better plan for abducting King Pascheega of Koka?" Vaid asked.

"No", Yuda replied. "This is a plan for a secret invasion of Koka"

Dron hit the high points: "Most of the standing army, about eight hundred troops, will make their way independently to Koka without any weapons. Suvaid and his legendary fortune will be right here to protect the castle. We will convert the Tunga into a floating armory by storing arms and ammunition in her keel. Then we will sail her down-river to the temple of Koka. On the next New Moon night, the troops will come to the Tunga to arm themselves, attack the Kokan castle and capture it".

"It is a good plan, your majesty" Vaid agreed. "If we maintain secrecy, Kokan castle will be defended by at most a hundred troops at night. And even those will not be on high alert. So, overpowering them with eight hundred should be possible. Our troops would probably not get in if they were armed when they enter Koka. But smuggling the arms separately on the Tunga is a good way around it".

Vaid was fuming internally that his plan had been so unceremoniously altered. But, he could not show it. As consolation, he told himself that if the plan failed, then his son could get into the act.

Ж

Balu silently tolerated three more days of uneventful imprisonment. He was given a meal of the flavorless goop everyday. He was also allowed out once a day between meals to clean himself in the river. He alternated between the prison clothes and his own clothes.

On the fifth day, he couldn't bear it any longer. At the very least he needed to know why he was being held. What had he done wrong? What was to happen to him now? And given that the guard was always the same man, hobbling around on his bad left leg, why was he being guarded by an invalid?

So, when the guard pushed his meal through, he tried again to start a conversation, to find some answers: "Sir!"

Silence from beyond the door.

"Sir!", Balu pleaded again. "I am in prison and I don't even know what I did wrong. Can you please tell me?"

"Really?" the guard mocked from the other side of the door. "Don't even know what you did wrong? Didn't they tell you when they dragged your sorry butt here?"

"I don't remember. They said something about embubble, I think. I don't even know what that means! And you accused me of stealing from the King a few days ago. I don't understand why anyone would say either of those things".

Silence.

"Sir!", Balu persisted in a reasonable voice. "Don't you

107

want me to repent for my mistakes? How can I do that if I don't even know what I did wrong?"

"It is embezzle, you idiot; not embubble", a suppressed smile in the guard's voice mitigated the harshness of his words. "And it means the same thing as stealing. You are accused of stealing from the Royal Treasury".

"What?" Balu was astonished. "I've never even seen the treasury. I've never had a grain more than the rations that the Praesha assigned me. If I stole, why am I still poor? It doesn't make any sense that ..."

"Quiet!"

Balu sat back, discouraged. But he was pleasantly surprised a few minutes later when the guard opened the cell door and beckoned him to follow. Balu stepped out into the prison courtyard.

"Go, wash up. Then we'll talk", the guard said in a reassuring tone.

All thoughts of the so-called food banished from his mind, Balu eagerly followed out, finished his bath in record time and rushed back to the guard who was resting on a boulder under a tree. Balu found a comfortable patch on the ground and sat down.

His speech, suppressed for five days, flowed out like the Amu. Without a preamble, he dove right in to describe how the older guards teased him during a game of Elephants and Camels, how he went away to sulk and how, as a result, he thwarted an attempt to abduct the king single-handedly. The guard looked on quietly, occasionally nodding his head.

"And I swear on Mother Amu, sir. That is the honest truth".

The guard just smiled.

"I am loyal to the King, sir. I can't imagine betraying Kunduj. I don't know why anyone would tell the King that I stole from him. And to be sent to jail with barely any explanation. It is so unfair!"

"So, you think the King is being unfair to you?"

"Not the King. But someone is telling him unfair lies about me. I hope you report back to him about how loyal I have been these past days in prison."

"What do you mean you were loyal in prison?"

"Well sir. I created no trouble for you. I stayed here almost ...".

"Almost what?", the guard gave him an encouraging nod.

"I stayed here almost of my own volition", Balu mustered up his courage to say, "because I don't want to disobey the King".

"What do you mean of your own volition? I have been guarding you the whole time".

"Well, I mean no disrespect sir, but it's not like you were trying very hard to prevent me from running away."

"Well, I mean no disrespect, young Balu", the guard countered. "But, it's not like you were trying very hard to run away."

"You let me out every day, sir. I could have escaped. I think I can outrun you."

"Yes, you could outrun me. But, never my arrow. However, I am glad that you did not try. I would have been unhappy if I had to kill or wound you".

There was no boast in the statement. It sounded like a matter of fact. Balu dropped the topic.

"You are right sir, I apologize. May I ask your name?"

"My name is Zvuk Meza".

"You are Zvuk Meza, the sound splitter?" Balu's voice was filled with awe and hero worship. Sound splitting, popularly considered the pinnacle of skill in archery, was the ability to shoot at objects, locating them just by sound.

"I am flattered that you have heard of me".

"Oh yes sir!", Balu rose up and bowed his head. "I apologize twice over. I was wondering why I was being guarded by an inva ... er, I mean someone limping on his leg. Now I feel honored. Please forgive me for underestimating you; I could never outrun one of your arrows".

"No need to apologize, young man. It is often a great advantage to be underestimated".

"Sir. It truly is an honor for me to meet you. Would you mind showing me your skill?"

"Sure. What do you want me to hit?" Zvuk picked up his bow and arrow and closed his eyes and partially turned the other way. Balu picked up a stone and hit a Shala tree about fifty feet away. Right away, an arrow swished through the air to plant itself on the trunk at almost the exact spot the stone had hit. Balu looked at Zvuk with speechless amazement.

"You don't have to be so amazed", Zvuk said. "That was easy because the tree doesn't move".

"Wait. Are you saying you can hit a moving target by sound?"

"Naturally. It is hardly useful in combat to only be able to hit stationary objects; you see the enemy doesn't stand still. And if I were not useful, the King would not have employed me for more than 15 years. Even now, after I've become an invalid - they still keep me".

Just then, they heard the cackling call of a pheasant.

"Do you want to eat well today?".

Balu, who had barely heard the cackle, was confused by the question but nodded his head. Zvuk quietly turned right to look intently toward the sound. Balu couldn't see much more than trees in the direction. Zvuk had squinted his eyes and was slowly turning his head both ways, trying to locate the exact direction of the sound. All the while, his loaded bow was pointed unswervingly in one direction. After a few moments, they heard the pheasant cackle again and Zvuk jerked to the correct direction and let loose the arrow. A moment later, they heard the agonized call of the pheasant as it breathed its last.

"Go get it", Zvuk ordered. "We'll both eat well today".

Ж

The meal of roasted pheasant and a few pomegranates, was delicious. With his hunger sated, Balu opened up again.

"Sir, I am deeply indebted to you for this meal. I feel like this was my first meal in a week".

"It is the truth. I won't force you to call that flavorless gruel as food", Zvuk laughed.

"Sir, how long did it take you to learn to split sound?"

"Stop calling me 'Sir'; I am not royalty. Just call me

110

Zvuk, or if you want to be formal, Zvuk Meza."

"Yes, si.. er, Zvuk. How long did it take you?"

"Sixty two days".

"Sixty two days?!", Balu exclaimed. "I would have imagined it took years."

"Well, I was formally learning archery for three years when I started learning this, so you could say it took years. And over time I still get better, so you could say I am still learning. But the initial learning period specifically for splitting sound, was sixty two days."

"You must have had a great teacher".

"Oh yes. The best. My Laushu is Commander Dron".

"Our Commander Dron? I didn't know he was ever a teacher".

"Yes, he used to teach. He is a great man and the best Laushu there ever was".

"But how do you remember the precise number of days it took? Why were you counting?"

"Well, it is a long story."

"Would you please tell me?" Balu pleaded and Zvuk started narrating.

Ж

I was in Laushu Dron's tutelage along with twenty other students. Our Kul was in the North Woods; even now, you can see remnants of it, if you know exactly where to look. One time, I came to Kunduj to visit my father and while returning, I was absent mindedly thinking about when I might get Laushu's blessings to leave the Kul and join the kings service. Perhaps Laushu knew someone in the castle and could help me.

I was startled out of my reverie by a bull hurtling toward me at breakneck speed. I jumped aside and saw that riding the bull was the most beautiful girl I ever saw. Her dark hair was open and was fluttering behind her. She was wearing a simple white tunic over her shoulders and green wraps around her legs. Purple Malva flowers were attached to her clothes. The look of sheer delight on her face, which made her even more beautiful, came from riding on a friendly animal. Freely. Without a cart. I was smitten. I had to find out

111

who she was. I ran as hard as I could and caught up with her near Darya lake. I hid in some bushes and observed her from about fifty paces away. She rested her bull and was trying to pluck water lilies without getting her clothes wet.

This was my chance to meet her; I came out from behind the bushes and asked what she was doing. She said that she needed sixty one water lilies by sundown for worshiping Rock Boha. But she couldn't get her clothes wet since these were her prayer clothes.

"I'd be happy to help", I offered.

"Also, I am not from Kunduj", she sheepishly admitted, "I am from Khiwani".

"That is fine. Pleased to meet you, foreigner".

"I mean", she persisted, "I do not have the King's permission for these lilies. I am sure he would be angry."

"Ah, don't worry. I will tell the King. You know, he appointed me to look after this lake".

A little white lie to impress a beautiful girl never hurt anyone. Right?

She did look mighty impressed, which made me feel as tall as that Shala tree. For the next two hours, she pointed out the lilies she wanted and I swam into the lake to pluck them. I learned that her name was Rasi. I also learned that on the day of Rock Boha worship, it is forbidden to change clothes or to wet them. That is why she could not go into the lake herself. Actually, she had gotten flowers ready the day before but, someone had gotten the temple elephant to trample her flowers. I thanked the elephant in my heart for giving me the chance to meet this girl.

When I came out of the water with the last of her flowers, she fashioned the long stem of one lily into a garland and put it around my neck. She gave me a hug, a kiss on the cheek and then wordlessly picked up the rest of the flowers got back on her bull. By the time I recovered enough to shout out "Can I come see you in Khiwani?", the bull was already racing away. But Rasi did turn around and flashed me a bright smile and a nod.

I was ecstatic. A few days later, I took Laushu's permission and went to Khiwani and met Rasi. She said her prayer was a roaring success; the queen herself had attended and had remarked favorably on the freshness of the flowers. The Queen's chambermaids were green with envy. Knowing that Rasi got the flowers the same day and that she did not have any help, they accused her of violating Rock Boha by undressing for entering the lake. Rasi related our encounter at the lake.

Queen believed the story and piously remarked that Rock Boha always sends help to those who wish to worship with a clean heart; the chambermaids burned with jealousy and refused to believe it. So, when Rasi took me to the other chambermaids to corroborate her story, they seemed angry. I did not care. What could they do to me?

Turned out, they could do plenty.

After spending a few hours with Rasi, I started to feel as if like I had known her all my life. I did not want to leave but needed to return to the Kul. I promised Rasi that I would come back before the next full moon and left.

As they say in Ivchean, Taleyi Chachali. As I was returning, my world came crashing down. Five strong men nabbed me and threw me in this very prison cell. The next day I was presented in front of the King. Prince Yuda, who was just a boy then, was also there.

Some official-looking courtier read out a complaint that I had "aided a foreigner. That too, to deplete the Darya lake of Lilies. That too without permission. That too while pretending to be a Royal Servant". The complaint made it look so sinister, as if I was conspiring with the enemy to topple the King. But the essential charges were true. Nervous and unskilled in argumentation, I saw no way to turn the narrative to my favor and simply admitted the complaints were true.

The King said he would pronounce punishment in seven days and ordered me back to prison. When some courtiers tried to get me punished immediately by pointing out that I had already admitted to my crimes, the King silenced them with a simple glare. I was absolutely impressed with his power. I learned later that day that the punishment for impersonating Royal Servants was death by head crushing. Suddenly all my admiration for the King was replaced by pure dread. Would I be dead before I see Rasi once more? What was to become of my aging father?

My Laushu came to my rescue. He worked what can only be described as magic in those seven days before my sentence. When I didn't return to Kul, he made inquiries with father, with his friends in the palace, and some of his students from Khiwani. He quickly pieced the whole story together, worked out a strategy for my defense.

So, seven days later when I was brought back before the King for the pronouncement of my punishment, there was a crowd of nearly fifty people including father, Rasi and Laushu Dron. The King regally walked in with Prince Yuda in tow. As he sat on on his throne, he patted the prince's shoulder and gestured toward the crowd as if saying I-told-you-so. Then he ordered:

"Summarize the charges."

A courtier stood up and spoke in clear, clipped tones.

"This young man aided a foreigner to steal Lilies from your majesty's lake. And he unlawfully pretended to be a Royal Servant. At the trial seven days ago, he admitted to these crimes".

He then looked at me and asked:

"Young man! Tell His Majesty if you still admit these accusations are true?"

"I do, Your Majesty".

"How many Lilies did you help this foreigner steal?" the King asked. This time, I mounted a small defense:

"It was sixty two flowers, Your Majesty", I replied. "She needed Sixty One for a Rock Boha prayer. I knew Rock Boha is one of Majesty's favorite Gods. Therefore I assumed that Your Majesty would not begrudge granting permission if asked. It was presumptuous of me; I should not have pretended to act on your authority. I apologize most humbly".

It didn't quite come out correctly. I had thought of much more to say but was too nervous. The king asked me with a playful smile:

"If she only needed Sixty One, why did you pluck Sixty two?"

"Your Majesty, I did not find out until later. I was getting the flowers from the water and she was counting. She made me get one extra to give back to me as thanks".

"Why did you tell her that you worked for us?" the king asked.

I hesitated a few moments because Rasi was in the audience. Then decided truth was the best choice and said:

"Your Majesty, I was stupidly trying to impress a beautiful girl".

That brought a laugh from the crowd and an understanding smile from the King. The king looked up at the crowd:

"Does anyone else have something to add?"

Rasi came forward and tearfully confessed:

"Your Majesty, it was all my fault. My name is Rasi and I am the one Zvuk is referring to. I should have come to you for permission. When Zvuk told me that he worked for you, I did not believe him; he looked too young. I knew he was just trying to impress me. So, I should have come to you after my Prayer - that was negligence on my part. So, please Your Majesty, give me punishment and spare Zvuk! He was only doing what any pious person would do to help with a Rock Boha prayer".

"No, Your Majesty", I interjected. "I am the Kundujan, I should have known better ..."

"Silence!" the king roared. "Does anyone else wish to add anything?"

"With your permission, Your Majesty", Laushu Dron came forward and spoke in an easy, confident tone. "I believe that there are foreign elements in Khiwani who are conspiring to misuse your dispensation of justice for their own ends. This young woman is unfortunate to have incurred the wrath of the chambermaids to the Queen of Khiwani. I believe they are conspiring to exact revenge, using your law as their instrument".

"I presume you have some basis for that statement, Laushu Dron".

"I do, your majesty".

"But you do not wish to present it publicly".

"His Majesty is very perceptive".

"Young man!" the King looked at me and sighed, "do you know that it is a serious crime to impersonate a Royal

115

Servant?"

"I did not know at that time, Sire". I replied. "However, I have learned since then".

"Your Majesty", Laushu Dron pleaded. "I appeal for clemency. My student's crime is less of impersonation and more of showing off to a girl. If His Majesty starts punishing young men for that, he might have very little virility left in the country".

As the king smiled and a titter ran through the crowd, Prince Yuda went up to the King and they held a whispered conversation for a few minutes while the crowd quietly observed them.   The King looked pleased with his Prince, nodded agreement and pronounced punishment:

"We can easily forgive stealing the flowers; it was done for a prayer. But we cannot forgive impersonating a Royal Servant. In great cities like our Kunduj, such behavior can lead to chaos.

"However, we too were young and foolish once. And we can understand the impulse to show off to this girl. So we find ourselves looking for a path between punishing and condoning this young man. And also this young woman.

"Upon the Prince's recommendation, we commute his death penalty and sentence both of them to Sixty two days of Utumcair - one day for each lilly stolen. We appoint Laushu Dron as Cairat to administer the punishment.

"You two are young and made a mistake. We applaud your truthfulness in admitting your error. Now that truthfulness will be put to a real test. Stay true and don't violate the Utumcair."

Utumcair means Blind Food. Starting at sundown the next day, both of us were to be blindfolded for Sixty Two days. Further, we had to hunt and gather all our own food. We couldn't accept food from anyone else. And no one was to offer us food, under threat of Royal punishment.

Of course, I did not know how to hunt blind and was seriously concerned that we might starve to death. So much for commuting the death sentence!

Anyway, upon Laushu's advice, Rasi joined me at home and we ate like pigs. Laushu told us to build up our reserves since the first few days will be the hardest. I could not quite understand how the later days could get any easier. Nevertheless, we followed his advice and ate seven very heavy meals by sundown the next day.

Then, we were blindfolded and sent to the Kul along with Laushu Dron who was to be our Cairat to administer the punishment.

Initially I thought Laushu would simply find some legal loophole and feed us. But his integrity did not allow such wiliness. Instead, he started sound splitting classes for me.

I thought it was a brilliant move. What could be better than learning a fantastic new skill as part of a punishment? Taleyi Chachali! Fate has ways of turning the greatest misfortune into fortune.

However, I soon had my doubts because the first eight days I did very poorly. My hunts were all completely barren; Rasi and I could only gather and eat small handfuls of berries.

I went to Laushu on the ninth day because I felt I would die of hunger. I thanked him for the learning he imparted me and told him my regret was that, despite all his efforts, I might die of starvation before repaying my debt to him. Laushu severely told me to desist from defeatist talk, to keep my head up and to keep trying. He said that he had faith in me and that I would not fail.

"But Laushu", I pleaded, "I am but a mediocre marksman. Even with a great Laushu like yourself, I probably cannot reach that pinnacle of skill in archery".

I thought Laushu would tell me that I was not so bad. But instead he downgraded sound splitting:

"I am only asking you to split sound; not reach the pinnacle of archery. The goal of archery is to hit your target. It does not matter whether you locate the target by sight, sound, smell, taste or by rumor. What matters is that you hit it. If you use only sound and have a near miss it is no better than having a near miss with full sight.

"You may work harder if you don't use sight. But if you miss, the pig you are hunting will not lie down just because you worked hard. The enemy will not stop after a near miss to marvel at your skill and to give you another shot. Even if you just want to make a living entertaining village folk with your talent, you will hardly be entertaining if you miss the target.

So, remember that sound splitting is no pinnacle. You can absolutely reach it, even if you think yourself mediocre.

"And don't think of it as just sound. Use all your faculties to locate your target and remember that sound is only one of them. I am having you concentrate on sound, only because it often is ignored when your eyes are open. But remember that you do have other ways of sensing your environment".

"But Laushu", I whined, "I am having absolutely no luck in hunting. These past eight days, we ate no more than a few berries each day. Rasi, a pious woman with some practice for fasting, is probably coping better than I am. But eight days is unbearable even for her. I feel ashamed that I brought her to this. Tell me, my Laushu, what am I doing wrong? Why am I failing so miserably?"

"It is because you are trying to see with your ears", Laushu reiterated in an unmoved voice. "Instead, try to get a sense of your surroundings using all your senses: sound, touch, smell, the small amount of light reaching your blindfolded eyes and most importantly, your mind. Imagine what your surroundings are like. Not what they would look like if your eyes were open, but what they actually are".

"My Laushu, I don't quite understand the distinction".

Laushu paused to think a moment and then ordered: "You will understand better if you hunt alone. So today, don't go with the hunting group, go into the woods by yourself and bring back food for yourself,for Rasi and for the Kul".

I hunted with the group because I thought it was safer. If I hunted alone, I might get myself hunted by a bear or trampled by a bull. I suddenly realized that Laushu was right; I was indeed depending on what others in the group were seeing, instead of trying to sense out the surroundings myself.

So, I took my Laushu's blessings and went alone that day. I knew our group usually went North, so I went West, away from the morning Sun.

It was a bright day though little light was getting through to my eyes. I felt my way from tree to tree and walked till about midday. I felt the Sun shining down directly on me and realized that I had emerged from the woods into a clearing. I wondered if this was what Laushu meant about using all senses. Anyway, I hurried back to a tree in order to prevent making myself an easy target, loaded my bow and waited, keenly listening.

After some time, I felt the ground trembling ominously. With my alertness sharpened by fear, it took me only a few moments to realize that it was a stampede of the aurochs. Instinctively, I returned my arrow to the quiver and scrambled up the tree as fast as I could. I was on a low branch, but at least I was off the ground and protected from the stampede.

As I heard the hoof beats rush toward me, my initial panic returned. When I suppressed that panic and calmed down, I realized that this was actually a very lucky event. All I had to do was hit one of the aurochs and we would have food to eat for at least three days. I reloaded my bow but the sound was all around me and it was impossible locate any one Auroch. I knew I had to hurry because the herd would soon pass me.

I thought I heard the loud snort of an Auroch and clearly felt I knew where the Auroch was running to and instinctively let loose an arrow just slightly ahead of there. I heard the agonized "Bah" from the auroch. I had hit it! I suddenly had a feeling I understood Laushu's lesson. Upon hearing a second "Bah", I shot out another arrow and hit it again! As the stampede continued, the auroch was also trampled. It cried out some more before going quiet. In the exhilaration of a successful hunt, I offered up a thankful prayer to Rock Boha, my new favorite God, and waited for the herd to pass before I got off the tree. I reached the carcass and was wondering how to carry the beast back to Kul.

Suddenly, an even bigger problem emerged when I heard the ominous growls of a pack of wolves closing in on me. I thought I understood fright when I heard the sudden onset of stampede. But that was nothing compared to the absolute terror I felt standing blindfolded in the middle of a jungle with Wolves closing in. The auroch may be mine but was I now to lose my hunt as well as my life?

I was wondering at the fickleness of the fate thinking "Taleyi Chahali" as I backed away toward my tree. The growls got louder and, in desperation, I let loose three quick arrows toward the growls. I must have hit them because the growls became howls of agony as they seemed to pause.

In fear and desperation, I almost peeled off my blindfold but before I could, loud sounds of drums, bells and human shrieks jumped out from the woods. After the wolves ran away, they came up to me. These were three of my fellow students; Laushu had sent them to come to my rescue if I got into trouble. They stayed far enough behind so I would not hear their cart. They had seen me killing the auroch as well as gamely trying to fend off the wolf pack. They congratulated me and, in their cart, we carried the carcass back to Kul. That got me a second hug and kiss from Rasi. All the fright I had to go through was paid back a hundredfold.

Not only was that auroch sufficient for a full two days for the whole Kul, the incident also broke a mental logjam in me. With the auroch stampede and the wolf attack, I clearly understood Laushu's lesson that I should not try to see with my ears but should sense my surroundings. From then on, I went hunting with the group but stopped depending on them. I caught something or other; my hunt was always enough to feed me and Rasi and usually had some left over.

My skill was getting better everyday. More importantly, through all this sharing of food, Rasi and I became really close friends. On the tenth day, Rasi's mother came to the Kul to convince her to ignore the punishment and come home. After all, the King of Kunduj had no authority on the citizens of Khiwani. To my pleasure, Rasi declined and said she did not want to abandon a friend like me. Her mother went back after warning me take care of her.

Even with my improving skill, we still went through three more episodes of starvation, each about four days long. On the forty eighth day, Laushu Dron called me into his Prayer Chamber and stated that I had surpassed the Laushu's own calibre archery. He said this was the greatest gift any student could give his teacher. Then he recited the Gratitude prayer to the Mother Oak and concluded: "It is for moments like these that I love teaching". I recited the prayer too and thanked Mother Oak for blessing me with my Laushu.

The final fourteen days of our punishment were almost pleasant and leisurely. The special bond between Rasi and I became very strong. Since I was useless for any chores around the Kul, we spent a lot of time walking and talking. By the end of the sixty two days, I was fully proficient in archery.

And that is how I got to learn sound splitting in just sixty two days".

Ж

Balu, listened with intent interest and said: "That is a beautiful story, Zvuk. But you cut it short at the end".

"That I did, Young Balu" Zvuk replied. "But there is not much more to tell".

"Of course there is!" Balu complained. "What happened to Rasi? Did she just head back to Khiwani?".

"Well", Zvuk replied. "Our blindfolds came off at the castle courtyard. After sixty two days of forced blindness, hers was the first face I looked upon and was smitten twice over, since now I also knew the real person that went with the lovely face. I pursued her and we got married about three months later. Twenty years later, I am still smitten with her".

"Wow. Congratulations!", Balu said. "I am so glad your life turned out well. Your service to the King in battle is legendary, but this life story really gives me a nice feeling ..."

"Thank you Balu", Zvuk interrupted. "It is getting dark. I know you must loathe going back to your cell. But, King's punishment must be fulfilled. Off to the cell you go!"

"Yes Zvuk", Balu acquiesced. "Meeting you has already more than compensated me for the imprisonment. Thank you".

The old King had finalized Zvuk's punishment within a week; but Prince Yuda had not even held a hearing for Balu and it was now rly ten days. Neither of them gave a thought to this decline in the dispensation of justice.

However, both found themselves hoping that Prince Yuda's punishment would improve Balu's life just like the old king's punishment had improved Zvuk's.

121

8. Anukra Charikram

The next day, Balu was pensive when Zvuk let him out. He wordlessly washed up and offered solemn prayers to both Mother Amu and the Sun. He then plucked a handful of flowers, offered them to Zvuk and said:

"Zvuk Meza. I am honored to know you and I thank you for telling me your inspiring story. I request you now to be my Laushu."

"Beautiful flowers! Thank you, Balu!".

Balu let the flowers into Zvuk's hands. He was disappointed that Zvuk did not accept his request. Or even acknowledge it. If people kept ignoring him, how was he ever going to get a teacher?

Zvuk sensed the strength of Balu's disappointment like a shove from an elephant and wondered: "Is he meant to be my student? Otherwise, how can I can sense his emotional state so clearly?" Zvuk smelled the flowers and added them to his pouch with elaborate ceremony. Then, pointed his index finger at Balu and gave his first lesson: "Balu you are a nice young man. But you do have one critical failing which will be your undoing, if you don't correct it."

"And what is that, Lau.., er... Zvuk". In his heart, Balu had already accepted Zvuk as his teacher. But there was no reciprocation, it was not proper to address him as Laushu.

"You give up too easily", thundered Zvuk Meza. "Ask me again tomorrow!".

The next day, Balu's pensiveness was mixed with a resolve. He repeated his prayers to Mother Amu and the Sun, returned to Zvuk Meza with a handful of flowers and requested him again.

"Zvuk Meza. I am honored to have known you and I thank you for telling me your inspiring story. I request you now to be my Laushu. Your skill is worthy of spending a lifetime to learn. Your respect for your Laushu and your devotion to King are worthy of emulation for a lifetime. Would you do me the favor of granting me access to your knowledge?"

Zvuk accepted the flowers and looked up at Balu with piercing eyes. Balu was shivering in the warm Sun and Zvuk Meza immediately sensed that it was due to fear of rejection.

"How did I instantly know what Balu was feeling?", Zvuk introspected. This was meant to be. It was time.

"Yes, I will."

Balu looked at him with a startle as if he was not sure whether he heard it right. With Zvuk's reassuring nod he realized that he finally had found his Laushu. With a release of tension from the past three days, he shed tears of joy.

"You will be my student." Zvuk continued. "Your responsibility will be to diligently learn your lessons and follow my direction. My responsibility is to teach you what I know and to look after your well-being. Do you understand and accept?"

"Yes, my Laushu". Balu had goosebumps just saying the word.

"I am pleased" Zvuk replied "I never thought I would have a student".

"I feel so fortunate that I have you as my Laushu, but", Balu asked a bit apprehensively, "may I ask a question?"

"You can ask me any question at any time. It is your duty to ask questions and to learn".

"Did I make a mistake in my original request? Why did you not accept me yesterday?"

Zvuk smiled. "You made no mistake. Your request was fine. But I wanted to get blessing from my own Laushu before agreeing to teach you. After all, this learning is his bestowal. I met him last night to seek his blessing and permission."

"So, if he had said no..."

"If he had rejected, I would have told you before you asked today. I had no desire to torment you. But, he said yes. He was very pleased that I found a student. He said that all skills are only one generation away from vanishing: if archers of my generation don't teach our skill, there will be no archers after we die. So, I will pass on my knowledge on to you. Apart from giving us both fulfillment It will ensure that the art of archery shall persist".

Balu stood beaming. Zvuk continued: "So, you are employing the strategy of Anukra Charikram, I am impressed."

Blank look on Balu's face indicated that he didn't

understand.

"You don't understand? It is the most famous line from Salarganyak".

More blank looks from Balu. And more astonishment for Zvuk.

"The Ivchean play!", thundered Zvuk. "Anukra Charikram means 'imitate my history'. All the Kuls around here teach that play to students to help them learn a little Ivchean. Aren't you too young to have already forgotten?"

"Actually, my Laushu", Balu replied with downcast eyes. "I never went to any Kul."

"What?", Zvuk was stunned.

"I requested about ten different teachers over the years, But no one accepted me. And I had no riches to offer as inducement".

"So, how were you accepted into His Majesty's service? And that too, in the castle?"

"This was the king's kindness, my Laushu" Balu elaborated. "My father died in some war when I was only 2 years old; I don't even remember his face. I remember my mother somewhat, but she she also died in the floods ten years ago. Talu took care of me for some time. When the old king heard my story, he said that since my father died in his service, it was his duty to care for me. So, he ordered Talu's rations doubled and ordered his kitchen to allow me to eat there. So, I was in the castle quite frequently; that is how I heard about you. After I grew up, the old king appointed me to the perimeter defense of the castle. When the Prince ascended to the throne, he assured me that I would be kept on. The Prince, er, the new king, has so far honored that word".

"Not really, my young student" Zvuk reminded him. "The Prince has sent you to prison".

"A prison where I met you, my Laushu", Balu countered. "Whether the king intended it to be so or not, this has been a great gift. And I feel sure that when His Majesty sees me, he will understand there has been some mistake. And he will let me out of this prison and allow me to learn from you".

"Anukra Charikram" Zvuk smiled. "You want to follow

my history".

"If you will allow me, Anukram Chakram", Balu mangled the saying.

"Anukra Charikram" Zvuk patiently corrected him. "My concern is that you have never learned any archery. I wonder if you are too old to start from the beginning. Especially if you are supposed to be in jail and ..."

"But Laushu", Balu insisted "I will work very hard. I will ..."

"I know you will", Zvuk interrupted. "I will not let you do otherwise. Don't worry, I am not giving up just yet".

Zvuk started with testing Balu's skills during the outside hours each day. He concluded that the situation was not as dire as he feared. While Balu lacked structured learning he was worldly wise. He did not have much practice with a bow and arrow but seemed to have a good aim when throwing stones. And he more than made up for any shortcomings with a burning desire to learn.

If Balu could stay out, he could learn so much faster; the requirement of staying in the cell most of the day was a great hindrance. So, Zvuk quietly initiated inquiries at the castle and was astonished to learn that no one seemed to know what Balu was accused of.

He tried to find the Praesha but he was away. At Koka, he was told. He wondered what was happening in Koka. He then waylaid Minister Vaid on the streets to complain. Vaid seemed genuinely puzzled that Balu was in jail and asked Zvuk to present himself for a private audience with King Yuda the next day.

Ж

"But, my Laushu", Yuda protested, "these things sometimes happen!"

"Perhaps, you are right. Perhaps you have reached your limit already!", Vaid responded with withering sarcasm. "You are the king of one city and ten villages. You already let things lapse and your only excuse is that sometimes these things happen? Remember, the only way you will be emperor is to use people: you must lead them to do your bidding. And you will certainly not get there if you ignore the ones so close to you."

125

Yuda's face went red. As only a Laushu could know, Vaid sensed that something had just snapped in their relationship; his sarcasm had been a step too far.

Yuda resented Vaid's sanctimonious lecturing. Yes, he had made a mistake in allowing the matter about Balu to be forgotten. But this was only a lowly guard on whom his father had taken pity. Besides, they were all busy with preparations for the invasion. And finally, wasn't it Vaid's job to keep track of such details. Vaid sensed Yuda's resentment and regretted his words.

"I am sorry, child!", Vaid tried to mollify. "Perhaps I am getting too old; that is why my tolerance for mismanagement shrinks by the day. Actually, on this particular issue, I am as much to blame as you. When you dispatched the Praesha along with Dron, I should have taken greater care to ensure all his duties were properly handed over".

Yuda accepted it with a nod. On other occasions, Yuda would have castigated himself and not let his Laushu take any blame. But not this time. Probably because this time Yuda recognized the truth in Vaid's cutting words. He really should not have neglected the matter of a man's life.

"Victory my King!", a guard noisily entered.

"I said we are not to be disturbed!" bellowed Yuda, venting his anger at the guard.

"Yes, your majesty", the guard bowed and spoke in clear, clipped tones. "But a messenger from Commander Dron is here and he insisted that he had to see you immediately."

Yuda and Vaid looked at each other blankly. Yuda nodded his head and ordered: "Send him in!". Within moments a messenger entered the room.

"Your Majesty!", he greeted "May Victory always be yours."

"Speak!", Vaid commanded curtly.

"A message from Praesha, your eminence. All preparations were complete but, in the last moment we hit a major obstacle. We have almost lost the Thunga".

"What?" Vaid exploded. "When did this happen? And what do you mean by almost lost?"

The Thunga was the biggest river boat Mother Amu had

ever seen. She was a floating armory but disguised as a pilgrim vessel. She was a key to Kunduj's surprise attack on Koka.

"It happened yesterday evening, sire", the messenger reported. "The Praesha moored the Thunga about half a Kos upstream of Koka. When his majesty decides, it would have taken less than 15 mins to launch the attack. But after heavy downpours of the past few days, the river was overflowing and the current was very strong; it snapped the Thunga's moorings and carried her downstream. I and some other men were on shore and witnessed the whole thing. We followed on foot and saw her crash into the control sluices upstream of Koka. Her keel is badly damaged. She was not yet taking water, but that is only a matter of time. She will not sail again unless major repair work is done".

"Does the Praesha or Commander Dron think that we have lost the element of surprise?"

"No, your Majesty", the messenger replied. "Kokan soldiers still don't suspect the Thunga; she was already decked as a pilgrim ship. And the Praesha thinks our other attack plans have not been compromised".

"So, the decorations were all done?"

"Yes your majesty. As of yesterday morning. And within half a day, we lost her."

"Where is the Praesha now?" Vaid inquired.

"He was about to come and report on the preparations himself, sire, but since we lost the Thunga, he decided to stay back with Commander Dron and assist with the necessary adjustments to battle plans".

Yuda reached a quick decision and looked up at the messenger.

"Go home and rest. We will have a message for you to take back this evening".

The messenger bowed and retreated. Yuda stayed quiet for a few minutes, planning next moves. When he finally looked up, Vaid asked: "What are your orders for me, Your Majesty?"

Though the words were respectful enough, Yuda felt annoyed; they sounded to him like a taunt. Or, like a Laushu testing a young student.   Somewhere something is broken, Yuda realized somewhat sadly. We will never go back to the old relationship. He put on a deferential mask and issued orders:

"We will continue with the plan. We will attack, the next New Moon day, fourteen days from today.

I want you to initiate a rumor that the Gods have started a black moon festival in Koka. Send rumor mongers to all towns within 20 kos from Koka with the News that, to celebrate the festival, Mother Amu has spontaneously birthed a pilgrim vessel. On this miraculous occasion, She will bless all those who visit Koka during the festival with children".

"Yes your majesty. It will be done".

"Ensure that they know the festival ends two days before New Moon. Mother Amu will bless the childless with fertility, children with long life and warriors with victory. Start the rumor in Koka and let it spread from there; it should reach Kunduj in a few days."

"Yes, your majesty. It will be done".

"Once the rumor gets here, send the remaining of our drafted soldiers to Koka, in small batches. Have pilgrim clothes made for all of them; they are to pretend this is a pilgrimage."

"Yes your majesty. It will be done".

"The Praesha reported that about a quarter of his conscripts are women. Ensure that they are matched up to some of the men. And send these conscripts through villages and towns so as to create a strong sense of miracle and people joining a spontaneous march."

"Yes, your majesty. This is brilliant. And it will be done."

Somehow, even Vaid's praise now grated on Yuda. Something had indeed snapped. Yuda soldiered on, hoping his irritation was not showing.

"Send a message back to Commander Dron that more soldiers are coming disguised as pilgrims but they will be ready for their role in the attack, when the time comes".

"Yes, your majesty. I will send the message right away". Vaid was in genuine awe at the cunning in Yuda's tactical plan even before the concluding master stroke:

"Spread a pious rumor through Koka itself: Mother Amu has appeared in visions and said She will bless the town with many visitors. But She wants the town to rest peacefully on New Moon night; She wants her children to procreate".

"Yes, your majesty", Vaid proclaimed "This will be done. And it will ensure that Koka is utterly unprepared, and sleeping, at the time of your victorious assault!".

"That will be all", Yuda said with a smile, hoping to convey that he had forgotten about the earlier altercation.

Vaid felt miffed that the king did not ask him, as he usually did, whether something was being forgotten. The fact that Vaid had nothing to add only deepened the hurt. Had his student outgrown any need for his advice? Yuda's smile felt to him like an irreverent smirk.

In spite of that, Vaid was genuinely filled with admiration for the plan. Koka stood no chance of resistance. They would be over-run by pilgrims in the next ten days. Koka did have a standing army, but it will be busy catering to the crush of pilgrims. Then as the pilgrims leave, they will be busy with cleaning up. And on New Moon Night, as they all slept, Kundujan assault will imprison them and take over the town. With brimming coffers to boot, Vaid added to himself contentedly. There will be minimal bloodshed while the king changes. Brilliant! Well done, my boy! I will implement it just as you ordered.

As he stepped out of the castle, Vaid was a bit startled when Zvuk Meza accosted him.

"Should I go in and meet his majesty now, your eminence?"

Vaid suddenly realized that they had never gotten to a final decision on Balu. Yuda had called his prolonged imprisonment a mistake but did he want him immediately released? Should he dare to make the decision? Given the fraying relationship, he decide it was not wise. So, Vaid said:

"Not yet. I will take you in shortly. Just wait".

"Yes, your eminence".

Vaid spent a few moments in the prayer room to meditate on the words he would need to use. Then he went back into Yuda's chamber nodding to Zvuk Meza along the way.

"Victory to you, Your Majesty". As Yuda turned to him, Vaid closed the door and proceeded. "Your Majesty, I neglected to get your final decision on Balu, the wrongfully imprisoned guard we were discussing earlier. His Laushu, Zvuk Meza is waiting outside. Shall I have Zvuk brought in, or should we discuss this case some more?"

The careful words were intended to avoid giving any offense. For Yuda, they sounded instead like those of a disappointed parent saying "Do whatever you want". He shrugged off the feeling.

"I think we should release Balu into Zvuk Meza's custody and allow his training to go ahead. We explain the imprisonment as a test which is close enough to the truth, anyway. I just want to be rid of this annoyance for now." Then in an attempt to mend the relationship with his own Laushu, Yuda pointedly asked, "Do you think that will suffice?"

"Yes, your majesty", Vaid replied. "I think that will make them both happy. And I think it will suit our present purposes also quite well".

"Good". Yuda clapped loudly and bellowed "Send Zvuk Meza in!"

Yuda observed Zvuk Meza with piercing eyes as he was escorted into the chamber.

"Your Majesty", Zvuk started with his practiced speech without being prompted, leaving Vaid and Yuda annoyed at the breach of protocol. "I am grateful to you for giving me an audience. I have accepted your young guard, Balu, as my pupil. He is presently imprisoned on your orders. I have attempted to ascertain what the charge against him is but have not been able to. I ..."

"So, you decided to walk in on my day and lecture me without prompting?" Yuda let his annoyance visibly flare into anger.

"I apologize, your Majesty. That was my mistake. But Balu's treatment after his recent heroic effort really rankled in my heart. Please excuse my breach of protocol as it results from my faith in your administration. Such injustice, which is impossible with you at the helm, nevertheless seems to be happening".

"I understand", Yuda appeared to soften a bit. "The imprisonment was part of a test we wanted to administer to Balu. From the reports I have seen, he is doing well. I am especially impressed that he gained a worthy Laushu in you. And you too have done well, in looking after his interests."

Zvuk waited a few awkward moments as Yuda simply gazed at him. Zvuk's hope that Yuda would immediately announce Balu's release was dashed. But still he couldn't let go of curiosity before voicing his appeal.

"May I ask, your majesty, what Balu is being tested for?"

"I cannot tell you, because you will divulge it to your student".

"But Your Majesty, I promise ...".

"No", Yuda waved him away. "Don't make promises you cannot keep. You are now his Laushu. We are impressed with how you are taking to being a Laushu. We do not want you to make any mistakes. If you deem it to be in Balu's best interests, we would fully expect that you will reveal any secrets to him".

Again an awkward pause. "By Ag, the king answers in nutshells, doesn't he?", Zvuk thought to himself. Out loud he said:

"Your Majesty. Is the test still ongoing or is it completed?"

Yuda gave him a look that said "you really expect me to answer that?". Zvuk quickly recovered and said: "Forgive me your Majesty. I asked the wrong question. The real question is: May I have your permission to take him out of the prison to my home?"

Yuda looked at him thoughtfully for a few moments and let Zvuk ramble.

"Your Majesty, this will enable me to teach him better. He will not run away. So, any punishments or tests that you wish to administer can be done at any time. I promise to keep an eye ..."

"Yes, you may take him home".

"Thank you, Your Majesty", Zvuk beamed.

Yuda gave him a wave of his hand and turned to Vaid, as if the topic was closed.

As Zvuk left the room Vaid could not suppress his admiration. Yuda had made the situation far better than it was before. The grave mistake that a person was left to rot in jail without ever being charged, did not even arise. By the time Zvuk relays it to Balu, the story would be embellished into a legendary story of King Yuda's sagacious justice. "Well done, my son", Vaid thought to himself. He dared not say it out loud for fear of coming off as condescending.

"Your Majesty. Please allow me to say that I think that matter was settled to the complete satisfaction of all parties. If I have your leave, I will start implementing your battle plan and will report back to you in the night".

Yuda nodded: "Stress the importance of secrecy. No one must know the real plan. If anyone spills the secret, I will spill their guts".

Vaid bowed and departed. What neither man saw was that the way others respond to their plan might not be as predictable as they assumed. Due to their inexperience with big invasions they neglected to consider the possibility that Commander Dron had suggested: that Koka might be blameless and that some other kingdom might have been behind the kidnap attempt.

Therefore, they failed to analyze how the real culprits would respond to this battle. How would they try to take advantage of this development? Yuda and Vaid also comfortably assumed that they could control secrecy and that no one would come to know until they announced it. Therefore, it was impossible that anyone else could meaningfully jeopardize their battle plan.

Ж

Yuda released Balu without any hint of apology for wrongful imprisonment. He even managed to make it seem like a magnanimous gesture which earned him Balu's undying gratitude. Yuda simply thought he was playing smart tactics to convert a bad situation into good.

But his impromptu decision set Balu's life on a remarkable trajectory. Arguably, Yuda might have done exactly the same thing even if he could foresee the long term

132

consequences of his actions. But he might have done so with a bit more trepidation and a little less self congratulation.

As it was, the king was pleased with himself and with the way he had turned events around. Needless to say, Zvuk and Balu were also both immensely pleased. But the most pleased of all was Rasi, Zvuk's wife. She was the unfortunate mother who watched her first-born turn a striking yellow color and die within days of birth. She had then lost three more pregnancies well before reaching full term. Indeed, each was shorter than the one before.

She had approached Seeress Groot and was told that this was simply God's will. That Rasi would never have children of her own. Therefore, she should consider all the World's children as her own. If her maternal thirst was not sated, she should adopt a child rather than try to conceive. With Balu's release, she would finally get a son who would be the same age as her first-born would have been.

Mother Amu was unperturbed that she was going to be cited in spontaneously birthing a pilgrim vessel. She had been accused of much worse. Whenever someone drowned in the river, there were always some who said that Mother Amu had eaten her children. There were many tribes that fearfully worshipped her in the form of a vengeful spirit, always ready to kill. This rumor about birthing a vessel was almost a compliment. While the slight rise in her currents did portend something sinister, at the moment, she continued to flow peacefully enough.

9. Sajje Nalti

"No, Mali", Jenon argued. "I don't want to take you, my pregnant wife, to an area where war might break out".

Mali was flummoxed. "What war? We are talking about Koka here. It is among the most peaceful places anywhere; even Urlapi has more fights".

"Yes, but Wars usually happen very suddenly. Pentia maga Peranga".

"What's that? War is sneeze-like?"

"Yes. War, like a sneeze, can't be predicted".

"Nonsense! Don't hide behind a proverb. I don't know where that saying comes from but you can usually tell when you are about to sneeze. And also when war is approaching".

With characteristic defiance, Mali was rubbishing a venerable proverb. Usually, Jenon loved that about her. But in this case, he felt annoyed and helpless. He was trying to convince Mali that it was a bad idea to go to Koka at this time just to see a vessel spontaneously birthed by Mother Amu. How can someone who thinks so independently be so slavish when it came to religion?

But his annoyance was not from that. It was from the fact that he could not tell her how he knew a war was imminent. Royal spies never divulged secrets, especially not to their beloveds; dragging them into the espionage game would be unforgivable. So how was he to convince her without revealing his reasons?

Silence raged for a few awkward moments as the couple cooled down their own emotions and tried to focus on the other. It was Jenon who first spoke in a hoarse plea.

"Why do you want to pray anyhow?"

"What do you mean?" Mali demanded. "Like I told you many times before, I pray because I want to reach Rock Boha in the after-life."

"But why?" Jenon pouted, trying to pacify her. "You know, the way I am going, I will never reach Rock Boha. So does this mean you will leave me in the after-life?"

"No, it means I have to pray twice as hard."

"What?"

"Not only do I have to get there, I have to gain enough influence to pull some strings for you too."

Jenon's satisfaction at turning the conversation playful lasted only a few moments because Mali was quite serious.

"Don't divert the subject! Why would you not want to …"

"I'm not diverting", Jenon interrupted again. "Just tell me one thing. Why do you want to go to a fertility prayer? You are already pregnant!"

"Je! This is fertility worship. It will be good for our baby. Can you tell me what you are hiding? Why are you so afraid to go to Koka?".

Jenon had always been weak in his ability to reject Mali's requests. Besides, what if she was right? What if this was good for the baby? So, with one more look at her pleading face, he threw caution to the wind and surrendered.

"Alright, we'll go. But, on two conditions".

Mali was willing to accept any conditions. It had been years since she had gone on a real pilgrimage. This would be wonderful! She just looked at him happily as if she had already accepted the conditions.

"No. These conditions are important, listen!", Jenon insisted. "First, don't ask me how I know anything about Koka - don't even try to reason it out. Second, when we are there, you will follow my instructions. I may insist that we leave in a hurry or that we leave incognito. Promise me you'll follow my instructions even if they seem strange".

"You are really afraid, aren't you?" Mali asked, alarmed. "Did you do something there?"

"Ah, that runs afoul of the first condition Dearling! Don't ask me anything about Koka. Perhaps I stole soma there". It was a reference to Bohamir, the mythological figure who was the object of Mali's Obstacle prayer. He preached teetotalism and played mischievous pranks on all drinkers by stealing their Soma at the most inopportune moments.

"Alright. I accept your conditions", Mali said cheerfully. "Even your secretiveness cannot spoil my mood now. This will be a wonderful pilgrimage. Don't worry about any war. Mother Groot says that the Amu is not in a war-like mood".

As Mali excitedly trundled off to share the News with Baegan, Jenon started worrying about his own precautions. How would he make a fast getaway, with a pregnant lady in tow, if war broke out? Kunduj had shown remarkable forbearance so far but that must be reaching its end.

He smiled to himself at the confidence Mali expressed in her surrogate mother. What, in Ag's name, did Seeress Groot know about reading the moods of a river? Did rivers even have moods?

Ж

As Jenon made elaborate contingency plans for how he would avoid war zones, he forgot to consider Yuda's old maid, Talu. He never even wondered what would happen if she came to Koka. She was an old woman after all and probably not interested in fertility rites. Even as he made all sorts of plans about war, he never considered any plan on what to do if he encountered her.

So, naturally, at about the time that Jenon was agreeing to Mali's proposal, a somber Balu sat next to Talu on the footsteps of Koka's temple.

"But, why did the king do that?" he asked, sounding perplexed.

"Look", Talu replied. "I had a long run with that royal family. They have mostly treated me fairly; Uh, I mean they have treated me most fairly. And I did make a mistake which almost caused the King's death. So, I have no bitterness. He wanted me out of the kingdom and I left".

"Yes, but your mistake was not intentional; it was quite innocent. I can ask my Laushu to see if anything can be done to let you come back".

"Oh, no!", Talu said forcefully. "I don't want to return to Kunduj. I will spend the rest of my days in the temple at Koka and focus on God."

"Can you at least tell me how it happened?"

"There is not much to tell, really. Four days ago, I accompanied King Yuda to the river when he went for his evening dip. Since I was waiting there, I also did my prayers. The king emerged from his prayers and I was tardy in handing him his change of clothes. He felt annoyed. He whispered to me, quietly, that my heart was no longer in his service, that I

136

was getting older, more pious and filled with other-worldly thoughts, that it was time for me to go so he can get some fresh blood.

"Then, in full view of the river waters and his other servants, he told me out loud that Mother Amu had just asked him to relieve me of all duty. Owing to my long service, he declared a full reprieve from any punishment for my mistake. He even told me I could go to the Treasury and collect some money before leaving Kunduj forever. He made a gesture as if he was helpless and compelled to follow Amu's commands.

"I am sure he thought it was a face-saving way out for me. I am equally sure that to the other servants, it sounded clearly like what it was: a banishment. Fair or unfair, once the king uttered it, it sounded to me like freedom. And I gladly accept it as gratuity for my long service. The King magnanimously offered me relief from an impossible situation. Ever since the kidnap attempt, I have felt suffocated in the castle and in the whole town. Everyone knew of my 'stupid mistake' and kept an appropriate distance from me. At my age, I don't need such ostracism. I considered fleeing but could not actually do it; I could bear the shame of being shunned, but never the dishonor of being a deserter.

"Anyway, I just thanked his majesty, bowed and left the only place I have ever called home. I felt enough shame after that exchange with the king, that I walked straight toward Koka, ignoring the king's offer of a severance pay. And no one tried to remind me".

"I still think it is unfair", Balu said. "That home you lived in was yours; you lived there all your life. To throw you out at your age to go live in a strange land is not justice."

"Ah" she snorted dismissively. "I will be alright; did I not run into you when I was vulnerable in the woods? Did you not bring me to this beautiful temple in Koka? This place is always crawling with pilgrims; there will be someone or other to help if I need anything".

"Perhaps.", Balu sounded unconvinced, "But I will protest to the king. You are my foster mother and he treated you unfairly".

"Don't talk like a rebel", Talu warned. "Just work hard and stay loyal. I am sure you will have a good position at his majesty's side for a long time".

"Should I help you get a position at some rich house, here in Koka? I hear there are plenty of such ...".

"Oh no!", Talu interjected. "It would simply put me into new servitude so soon after getting out of an old one".

"Perhaps I could take you back to Kunduj so you can collect your severance".

"Again, No. The scorned should stay away from the shunning grounds".

"I can't just abandon you here!", Balu cried. "When my Laushu took me in, I knew I was getting a Shumi. And Shumi Rasi has shown me so much affection that I feel like I gained a real mother. But now that I have her, do I need to lose you?"

"Balu", she said, touching his face tenderly. "You are a good boy. May Rock Boha grant you all that your heart desires. Go back to your Laushu in Kunduj and continue your studies. Become the greatest warrior there ever was. Even greater than Zvuk Meza himself. All while basking in the affection of your Shumi. That is the gift you can give me. Allow me to live the rest of my days here in Koka. The piety, the river and the temple will do my soul a lot of good. You are not abandoning me; come by often and spend time with me."

"Agreed?" Talu prodded him when he did not respond.

He turned to her with tearful eyes and nodded his assent. He gave her a big hug and whispered that he would be back before the new moon to check on her.

As he set out, back to Kunduj, Balu reflected on the fact that his Shumi had already done him a great favor. Having started training, both he and Laushu Zvuk just wanted to keep going. But Shumi Rasi had insisted on a lonely pilgrimage to Koka as an initiation prayer, before embarking on training. Without God's blessing, she proclaimed, no learning will stay in your mind. If she hadn't forced him, he would never have come to Koka. Nor would he have come upon Talu, off the beaten track and lost in the woods. In that case, Talu would almost certainly have perished.

"Thank you, Shumi", he quietly prayed, "your insistence led to my being able to pull my foster mother to safety".

He walked past the boat that they said was

spontaneously birthed by the Amu herself. He was raging internally about how the King could dispense such injustice. It would have been understandable to remove her from duties but banishment was definitely too harsh. He forcefully suppressed the thought, remembering back to Talu's admonition not to think like a rebel.

That is when he noticed Commander Dron standing by the side of the road, in civilian clothes, in the midst of a group of men. With no misgiving about troubling a great man, he went up to Dron and touched his feet.

"I pay my respects to my Grand Laushu."

"Who are you?"

"I am Balu, the new pupil of Laushu Zvuk Meza. You are his Laushu and therefore my Grand Laushu. My pilgrimage to Koka is now special because I have seen you. With your blessings, it will attain completion, Commander Dron!".

"May you learn well and attain success", Dron said with an upturned raised palm gesture which was simultaneously benediction and dismissal.

Balu bowed and departed with a sprightly step, more confident than ever, that it was now his destiny to become a sound splitter. If he knew what destiny actually had in store for him, he might have raised his ambitions just a little.

Ж

That little scene of Balu paying his respects to Commander Dron, which lasted barely ten breaths, led to events that could not have been predicted by any of the participants. One of the onlookers was a young woman, a devoted patriot of Koka who was learning Ivchean spy craft. She got a nagging sense that something other than a fertility miracle was going on.

She reported back to her Laushu that legendary Kundujan commander Dron was loitering in Koka for the fertility prayer. But he did not have his wife with him. Her laushu conveyed it back to Pascheega, the king of Koka. The King sent young women, disguised as pilgrims, to quietly investigate the Kundujan men who were watching over the vessel.

Dron was a great commander but even he was no

139

match for the powerful allure posed to his men by these young women. It took him a while to notice that among the worshipers there was a sudden uptick of the number of unaccompanied young women. He sensed something and forbade his men from fraternizing. If he had known anything about Kokan espionage, he might have called off the attack completely. As it was, he simply thought that an unknown amount of information had seeped out; this was a problem that surely could be managed for a week.

Ж

Into that environment, arrived the entourage of Khet's King Mayun which included Queen Nuri, Jenon and his wife Mali and several other aides. They encamped just outside of Koka, sent word and awaited official welcome from King Pascheega.   It was a formality, since Koka never forbade anyone from worshiping at her temple and most ordinary pilgrims simply walked in. However, it was a courtesy that Royal families afforded to Koka; to not do so was as rude as an invasion.

Mali was disappointed. She had imagined a private pilgrimage with just herself and Jenon. How lovely that would have been! But when Jenon had asked permission to leave, the King had not only granted it, but had offered to go along. Queen Nuri also joined and before long, a whole entourage was departing. Granted, they traveled in far greater luxury than they otherwise would have for which Mali's tired pregnant body was very grateful. But the young soul in that pregnant body simply craved more alone time with her husband.

Jenon was also disappointed about joining a royal entourage rather than being alone with his wife. But he was also very caught up in his Kokan Gambit. How had it worked out? Would there be fighting between Kunduj and Koka? Why hadn't they heard anything about movement of armies? He tried to analyze the situation with his "Chief", but Mayun told him to not rush it. They did not yet have any information. The time now was to simply observe what happens and let the story play itself out. Trying to conclude prematurely can make one blind to observations that don't fit one's storyline.

Ж

140

When the entourage was allowed into town, Jenon took an eager Mali to the Tunga, the fertility boat spontaneously birthed by the Amu. Jenon was impressed by the crowds and was intently observing all the goings on. This made Mali, who mistook it for pious prayer, very happy.

When they got on board the Tunga, Jenon sensed something was amiss but could not put his finger on it. He saw devotees, young men and women, streaming in and out and praying. Some men were working on the prayer dais and others on the boat. There was a shrine for Mother Amu at the aft end of the boat; she was depicted as a woman with multiple arms and a suckling babe at her breast. To him it all seemed a fairly normal pilgrim site. But then he bemoaned that he hadn't ever observed other pilgrim sites keenly enough to notice if something was amiss here. Most times Mali dragged him to a temple, and he was more interested in teasing her for her piety than in actually praying.

After some time, Mali gently elbowed him to ask whether he was ready to go. This was very unusual. After they left the Tunga, he asked:

"Is something wrong?"

"No," she replied unconvincingly. "Why do you ask?"

"Well, typically I have to plead and drag you away from a temple.   But here, you asked me.   That is uncharacteristically unpious of you. At this rate, I will have to pull strings for you with Rock Boha in the after-life".

Mali mumbled something inaudible.

"What's that?"

"I said", she replied in a higher voice, "I don't think Rock Boha is on that boat".

"Why do you say that?" Jenon had never thought Rock Boha, or any other God, was on the boat. But he was curious to know why his pious wife, who saw God in most things, would write off this particular place.

"Well", Mali hesitated. "I shouldn't say things; Sajje Nalti, and all that you know. But most of the people on that boat were not there for prayers. And did you notice they put the babe on Mother Amu's left arm?"

"You are right about Sajje Nalti: one should find faults

at a pilgrim site. But, Mother Amu in that depiction had like 6 arms. Does it really matter which arm they depicted the baby in?"

"It was eight arms, actually. And yes, it does matter! The Amu always floods on her left bank. That is why most villages are on her right bank. It is inauspicious to put a baby on the left".

"Dearling! Amu doesn't flood the right banks as much only because she goes by hills and cliffs on that side. It is not her fault if people build villages on her left, which is her flood zone. Anyway, don't you see that Koka is in fact on the left bank. Perhaps in Koka, it is a sign of pious confidence to put a babe on the left. I guess that proves Sajje Nalti: it is never faulty if it is at a pilgrim site".

"May be", Mali sounded unconvinced but gave in. They walked quietly for a few minutes and suddenly it hit Jenon that he had missed something more important in Mali's observation.

"You said that most people on that boat were not praying. What made you say that?"

"I saw a bunch of the Kundujan men working on that boat. They were more interested in the girls around them than in any worship. I shouldn't criticize other people's praying. I mean who am I? But they were definitely more interested in ... "

Mali tapered off. And Jenon realized that the same thing was bothering him, though he hadn't understood it till just then. What did that mean? He definitely needed to find out.

"Oh wow!" Mali stopped in her tracks and looked spellbound. Jenon saw her staring at the Kokan temple, stunned at its simple majesty like any first time visitor. He simply stood by her side, an arm around her shoulder and enjoyed the moment. After a while he quietly whispered "Shall we go in?". Mali simply nodded and they walked toward the temple, hand-in-hand.

"I can tell, even from far away, that this place has Rock Boha in it. As well as every other God. It radiates tranquility, peace and a very approachable and welcoming, Majesty".

"Save your hyperbole, Dearling! Wait till you see the

inside".

She threw him an ecstatic glance and quickened her step. They didn't exchange another word as a spell-bound Mali completed a soul-cleansing visit to the temple in silence. As they walked back to their tent, Mali teased Jenon: "You know I don't have to pull strings for you anymore. Just by bringing me to this wonderful temple you have bought your own way".

That night, after that peaceful sojourn in the temple and a view of the full moon, Jenon was tempted and just forget all about political gambits, and wars and the inconsistencies with the Tunga. He simply wanted to take a long walk along the river with his beloved Mali at his side. However, Mali had other plans and was getting ready for something.

"Where are you going?" Jenon asked.

"They are doing the Full Moon prayer for Mother Earth in the temple. I want to go."

"Hoo hoo", he whined in a childish whimper. "I wanted to go on a walk along the river. We just finished a prayer. Why another one?".

"We can go for a walk after the prayer. Around midnight. Please! I will make it up to you".

He tried to gather her in an embrace. She melted into his arms, gave him a loud wet kiss on his cheek and but then firmly pushed him away.

"Later!", she warned sternly. "Now, the time belongs to God."

"I thought all time belongs to God!"

"Yes, oh Seer of Seers! All time does belong to God. But now is the time for us to go in service of God!"

Jenon clearly was not looking forward to spending two more hours at the temple.

"Come on! Don't be like that", Mali pleaded. "Look, I am not asking you to come. Let me go now. You come to the temple around midnight and we could walk back together".

Jenon gave in but walked with her all the way to the temple. After she was well ensconced, he left to make a surreptitious visit to the Tunga. He noticed two men depart from the Tunga, talking. He shadowed them and tried to listen in on their conversation.

"You know, the commander says we should work together because we are all Kundujan. But I don't know about some of these men and women. I've never seen them around." the first one said.

"I know", the second one replied. "I believe many of these new ones are from outside of Chelivas. Some are from outside the city of Kunduj altogether."

"I wonder why", the first one said. "It is not like we can't handle this by ourselves!"

"Hush!", the second one said fiercely. "Do you really want to question the strategy of Commander Dron? And of Vaid's pupil, his majesty King Yuda?"

"Well, no", the first one replied as they parted ways, each to go his own way.

That was Jenon's lead.

Ж

Jenon was ushered into the King Mayun's private tent and saw Mayun talking to Queen Nuri apologetically: "Pardon me, milady. This important affair cannot wait. And we don't have a secret conference chamber while traveling".

"Understandable, milord", Nuri replied. "Would you like me to retire to another room?"

"No, not at all. Please stay!" Then he turned to Jenon.

"Chief, I think the Tunga herself is the Kundujan platform from which they will launch the attack" Jenon went straight to the conclusion.

"What?! How sure are you about this?"

"Almost certain, Chief"

"How do you know?" Mayun demanded. "Tell me everything".

"Mali wanted to go to the midnight prayer ceremony. Earlier tonight, I dropped her off at the temple and went to the Tunga to investigate. I overheard two soldiers leaving the boat and talking suspiciously. So, when they split up to retire, I approached the younger one and asked him where the house that sold Soma was. He pointed me in a direction and asked me if I was not local. I acted a bit mysterious and told him,

144

that this was actually my first visit to Koka. I asked him if he would join me for some Soma and he agreed.

"So for the past hour, I have been squeezing information from him. I pretended to be an Ivchean mercenary serving the Kundujan cause who was dying to say more but couldn't. I pretended to slip up and blurted out some crucial details about how King Yuda was abducted. I also let him know that I knew that the Kokans were responsible for the abduction. Then acted like I didn't care, because I would work for anyone that pays me.

"All that pretense opened him up as he tried to show me that he knew more about the strategy than I did. It turns out the entire contingent of men and women working on the Tunga are soldiers. They are preparing for an attack this coming New Moon night. There are a total of nearly six hundred soldiers already here and another two hundred on the way. He might have exaggerated the numbers, Chief. But the overall battle plan is clear: it will be executed New Moon night when most of the town is supposed to be asleep after the long festival"

"We must warn Koka" Mayun said thoughtfully. "We can't let Kunduj occupy her. But how do we pass on a warning without raising suspicion?"

The distant crescendo of temple bells indicated that the prayer was reaching its end. It fell quiet and minutes rolled by as Jenon was getting anxious to leave. To go to the temple and walk back with Mali. In the end it was Queen Nuri who broke the silence. She made a slight gesture with her palm which was very unobtrusive and attention grabbing at the same time.

Jenon allowed himself a little ethnic pride. The Queen was Ivchean like Jenon. Like they say: no royalty like Ivchean Royalty, Jenon quietly marveled; even in a room that included a king, she only needed to make the slightest gesture to completely command the room.

"With your permission, My Lord, I can help", Nuri offered up a simple solution. "After my prayer tomorrow, I can invoke custom and take Haridra offering to the Kokan Queen. It has not been planned but she'll never reject Haridra. The offering ceremony will give me a few minutes alone with her and I can pass on any message you wish".

It was the stroke of a genius! Message conveyed at the highest level with no middle-men. And in such a natural way that no one would suspect it. Before King Mayun or Jenon could express any admiration, Nuri shut down the discussion by talking to her husband in a more informal tone.

"And now my dear, you should send this young man away to collect his wife from the temple. It is past midnight and the silence of the temple bells indicates that the prayer is completed; she must be waiting for him".

As Mayun nodded, Jenon bowed and left, his respect for the queen and king doubled because of that simple show of personal concern. He rushed toward the temple and met Mali on the way, walking back alone. As he extended his hands she held his arm and sighed.

"Such a beautiful night! I'd love to take that walk by the river with you".

Typical Mali, Jenon thought. No rancor or annoyance at the delay but going straight to joy at being together on a pleasant night. He squeezed her arm.

"Are you sure you are not tired? That was a two hour prayer ceremony!"

"Yes and it was wonderful. I am not tired. I feel peaceful and invigorated at the same time."

"As you say, Dearling!"

The couple walked happily, hand in hand, to the river bank and then up a walk path along the river, dimly lit by the almost Full Moon. The reflection of the iridescent moon shimmered on the water which made babbling sounds as it lapped against the shores. The whole town had gone to sleep leaving a silence which felt eerie so soon after the noisy prayer ceremony.

"You know you were right when you said it. I should overlook the Tunga's faults because Sajje Nalti. I owe the Tunga an apology".

"What makes you say that?"

"Do you know what made tonight's ceremony so wonderful?"

"The fact that I was not there to make wise cracks?"

"No, it was the old lady who led the worship. They have a beautiful tradition here in Koka. One night every month, which happens to be tonight, a lay person rather than a priest leads the prayer. Tonight they chose this old lady named Talu, a helpless migrant from Kunduj who sought refuge at the temple. She paid homage to the great temple saying that so far she had never gone hungry, surviving on devotees' offerings. She said tonight's honor was another sign from Mother Herself that this was the right refuge for her."

Jenon stiffened at the mention of Talu. But it was a common enough name that he willed himself to believe that it was a different woman and asked: "So, what made her prayer special? Was she an expert on the ritual?"

"No, she broke every rule of the ritual. When people leave a messy temple they generally wash their feet but she forbade it. Her rationale was that Mother Earth had showered her blessings on us. We should let them stick to us and not wash them away. One is supposed to circumambulate starting Westward. But she made us go Eastward, saying this is how we can face the other great devotees of Mother Earth who circumambulate westward: the Sun, the Moon and the stars. She offered the food with her left hand, saying in case the Mother granted something, she wanted to keep her right hand free. Usually we offer food to God before we ourselves eat. However, she made all of us taste the food first and then offered it to Mother Earth. Her thought was that no mother would like to eat before her children. So, unless we had eaten, Mother Earth would not be happy consuming the food we offer".

"I knew it!" Jenon interrupted with a twinkle in his voice. "Just so we agree, you are admitting that all those times you chased me away from food because the prayer was not yet completed. You are admitting that you were wrong and I was right on all those occasions. Right".

"No", Mali laughed. "I am simply admitting Sajje Nalti: that there are no faults at a pilgrim site. In fact she proved the anti-proverb Sajjaam Halti: that faults happen only at pilgrimage sites. She made so many mistakes and yet, she was so full of devotion that she made it alright. All her Haltis were in a cause: to bring us into a closer relationship with God. I truly feel like I am now adopted by Mother Earth and that I can deal with her as informally as I would with my mother. Any imperfect ritual that can accomplish that, is far better than a perfect one. It is like I went in seeking to find the route to God and this lady simply took me straight to Her presence!"

Jenon did not make any more jokes about what was clearly a moving experience for Mali. Besides, he was partial to folks who ignored ritual and got straight to the point.

"Wow. I guess I missed out on a wonderful prayer ceremony. I should meet this old lady, Talu, and pay my respects".

"Yes, we can go tomorrow and meet with her. She is always there on the temple steps. We would have seen her earlier today except that she was inside preparing for the service".

They walked in silence with arms around each other.

Mali asked: "Remember you were afraid to come here because some war might break out! Can you imagine, this peaceful night, three nights after Full Moon, that anything like war is imminent?"

"Hmm" Jenon was non-committal.

They got farther from the temple and walked toward a small hillock just outside of town. Atop the hill was a pair of boulders. They sat on one of the boulders to enjoy the breeze and the peaceful sounds of the river. After a few moments Mali pointed to a deodar sapling growing between the boulders.

"This sapling is in such a perfect spot", she remarked. "It is as if a gardener chose a perfectly protected spot and planted it here".

"So typical of you to observe such strange things", Jenon remarked moving closer to her and kissing her lips. "I have a proposal".

"What?"

"I say this will be our tree. We will visit this spot every time we are in Koka to check on it".

"What strange declarations you make!", Mali remarked, returning his kiss. "I love it. Yes, this shall be our pilgrim spot in Koka. May this sapling grow to be a great cedar!"

Neither Jenon nor Mali had any idea of the role Jenon played in planting the sapling in this perfect spot. Mali of course knew nothing; Jenon remembered floating downriver on a deodar log but had no idea that it was the parent of this sapling.

Neither of them could scarcely imagine that Mali's pronouncement of this one becoming a Great Cedar was in fact the sapling's destiny.

The sapling swayed in the gentle breeze as if to say they were always welcome to his shade. Great trees are magnanimous even in their sapling days.

10 Nooham Farar

"Nooham farar!" laughed Queen Nuri contagiously.

Jenon smiled at the witticism. It was the famous last phrase from a popular play about Utapani, the cowardly but extremely boastful prince. Utapani once went hunting and took great precautions to protect himself from the likes of tigers, elephants and crocodiles. He was confident he wouldn't have to run away and could act brave. However, once in the jungle, a field rat got close to him. He got mortally afraid and immediately fled with his whole entourage. He expected to be running away from a tiger or a lion but ended up fleeing from a rat. Nooham Farar, the last phrase, famously summarized that he fled from the most unexpected thing.

"Indeed, milady!" King Mayun guffawed. "Indeed! Jenon here was afraid he might have to flee from a great big war but instead he is running away from a little old lady!"

"I am not fleeing, Chief", Jenon protested. "It is just that after Mali told me her name, I checked and it turns out Talu is in fact the same old ..."

"We know, we know", Mayun interrupted. "But it is still funny".

"Yes sire, it is" Jenon conceded.

"So, what do we do now?" Mayun inquired. "After coming in so publicly, the queen and I can hardly leave in a rush. But we do have to ensure that she cannot see you in our entourage".

"The best way", Nuri reasoned, "is to send Jenon away on an errand. No offense, but except his wife, no one will miss him if the rest of the entourage is still here. So, Jonon! I order you to go back to Khet immediately to fulfill a ritual that I dreamed about last night. Take this necklace to our Ag Myra in Khet. You are to purify it by the fire in the holy fire pit. When everything except the precious stones are turned to ash, collect them in an urn along with some of the holy ash. When the prince is born, these purified stones will form his first necklace. This purification must happen before sundown today. Understood?"

"Yes, your majesty", Jenon replied with alacrity. "I understand, and it will be done".

"I am impressed with the job you did", Nuri reassured him. "I am loathe to separate you from your pregnant wife, in the name of false duty. But do not worry about Mali. She will meet Talu this afternoon as planned. I will accompany her myself, and perhaps I can get more information about Kunduj. And tomorrow morning, I will send Mali home with a couple of trusted men."

"Thank you, your majesty!", Jenon bowed with visible relief. "Thank you for your thoughtful consideration."

"I am fortunate indeed", proclaimed Mayun, "to have at my side, such beauty and sagacity."

"Meh", Nuri waved her hand dismissively.

Ж

"For a recent refugee like me, it is a great honor to be in the presence of two little Bohamirs" Talu said as she touched and blessed the pregnant abdomens of both Mali and Queen Nuri. And then, as if realizing her faux pas, looked up to the Queen and bowed "It is an honor to meet you too, Your Majesty".

Queen Nuri, amused by the quick correction, gave her an understanding smile.

"I apologize my husband is not here, Mother Talu" Mali explained. "He was called away on duty. I hope he gets to meet you sometime real soon."

"I understand that duty comes first", Talu replied. "I also hope to meet him sometime soon".

"Did you say you are from Kunduj?" Queen Nuri started prodding for information.

"Yes, your highness", Talu replied wondering how much a foreign queen might know about the goings on in Kunduj. "I just moved here a short time ago, Your Majesty".

Nuri made a gesture as if to dismiss her "Oh, don't call me Majesty. I moved this far west after marrying His Majesty King Mayun of Khet. Seeing you reminds me of my own mother, back in Ivchea. Especially at this time of pregnancy, I bitterly miss her. I have servants more than enough who fulfill my every command. But what I long for, is the presence of my mother who will issue commands to me with affectionate informality. So, please don't call me this Highness and that

151

Majesty".

Talu smiled awkwardly as if to say, I understand. But instead the smile only announced her discomfort. Nuri knew that discomfort was her route in. So, she piled on.

"I did not realize", she said "that the ordinary people of Kunduj were affected by the recent happenings to the extent that they have to leave as refugees".

"No your er...", Talu stammered. "The people are fine. King Yuda looks after his kingdom well".

"Oh, that is good" Nuri said as if recovering from a mistake. "I am sorry, when you said you were a recent refugee I thought... Anyway, it is good to hear that your leaving had nothing to do with the recent abduction attempt on your king".

"Actually, it was the main cause ..." Talu suddenly quieted, thinking it would be a bad idea to divulge too much. After all Nuri was a foreign queen.

Nuri pretended to stiffen at how suddenly she stopped talking. Then she said, in a hurt voice: "I am sorry Mother Talu. I have made you uncomfortable with my questioning. I should not have come to this private meeting between you two. I will leave you alone".

With that Nuri turned and walked away. She felt bad for emotionally manipulating an innocent old lady in this way. She almost hoped that Talu would not fall for it and would just allow her to walk away. But she knew people, and knew that Talu would behave to the stereotype.

Mali was paralyzed by the sudden turn of the conversation and was at a loss about what to do. Talu was affected similarly but recovered and went after Nuri before she took five steps. "No, no your highness. Please come back and sit down".

She held Nuri's arms, gently walked her back, and bade her sit down on the dance platform in front of the temple. A number of legendary performances were conducted there but this afternoon it was unused and empty. She also made Mali sit next to the queen, both young women facing the temple.

"I have raised enough babies to know that the babies you two are carrying are as divine and precious as Bohamir Himself. I am not going to upset you and therefore upset the little child you are carrying. Besides, my story is unfortunately very well known in Kunduj. It is no big secret. Perhaps it will do me good to just talk about it".

"Now even my curiosity is piqued", Mali chimed in. "Are you saying your leaving Kunduj is related to the King Yuda's abduction?"

"Oh no!", Talu despaired "you have heard about it too? I thought it was just the politically inclined folks like her majesty who paid attention to it. You are a simple pious girl. If I have to be shamed in front of you too, I have no redemption!"

"Shamed!?" Nuri exclaimed, "Why would you be shamed? You were not a soldier or a palace guard". After a little pause, "Were you?"

Talu took a deep breath and narrated how her life took an unexpected turn a couple of months ago when two men named Kanavata and Vrajavoora came to her home. As she went through the whole story, Mali and Queen Nuri heard intently only supplying exclamations like "Oh" and "Really?" in the middle. When the story ended, Talu concluded:

"That is why it is my shame. I let my king down and because of me, he went through a traumatic experience. I am fortunate that he did not punish me more".

"No you are not!" Nuri retorted, enunciating her words very clearly.

Both Mali and Talu looked at her in surprise.

"I should not criticize fellow royalty, but you did nothing wrong. Nothing worth punishing".

"Keeping my Raha Daur secret ...".

"Is as it should have been!", Nuri interrupted emphatically. "I have had servants all my life, but I have never thought that their souls belonged to me. Your relationship with God is your own - it has nothing to do with the King unless it impacts your performance of your duty".

"But it did affect my duty. I missed attending to my duty on that ominous night".

"That too is not your fault", Nuri insisted. "These men drugged you unconscious. They might easily have killed you. If they had, whom would you blame then? The fault lies not with you, but with the palace guards who allowed these two to get so close to the King".

Mali viewed her with admiration and pride and thought "Certainly sounds right to me. That is how MY queen would dispense justice.

After a little pause, Nuri continued.

"I should not get so passionate about the goings on in other people's courts. Anyway, you must be really angry with those two men. If it were not for them, you would be spending your old age comfortably in your own home".

"Actually, no. I am not upset at them", Talu replied. "Almost as soon as the king pronounced his punishment, I felt free. I should have left years ago to serve God in my old age. But I never knew how to raise the topic with the King. And I never considered desertion.

"These men did me a favor and released me from there. Now, finally, I have the freedom to be myself. I am conversing with a queen and telling her my story. This would never have happened if I stayed on. This life is much better. So, I thank Kanavata and Vrajavoora for having brought me to this pass. My initial resentment toward them has completely morphed into gratitude".

"You are a remarkable woman", Nuri praised Talu. "If you ever run into trouble, remember our kingdom Khet. I can ensure you are taken care of."

The moment those words came out of her mouth, Nuri regretted it. If Talu were to ever actually come to Khet, it would stir a hornet's nest of complications and divided loyalties. Mali added on to Nuri's magnanimity by expanding on the promise.

"In fact, Mother Talu" Mali said, "Seeress Groot has her cloister very close to Khet. If living here ever becomes difficult, you should go there. I am sure Mother Groot would be very happy to have you. I will talk to her when I go back."

"Thank you very much, ladies. Your words cheer me immensely."

Nuri felt a sense of shame. She should have been here to simply enjoy the togetherness of these women. Instead she was here for espionage and digging up information. Even though she had crucial bits of information which would make Talu's story complete, she could not divulge any details. This sacred place was defiled by her duplicity. That strong emotional response brought tears to her eyes. Talu noticed and immediately took on a maternalistic tone to ask in a concerned voice: "My dear! Are you OK? Did I say something to upset you?"

Nuri decided to confess even as she noted to her rational self, that pregnant women must be removed from the spy pool. They were too emotional to keep a detached aloofness.

"Mother Talu" she started. "I feel ashamed. I had an ulterior motive in coming here. I wanted to get your story because it may have an impact on my Kingdom. I then emotionally manipulated you, so you would feel kindly toward a pregnant lady and reveal your story. I should have come here for companionship. Instead I came for espionage. Will you please forgive me?" Nuri put her hands together in a salute.

Talu put her arms around Nuri, wiped her tears away and said: "My dear! You have done nothing wrong. There is nothing to forgive. It was good for me to tell my story. It was even better for me to hear you defend my actions so vociferously. I am honored that your Royal Highness would take such an interest in the story of poor old Talu. If my story was at all useful to you, I am gratified."

"Yes, it was useful. More than you can know. When such dramatic things happen so close to our Kingdom, it is better to know as much about them as possible."

The three women sat in silence for a few minutes enjoying the peace and serenity of the temple. Nuri decided that she would not let this woman suffer because of what her kingdom had done. Nuri could live with the guilt for the past. That guilt was her punishment for the heartless way her kingdom had used Talu. But, she could not stand by without making amends for the future. Steeling her resolve she said:

"Mother Talu, I will reiterate. If you ever run into any trouble, please do come to Khet. I will personally ensure that you have a home in my domain. And as Mali said, you might also enjoy spending time with Seeress Groot."

That magnanimity moved both Talu and Mali because somehow they knew that Nuri meant it. Perhaps this is why there is no royalty like Ivchean royalty: they command trust and respect almost instantly.

"Thank you, your highness", Talu replied. "That is very generous of you".

Ж

King Pascheega of Koka was aware that some mischief was afoot from Kunduj. Maddeningly, the warnings of trouble were just not specific enough to take any action.

Pascheega was an older man and most of his thoughts were too other-worldly to spend too much effort trying to piece it together. After the floods ten years ago, he lost both his sons to a mysterious illness that had engulfed his kingdom. He and his wife were spared and he did not know why. Shouldn't the old die before the young?

When the Kokan people were suffering in the floods, his sons had gotten personally involved with providing relief. Pascheega had told them to stay in a safe place. There were others who could do the actual work; the princes only needed to command the troops. But the idealistic young men, had disobeyed. Perhaps as a consequence, they contracted the illness and succumbed to it.

Thus Pascheega was now heir-less, and a number of the neighboring kingdoms were eyeing Koka. It did not surprise the king that Kunduj, with a brash young man at the helm, would cook up some nefarious plans. But his spies had only provided a partial picture. Now his entire court was busy with the administration of this new spontaneous birthing of a boat which had brought many pilgrims. And the pilgrims were rich enough to spend a lot as well. In all that ruckus, the details of Kundujan plans were left hazy.

What about Khet? Did the message from Queen Nuri, sincere as it seemed, have ulterior motives? Pascheega invited King Mayun and Queen Nuri to a special state dinner. While there, Mayun willingly supplied many details; details that helped Pascheega understand the whole scheme.

Mayun had also offered help, military and otherwise. Pascheega smiled to himself wondering what tiny little Khet could do to help. Then he cynically thought: they can do plenty. Especially, when we are busy fighting. They can wait for Koka and Kunduj to get weak and then gobble them both

156

up for themselves.

Then we will have a Nooham Farar for the ages, Pascheega thought: we expect to flee from fierce Kundujan invasion but instead have to run from the cunning of tiny Khet.

However, as Pascheega pondered, one thing did not make sense. Why did Mayun divulge the whole Kundujan plan? It would have been better for him to stay quiet and let the two powers fight each other to exhaustion. Was Mayun's pilgrimage a gambit to be close during the fight so as to take advantage? If so, why did he expose the Kundujan plot? With all those inconsistencies, Pascheega just could not be sure of Mayun's intentions.

He politely asked Mayun to leave with his entourage before any troubles begin. He also gently refused Mayun's help and sagely opined: Unless a country can defend itself, it risks becoming subject to someone else's hegemony.

"I hope", he added, "if and when I am in real trouble, Khet's offer of help would still be open".

King Mayun pledged that it will be and left with his entourage, five days before New Moon.

Ж

"Apotheker! Apotheker!" shouted a breathless Balu as he ran to the apotheker's house in the Chelivas section. Initially annoyed, the Apotheker made way for him when he saw that Balu was carrying a wounded woman on his shoulder. He bade him put her down on a mat and asked what happened. Through catching his breath Balu quickly explained: "This is our legendary warrior Chetu. I found her, wounded and bloodied limping toward town near the Amu. She gave me a message to convey to the King and then collapsed in my arms."

Apotheker nodded and started to check her. Wordlessly, he got a small pitcher of Amu's water and dripped a couple of drops into Chetu's mouth.

"Balu, you have done what you could. But she is gone. Her wounds were too serious. Go on and give the king your message. I will inform her family."

Balu shed tears and collapsed to his feet at hearing the News. Chetu had teased and taunted him relentlessly. But she

157

had also taught him many valuable lessons about discipline and about being an honorable servant of the nation.

As he turned to leave, Balu saw that Minister Vaid was standing there in silence. After a few moments, Vaid turned and signaled Balu to follow him so they could give the message to King Yuda. Shivering at the gravity of what he was about to report, Balu accompanied Vaid to the castle.

When they went into the king's audience chamber, Yuda was talking to twelve of his men about something. A subtle facial gesture from Vaid was enough for Yuda to adjourn the meeting. When everyone had departed, Yuda turned to Balu and demanded: "Speak! What happened?"

"Your Majesty, Warrior Chetu is dead", Balu reported in a voice breaking with emotion. "She gave me a message to convey to you: We have been betrayed. The invasion was a complete failure."

Yuda's frame became taut with fury and frustration. How could this happen? Only three days ago, they had reports from inside Pascheega's palace that all was ready. The enemy was completely unaware of the invasion.

"Where did you run into her?" Vaid inquired.

"Just south of town your highness, near Mother Amu". Balu neglected to mention that he was going to Koka to visit with Talu. Since she was banished, it was not clear how the king would react to keeping contact with her.

"Continue", Vaid commanded.

"I was happy when Laushu Zvuk informed me earlier today that I had passed the second level of target accuracy. Shumi Rasi asked me to get sacred water from Mother Amu so we could perform a Gratitude Prayer. About a hundred paces from the river I saw Warrior Chetu. She was injured and bloodied. She was limping toward town and I saw her fall to the ground.

"I ran up to her and asked what happened. She fiercely quieted me and asked me to listen very carefully. She said that she did not expect to survive but that her message had to reach his majesty forthwith. These are her words:

"Tell his Majesty that our invasion was a complete failure. We have been betrayed. They were fully prepared for us. I was at my post, attending the Praesha and Commander

Dron on the Tunga, when a few soldiers from the rearguard of each of our six attack contingents reported back. The stories were all the same: they got past a fortified threshold easily. But immediately after, each ran into a heavy bombardment which killed the front guard and took the others captive. Soon after that, the Tunga herself came under attack with a heavy barrage of arrows. The Praesha, Commander Dron and all the rearguard soldiers who reported back were hit and took on serious injuries. I counted nearly thirty of our warriors dead on the Tunga. And who knows how many more in the attack squadrons. I got hit too but somehow my wounds felt superficial and I ran. But now I can feel, my life ebbing away. I am not long for this world. Never mind about bringing me to the apotheker. First report this to his majesty. Go!

"Then her breathing got shallow and her eyes closed. I apologize your highness, for I disobeyed her directive. I picked her up on my shoulder and carried her, as fast as I could, to the apotheker's house. He pronounced her dead and I ran into your highness."

"I understand, Balu", a stunned Yuda said. "You did the right thing in taking her to the apotheker first."

Balu bowed and stood. After a moment's silence, Yuda gave orders to Balu.

"This night is for mourning. There shall be no Gratitude Prayer tonight anywhere in Kunduj. Go back to your Laushu and stay there. We will have more orders for you later".

After Balu left, Yuda vented his anger. "Hey Ag! God of Gods!!", he despaired.

Then turned to Vaid and bellowed, "How in the world did this happen? What did we overlook?"

Vaid was quiet for a little while. But the silence combined with Yuda's searing gaze got unbearable. So, against his own better judgement, Vaid found himself talking.

"Even two days ago", he started, "all our information was favorable. We had no reason to lose any confidence. We had six lines of attack - so even if one or two were compromised, we would have others. There was no hole in our plan."

Silence reigned again with Yuda fuming. It was clear that if Vaid hadn't been his Laushu, Yuda would have said some harsh words. Vaid helped him out by saying them himself: "Clearly there is a big hole in my analysis or the plan would not have been such a spectacular failure."

"There is no point in blaming anyone", he said and paused looking pointedly at Vaid, as if to clarify whom exactly he blamed.

"I will ponder the next move. I cannot accept the loss of almost all my army in my very first war of conquest."

It was clear dismissal and a slap in the face for the Minister. The king was essentially saying that he could not depend on his minister to come up with a plan to get him out of this jam. He had to ponder it himself. Stung by the rebuke, Vaid stood up to leave the chamber. But half way, he turned to say:

"I cannot accept the loss either. But what can we do? It is not like we can go to Pashcheega and ask him to return our troops. He is likely to castigate us for a sneak attack. And he will disclaim any part in his sneak attack on us. I think we may have to accept these losses and start building again. We must consider this simply an obstacle to overcome and move on".

It was an emotional response of an elder cut down to size by his younger. It was based more on a presumption of authority than on what the king wanted to hear. Yuda's fury flared up at the response and that fury did not allow him to limit himself to unspoken rebukes.

"Oh really!", he asked sarcastically. "You gave me grief about Balu: a single low level soldier that was ignored in a busy period. You scolded me that perhaps I had already reached the limit of my accomplishment because it was my fault. But now you are willing to let go of hundreds of soldiers without a fight? You never put a single day's thought into what could go wrong with the invasion and how to overcome any problems. Not a moment's thought into how to improvise when things went bad.

"Perhaps, it is not me but you who has already reached the pinnacle of his achievement. If a simple sneak attack, with the full element of surprise, on an unprepared adversary is beyond your abilities to plan, maybe you are not fit to be an emperors minister.

"I heard tonight that I lost my Praesha, my Commander and most of my standing army. And all you can advise is to accept losses and start building again? What would we do if Pashcheega were to attack in the meantime? And now that he can claim moral superiority, we can't even depend on him to restrain himself. Perhaps even if we lose the kingdom, we simply accept losses and start building again. Right?

"Why am I even arguing with you? You are always more interested in lecturing me than in advising me. You just viewed this whole invasion as some intellectual exercise you gave your student never as the true plan of your king for you to iron out all wrinkles.

"Now go! Come back when you have a plan for getting my army back. Or when I call you back to the castle."

Yuda turned his back. Vaid, his face turned crimson at the rebuke, took a deep breath and walked away.

Ж

"Our Laushu died serving the King" said Rasi with tears flowing down her cheeks. Zvuk Meza shed his own tears and added: "He was the best Laushu a student could ever have."

Balu felt guilty at having brought them this News. "Does this mean the king is in trouble?"

"Yes, it probably does", Zvuk replied. "And we will be always at the ready to serve him. But we need to wait till he calls us. It would not do for us to disturb him at this time."

Balu almost did not hear most of it. His voice breaking with emotion, he broke down in tears saying.

"Did we really lose thirty of our warriors? It must include a lot of the Praesha's troops. It must include a lot more like Chetu."

"Control your emotions, Balu!" Zvuk said sternly. "As warriors we always carry the risk of death, especially when we are ordered into a war. We may mourn our fellow warriors but cannot let it come in the way of our work, which is to secure the release of those that are still in enemy hands. We must help the King with the attempt at retrieving them. And if necessary, be willing to die in the attempt ourselves."

Even as he was saying it, Rasi embraced Balu and wiped his tears, fulfilling her role as his Shumi. At the last

161

sentence, she looked angrily at Zvuk and closed her ears reciting the usual antidote to unpleasant utterances: "May the inauspicious words be rendered powerless!" Then she gave Balu a softer message than Zvuk Meza's stern truth:

"The ones we lost are now in heaven. They are fine and happy. We grieve not for them but we are going to miss them. So, our bereavement is about us, not them. However, we have a duty toward the ones who are still alive. We will help them, try to bring them to their families. You have proven yourself once to the king already. You have nothing more to prove. Simply follow His Majesty's orders as and when they come. Understand?"

Balu nodded his head and wiped his tears. The three sat in silence for a few moments while Rasi recited the Farewell Prayer in a low voice:

Hey Rock Boha, wouldn't you kindly,
    Tell the other Gods about our friends,
    Who today reached the end of their history,
    Who today attained the right to be heavenly,
    Who today did acts deserving your sympathy,
    Who today have become purely Soul-ly.
    We pray you and your fellow Gods to
        Welcome them to your heavenly abode,
        Teach them the ropes of the afterlife.
        Even as we remember them,
        Help them break their bonds with us.

Zvuk Meza and Balu mumbled along with the prayer. All three fully believed the prayer that their friends were indeed better off, now that they were on a higher plane and interacting with Rock Boha Himself.

Rasi patted both Zvuk Meza and Balu on their backs. "We should sleep now so we are ready when the King summons us tomorrow."

Balu felt tense. Just like when he was suddenly imprisoned, the world was crumbling all around him. The last time had ended very well for him: he gained a wonderful Laushu and a loving Shumi. How would it turn out this time? Also, going to Talu before New Moon, as he had promised was unlikely. He wondered if he would be able to go there any time soon.

Next morning summons came from the castle assigning Balu to interior palace guard. He had been away from the castle for a while but now he was back in service and immersed into the protection of a castle that was short on staff.

Ж

Over the next week, Balu witnessed King Yuda acting very distressed and agitated. He chalked that up to the loss of so many fine people. He witnessed Minister Vaid coming and going, each time looking more angry and sad than the last time. To escape the king's fury, the other guards took to avoiding the King. In the middle of this tense and distressed atmosphere Balu could not ask for time away in order to visit Talu. And he definitely did not anticipate that within days he would be off on an official trip to Koka.

The town of Kunduj was also getting more tense through that week. Chetu's cremation served as a meeting place for fellow warrior families where her last message to the king spread and was amplified into exaggerated rumor. No word was forthcoming from the castle about who was lost and what was being done to retrieve the others. Though no one could advise the king on what exactly he should do, many warrior families were desperate for him to do something. Anything.

On the thirteenth day, the day after Chetu's Tilar Jal (final farewell prayer), Balu came in for his guard duty in the evening. The other guards told him "The king is furious, be careful" and left hurriedly. A few other guards, keeping night watch with Balu, quietly slipped away into invisible corners of the castle. Balu was left alone in the front chamber when the door to the secret chamber cracked open in the wind and he could hear the conversation inside.

"So, what was the point of all that subterfuge?" King Yuda was asking angrily

"Well, your Majesty", Minister Vaid was countering. "It was a gambit - we knew all along that it might not succeed. Somehow Pashcheega got wind of it and ..."

"How? Does he have spies planted here?"

"Not necessarily, your majesty. Even without spies ..."

"No!" thundered Yuda. "I think Pashcheega does indeed

163

know what is going on in our castle, because he has sources here. That is why all our gambits have come to naught. Let us assume this: whatever we plan, it will be known to him. Then what can we do?"

Silence reigned as the Minister seemed to admit there was nothing that could be done.

Finally, the king dismissed Vaid: "That will be all. I would like to be alone."

Vaid looked distressed and ashamed when he came out of the chamber. He left the castle with nary a glance at Balu, as if even he wanted to escape from the King.

Balu was naive enough to feel sorry for the King. A few minutes later the king summoned help with a stentorious "Who's there?".

Balu went in and bowed "Your Majesty!"

"Get me a drink!"

Balu fetched Soma from the kitchen in a goblet of fine Ivchean ceramic. After serving the king, he bowed and asked if there was anything else: "May I serve his majesty in any other way?"

The king was preoccupied and did not respond with the usual dismissal. He just looked at Balu thoughtfully. Balu looked into Yuda's eyes and saw depths of pain and disappointment. With genuine sympathy for his king, Balu continued.

"Your Majesty. It pains me to see you in this much distress. My life is wasted if I cannot lessen the load at least a little."

"What can you do?" Yuda asked angrily, irritated by the sympathy from a lowly soldier. "You brought me News of Chetu's death. And brought me her disastrous message that my army is totally lost. Can you undo either of those events?"

Stung by the angry response, Balu just stood there. Yuda hung his head down to look at the ground and whispered, as if trying to fathom the magnitude of his loss.

"My army is totally lost. My beloved army. My whole army."

Balu stood mutely. The king looked up at Balu and said pacifyingly.

"You are a good servant, Balu. The others hide from my anger, you come forward to offer help. You are a good soldier too, one to whom I was pleased to give the arrow honor. But for right now, there is nothing you can do: just keep the soma coming."

As the King got more drunk, Balu decided that the king had enough. He went into the room unsummoned and said:

"May I help you to your bedchamber, your Majesty?"

"Why? You think I should not drink anymore?"

Silence.

"You are probably right", king said in a slurred voice. With a hand on Balu's shoulder, the king started, with uncertain steps, for his bedchamber upstairs. "But I won't stop drinking unless you make me one promise."

"Anything, your majesty!"

"Bring back my army from Koka!"

"Your Majesty! How?!"

"No, you already promised. You must fulfill!"

"But, your majesty. I don't know how to go about something like this. And I don't even know the details of what happened, just rumors."

"Oh, don't worry about that. I'll tell you all".

"Your majesty, you know I will do anything, even give my life, in your service. But this is not a good idea. I don't know anything about commanding an attack squad."

"Ha ha", the king guffawed. "There is no attack squad for you to take."

"I also know nothing about diplomacy or any other ways of getting them back. I ..."

"Hey you!", King Yuda yelled, summoning a servant. "Go and get Minister Vaid, right now"

After a moment of slight hesitation, the servant bowed to the king's glare and left. Balu and Yuda continued on upstairs.

"Your Majesty", Balu continued. "I don't know about attacking, or diplomacy. I don't even know how to build up a conspiracy."

"Hah!" Yuda exclaimed victoriously. "You do know! You

know that the three methods to try are attack, diplomacy and conspiracy!"

"No Your Majesty", Balu replied with disarming honesty. "I don't really know. I only remembered because my laushu taught me about them yesterday".

"You are really unique", the king said. "Anyone else in your position would have played up their knowledge. I want someone with your honesty on this problem".

"But sire. I really don't know of any way for accomplishing this."

"Neither does anyone else! But they have still tried all the methods. And failed. Now, I'll tell you every detail of what happened and you will try to bring my army back. And you will succeed."

Balu didn't know what to say.

"It all started with the abduction attempt which you thwarted." the king began to explain all that happened since that fateful night.

Minister Vaid arrived and saw that Balu was sitting on the floor. The king, sitting on the bed, was divulging details of the invasion and its failure.

"Come, come my Laushu!", the king said as Vaid tried to interrupt. "I have come up with a foolproof plan to bring our army back. Balu here will go and get them."

"But, your majesty ..."

"As they say, *Veerya mael pakya*, my Laushu. Luck is better than valor. And I can tell. Balu here is very lucky."

"Your Majesty, you are drunk. You cooked this up, unpremeditated, in a drunken stupor." As laushu, Vaid was entitled to give that stern truth to the king. Balu hoped that would somehow dissuade the king out of this insane plan.

"As if our premeditated plans have delivered bountiful results", the king mocked and then turning to Balu. "See! No one believes in you except me. You won't let me down will you?"

"Your Majesty!", Vaid responded again in a stern voice. "In the morning you will see that this is not a good idea and will change your mind."

"Really!? You are probably right. Well, I know how to fix

that. Tell Balu all he needs to know about Pashcheega right now. I want him on his way before sunup." And then turning to Balu, he said pointedly "Decamp to Koka before sunup. Go there and do what is needed to bring back my army. That is an order!"

Balu could scarcely respond with anything other than "Yes, Your Majesty!"

As the king lay down on the bed, Vaid looked at Balu with a mixture of apology and pity.

Ж

Balu got home in the middle of the night and woke up Zvuk Meza and Rasi. He explained the whole situation as he prepared to leave for Koka. Zvuk and Rasi wished they could join Balu, but there was a Royal Decree that all servants in the Chelivas sector must stay in town.

Balu touched Zvuk's and Rasi's feet to seek their blessing. Rasi, tears flowing down her eyes, blessed him with victory. Zvuk Meza gave Balu some much needed courage with a pep talk: "Rock Boha entertains himself by creating strange situations for us. Why would he arrange events so? Why make the king send his least experienced warrior on an impossible mission?

"Perhaps in order for one to ascend like a volcano's breath, there must be the possibility to crash like a shooting star. Perhaps for greatness to come to anyone, they must be forced to attempt the impossible. Even for Rock Boha, there is no other way to impart greatness. He is sending you on this mission because He has a plan for you. Keep the faith and go! Rock Boha is with you!"

As Balu hurried to leave before sunup, he pondered that this was his own Nooham Farar: he never expected to be running away from sunrise.

167

Story of the Story - 5

"This is important, Man!" Jalal's plaintive appeal from the other side of the phone, really got to me this time.

"Yeah well, so is my life!" I replied angrily. "You mat not be remotely aware but I do have a busy life outside of this translation. So, no! I cannot spend any more time on it. I cannot make it go any faster."

"Come on! Don't treat this as just another intellectual exercise", he chastised me without a hint of irony in his voice. "This is the key to the salvation of my eternal soul."

"No, you come on!" I retorted. "In spite of whatever mystical nonsense you experienced with the Haji, that is bull shit! This ancient book is interesting. But still, it's just a book. It has nothing to do with your soul. The sooner you realize that, the sooner you can find some peace".

I hung up the phone. I really wished it was a handset so I could slam it down. I was angry! Who the hell did he think he was? Expecting me to spend all my time on his hobby. Sheesh!

After I cooled down, I regretted some of the things I said. I knew the book had deep meaning for him. I should not have blown up like that. I tried to call him back and conciliate, but he did not pick up his phone. I tried again several times to call and text him with the same result. I hoped I had not broken our relationship beyond repair.

Next day, I got a call from DubDee.

"Hi DubDee. Why is Jalal ghosting me?"

She just sighed.

"What happened? Is he really that upset at me? Please tell him I am sorry for what I said".

"It's not that", DubDee replied. "I am calling from the hospital. Jalal is re-admitted".

"What?! Why? Did he fall again?"

"No. Two days ago, tests revealed that his cancer has recurred. He tried to keep it from everyone including me. I have been away for a week, managing a corporate retreat in Bar Harbor. But yesterday when I came back and checked in on him, he was lying on the floor. He said he had fainted. When I took him to the hospital, the whole truth came out".

"Oh no. I am so sorry."

"Yeah. The doctor said the prognosis this time is poor. There is a only a five percent chance that he will survive another year".

DubDee's voice broke down. I mumbled that I was sorry to hear it and added, "Well, he beat the odds last time, Perhaps he will do it again".

"Yeah", she said simply.

It was another day before I was able to get Jalal on the phone. He seemed in good spirits and talked cheerfully enough.

"I am sorry for the things I said last time", I apologized. "It is just that I was frustrated with too much travel and work at the office and I ..."

"No", he interrupted me. "I should be the one to apologize. I should not have said you were slacking. I know you spend a great deal of effort on this and I am very grateful".

"Don't worry, Jalal", I tried to console him. "May be you will beat the odds again. I mean, you did it last time. Who knows?"

"No, my friend!" he replied with some resignation in his voice. "I can feel it this time. This is my time. My doctor said I have a five percent chance to live one more year. I think she is over-estimating. I think I have six months, tops".

"Come on! Don't give up like that. It can be important to keep a positive ..."

"Wait!" he interrupted me again and sighed. "I am not worried. I am ready. I have all my affairs in order. But can I ask you for a favor?"

"Sure", even as I said it, I was not sure. What if he asked me to spend more time on the book? Where would I find the time? But he surprised me.

"Can you please come to visit me? I would like to meet you and your family in person".

I reflected on the wonders of twenty-first century communications technology. We had embarked on this remarkable collaboration but had never met so far. It was clearly over-due.

"Absolutely! Let me check with my wife and I'll let you know the dates".

We found time for three weeks out to visit him. In the mean time, I neglected my day job a little as I tried to hasten the translation of the book.

11. Niji Sheng Saaban

"Your Majesty," Minister Vaid explained. "You were drunk last night and sent that boy, Balu, as your emissary to Koka."

If Vaid expected Yuda to express dismay and regret for a foolish act, he was disappointed. Yuda was nonchalant.

"I know. I was not so drunk that I don't remember."

"Your Majesty. I did not want to correct you in front of the men yesterday. But, that was not a good move."

"Oh!? And why not?"

"So many reasons," Vaid was exasperated. "He is no ambassador. He has no experience with statecraft. He is not a great warrior; nor even a mediocre one. He is not even a spy who could dream up some surreptitious jail-break."

"So what? You have tried deceitful gambits by experts in espionage. You have tried to send warriors. You have tried our best diplomats. You have tried all that during the past ten days. Did you have any success that you can report?"

"No, but that just means we have to think of even better plans and find even better diplomats".

"We are running out of time. If we don't get them out soon, I fear we will lose them forever; king Pascheega might execute them".

"I agree, Your Majesty. But that does not mean that we use someone who knows nothing about statecraft."

"Why not?" Yuda retorted. "It is not like we have much to lose. Why not send a loyal soldier like Balu? Do you know he is very beloved. He has a large number of well wishers."

"I did not know that. But that is irrelevant. His well wishers, his loyalty are both irrelevant."

"It is relevant!" insisted Yuda. "I have found that having a large number of well wishers often translates into better luck. And anyway, the usual has failed. Repeatedly. So, why not just try the unusual?"

A guard came through the door saying "Victory Your Majesty". Yuda looked at him and barked "Report!".

"Your Majesty! I bring some bad News from Koka. Early this morning, Balu was arrested for trespassing into Koka without permission. Apparently, he claimed to be a Royal

Messenger from you. But instead of waiting outside town for permission he just walked in. When confronted, he readily admitted that he was a Royal emissary. He is in jail; unclear what happens to him now."

Yuda sighed and rubbed his forehead: "Any News on the other members of our army?"

"No Your Majesty. And I have to say, that lack of News is good News. It means that they are all still alive and that King Pashcheega has not decided what to do with them".

"Go back to Koka and send me messages when anything happens. That will be all!"

When guard left, Vaid could not resist a dig tantamount to I-told-you-so.

"And that is why we don't just 'try the unusual'."

"That's OK", Yuda shrugged. "It is no worse than our other gambits which also failed".

"Yes, it is worse. Don't you see? This one didn't even get started. He got arrested even before he could do anything. You must understand it is never a good idea to make a desperate attempt when you are drunk and ..."

"Enough", roared Yuda. "That will be all, Minister!"

Minister Vaid bowed and left the chamber, chagrined at how his relation with the king seemed to be getting worse by the day.

Ж

It was a beautiful sunny day in Seeress Groot's cloister. The first warm day of the season. It seemed to hold promise of nicer days to come. But Queen Nuri was filled with foreboding that some form-less danger was fast approaching. Having resolved to do something about it, she had come to the Seeress for help with a special prayer.

"Are you sure, Your Majesty?" Groot asked.

"Oh please, Mother. Don't be formal and call me 'your majesty'. I am here as an ordinary devotee who needs your help with Niji Sheng".

"Ironic. Since you would not even qualify for this prayer if you weren't the queen."

Silence.

172

"Because you are talking about sinful things committed not personally by you but by your kingdom. Right?"

"Yes".

Groot took a deep breath and attempted to summarize: "So, you think that your kingdom has done some sinful things. And you are afraid that all your people will get punished for those sins. So, you want to take a Saaban. An oath. You want to take an oath that all those sins are your responsibility."

"No. That is too declarative and some people might disagree. I don't care who IS responsible for them. I want to shoulder the responsibility for any bad consequences from them."

"OK", Groot continued her summary with unnecessary repetition. "You want to pray to Rock Boha to spare your people the fallout from these sinful actions. You wish to bear the burden of all punishment for those actions. You want to take the oath of Niji Sheng, of self sacrifice, in order to spare your subjects. Is this what you are saying?"

"Yes."

"You know, that is not how divine justice works. Punishment is meted out to the people that commit the sins, not to the ones that want it."

"But I want it to work that way in this case."

"You are pregnant and will give birth in two months. Punishing you will also punish the child. How can you want that? And how can you expect the Gods to dispense such injustice?"

Nuri had tears in her eyes as she replied: "No. I don't want that. That is why I take this oath. I pray that my child be spared along with all my subjects. If someone must be punished, I offer myself as sacrifice. I have always believed that because royalty are given enormous privilege, our lives are forfeit for public welfare. I cannot tolerate punishment to my people in order to spare my child; my people are my children too."

Now, it was Groot's turn to have tears in her eyes as she looked upon the queen.

"Your Majesty! That honorific does not do you justice. I

have met many so-called 'great' kings and queens. But never seen anyone express this much concern about their people's welfare. Your Niji Sheng Saaban, your oath of self sacrifice, will become a beacon to all royalty showing them the path of righteous behavior. You truly are great."

"Mother Groot! Help me so it is successful. You are the greatest seer there ever was. If anyone can make a success of this prayer, it is you. I want the Gods to hear my prayer and our people to be spared."

Groot said after a thoughtful pause: "Two questions must be answered to ensure its success. First: What does the King think of what you are doing?"

"His Majesty King Mayun does not know that I am doing this. But I know he thinks that he is the one responsible for the sins and that the punishment will come to him anyway. He always stands ready to lay down his life to defend the kingdom. So, he does not think he needs to take any oath such as this".

Groot just looked at her.

"But that is not what you are asking" Nuri conceded. "I admit, if he knew I was doing this, he will try to stop me. He will try to sit in my place."

"Understood. That leads me to my second question: What are these sins you are repenting for?"

"I can't tell you that."

"But you are revealing without saying it that the King was more involved in planning and executing them than you were."

Silence.

"So, Queen Nuri. Why *not* let your husband take this oath? If it was his sin, and he would gladly take the rap for it, why not let him take the Niji Sheng Saaban?"

"Because the Nation needs him more than it needs me. He is both a warrior and a Commander. I am neither. If the punishment weakens him in any way, the country will suffer"

Groot silently meditated for a few moments.

"Alright, I will help you with this prayer. Call in one of your aides. I will send him to bring some prayer materiel."

An aide was summoned and Seeress Groot gave him a

long list of things to fetch for the prayer. The aide received an approving nod from the queen and left.

"Now, Queen Nuri. Face North-East and pray to Rock Boha. Specifically think of the sins that were committed and express your repentance for them."

Nuri nodded and sat quietly inside Groot's hut with eyes closed and meditated over "her" sins. When there was fear of an attack from Kunduj, it would have been honorable to get ready to fight. Or to sue Kunduj for peace. But Khet had done neither. Instead it had devised a sneaky and dishonorable counter-attack to abduct King Yuda in the middle of the night. When that failed, the retribution was cunningly diverted onto innocent Koka.

As a direct result of all this, a pious devotee of Mother Earth had become homeless in her old age. Several Kundujan soldiers had died. And hundreds more were held captive and it is possible they would be executed. How many children would be orphaned for our chicanery? And what would happen when Kunduj inevitably learns the truth and turns its wrath on Khet? How many of our people will die then? How much more suffering?

Oh Mother Earth! Oh Rock Boha! Oh Bohamir! Oh Mother Amu! Hey Ag! Please do not let my people suffer for these misdeeds. I pledge that I will make amends for them for as long as I am alive. And if you have to punish someone, I stand ready. My kingdom initiated all this; so, let the misdeeds be mine and focus all your punishment for it, on me. As Gods, nothing is impossible for you. So, please spare everyone else.

The queen had barely completed her prayers when commotion erupted outside the hut.

"Help! Seeress Groot! Please help me!"

Seeress Groot, who was sitting on a tree stump, signaled the petitioner to slow down.

"Who are you? And what is the trouble?"

"My name is Talu. I met your Queen Nuri some time ago in Koka. She promised to help me if I was ever in trouble and advised me to go to you. I don't know where else to turn. Please help me!"

"What is the trouble?" Groot prompted Talu.

"My son, actually my foster son, I helped raise him and think of him as my son. His name is Balu and he is a loyal soldier of Kunduj. He is presently imprisoned in Koka. As a poor old woman, I have no resources. Will you please save him!"

Nuri came out of Groot's hut and heard Talu's explanation. She regretfully closed her eyes, and thought: Oh Mother! Is this one more innocent person getting punished for my misdeeds? Talu saw the queen and stopped talking.

"Your Majesty! Why are you here? Is your pregnancy running into any problems?"

"No, I am fine" Nuri replied. "What happened with your son? Why is he in prison?"

The queen sat on a comfortable flat stone on which was spread a mat of deer skin. Talu sat down on the ground. Looking alternately at Queen Nuri and Seeress Groot, she narrated.

"This past New Moon night, I was sleeping on the temple steps wondering why my foster son Balu had not visited me like he said he would. I felt sad thinking that he was just one more young man neglecting the old. I am not even his real mother and so have no claim on his affection. Thinking on all this I had trouble sleeping.

Mid-night I heard a commotion. The Tunga, the boat that was spontaneously birthed by Mother Amu, was under attack. In the dim light of the temple lamps, I saw people fighting on board and around. It was over very quickly. Next morning, word came from the palace that there was a major attack on Koka the night before. Several enemy soldiers were killed and hundreds were captured.

"The ordinary people of Koka were not affected by the attack; everyone listened to the account with finger-on-the-nose amazement. They almost did not believe it until senior ministers and temple priests vouched for it and until last rites were held for the dead enemy soldiers.

"I did not think much more about it until my Balu came to me yesterday, a few hours before sunup. I was happy to see him and even more happy when he explained why he could not come to me before: he had been called into duty by King Yuda. Apparently, Kunduj had lost almost all her army to

Koka; they were all captured or killed. King Yuda had made several attempts to retrieve his army but all had failed.

"So, in the end, King Yuda turned to my Balu. He is just a boy and has no experience in statecraft of any kind. And yet the king thought to turn to him for getting his army back. Being a loyal soldier, Balu accepted the order though it was a mission entirely beyond his ability.

"Anyway, Balu took his morning dip in the Amu and offered prayers. As he was coming out of the river, four security guards surrounded him and made him drop his spear. Then they shouted questions at him to ask whether he was an agent of King Yuda and whether he was here to take the Kundujan army. Balu admitted that he was. They immediately arrested him saying that, as a Royal Messenger, he was supposed to wait outside the border. By coming in uninvited, Kunduj had invaded Koka for a second time.

"Balu protested that he had come to visit the temple several times before and had never sought permission. That he was sorry. That he was not aware of this new rule. That this was not an invasion by any means. That he had come alone and had no way to use force. That he was going to seek an audience with King Pashcheega and pray him to release the army.

"The guards laughed and said that if he now got an audience with His Majesty, it will be as a criminal and not as a Royal Messenger. Balu had forfeit all ambassadorial privileges when he rudely entered the kingdom without permission.

"I considered stopping them. I wanted to tell them to take me and spare my son. But I knew that would only get both of us thrown in jail. So, I thought back to your generous promise, your Majesty, to help me if I was ever in trouble. That I could come to Seeress Groot's cloister to seek solace. So, I have been walking almost non-stop for a whole day to reach here. Your Majesty! Seeress Groot! Will you please help me save my son?".

Groot looked at Nuri's face and wondered if the changing expressions on her face from regret, to guilt, to resolve, meant that this had something to do with the sins she was referring to. Before Groot could talk, Queen Nuri responded.

"Yes, Mother Talu. We will help you. We will get your son out of prison. First, please take a meal and rest awhile. Allow me to think of how to go about doing this."

About an hour later, a messenger came to announce that a small entourage from the castle was coming to the cloister; it included the aide with all the materiel that the seeress had requested. But it also included the king.

The queen was annoyed. She had wanted to avoid an argument with the king till the prayer ceremony was completed. Seeress Groot sensed the queen's displeasure.

"Your Majesty" Groot said, "Don't be annoyed at your aide. It is not his fault that the king is coming over here."

"Oh?"

"I deliberately chose my list of materiel to include things for which he had to go to the castle and had to get the king's permission. It is my fault that the king was informed and is coming over."

Queen sat silently with pursed lips.

"Your Majesty!" Groot continued in a softer voice. "You wanted my help in ensuring that the Gods hear your plea. That will not happen unless you and your husband are together on this. You cannot avoid that confrontation. It must be completed before the prayer."

More silence.

"You understand?"

As the queen nodded, the king rushed into the hut looking furious. He backed down a bit upon seeing Groot.

"Greetings Seeress."

"May you always be victorious" Groot blessed.

"Did I hear this correctly, Seeress? That as protection against deeds done as part of statecraft, you are going to perform a Niji Sheng Saaban for the queen?"

"I am simply fulfilling Her Majesty's wishes."

"Milady, this is outrageous", Mayun turned to Nuri. "What I did in statecraft was not a misdeed. It was what needed to be done."

"Really, My Lord?! When I think of all the consequences to innocent people, I can hardly sleep."

"I will step out while you two talk this out", Groot said. "But, allow me to say one thing before I leave: Think not of this as a confrontation but as a chance for each of you to understand the other's point of view. Only that will save your domain and your people."

The two looked at her angrily. After Groot stepped out of her hut, silence reigned for a few moments. Nuri spoke first.

"I am sorry my dear. I have this foreboding fear of a calamity about to befall our people. And I fear it will be retribution for our misdeeds."

"What misdeeds?"

"Did we really need a dishonorable sneak attack on Kunduj when we heard about their plan to invade?"

"Yes, we did" Mayun insisted. "And no, it was not dishonorable. You remember when we went to his coronation? How Yuda was friendly and tried to lull us into complacency? All the while he was hatching a plot to invade us. It was he who was being deceitful and dishonorable. What choice did we have? We could not fight back; he has a standing army ten times bigger than ours. We couldn't sue for peace; how would we be fulfilling our obligation to protect our people if we let them be dominated by this brash young man? It was our best option. You can poke holes in the plan and criticize it if you want. But, please don't call it dishonorable."

"What about deflecting the blame onto Koka when the abduction failed? They could have been seriously hurt."

"No they couldn't", Mayun defended again. "Koka has a much stronger army and would have easily repelled any attack by Kunduj. It was an edhir mael pakdhir gambit. A well accepted ploy in statecraft. And it worked beautifully. There was nothing dishonorable about it. Besides, we were in Koka at the right time, and helped minimize damage down to nothing. In the end, we successfully defanged that snake, Yuda. In fact our gambit has brought peace to this whole region, without shedding too much blood".

"I don't question your statecraft, dear. I really believe you planned brilliantly and executed flawlessly."

"Then why ..."

"Because I saw another angle to the whole affair when I met with Talu in Koka. In the midst of all these strategic ploys and statecraft, we forgot to pay attention to what happens to ordinary folks. Do you remember that she is homeless now?"

"Yes. But don't forget that she is happy about it. It was deliverance for her."

"What of the Kundujan soldiers that were killed? And the hundreds that are imprisoned."

Mayun paused before he responded.

"I think of myself as a soldier too. So, I do feel bad for them and their families. But we soldiers stand ready to die for our kingdom. Soldiers are nurtured by the king even in times of peace and their sole purpose is to absorb blows like this; they are willing participants in war. Therefore, soldiers are always fair game. It may sound harsh, but it is the truth. Besides, those very soldiers would have invaded us. And I don't believe they would have had any hesitation in killing our soldiers in order to take over our villages. So, even though I feel bad for them, I have to say they deserved it."

"So, you think there was nothing wrong with what we did."

"Absolutely."

"Then why do you want to stop me?"

"Huh?"

"I am only requesting the Gods that any bad consequences from our actions should be focused on me. If, as you think, there will be no bad consequences then nothing will be focused and, no harm will be done. So why do you stop me?"

"B .. B.. Because, ..." Mayun was stumped, unable to think of a way out of his logical fallacy. Nuri approached him, put her arms around his neck and spoke tenderly.

"Dearest. I truly do admire the way you dealt with this threat. It could have been far worse for everyone if you did nothing. My oath is not a criticism of those actions. It is possible that my pregnancy is making me too emotional. But since I met Talu, I have been seeing the other side of war. And I feel afraid that the Gods will rebuke us. So, I would like to pray to them to send any bad consequences of these actions to me. If what we did was right, there will be no harm. If there will be some punishment, I want to bear it and spare our people. Please, let me do this."

"Yes dearling, you are getting too emotional" Mayun replied. "But they say being emotional is just the inability to see the middle ground between right and wrong. So, if what you say is right, let me take the oath. I will sit in the prayer."

"It won't work", Nuri shook her head. "Because you don't really believe anything wrong was done. Besides, as a soldier, some punishment will be dished to you anyway, even without the prayer. Finally, if Kunduj realizes our role and attacks, we will need you, the soldier and commander, much more than me. Remember with the depleted army, they are matched about right with us."

Nuri paused meaningfully, laid her cheek on Mayun's chest and concluded in a low and intimate voice.

"Besides, you are overlooking the obvious reason I am the right choice for this. I have my brave soldier to protect me from any punishment. All you have is your timid girl. Let me do this and protect me, as you would the entire kingdom."

Brave soldier and timid girl were monikers they used when teasing each other. Mayun embraced her, took a deep breath in acquiescence.

"I could never say no to you."

"Do you know that Talu is here in the cloister? She came by seeking help because her son is imprisoned."

"Really? How? Why?"

Nuri repeated Talu's story to the king.

"Wow" Mayun exclaimed. "That is quite the situation the young man is in. I am not sure there is much we can do to help though. Pascheega does not brook any external interference. And especially in a matter of justice like this ...".

"I know", Nuri said. "I've been thinking about that and I agree that any interference directly from us will only make matters worse. How about someone else though? Someone like, say, Gramani. Do you think he can help?"

"That is a great idea! Yes, I think he can help. Rather, I should say, if he cannot help, then no one can!"

An hour later, the whole cloister gathered together along with a number of castle workers. Queen Nuri took a dip in the sacred Amu, sat in front of a fire pit and took an oath of

Niji Sheng. Most attendees did not know the details of her real reason: they just thought that she was re-dedicating herself to the kingdom and wanted the Gods to protect her people. King Mayun, who knew the real reasons, made a moving speech:

"Her Majesty, Queen Nuri has just shown the way for all royalty all over the world. I learn from her example that our lives are forfeit for the welfare of the people. From this day forth, Khet will not be known as my kingdom, but rather as Her Majesty's Queendom. That I pledge my love to my queen will come as no surprise to any of you. Now I also pledge my life to the service of her Queendom, for as long as I draw breath."

The whole assemblage sloganeered: "Victory always to Queen Nuri!".

Talu, who was in the audience, was inspired to take a Niji Sheng Saaban of her own for a much more private goal: "Oh Bohamir! Please let my life be forfeit for that of my son. Please spare my Balu. If there must be some punishment, I am ready."

A single person's Niji Sheng often leads to several others copying it. So, it was not surprising that Talu followed the queen. However, no one could have imagined that hundreds of Niji Sheng oaths were to follow this one with remarkable consequences to the arc of history.

Ж

"Kanavata! And Vrajavoora!", Talu exclaimed.

Mali looked at them confused. Jenon and Vika were stunned into silence.

"Wait", Mali asked Talu. "You know them already?"

"Yes, my dear," Talu replied. "These are the two men I told you about, Kanavata and Vrajavoora, the ones who stayed in my home for a month. And then almost succeeded in abducting King Yuda in the dead of the night".

"No, mother Talu! This is my husband Jenon and his brother Vika. You are mistaking them for some other people."

Even as she was saying it, Mali's voice lowered as she looked at the expressions on the men's faces and realized that Talu was right. Mali felt weirdly proud of her husband. She

182

thought he was a simple soldier. Instead he turns out to be a heroic superspy that the king sent on a clandestine mission. When did that happen? And why had he not told her? And then she felt ashamed of her pride. Disturbing her from the reverie, Jenon and Vika sat down in front of Talu. Jenon held Talu's hands and spoke for both of them.

"We apologize, Talu. It was inconsiderate and cruel of us to have used you in that deceitful way. Please forgive us?"

Talu squeezed Jenon's hands and put her hands on Jenon's and Vika's heads. "There is nothing to forgive. I understand why you did it and it brought about a very good change in my life. I am now banished from Kunduj and am living the life of a free spirit in Koka. Truly, I have nothing but gratitude for you two."

"Yes, we heard that you got banished".

"Well, the king blamed me for the fiasco and banished me. So I left Kunduj and have been living in Koka."

"We are truly sorry about that" Vika said.

"No, no. Thank you both. This has been very good for me. A very peaceful and enjoyable life. And by the way, did you know the soldier who stopped you is my son, er foster son, Balu."

"No I did not" said Vika, astonished. "What connections Rock Boha makes!"

"And so, from the day that he saved the king, my Balu's role and profile have been growing".

"Oh!? I am glad to hear that", said Jenon, thinking back to how he had almost killed Balu that night.

"Yes. The king had your abduction attempt investigated and concluded that you two were from Koka. So, he organized an invasion of Koka which was an epic failure; Kunduj's entire army was captured. King Yuda tried various diplomatic means to get his army back but all those attempts also failed. So he turned, again, to his most trusted associate: my son Balu. Asked him to go retrieve the army".

"Wow. That is quite a job for such a young man" Jenon said.

"You are indeed correct. Since he is inexperienced in any diplomacy, Balu did not know that you had to wait for a formal permission before entering Koka. Instead he simply walked into the kingdom like an ordinary pilgrim. He was arrested and promptly thrown in jail. I came up to meet Queen Nuri to see if she will help get my son back. I met her the day she took the Niji Sheng Saaban. Did you hear, at that ceremony, King Mayun declared that this is now a Queendom and that Queen Nuri is at the head."

"Yes, I heard" Jenon waxed eloquent with admiration in his voice. "The queen has shown supreme nobility in this. Everyone talks about willingness to give their life for the people. But the Queen actually did it. Where everyone prays to escape Gods' wrath, she actually asked the Gods to focus their wrath on her. With this incredible act of kindness, she has shown herself to be not just Queen of Khet but rather empress of the world".

"Anyway", Vika said in hushed tones, surprised at the depth of Jenon's feeling. "Did she help with your son's situation?"

"Oh yes, she did. She gave me a necklace and advised me to approach someone called Gramny. He is this old man in Khiwani who has made a study of the justice in all the kingdoms of this region and he can give advice on how to proceed. I was to offer the necklace as payment for his advice. Also, some family was going that way in a caravan of bullock carts. Upon the Queen's request, they allowed me to ride with them up to Khiwani. So, yes. The queen helped a lot."

"I do not know of this Gramny", Jenon said.

"He is now more than eighty years old" Talu explained. "In the old days he used to be Khiwani's Gramani, the official who administers the village. In that capacity, he studied the ways of law enforcement, not just of Khiwani but of all kingdoms in this region. For the past 20 or so years, he has been helping people escape Royal wrath and people gladly pay for his advice."

"So, what did he say? Was he helpful?" Mali asked.

Talu, was rather enjoying being the center of the conversation. It was not often that she got to tell a story that three people were listening to with breathless anticipation. She savored the feeling and continued the story in a leisurely fashion.

"Well, when I reached his home, Gramny was sick. The apotheker was there attending to him. I waited outside the house, hoping he would be strong enough to talk to me soon. And guess whom I met there?"

"Who?"

"Zvuk Meza and his wife Rasi" Talu paused meaningfully.

"The Kundujan sound splitter?" Vika asked perplexed. "Why was he there?"

"As it happened, my Balu chose him as his Laushu and is right now studying archery with Zvuk Meza. They were there for the same reason as I: to see Gramny and figure out a way to free Balu. Apparently Rasi grew up in Khiwani and knows Gramny quite well. And of course she is now Balu's shumi. It seems Rasi has had trouble bearing children and so she has taken to Balu with the affection of a real mother. Sometimes she even forgets that I was there first; Balu was my foster son long before he was anything to Rasi."

"So, did Gramny see you?" Vika asked, trying to nudge her back to topic.

"Yes. Since Rasi is familiar with the family, she went in right away to help attend on Gramny. He rested for a few hours and then was strong enough to talk. I bet if Rasi had her way, she would just have spoken to him and gone her way, without involving me at all. But, since I was eye-witness to Balu's arrest, Gramny asked for me and then talked to all three of us: me, Zvuk and Rasi.

"After listening to my narration, Gramny summarized our challenge with the ease of someone who has done it a thousand times. He said we face a three layered challenge.

"First challenge, how to get an audience with the king in open court. Without getting an audience, nothing could be done. But getting it in open court would be preferable because that would allow us to get very subtle with our arguments. And the king might give in, just because he appreciates the subtlety of our argument.

"The king has a Justice Gong in the temple. If we ring it, the head priest will be obliged to take our complaint to the King and it will be heard in open court the next day. Gramny said people are often afraid to use this because the King can be very strict in open court. But in this case, it is our only recourse.

"After talking to Gramny, Zvuk had to go back to Kunduj. So, Rasi and I were rushing to Koka to ring the gong. There was urgency because there is a chance that Balu might be executed. I slipped and injured my foot during the rushed walk. I asked Rasi to hurry on ahead and that I will follow later. Mali found me and helped me get here."

"That explains how you got to be at our home" Vika nodded. "But just getting an audience with King Pashcheega in open court won't do it, right? Don't you have to know what to say, how to argue?"

"Ah yes. That brings us to the second challenge Gramny listed: How to get Balu released. Balu can argue for himself. But apparently Rasi learned a lot from Gramny in her younger days; so she can argue the subtler points better.

"Gramny said to stick to the truth. Yes, Balu did walk into town uninvited and unannounced. But Gramny said to argue the subtle point that only the temple and the castle were 'Koka'. Even there, King Pashcheega's father had proclaimed long ago that admission to the temple was open to all people from all over the world. So, the permission requirement, in truth, only applied to entering the castle. Even though over time 'Koka' had come to mean the whole town, the law still applied only to the castle. I could never make such an argument confidently, let alone making it in open court. So, I am glad it falls to Rasi."

"I am dubious about this", Mali chimed in. "I am not sure it will work in getting your son out. Would a king's wrath really be melted by such convoluted reasoning? I mean, it almost amounts to openly defying his authority."

"I had the same doubts" conceded Talu. "Gramny told Rasi that this was just an outline. She would have to keep on her toes and grab on to any opening that may present itself. If anything appears be impacting the King's thinking, latch on and keep emphasizing that point".

"But, what of Yuda's army?" Jenon asked. "Even if he is released through this miraculous argumentation, does Balu have a future if he fails to secure the release of the Kundujan army?"

"That" sighed Talu "is the third challenge Gramny enumerated: how to get King Yuda's army released. There even Gramny was at a loss what approach to take. There was no reasoning to provide a righteous rationale for King Pashcheega to release them. Gramny said to plead for the King's mercy and ask him not to execute them. That might be granted because the king is not blood-thirsty but that was the best that could be hoped."

There was silence for several moments while everyone contemplated the failure that Balu was condemned to. Jenon tried to change the topic.

"So, did Gramny like the Queen's necklace?"

"He liked it very much. But he did not take it. He said this advice was for Rasi, his old student and apprentice. He made Rasi promise to come back and tell him about how it all went. That was all the payment he was willing to accept."

Ж

"So, Chief", Jenon said after summarizing his conversation with Talu. "With your permission, I would like to take Talu to Koka. This trial would be interesting for us to watch."

Mayun glanced at Minister Byram.

"Sure. Help her get to Koka. Then I would advise killing both Talu and Rasi", declared Byram in a matter of fact voice.

"What!?" Jenon asked, outraged. Mayun also was taken aback but did not voice any opinion.

"Your Majesty" Byram tried to justify his opinion. "Talu is the only one who can identify Jenon and Vika. Without her, there is no path for Yuda to know that Khet was the source of his humiliation. And Yuda has already disowned her. So no one will miss her. She must be eliminated to protect our kin .. er Queendom from any suspicion. And then there is Rasi. There is a chance, however small, that she will succeed in getting Yuda's army released. Why take the risk? Eliminate them both. From a humanitarian point of view, lives of two women are not more valuable than the hundreds in your .. er Her Majesty's .. domain".

Byram's arguments were coldly logical. Mayun could not find a flaw in the reasoning. And suddenly he saw the side of statecraft that had distressed Nuri enough to take the Niji Sheng Saaban. Jenon desperately interfered to say:

187

"But Minister Byram. Her Majesty has implicitly granted dauntlessness to Talu. It would not do for us to then kill her."

"It is just statecraft", Byram replied in a cavalier voice. "We simply need to do it in a way that does not implicate the Queendom".

"No", Mayun interjected. "Our promises are not broken so easily. Protect Talu to the best of your ability so no harm may come to her."

"Yes, chief" Jenon replied with alacrity.

"Apologies, your Majesty" Byram said. "I did not mean to cheapen the meaning of Her Majesty's grant of dauntlessness. I was simply pointing out options. I will not raise the topic again".

Mayun nodded and wondered if he now had to keep an eye on Byram to control his seemingly violent impulses.

Ж

The open court was crowded. There were many friends and family members of the imprisoned soldiers in the court. There were also many citizens of Koka who were curious to hear details about the foiled Kundujan invasion. The high priest was sitting on a chair on a raised platform. The king's throne was set on an even higher platform but was empty at the moment. Rasi was standing nervously in front of both and trying her best not to fidget. Just then Talu walked through the crowd up to Rasi, huffing deep breaths. Jenon parted from Talu saying he was going to the temple. He wanted to watch the trial but not be a central participant in it.

"Thank Bohamir!" Rasi exclaimed to Talu. "I am glad you made it just in time. The trial will begin as soon as his majesty arrives."

"Anything you need me to do?"

"No", Rasi replied. "Just stay here with me; the company and the sense of not being alone will give me some confidence."

She stopped as Laudators' voices boomed through the hall, each praise of the King punctuated by an emphatic drum beat.

"The Ultimate adjudicator. The One who fits the right

188

punishment to every crime. Justice Incarnate. The Master of Koka and its magnificent temple. The best among Kings. His Righteous Majesty, King Pashcheega is arriving".

The hall fell silent as the king swooshed his robes to regally occupy the throne. The laudators initiated another round of panegyric but Pashcheega raised his palm signaling for them to stop. The king nodded at the high priest and crisply ordered: "Bring in the criminal".

Balu was brought in. He was wearing shackles on his hands and feet. Forgetting her position as the Gong Ringer for the accused, Rasi went up to him and hugged him in open court.   This open breach of protocol caused a collective indrawn breath from the audience. Ignoring this reaction, she touched his face with the palm of her hand and asked whether he was OK. Balu nodded his head and tried to ask what was going on. The high priest was annoyed.

"Attention here!" he commanded in a stentorian voice.

Rasi reluctantly faced forward to the King and priest. Balu did the same, as did Talu.

"Your Majesty," the high priest continued. "This young man is Balu. He has admitted that he is an emissary for the wily king Yuda of Kunduj. He has admitted that he is here to gain release of the treacherous Kundujan army. He has admitted that, he has entered Koka without permission. And as you just witnessed, even his gong-ringer has no regard for the protocol of open court. None of this is in dispute, your Majesty. This woman, her name is Rasi, still insisted on ringing the gong and on wasting your precious time.   I challenge her to contradict any of my statements".

It was a most devastating opening argument. Typically, there was a counter argument and the high priest would present both sides, even if he emphasized just one side of it. But here, there was no defense, the priest had declared and had challenged Rasi to argue it.

Rasi cleared her throat, came forward and bowed to the king with elaborate reverence. She was playing for time to formulate her response. Suddenly Rasi remembered what Gramny had said: argue morality more than procedure. She looked up defiantly at the priest and enunciated clearly.

"If a mother's love breaks protocol in this court, your

highness, I admit that I broke protocol just now in receiving my son. Because, your highness, I am not just Balu's gong-ringer; I am also his Shumi. He is my husband's pupil. It is mother's love that made me receive him so".

"And who is your husband?"

"Zvuk Meza".

"The sound splitter in Yuda's deceitful army? He could well have been used by Yuda in the invasion. And be among the prisoners right now."

After a short pause the high priest continued in a chilling voice. "Beware. King Pashcheega the righteous, has no patience for such insolence. You break all the rules and then criticize our rules for being against motherhood?"

"Your highness, insolence was not my intent. I humbly apologize for giving that impression. I was merely explaining the lapse in my own behavior by stating that it was caused by my motherly affection for Balu."

This was not at all going according to the plan that Gramny had recommended. Rasi had to change the direction of the conversation. So, thinking quickly, she turned to Balu and said in a stern voice.

"Balu, step forward! Explain to his highness, his majesty and all the audience why you entered Koka without permission".

"I was not aware", Balu said with genuine confusion in his voice. "I did not know that permission was required. I have visited Koka and its magnificent temple many times and have never sought permission. And I have never heard of anyone else seeking permission either".

"But this time, you were traveling under the Kundujan flag!" thundered the high priest.

"Flag, your highness? That honor was never given to me".

"What? Are you now claiming you were not sent by King Yuda?" the high priest was rattled.

"I was, your highness" Balu was genuinely confused. "I came on a mission from my king to plead with King Pashcheega for the release of our army. But I didn't carry our flag".

"How dare you play word games with me?" the high priest roared and stood up.

"Your highness", Rasi interceded in a pacifying voice. "As you can see, Balu is an innocent young man, not steeped in the diplomatic traditions and language. It is this unfortunate lack of knowledge which caused him to run afoul of the protocol that he was supposed to seek permission before entering the city. This was certainly not meant as an insult or as defiance of His Majesty's authority. I plead with you to forgive him this trespass of ignorance".

Gramny would have been proud of the cogent pithiness of her argument. And she didn't even have to resort to arguments about the borders of Koka. Rasi hoped it would do the trick. The entire audience was quiet. Even the high priest fell silent because Pashcheega raised his palm. Whether to forgive, was now clearly up to the king. He looked down straight to Balu and spoke simply.

"You say you are here to plead with me. Go ahead."

Balu bowed down to the king.

"Your Majesty. I plead with you to release the members of our army that are in your custody".

Upon a nod from Pashcheega, the high priest spoke again in a voice that expressed surprise and not a little condescension.

"His majesty can understand your act as a mistake born out of ignorance and might forgive you. But why would he forgive an invading army? That kind of offensive action deserves strong punishment".

"But your highness" Balu said. "It was not really an offensive action".

"Of course not" the high priest's voice was dripping with sarcasm. "Sending eight hundred soldiers to coordinate an attack on his majesty's castle in the dead of night was not an offensive act. It was merely defensive Kundujan crouch".

"Not defensive, your highness" Rasi interceded again. "Balu merely meant that it was done in response to recent events".

"Explain!" demanded the high priest.

Rasi did not want to get into this. Gramny had said it

was a lost cause to dig up the abduction attempt as justification for the invasion and that it was better to focus on Balu. But now there was no turning back. She decided to risk it. She would tell them Balu was the one that stopped their abduction. That might raise his stature. Or it might focus their vengeance on him.

"As your highness knows,", Rasi replied. "A few months ago, there was a sneak attack on Kunduj when two men attempted to abduct King Yuda in the middle of the night. Balu was the soldier that foiled that attack".

"We heard of the attack. But this criminal's heroics in that episode don't concern us here".

"No, your highness", Rasi found it difficult to be any more direct without coming off as an accuser. "I was merely trying to explain that the Kundujan attack was not quite offensive because it was merely in response to that event".

"Silence!" roared the high priest. "This is like the thief castigating the Gramani. Are you daring to accuse his majesty of that cowardly attack?"

Balu was yet to master the art of controlling his tongue. Confused by the high priest's statement, he came right out and asked.

"Are you saying, that you did not order the attack? Based on their investigation, King Yuda and Minister Vaid were convinced that it originated from Koka".

"Just for that accusation, we should execute you. How dare you ...".

High priest fell silent when King Pashcheega stood up. It was usually a sign that he was ready to pronounce his judgment. But that was not to be this day.

"This is an open court of justice", the king began. "If an accusation is made here, even if it is against me, it must be heard. I stand as any criminal here would. What did your investigation reveal, young man?"

This magnanimous gesture from the Justice Incarnate drew loud applause and slogans of "Victory to King Pashcheega!" from the appreciative audience.

"With your permission, your majesty, I can summarize the evidence that was uncovered". Rasi interceded in a trembling voice full of trepidation guessing that Balu would be out of his depth in summarizing the evidence. "First and Foremost, it is important to note and concede that there is no evidence to connect the culprits personally to your majesty. So, I do not state the following to hold your majesty responsible or to accuse your majesty".

"Fear not!", Pashcheega said. "We grant you dauntlessness. Freely summarize the evidence against us!"

No one noticed the uncomfortable squirming of Jenon and Talu.

"First, while searching for the culprits, our soldiers found a shaman in the forest who had met the perpetrators. He said that they claimed to be from Koka. Second, a deodar cedar was cut down near Kunduj and was used by the culprits as a makeshift escape raft. That cut down tree was found in the Amu sluices just upstream of Koka. And third, during preparations for the invasion, some of our soldiers met Ivchean mercenaries who also claimed to have met the perpetrators in Koka".

When Rasi fell silent, Pashcheega spoke in a grave voice.

"We take pride in the way we do justice in Koka. Your summary of the evidence shows that our pride is well-founded. This may pass for evidence in Kunduj but holds no weight here in the logical world. Even if every word of what you said is true, it still does not tie the attack to us.

"First, the Shaman might have been lying, or the criminals might have lied to him. Second, the perpetrators would be expected to swim ashore somewhere along the way. It surely seems reasonable that they did not carry the tree with them but probably abandoned it in the river. Our sluices are designed to catch debris like that, so it is no wonder that you found the tree in them. Third, there are no Ivchean mercenaries in Koka for they would be under arrest. Even if we missed some, they would certainly have no information about what our city does".

Jenon in the audience cringed as each piece of the evidence he had fraudulently supplied was systematically demolished. Pashcheega continued.

"We reject your accusation in totality. We are shocked

that any city would be naive enough to mount an invasion on the basis of such flimsy evidence. Finally, just to inform this discerning audience, we categorically proclaim that whoever committed that crime did not work for us, was not commanded by us, was not related to us and, as far as we know, does not live in Koka".

With that Pashcheega sat down regally and gave a determined nod to the high priest; it looked like an order to tear into Balu. Rasi got frightened and started before the high priest could begin.

"Your Majesty. We apologize most humbly. Balu was given to understand that Koka was behind the attack. He is a humble soldier simply doing his king's bidding. We understand your anger at the king. But you are Justice Incarnate; I appeal to you to not punish a soldier because of your anger at his king".

The high priest stood up but did not interrupt Rasi. He had a bemused smile on his face which unnerved Rasi; he was telling her to go ahead and dig her own grave. She ploughed ahead in a nervous shaky voice.

"Your majesty. I appeal to your love for this precious commodity: the loyal soldier willing to lay his life down for his king. My Balu is simply that precious commodity. I pray you to forgive his trespass and let him go".

Rasi bowed and fell quiet. She gestured to Balu who also bowed down and quietly waited. The high priest regretfully shook his head, made an elaborate gesture up to the sky and toward the temple as if to say, he had no choice. And then he zeroed in for the kill with a devastating closing argument.

"Madam Gong ringer! I respect your position and applaud you for speaking the truth so clearly. You have made my argument for me. It is *because* Balu is a loyal soldier and because he is willing to lay his life down for his king, that His Majesty cannot let him go free. Or let the rest of the Kundujan army go.

"His Majesty's spies were able to detect this attack in time. But it does not stand rational scrutiny to say that now he should let them all go so they may try again. And perhaps do it better next time. His Majesty rules Koka as a peaceful realm for the pious of the world and for citizens of Koka. Kunduj has already proven itself to be vicious. As much as his Majesty desires peaceful relations with all neighbors, does it make sense to strengthen the army of such an aggressive neighbor?"

Rasi was stupefied by the skill with which the high priest used all her own points against Balu.

"But your highness", she pleaded "Balu is but an innocent soldier simply serving his king. I plead to His Majesty's kindness for leniency."

A commotion started around the assembly as it became clear that Balu and Rasi had lost. Rasi seemed gutted but Balu stood in the middle with his head held high and a stoic expression on his face. Pashcheega stood up and the high priest went to him briskly. The assembly quieted down as the priest finished his conversation, stepped away and enunciated in a clear voice.

"His Majesty King Pashcheega has heard all that he needs to hear about this matter. He will ponder the matter, pray to God and render justice on this tomorrow morning. In the meantime, Balu is confined to custody along with all the other *loyal* Kundujan soldiers".

The high priest put the slightest emphasis on the word loyal. It felt to Rasi like he was twisting a knife in her belly. But the adjournment was conclusive. The king and priest left the dais as some soldiers came to take Balu back to prison.

Rasi held Balu's hand and tearfully whispered "I have failed you". Talu joined in, with some acrimony, and said to no one in particular: "I wish Gramny was able to come". Rasi was distraught enough to be oblivious to the dig, and replied "Me too". Balu comforted both of them as the soldiers pulled him away.

"Don't worry. You both were wonderful to come to my rescue. Shumi, you presented my case truthfully, the way I would have wanted to speak of myself. If they damn me for who I am, I stand ready for punishment. And don't worry it is not done yet. Let's see what the King says."

Balu walked away with the soldiers, solemn and dignified. Both Talu and Rasi were struck by his almost regal gait with a straight back and head held high. When had their little boy grown up so much?

Ж

Rasi followed Balu as he was taken to the Tyaagbumi just south of the castle. It was the large ground where the King conducted sacrificial rites. This made sense because there was no jail which could hold eight hundred people. The Tyaagbumi was easy to guard because it had only one entrance and exit, leading to the Amu. Rasi hoped it was not to be the sacrificial ground for all these soldiers, including her boy.

Sooner or later the king would need the ground for its usual purpose of holding ritual sacrifices. So, having all these people in the ground was clearly a temporary arrangement. She worried about how it was to end: in the release or in the execution of them all.

Two hours later, Rasi found herself at the entrance to the Tyaagbumi along with Talu. They were trying to convince the chief guard to let them in to spend some time with Balu. The guard was unmoved by their pleas that he should help two mothers spend time with their son.

"I have no reason to help you", he said. "There is nothing in it for me. Or for Koka."

Instinctively, Talu pulled out Nuri's necklace, which Gramny had declined as payment: "Will this gift be acceptable recompense?" she asked.

"Looks very valuable" said the guard with wide open eyes.

"It is", Talu replied. "It belonged to Queen Nuri, before she gifted it to me".

The guard quietly snatched it and allowed the two women to enter the yard.

As Rasi and Talu sat with Balu an ever-growing circle of audience built around them. They were surprised to learn that only eleven warriors were actually killed during the ambush. Twenty two others were injured but were appropriately treated. The unhurt soldiers were treated humanely and with decency.

But, that meant there were nearly eight hundred men and women in this yard and it was difficult to see how

196

Pashcheega would deal with them. To execute so many seemed totally out of character for him; he was just not that blood-thirsty. Rasi wondered if that was the weakness of Pashcheega's position. But, what the high priest said was also right: releasing them would truly be folly. There was no clear solution and perhaps that is why the king had not yet made his decision. Was there some way to take advantage of this?

Balu did not want to talk about any of that. He just wanted to hear about what had been happening the past few days. He expressed admiration for Queen Nuri when he heard of her Niji Sheng Saaban. He profusely thanked Talu for her extensive walking and massaged her feet for a few minutes. Talu told him, in front of several other warriors, that she just learned that it was in fact Khet that organized the abduction attempt.

However, the moment the words left her mouth, she regretted it and wondered what ill consequences that disclosure would bring. If these people were released, it would become open secret in Kunduj. Had she just initiated a war?

Balu expressed gratitude to Gramny. He told Talu and Rasi to not worry and just wait to see what would happen in the morning. Finally, when the guards came and asked the women to leave, he hugged them both and touched his Shumi's feet.

Ж

Jenon slept on the mound by the river next to his deodar sapling. It had grown to about knee level and was looking very vigorous. Jenon held a conversation with the tree and confessed to his role in the entire affair. The cedar listened in grave silence and gently waved in the wind. Jenon took it as forgiveness and slept soundly.

When he awoke in the morning, he felt no guilt, only curiosity about how it would end. When he reached the courthouse, the king and the high priest were already there facing Balu along with Rasi and Talu in the middle. Jenon melded into the crowd and watched as the high priest said:

"His Majesty is about to pass judgment. Do you want to say anything before he does so?"

"Yes, your Highness", Balu replied.

Rasi looked at him in surprise.

197

"Proceed", the high priest intoned.

"Your Majesty", Balu knelt down and addressed the King directly. "I wanted to let you know that last night I took a Niji Sheng Saaban for Koka's safety. If the Gods were to ever consider sending danger toward Koka, I appeal to them to send that danger to me. If the danger is from other men, they will first have to deal with me. As long as I am alive, I will defend Koka from all danger".

There was a collective in-drawn breath from the assembly. Even the high priest was confused and taken aback. Rasi noticed that King Pashcheega bit his lower lip and made a fist as if the knot of his conundrum had been resolved. And then it hit her: of course, this is the way! Before she could say anything, Balu continued.

"Your Majesty, I spoke to all the Kundujan warriors in your custody. Every last man and woman among them has also taken the same oath. We will all be here to help defend Koka if she were ever in danger: whether man-made or divine".

Balu stood up, bowed to the king and stepped back. His statement was done. He had not done it with any strategic intent but rather as moral recompense for his part in an illegal invasion. Nevertheless Rasi jumped on the huge strategic opening it provided. She thanked Gramny in her mind for all his advice. When a small opening shows up, pry it open and take full advantage, Gramny had said. The fact that the King considered the Saaban important and that he was not blood-thirsty was her opening. She stayed alert to see how she can take advantage. It came about fairly soon.

"Do you expect that His Majesty will set you free just because of this oath?" the high priest asked indignantly.

"No, your highness", Balu replied in a confident monotone. "I have no expectation of His Majesty. I am ready to receive whatever judgment he pronounces."

"Oh really", the high priest appeared really annoyed now. "So, you have no request of him. What if he gives you the death penalty right now."

Balu appeared a bit confused, but before he could answer Rasi jumped in.

"As his Shumi, your highness I would be very sad but would be happy for my son". Rasi let everyone stew in confusion for a few moments before continuing. "That punishment would allow Balu to completely fulfill his oath. He has taken an oath to protect Koka for the rest of his life and if His Majesty cuts that life short, his oath will be fulfilled easily. Not many people get to take an oath this momentous and fulfill it with such ease. So, if that is the king's pronouncement I would be happy for Balu".

The assembly was impressed at this reasoning and broke out in applause. The high priest was taken aback at this brazen fearlessness.

"And what if he is sent back to prison for life?" the high priest threw down the gauntlet.

"If that is his majesty's justice, Balu will of course accept it", Rasi replied carefully. "For that will also allow Balu to fulfill his oath with relative ease. Unless some danger befalls Koka, Balu will be in jail, supported by the kingdom. If and when there is danger, he will try to get out of jail and protect Koka. And ...". She stopped abruptly as if preventing herself from committing a faux pas.

It was a trick of legal argumentation that Gramny had taught her long ago. It was designed to coax the other party into forcing her to say what she wanted to say anyway. The high priest fell for it completely.

"Proceed! And?" he commanded.

"Your highness, I was about to present my analysis of the situation. But given his majesty's sagacity, it is superfluous. So, I stopped myself".

"Go ahead", the king himself intervened. "What is your analysis?"

"Your Majesty", Rasi replied with her closing argument. "Because of this oath, these soldiers are effectively part of your army. If you have any doubts about that, your high priest, who is skilled at these things, can re-administer the oath in such a way that anyone who attempts to break it, will be subject to tremendous divine wrath. So, whenever Koka needs them, you can count on these folks. The only question is how much resources you will spend to have them at your beck and call.

"You have three choices: first is to execute them. With this, you will spend resources on the executions and you will not have their help during any future time of danger. Second choice is to send them back to prison. There you will spend a lot of resources on keeping them confined but will have their help when needed. Third choice is to grant them freedom. They will live their life and take care of themselves without your having to spend any resources. And you will still have them available when you need them. Out of those three, the preferred choice appears clear to me, Your Majesty. But I am not Justice Incarnate; you are. I plead with you to do justice as you see fit".

Even Gramny could not have made a better closing argument. Nevertheless, Rasi felt nervous. Had she over-stepped? Would the king get angry at essentially being told what he should do? But then, what other way was there? If she had to analyze it, this level of prescriptiveness was inevitable. She stood next to Balu and bowed her head down in reverence but also to ensure that expressions on her face were not out in the open. She did not have to wait long for the King stood up, and pronounced his verdict.

"Madam Gong-ringer has made cogent arguments and summarized our choices succinctly. Rock Boha teaches us that punishment that fits the crime is one that changes the criminal's heart. This is a prime example of such a punishment. We sentence all eight hundred Kundujan soldiers to re-take the Niji Sheng Saaban as prescribed by our high priest. Thereafter, they are free to go but they will follow their oath. Wherever they are, they will work for Koka's benefit. If Koka is ever in danger, they'll make themselves available to help."

The assembly broke out in thunderous applause and cries of "Victory to Justice Incarnate" rent the air.

Ж

The Chadans called the tree Devadaru or the timber of Gods. At less than a year old, the deodar sapling was only knee-high. It did not have much timber to speak of, for Gods or for men. But befitting its glorious future, it was witness to a momentous week where a parade of seven hundred and ninety three men and women undertook the Niji Sheng Saaban. It was probably the first time in history that so many people offered to sacrifice themselves for the safety of a community that they did not belong to. How many more such historic events would the cedar witness in its long life ahead?

The high priest gave a moving speech to all the oath takers standing on the high ground right in front of the sapling.

"Well, you may sigh in relief that you have gained your freedom. You may even think that you hoodwinked the King of Koka, to get away with invasion. But do not ever think that this oath of yours was mere words. This oath is truly powerful. I cannot bind you to Koka any more than you have bound yourself to her through this oath. As long as you are faithful to her in thought, word and deed, the Gods will ensure that you prosper. And Koka's divine blessings shall be with you.

"If you ever betray her, you have just requested the Gods to show you their wrath. And believe me, they will not disappoint you.

"Koka is a special place, not just for the residents of this town but for all humanity. It is a special place with a divine temple and is the true abode of Gods. That is the reason people seek and find refuge here. That is the reason that people seek and find forgiveness here. Just as a mother whole-heartedly forgives an errant child, you are absolved and forgiven. Therefore, from this day forth, you are all Kokans, children of Koka. Go on and live your life to the fullest. And always pray for Victory to Koka!"

Everyone chanted "Victory to Koka!". As they left, they paraded around the magnificent temple, kissed the ground in front of it and vowed to never ever partake in any activity that would bring harm to this serene place. Gratitude filled their hearts for their second chance. Many had tears in their eyes as they walked away.

Story of the Story - 6

Jalal opened the door when we rang the bell and vigorously shook hands with all three of us: me, my wife and our son. "It is such a delight to meet you . Thank you all for coming".

After greetings and a brief tour of his home, we were all seated under an awning on his backyard deck. DubDee texted Jalal that she is stuck at the office and will join us in about an hour. A gentle breeze pleasantly cooled us down on the bright sunny day. Jalal seemed physically a bit weak but in good spirits as he opened the serious part of the conversation.

"You know that I don't have too much more time to live in this world".

"I am ..."

"No, please. Let me finish. I know that you are busy and can't spare any more time on the translation. And I understand. I really do.

"But I will still keep pestering you (laughs). And we will continue to have our fights till the day that God punches my ticket.

"But, I want you all to know that leaving the book and its translation in your committed and capable hands gives me a great deal of peace".

"Committed, sure!" I replied "But not yet fully capable. My Dari is weak and my Brahui is hopeless. So, without your help with those two main languages in the book, our current frustratingly slow pace would look like Warp 10. So, definitely need you to ..."

"And I definitely need your help," he interrupted again, "to produce the Dari and Brahui in the first place. Despite working with you these last few years, I still can't somehow decipher them. Perhaps I am just too old".

"Yes, Captain Obvious and Admiral Self Evident!", mocked my wife with a smile on her face. "It is clear that both of you are needed to complete it. So, the less time you waste on quibbling, the better".

"Agreed, my dear", Jalal replied. "But let's be clear eyed: I am not long for this world. So, either we complete it before I am gone. And I know! I know! That can be very hard *for you. Or, we accept the alternative that you work on this by yourself after me – however slow and painful that might be".*

Just as we were squirming, trying to change the topic, DubDee came to our defense by breezing into the backyard. We spent the next few minutes with greetings and handshakes.

When my son piped up to point out to DubDee: "You are not in a wheelchair anymore!"

"No, Cutie Pie! I am not" she replied as my son, the college senior, visibly blushed at being called by his childish name. But that gambit drifted the conversation completely away. We talked about how she got a prosthetic leg seven years ago and how her life had changed since then.

Ж

That night, we regrouped for more conversation. DubDee had ordered some pizza, soft drinks and Tiramisu for dessert. As dinner was winding down, Jalal revisited the uncomfortable topic.

"Folks! I tried to say this earlier today but the conversation drifted away after DubDee came in. But I am glad because I wanted her to hear it too. I know I am the reincarnation of Jenon from the historical book we are translating ..."

"Come on Jalal!" DubDee interrupted. "Don't go there again! Let's just have a pleasant dinner".

"No!" Jalal replied firmly. "I need to put this out there. And this might be my last chance. I don't mean to make you uncomfortable .."

"You don't make me uncomfortable!" DubDee interrupted again. "I just think you are tormenting yourself by believing such mumbo jumbo".

"... but it is what it is" Jalal continued as if he was not interrupted. "I am reincarnated Jenon and DubDee here is reincarnated Nuri. We are friends in this life because we are to safeguard this story. It is a very important chapter in human history and it should not be lost. My life's purpose will be unaccomplished if ...".

"Wait!" I interrupted him. "You said before that you are a direct descendant of Bada Ravi".

203

"Yes. In fact my last name, Badrawi, is simply a corrupted form of Bada Ravi. But, the two ideas are not mutually exclusive. I am Jenon, re-born in the lineage of Bada Ravi to keep this book alive for the next thousand years".

"Dude!" DubDee joshed him. "That is a psychotic thought. May be this is a new disease: Cancer Psychosis. If it is not already a known diagnosis, someone should write a medical paper reporting your case. Anyway, you can stew in it if it gives you peace. But why are you dragging me into it? Why are you calling me a character from this novel?"

"This is not just a fictional novel", Jalal said with conviction. "It is a recounting of what truly happened. And I am not dragging you into anything. It is simply a fact that you are Queen Nuri, reborn now. That is why you were so instrumental in preserving this book and getting it translated".

"Come on! I don't ...".

"Don't fight it, DubDee!" I laughed. "Nuri is probably one of the most noble characters in the book. So, it is quite the compliment he is giving you".

"It is not just a compliment" Jalal said. "It is the truth. And you, my friend, are like Bada Ravi a thousand years ago. You are not involved with the story but will be the impartial chronicler to translate it with a neutral voice".

"If I may", DubDee again chimed in. "I thought this was about events from thousands of years ago. So, if this is my rebirth, what have I been doing since? Hanging in purgatory?"

"No", Jalal replied. "I don't think is this your very next birth. I am quite sure you have had many births between then and now. But your purpose in this birth is to ensure the survival of this story".

"Kooky!", DubDee laughed. "No doubt about Cancer Psychosis now. I will ask Dr Garcia to write up your case in a medical journal".

Jalal joined in the laugh but did not press the point further. The rest of the night was filled with lighter conversation. Jalal, having gotten this off his chest, seemed content to simply enjoy the dessert and the company.

The Third Conspiracy

Spring of 3657 BC

12. Alli Manna, Illi Channa

"Are you sure?" asked Suvaid, the fortunate. He was sitting on a boulder on the banks of the Amu, facing the river. It was about half a kos outside the borders of Kunduj.

"Positive", Jufen replied. "I heard it independently from seven different women who were imprisoned in the Tyaagbumi jail in Koka. They all heard it directly from Talu that she saw the abductors in Khet; that she knows they are in the court of King Mayun of Khet".

"That is very good to know".

"But what is the point?" asked Jufen. "It is not like we can avenge the king's abduction just by ourselves". There was not much enthusiasm in Jufen's voice.

"No but we will avenge Chetu, your beloved daughter and the love of my life".

"By targeting those abductors?" Jufen sounded totally confused. "Are you saying they are responsible for Chetu?"

"No, no. We definitely do not target the abductors. They are simply tools. I want to take revenge on the archer not the arrow".

"Huh?"

"Let me take a step back and explain. First, the kingdom – excuse me, the Queendom – of Khet cooked up a conspiracy to abduct our king. And it failed. Then, our kingdom made a mistaken analysis and conspired to conquer Koka. And it failed. Ours will be the third conspiracy. It will be to simply avenge our beloved Chetu. And it will succeed because it is not by a kingdom or its army but by us, ordinary folks. We will be able to keep the conspiracy a secret and ...".

"Haha", Jufen interrupted with a mirthless laugh. "Funny to hear you, the only son of the Elite Minister, call himself ordinary folks".

"*Former* Elite Minister. And I was employed just by my father – not the king. So, at this point I have no contact or position at the castle. I am in fact ordinary folk – without a job".

"So, what can we do? Perhaps we should take this News to the King? And leave it in their hands?" Jufen asked doubtfully.

"No" Suvaid replied with carefully chosen words. He had to induce Jufen to cooperate with his scheme. "With so many people knowing it, I have no doubt that the News will reach his majesty on its own. And king Yuda will avenge the abduction attempt. I am content to leave that up to him. Personally, I only want to focus on avenging Chetu".

"But how?" Jufen asked.

"First things first", Suvaid replied. "There is no doubt in my mind that that first conspiracy to abduct our king was the ultimate cause for Chetu's killing. We must, both of us, must go to Khet, identify the culprit and exact revenge from him".

"But how would we identify him?"

"Hey, I am Suvaid the Fortunate. Kaidbar the slayer of bad luck. Leave the how up to me. For now, I need to know if you will go to Khet and help me avenge Chetu".

"How will gong to Khet help?"

"Well, being here and doing nothing will definitely not help. We know our revenge will be directed there – probably toward someone in the royal household. Now that I know this, I cannot continue to stay in Kunduj. My mind is already there. Alli manna Illi channa. My mind is there and, the (left over) trash – my body – is here. So, I am going there. Will you join me?".

Ж

It was well past sundown when King Mayun entered his private chamber. Lamps were lit low and Queen Nuri was resting with her eyes closed. The new maid was sitting on the floor next to the bed and was dozing. Mayun didn't remember her name but she was to be the queen's midwife and also a duenna for the prince after birth. She realized that the King had come in and jerked up. He gave her a wink and signaled her to leave the chamber. Queen Nuri opened her eyes and greeted him in a sleepy voice.

"Hey my brave soldier".

"How is my timid girl?" Mayun lay down next to Nuri and caressed her abdomen. "Sorry to have awakened you".

"No, I was just resting and waiting for you. Seeress Groot was here earlier today and she said that the baby

208

should be coming any day now, possibly in a week".

"Did she say all was well?"

"Yes. Everything is alright".

This was Mayun's favorite time of day. A time when he discussed issues of state with the Queen. She was the best of his advisers: always calm, always incisive, she quickly honed in on the crucial aspects of any situation. If anyone could make sense of his current conundrum, it was her. He sighed and continued.

"Good. I got some News out of Kunduj that kept me longer than expected."

"Oh No! What now?"

"Apparently, Yuda now wants to invade us by water; sail down the Amu and then march on us".

"What?!"

"Yes, I was stunned too. Previously we thought it was a land invasion which would have taken them a month to prepare. A river invasion could happen within a week".

"But," Nuri was confused. "The 'previously' was only a week ago. When did they change their minds?"

"I don't know" Mayun shrugged.

"But wait", Nuri objected. "Didn't you say that a water invasion was so much more dangerous for them and so much easier for us to thwart? So, why would they take the risk unless there is some rush for it?"

"I don't know", Mayun shrugged again. "Doing this hastily makes no sense. Not like we have some great reinforcements coming in. Maybe the great shake-up resulting from their misadventure into Kunduj has left them confused".

"OK, let's analyze this carefully", Nuri said. "What do we know about 'the great shake-up', as you put it".

"Let's see", Mayun summarized. "When he returned triumphantly to Kunduj with the whole army, the king was impressed with Balu. Since Commander Dron and the Praesha were both killed, Yuda appointed Balu to both those posts, a dramatic rise for the inexperienced young man. Then a week later Minister Vaid was deposed. As far as we know, Vaid is no longer in Kunduj".

"Well", Nuri replied. "You remember Jufen, our new duenna? Not only is she from Kunduj, she was also a maid servant for Vaid. She tole me that Vaid criticized Balu's victory saying that the Kundujan army was now crippled because it was oath-bound to protect Koka. And, when Balu proved immensely popular with the forces, Vaid responded in a rash of jealousy and told Yuda: 'Now there is no way for you to ever get rid of him'. Yuda must have got tired of all this negativity. He deposed Vaid and sent him off on a pilgrimage. Not quite banishment, but close enough".

"Interesting" Mayun replied. "Byram himself has been in Kunduj to keep an eye on things. I wonder why he did not find out this back story. He has been sending other information though. First came word that replacement for Vaid was going to be his son Suvaid, the Fortunate. Then suddenly, it turned out to be Rasi, Balu's shumi and Gong-ringer. This woman, who was a simple house wife till recently, is the new Prime Minister of Kunduj".

"You know", Nuri replied. "when you summarize it like that, it is incredible. Dramatic fall from grace of a venerable minister is rare enough. Combine that with a whole army getting caught. And an inexperienced guard along with his Shumi succeeding in dramatic fashion where experienced diplomats failed. And then for them to be rewarded with high posts in the country. I've never heard of such things happening. It is more like a play than real life".

"Ah, their army", Mayun continued. "First word was that all the forces were being disbanded and sent back to their homes. Then two weeks ago, they were regrouping and preparing for a massive land invasion – on us – in a month. And now this invasion by boats within the week. They seem totally confused".

"I wonder", Nuri sighed, "If Byram is the one causing the confusion".

"You mean he is betraying us by deliberately sowing confusion".

"No, not that", Nuri replied. "Perhaps he is being supplied misinformation and is falling for it".

"Hmm" Mayun said tentatively. "Also, it is curious that if there is so much confusion, Byram has not proposed any way to take advantage of it."

"In any event", Nuri replied, "we have no choice but to believe him ...".

"Victory your majesties!" a breathless chambermaid barged into the bed room. "Humble apologies. But another messenger from Minister Byram has just arrived and insisted that you will want to hear his message right away".

"In the secret chamber!" Mayun dismissed her and muttered "Now what?"

"Maybe Yuda actually wants to abdicate and give us his whole kingdom" Nuri said in a deadpan voice.

"Heh heh. I'll take it", Mayun chuckled as he left the room. He was back in about ten minutes.

"Here is the update: Byram does now know the reason for Vaid getting deposed; and it is similar to what the duenna said. He also reports that they have readied a flotilla of fifty boats; water invasion is for real".

"Oh my!"

"Yeah. He counted the boats himself. And most of the troops recently released from Koka are getting ready. And has has also suggested that all these multiple changes in tactics are due to him".

"Hmm?"

"He did not send the details but apparently he has been able to sow some misinformation which caused them to rapidly change tactics".

"Oh. He made them change their tactics so it is easier for us to counter them. So he did do something to take advantage of the confusion".

"Yes. We will send about five men each to the west and north frontiers and have them make loud noises as if there are many more of them"

"So, if the Kundujans visit, they will think we are really prepared for a land invasion?"

"Right".

"So, what about direct counter measures for a water invasion?" Nuri asked.

"Let's see. The best place for them to land, rather, the

most probable place they will land is just by the fern forest. We will set up three ambushes between there and the castle. If any of their troops get through all three ambushes, we plan to start a forest fire to entrap them. Tomorrow, we will put all those plans in place".

"What about the village?" Nuri asked.

"Well, I don't think Kundujan soldiers will target the village. Can't spare men to defend ...".

"No dear", Nuri interrupted him. "We have to get them to a safe place. We can't create three ambushes to protect the castle but abandon the village".

"Of course you are right! Let's see. How about the temple? Perhaps we should move the vulnerable there and station men to protect them".

"I think that will work. You can put Jenon and Vika to work to make a plan to evacuate the whole village into the temple".

With the plan of action decided, the couple fell into a companionable silence before slipping into slumber.

Ж

Next morning, Mayun summoned Jenon and gave his orders.

"Work with Vika and set up a quick way to let the whole village know that they should move to the temple. Start the cleaning of the temple and make it so our folks can stay there. I've told the Praesha to have at least ten troops to guard it. And once the enemy lands, we will send word back to the village and I will need you in the first ambush. We know you are an expert lance thrower. Your job will be to ensure Kundujan soldiers will not land on our side of the river. Understood?".

"Yes, Chief", Jenon said without much enthusiasm in his voice.

Queen Nuri breezed into the chamber. Jenon stood and bowed while Mayun looked puzzled. Nuri's maid followed her with a plaintive request.

"Nuri Niang. We need to finish with your massage". She saw the King and fell silent.

"In just a bit. I need to speak to ..."

The maid boldly interrupted the Queen. "You have always been like this since you were a child. Always off on to something else. Pregnancy is not a game, you know. Much more important than any state craft and …".

"I know, I know, Choon Ti", the Queen sounded almost like a petulant juvenile. "I promise I'll be right back. Just give me thirty minutes."

"Thirty minutes", the maid said, pointing her finger at the Queen. She left the chamber with an eye roll and a shake of her head. Jenon watched in bemused silence. Only Ivchean Royalty would allow a maid to speak with such impudence.

"Can't stop your rebellious behavior toward old Choon, can you?" Mayun teased.

"She raised me since when I was little and she is overprotective like a mother. So yeah. It is only natural that my rebellion is directed toward her. So, Jenon! Did you hear about the plan?"

"Yes, your majesty. The chief was just giving me his orders. I will start on it as soon as I can arrange some things. Probably tomorrow".

"You don't sound too enthusiastic".

"I know", Mayun jumped in. "I thought you would be excited about this plan."

Jenon stood quietly fidgeting.

"Come on, just say what is on your mind", Nuri laughed. "I only have 30 minutes".

"Your majesty", Jenon replied. "Mali, my wife, is pregnant. Seeress Groot was by yesterday and said that the baby may arrive any day now. I am just worried about both me and my brother Vika leaving her at this stage".

"Ah, of course" Mayun intoned. "Alli Manna Illi channa. Mind over there – with Mali - and the left-over trash (just the body) in the village, organizing the evacuation".

"Alli Manna Illi Channa, indeed", Nuri mumbled. Then she turned to Mayun and said, "We can't use him. Let's find someone else".

"No, no Your Majesty", Jenon replied defensively. "I will move Mali to Seeress Groot's cloister. I will ask my brother Vika's wife Baegan to move there as well and then I will start;

just might take a day or so to arrange all that".

"Don't do that!" Nuri thought for a moment. "This mission is important for the safety of the whole kingdom, including your wife and child. Why don't you bring her here? To the castle? We have a new midwife, if needed. It will also be good for me to have another pregnant woman around".

"Thank you, your Majesty. But the cloister will be good enough. Mali thinks of Seeress Groot as a Mother".

"I know. But Mother Groot will likely be here to attend to me. And our new midwife, Jufen, is here. Even my beloved loudmouth Choon Ti, is here and will fuss over Mali. There will be plenty of people to take care of her. This will be a much better place than the cloister. Bring her here. And then go with complete peace of mind. We need you Alli Manna, Alli Channa: mind and body together over there to accomplish this important mission."

"Yes, your majesty", Jenon said. "May I also bring my sister-in-law Baegan to accompany Mali?"

"Sure".

"Then it is settled", Mayun said. "I feel a whole lot better now. We will be prepared!"

Ж

That night, momentous things were afoot in the Royal Castle of Khet which would negate that confidence. Well, near the castle anyway. Because we start in the temple, just a five minute walk outside the castle compound.

Jufen entered the temple and apprehensively looked around the prayer hall. Plans were afoot to cram it with the whole village, if needed, But, it was deserted for the moment. Relief washed over her when she saw Suvaid emerge from one of the many nooks and crannies of the temple. He prostrated himself in front of the deity and whispered to her: "Go top side". Jufen left the prayer hall and climbed a small hill which provided access to a flat terrace called top side.

"You are late!" he said in an accusatory tone. "I have been waiting since mid-day!"

"I could not leave. Jenon just brought his wife, his brother and his sister-in-law to the castle. There was too much activity. I just could not leave in the middle."

214

"Why? What are they doing in the castle?"

"Jenon's family? I don't know. Jenon and Vika are not there anymore. They dropped off Mali and Baegan and left".

"Where to?"

"I think the King asked him to prepare an evacuation plan for the village".

"Good" Suvaid said with a smile. "My luck is still with me. That will be very useful for us".

"What are you talking about?", Jufen sounded exasperated. "Even earlier, there were too many people in the castle. And now there are even more. And you think this is good!?".

"Don't worry, I'll take care of that. I have planted enough misinformation to divert their entire attention away from you".

"I don't know. I am worried".

"You must continue. This must succeed. This is for Chetu"!

"Oh, I will continue; I have no intention of stopping", Jufen replied. "But as for success, it may just have become more difficult".

"Not really. They will all be gone. The castle will be mostly empty by tomorrow".

"Are you sure?"

"Yes. But, if you wish, we can just do it tonight when the chaos from all this activity gives you cover ..."

"No, no no", Jufen vehemently interrupted. "As a midwife, I know that the baby is a little Bohamir. As much as I want to avenge Chetu, I cannot harm the baby. So, as long as it is in her womb, I cannot harm the queen."

"Well, it is just a matter of time" Suvaid said coldly. "Soon after she delivers, you will stab the queen with your gal pihiya and kill her".

Jufen gasped. She knew the plan. But stating it so harshly was still jarring. Gal pihiya was a sharp stone tool used to cut the baby's cord; using the sacred tool for murder sounded obscene.

"Having second thoughts?" Suvaid probed.

"No. Well, yes. The queen is a nice lady. She was asking me about my life in Kunduj and whether Minister Vaid's departure had any impact on me. She took a real interest in my life. I have never seen that from any royalty. Anywhere".

"You are so naive!" Suvaid guffawed. "Did it ever occur to you that she was simply getting more information from you? So that they could create more mischief in Kunduj".

"More mischief?"

"Yes! Meaning more warriors like Chetu would die. And more venerable people like my father would be humiliated".

Jufen looked down to the ground, conflicted. Suvaid spoke again.

"Think about it this way. Is there any doubt that Khet was behind the abduction attempt on our King?"

"No. I met Talu at Koka and also met Jenon and Vika after I arrived here. I know that they were the ones. I have no doubt".

"Alright then. Do you accept that Queen Nuri's *Niji Sheng Saaban* is admission that she was the architect of that cruel hoax? A hoax almost succeeded. And even in failure, it ended with the death of Chetu: your daughter and the love of my life? A hoax that ended in deposing my father?"

"I don't think the queen was actually the architect ..."

"It does not matter! She pledged Niji Sheng. She publicly and willingly accepted the responsibility. Now you say you don't want to punish the baby and I respect that. But, as soon as the baby is out, let;s send the queen up to Rock Boha".

Jufen was silent.

"You will dishonor Chetu's memory if you don't do this. Knowing who is responsible, if you don't avenge Chetu ..."

"I know, I know", Jufen cried. "Chetu was the reason for my living. Light went out of my life that horrible day. You don't have to keep reminding me why I am doing this. Just that it feels awful to kill a mother in labor".

"I know", Suvaid replied simply. "War always feels awful. And this is war. A war that Khet has launched on Kunduj. It is a war that even my father was too late to recognize. If I was the new Minister, I would have convinced the King and there would be a reckoning. Instead we have an incompetent blockhead as the new minister. It will take her forever to even acknowledge it, let alone engage in this war. So, as awful as this feels, it really is up to us, you and me, to save Kunduj. If we fail, Kunduj will fall. And, hundreds more will be killed. Hundreds more just like beloved Chetu."

"If we succeed, do you think the King will make you the new Grand Minister?"

"I am going to try my best to make that happen. But, let's face it: this mission is dangerous; I might not even survive it".

Jufen gasped again.

"Yes. I might not survive. But I still want to do this. For the love of Kunduj. For the love of Chetu. And for the love of my father".

"Wait." Jufen asked. "If you get killed, who will guide Kunduj? How will it help ..."

"Don't worry," Suvaid replied. "They call me the Kaidbar: one who defies misfortune. I don't intend to die but let's just see what happens. The biggest long-term danger to Kunduj in the next ten years is from Khet. This king is getting ambitious and very brazen. Think about it: he tried to occupy Kunduj by kidnapping our king! How brazen!Killing his wife, will break his will and break his ambition. Just that, is worth dying for".

"All well and good, but how do we do it? The castle has more people than the temple on the fifth of Spring. And they are all doting over the queen. It is not like I am some great warrior, to overcome all that".

"Jufen", Suvaid replied, "we are going to prove that ordinary riff-raff like you and me can change history just as much as any great warrior can. Believe me, the castle will be empty. You just stick to your job and I will stick to mine. Together, we will make it happen".

"You keep saying the castle will be empty. Why? How will you make them all leave?"

"Alright Jufen", Savid said as if giving in. "I will tell you but you have to keep it to yourself".

"OK".

"As you may guess I have friends in the castles of all the kingdoms around here. First I planted a seed of an idea which led to the high priest of Koka to send word to Kunduj that he wishes the warriors to come back to Koka and renew their pledge. So, hundreds of Kundujan soldiers, who were just recently in Kokan jail, are now going on a pilgrimage to Koka's magnificent temple. Next, I have planted the notion in Khet that Kunduj was going to invade".

"How? Even if you told them why did they believe you?"

"You know I am Suvaid the Fortunate, Kaidbar, the slayer of …"

"Yeah, yeah. It is easier to light up the field on a New moon night than to separate you from your luck. But how did you do it?"

"Hey, that's not bad. From now on whenever I refer to my luck I will mention some impossibility as easier than me losing luck" Suvaid grinned.

"What?"

"Yeah. Like: I am Kaidbar the slayer of misfortune. It is easier to separate Bohamir from the soma he stole than it is to separate me from my luck".

"Yeah, yeah, whatever! But how did you get Khet to believe your lies?"

"It was actually easy. By luck – see she never deserts me – I noticed that Khet's Minister Byram himself was sent to Kunduj to spy on our intentions. I didn't notify the king about the spy among us – after all I am not working at the castle anymore. I simply had a friend of mine tell Byram that I, Suvaid, was disgruntled with the kingdom for deposing my father. And that I had some valuable information about an upcoming invasion. Then, it was fairly easy. I just played hard to get and actually had him give me a substantial payment in exchange for my lies".

"What!? He paid to get deceived?!"

"Indeed. It is not uncommon in spy craft. It was a good thing – a lucky thing you might even say – that Byram was there. He may be a good minister, even a great strategist. But he is no field. It was not too hard to trick him".

"Like you have put in many years as a spy on the field"

Jufen mocked.

"You know, you are right", Suvaid conceded. "I am also no field agent. But again my luck came in handy. Me misunderstood my first missive to mean that Kunduj was planning a massive land assault. They have no way to repel it, so he was panicking. The next time I saw him, he was pleading with me. He told me to remember my father's humiliation and actually requested me to figure out a way make the invasion to come by the river – because they know hoe to repel it".   Suvaid could not help but laugh out loud. "So, naturally, I charged him some more money and obliged him – made the invasion come by river".

"Wow! So, they were panicking about a land invasion. Now, they are preparing for an invasion by river. But actually no invasion will ever happen".

"Yes".

"Why not let it happen? If our king is sure to win a land invasion, isn't it better advise him to go about it?"

"I did. In fact I did talk to the new minister – or to the sorry excuse that occupies that post now. She is so naive that she told me to forget about all that – because it is best to cultivate good relations with neighbors. Can you believe it? In a way, I am glad for her rejection. Because an invasion might succeed in allowing Kunduj to occupy Khet – but it will not avenge Chetu. King Mayun and Queen Nuri probably both live. They might even stay on the throne as King Yuda's Vice Regents. That would not have been satisfactory fr me".

"Alright – I salute your tangled web of a conspiracy. But I still think it will be difficult to empty out the castle at the right moment. How long would it take them to realize the invasion is false? And then they will come right back. If the queen has not delivered by then, I won't harm her. Of that much, I am certain – not even to avenge Chetu".

"That's fine. Tomorrow, I'll be in touch with you and at the exact right moment, I will introduce further misinformation to induce panic so they will all leave the castle empty".

"What is that right moment?"

"When the queen goes into labor".

"Are you mad?" Jufen asked. "Do you know how busy I

will be when there is labor? I won't be able to leave the queen's side for even a minute. How will I pass a word to you?"

"Oh".

"Oh, indeed", Jufen said triumphantly. "And Induce panic? How will you do that?"

"Yeah" Suvaid replied in an absent minded voice. "I was thinking of sending a message saying oh say, that their ambush was a failure and the king has ordered all hands to the third ambush as reinforcement".

"All that works fine" Jufen sighed. "But the time window is too short. We can't guarantee we'll be ready by then. It is not like I can control when the queen goes into labor".

Jufen sounded almost relieved. She wanted revenge, but she still was a midwife. To use a Gal pihiya not for saving a mother but for taking her life was too abhorrent to her.

"Hey", Suvaid appeared to have a brainwave. "Why can't you control the time of labor? What if you induced labor at the same time that I induce panic?"

"What? With like Aloe vera?"

"Yes. We may then be able to use the chaos of the crowd to our advantage".

"I don't know. Where will we even find the herbs?"

"Leave that all up to me" Suvaid roared in a severe voice. "Tonight, I will leave a bundle of Aloe vera and Jujube seeds in front of Mother Amu. Come back to the temple tomorrow morning and pick it up. At midday, powder the Jujube seeds and make a philter adding the Aloe vera pulp to it. Serve it to both pregnant women. Don't worry, they won't complain. It tastes quite good".

"Stop with ordering me around", Jufen retorted. "You may be Suvaid, the fortunate, the son of Grand Minister Vaid. But, I am Jufen, the mother of Great Warrior Chetu".

"I apologize for my tone", Suvaid conciliated. "Since we are so near to our target, I get a little excited. But listen. If you do that by evening of day after tomorrow they are guaranteed to go into labor during the night. When the queen goes into labor, they will likely send Vika and a few others to fetch Seeress Groot. I will create a blockade to ensure that the Seeress does not arrive until it is too late. I will also create diversions so the King, along with most guards, will leave the castle. So, you will be the sole midwife in the middle of the night in a castle with two women going into labor. Use that authority! Order people around and send them on errands to ensure you are alone with the queen".

Jufen nodded with a resigned determination. "I will pick up your herbs from the temple and will serve the philter to both Mali and the queen tomorrow everning. You will create a distraction to pull the king and most others out of the castle. I will dispatch whoever is left on some errand or other. After she delivers the baby, I will kill the queen. For Kunduj. And for my Chetu".

"No. First for our Chetu. Only second, for Kunduj" Suvaid replied pointedly.

Suvaid and Jufen departed from the top side of the temple.

Jufen, as Chetu's mother, was committed to the plan. "If I don't avenge Chetu, how can I live with myself?" she thought. But as a midwife, she was deeply conflicted. "Am I not as responsible for the mother as I am for the baby? How can I live with myself after killing a mother in labor?"

The contradiction was too grave and Jufen resolved that this was to be the end of her life. Once this dreadful deed was done, she would bid good riddance to her wretched life: Chetu, dear! I will see you in a few days days, after committing a valuable service to Kunduj.

Ж

Next night, Suvaid was resting under the shade of a Chir pine in the temple compound. He was tense and excited about what was to happen the next night when he noticed Jufen walk in.

"Did you not find the bundle I left?" Suvaid asked anxiously, as soon as she neared.

"Yes, I found it", Jufen replied. "I saw that you already powdered the jujube seeds; it was one less thing for me to do. And you included a chalice of honey which made the drink more palatable".

"Wait", Suvaid interrupted. "You already gave it to them?"

221

"Don't worry, I did not add the aloe vera yet. I just wanted to get them used to getting a drink from me".

"Good thinking. Any complaints?"

"No. That poor girl Mali even thanked me for a delicious drink. I told her that pregnancy increases one's appreciation for it. The queen also liked it. But it had to go through Choon, who insisted on tasting it first before giving it to the queen".

"Sounds like your idea worked. Now there will be less scrutiny tomorrow. So, not to be untactful, but why did you come back here?"

"What is it to you?" Jufen retorted. "This is a temple, is it not? Can't I just visit Mother Amu?"

"Sorry, I didn't mean it that way".

"Yes you did!", Jufen hissed. "Very easy for you to say: just do your job and I'll do mine. When all you have to do is bring some herbs while my job is to kill the queen. A queen who is always under protection and now doubly so".

Her resentment stung Suvaid. He waited a few moments and then said in a low voice.

"You think my job is easy? Don't you remember all the misinformation I talked about. You think planting that is easy? I stopped counting the number of times I have shuttled between Kunduj and here – I am developing blisters on my feet. Youthink that is easy? But that is nothing compared to tomorrow. I am going to have to put my Kaidbar title to a full test: let's see how much misfortune I can handle. Believe me, if I cannot ward it all off, tomorrow will be the last day of my life".

"Why? What are you going to do?"

"Better to not tell you. The less you know, the better. Suffice it to say, I have a busy day to ensure that almost everyone leaves the castle by nightfall".

"My resolve is flagging", Jufen confessed. "A midwife like me should not be complicit in the murder of a mother in labor. Enough women die in labor without such treachery".

"I know. But don't think of Nuri as an ordinary mother in labor. She is not. She is a queen bent on bringing ruination to our beloved Kunduj. And she is the one that caused our loved ones to be humiliated and killed".

"Hmm"

Suvaid used the method of applying maximum pressure by leaving Jufen with total free choice.

"Well, I am clear about my duty, Jufen. And I am going to get it done. The castle will be empty by nightfall tomorrow. I may die in the process, but I will get it done. Then killing the queen won't be as challenging as it looks now. But, it is up to you to decide what your duty is".

"How can you be so sure about your duty?"

"Because", Suvaid raised his voice, "I know what I owe to Kunduj and to my father: my whole life. I know what I owe to Chetu: my heart and my love. I know what I owe to the warriors in the Kundujan army and even the Khetan army: a fighting chance to avoid a needless war. And I know what I owe Bohamir: a chance for peace in His domain.

"I am able to accomplish all that by taking the life of just one queen. I am willing to lay my life down for that gamble. That is how I am sure of what my duty is".

Jufen slinked away quietly, prayed to Mother Amu and left the temple.

Suvaid was unclear whether she was committed to follow through. He would have to go back to the castle tomorrow to keep Jufen on the planned path. It would be a busy day. He lay down on the ground and went to sleep.

13. Tanithai Judwai

Everyone in the castle was nice to Mali. Jufen, the midwife, was especially solicitous; she had brought a delicious philter of jujube seeds last night. Baegan was always around and Vika was just outside the castle, just a shout away. There were fifty eight people in the castle to take care of every eventuality, and her every need. True to promise, any food or comfort she requested was promptly provided. In a word, she was getting pampered.

And yet, Mali wanted to go home. This was the Queen's castle and the Queen's pregnancy was understandably paramount. Despite everyone's best intentions, Mali felt secondary. If she went home, she would be the only pregnant woman around and she would be everyone's primary concern. Nevertheless, because Jenon was away, she was scared to go back home.

Physical discomfort of full term pregnancy made her wish that the baby would be born soon. Emotional discomfort of being away from her husband made her wish the pregnancy would go on just a little longer. Just till these political shenanigans were finished and Jenon was back; hoist that physical discomfort on a trident!

Her physical discomfort must have won the argument because Mali's labor pains began before midday causing considerable hubbub in the castle. Upon hearing the news, Jufen felt relieved that this happened without her having to induce labor. King Mayun dispatched Vika and three other guards to fetch Seeress Groot. The queen asked Jufen to stay with Mali and Baegan.

"But your majesty", Jufen protested. "My place is by your side; you may also go into labor".

"Well", the queen reassured her, "I am not yet in labor. Choon Ti, who was a midwife long ago, is adequate for now. Anyway, there is plenty of help to go around. And in a few hours, Seeress Groot will be here".

Jufen bowed in agreement. Somehow, that exchange added to Mali's uncomfortable feeling of being secondary. She wished that Mother Groot would get there soon.

After one of Mali's contractions subsided, Baegan

mumbled that she needed water and left. She used the Khet-specific slang of "needing water" meaning going to the women's area outside the castle to answer Nature's call. After a few moments Jufen also left saying she needed to run an outside errand. "Running an outside errand" was a Kundujan euphemism, also for answering nature's call.

Mali was versed enough in both that she understood both women. With a linguist's delight, she wondered whether Baegan and Jufen would have understood each others expressions.

After a while, which felt altogether too long, Baegan came back looking concerned.

"You look worried. Is something wrong?"

"Even in your labor pains", Baegan said affectionately, "you notice that I look worried?"

"What's wrong?"

"I just saw Jufen talking to a young man", Baegan whispered. "He is not from the castle; I don't think he is even from Khet".

"Well, we know Jufen is not from Khet. So, maybe she met an old acquaintance".

"I suppose".

"What were they saying?"

"I don't know", Baegan replied. "With this storm approaching, there was a lot of rustling and I could not hear their words. But the way they were talking, looking around surreptitiously and making several gestures toward the castle, left me very uneasy. I wish Vika would get here soon and bring Seeress Groot."

"You and me both" Mali murmured. "Maybe there is an innocent explanation. Let's ask Jufen when she gets back".

"We could" Baegan conceded reluctantly.

"Wait! Jufen said she was going for an outside errand".

Baegan gave her an empty look.

"It means going to the women's area", Mali helpfully supplied.

"No", Baegan hissed emphatically. "She did not step foot there. She had a long conversation with this man and came right back".

"Hmm", Mali was worried. "I wonder why she would lie?"

"I know!" Baegan sounded exasperated.

"Don't worry, I am back!" Jufen said as she re-entered the room. "Sorry it took me so long".

"That is alright", Mali said, pretending a nonchalance that even Jenon would have been proud of. "After all, this is a very busy time in the castle. You probably had to meet someone".

"No, no meetings", Jufen said, protesting a bit much. "I just went to an outside errand and then just now gave a jujube philter to her majesty. Would you like one, dear?"

"No, I am fine ..unnggggg!" Mali squealed as the next set of contractions hit her. Jufen and Baegan sat to her two sides holding her hands.

When her contractions subsided, Jufen patted Mali on her hand and stood up. "What about you, Baegan?", she asked. "I have more jujube powder and am going to make a philter. Would you like me to get you a drink?"

"Sure".

As Jufen left the room, Baegan eagerly turned to Mali and said: "Now we know she is lying. I wonder why".

"I am scared. I wish we had never come to this castle. Where on earth is Vika?!"

Baegan just looked worried.

"We need something to defend ourselves", Mali said. "I wish we brought my bow and arrow from home! Perhaps we can get something from the armory here."

"It is empty", Baegan declared. "I accidentally went there last night, just walking around the castle. There are too many soldiers around and they are all armed to the teeth, ready to defend the queen. Looks like they are also expecting some trouble. The arms have all been distributed".

Mali looked crestfallen. Baegan reassured her: "Don't worry. I am here; I won't let anything happen to you or the baby."

"Perhaps we could just go home".

"No" Baegan said sagely. "Your labor pains have begun. It would be dangerous for you to walk home now. Besides, Vika and the Seeress would come here. And the Seeress might not even come to our home if the queen goes into labor in the meantime. I'd have to get Kuni's wife home to help midwife you. It is not a good idea to do all this in the middle of labor".

"Hmm", Mali said thinking. "Perhaps you could go home ...".

"No way. I am not going to leave you, in the middle of labor".

Baegan fell silent as Jufen returned. She bowed with an elaborate flourish and offered Baegan a chalice.

"Your jujube drink, milady!"

Baegan nodded with an embarrassed smile and mumbled "Thanks". It was hard for Mali or Baegan to imagine that Jufen, this kindly and jovial old woman, could somehow harm Mali or the baby. Mali turned to Jufen and asked:

"So, how long do you think it will be, before I deliver? Will Mother Groot get here before then?"

"Probably another six or seven hours", Jufen smiled. "Don't worry. Whether the Seeress gets here or not, you will have a baby at your breast before the sun comes up again".

Suddenly, there was commotion outside and a maid popped in to announce that labor pains had begun for the queen as well. Still, Jufen stayed by Mali's side and held her hand reassuringly.

"How do you feel, Baegan?" Jufen asked.

Baegan felt uncomfortable. It was a strange question to ask Baegan when Mali, who was in labor, was in the same room. Baegan replied dismissively "Oh, I am fine!"

After the next contraction had come and gone, Jufen left again, saying "I will be right back".

"She is vexing me", Baegan whispered to Mali. "Did you see the way she was observing me? Asking me how I was and ..."

"Wait", Mali interrupted. "Do you feel well enough to follow her to see what she does?"

"But I don't want to leave you ..."

"I'll be fine" Mali interrupted again. "Go, or you may not find out where she went". Baegan hesitated and Mali added forcefully: "Go! Now!"

Baegan quietly left and was gone for about fifteen minutes. Mali had one set of contractions come and go in the meantime. She quietly bore it but then started to get deeply anxious and a little scared at being alone. She was about to call someone else for help when Baegan hurriedly came in and sat next to her heaving a bit breathlessly.

"What happened? Are you ..."

"Shh", Baegan interrupted. "I'll explain later. I'm going to pretend to be sleepy when Jufen gets here. Don't be afraid, I am not actually sleepy".

"Yes, but..."

"Later" Baegan interrupted again just as Jufen came in. But right behind her was one of the Queen's maids.

"Jufen!", she cried. "There you are! Mother Choon wants you in the Queen's chamber right away".

Jufen turned to Mali, who nodded to her to say it was OK. Baegan, yawning expressively, waved her away.

"We'll be fine, go! I can keep Mali company. Go find out if all is well with the Queen".

Jufen left with the maid and Baegan related what she saw in a jumbled hurry.

"She met the same man again, this time in the backshed. They probably would have met outside but I think Jufen wanted to avoid getting wet in this rain. Anyway, I know they are planning something bad. I didn't clearly catch his name. Something like Gyde Par.."

"You mean Kaidbar? It is a Kundujan name that means one who defeats misfortune."

"Yes, that's it! He kept boasting that his luck is still holding. He said his plan would empty the castle in the next fifteen minutes. He told her, er Jufen, to use osilla to sedate the rest and then 'finish it'. They never said what 'it' was but it did not sound like a happy thing. She told him that she had added osilla to my jujube drink. She thinks it will make me sleepy but, osilla has never had any effect on me. Now I don't want Jufen anywhere near you. I can midwife you myself".

"But, that is not enough ...unnnnng!" Mali stopped as another set of contractions hit her. After they subsided, she continued: "We have to help the queen. We can't let Jufen to harm her. The queen would be very vulnerable, especially if they are emptying the castle. Go out and try to tell the King that some conspiracy is going on and that he should not leave the castle".

Ж

He assured himself that he was Kaidbar. It would be easier to steal a ruby stuck in the teeth of a live crocodile than to molest his luck. Suvaid was confident of that.

When Vika and a few others went out to Seeress Groot, Suvaid followed them to the cloister. When they started back, he tricked them into a trap he dug in the ground. This late at night, no one would happen by to come to their rescue. They would probably not be harmed but there was no way any of them could get out of the trap before sunup the next day. His luck seemed to be steering his plan beautifully.

He told himself he was Kaidbar. It would be easier to part a mother bear from her cubs than to part him from his luck. Suvaid was positive about that.

Suvaid next turned to their ambush strategy with three sets of guards. These were positioned, one behind the other between the castle and the probable landing point for the Kundujan army.

And then there was a fourth set of soldiers about a kos south-east of the castle. They were the Fire Cluster, ready with torches to start a forest fire and destroy whatever Kundujan troops made it through the three ambushes. The strategy looked strong, even against a much larger force. But it was pitifully mis-guided against a non-existent attack.

He told himself he was Kaidbar. It would be easier to foil a plot by a nest on its own resident birds, than to foil his plan. Suvaid was convinced of that.

After stranding the Seeress and others, he went first to the outermost layer of guards. He told them that he was a messenger from Minister Byram with a warning that an invasion was coming from Kunduj tonight. Then he went to the castle and let the king know that he was deputized by Byram to inform him that the invasion force was even larger

229

than originally thought and the Fire Cluster must be reinforced. Mayun personally led the remaining guards to the Fire Cluster.

He told himself he was Kaidbar. It would be easier to storm a fortress on an island surrounded by stormy seas than to breach his plan. Suvaid was sanguine about that.

Soon after Myun left the castle, the skies opened up. A cloudy and windy day suddenly turned into a stormy night with incessant rain as if someone had upturned pots full of water.

Suvaid next met Jufen and gave her twenty doses of osilla and told her to use it to put whoever was still in the castle, to sleep. That was poetic justice because these Khetans had used the same drug to incapacitate King Yuda during the attempted abduction. Jufen refused to use osilla on the queen before delivery as it could harm the baby. Suvaid was OK with that because he also wanted the baby to be born safely. He had bigger plans for it.

With the castle almost empty and those in the castle drugged, he was sitting pretty. He had to work hard on Jufen to reassure and convince her to stick to the plan. Still, she was a good accomplice; conflicted about the mission but committed to it.

He told himself he was Kaidbar. It would be easier to squeeze a rock to extract oil than to squeeze his plan to extract failure from it. Suvaid was self-assured about that.

His plan worked beyond his best hopes because Mayun himself joined the Fire Cluster. Suvaid did not know it but Mayun also missed Baegan's warning about Jufen. Baegan tried to warn the five guards left in the castle but she found them already in an osilla-induced stupor.

He knew he was Kaidbar. It would be easier for a single swordsman to repel a locust swarm than for a whole army to repel his lone attack. Suvaid was blindly presumptuous about that.

Suvaid was unaware that Baegan had seen his meetings with Jufen. Nor that she was resistant to osilla. Nor did he know that Baegan actually heard portions of his second conversation with Jufen. He was oblivious to these chinks in his armor of good fortune.

He reiterated to himself that he was Kaidbar. It'd be easier to separate water from diluted milk than to separate him from his victory. Suvaid was fearless about that.

Unaware that his armor of good luck has some chinks and that his accomplice now had an antagonist, Suvaid was patiently standing in the pouring rain at the west-end of the castle, just outside Queen Nuri's window. He had used the past hour of the night to arrange hay bales in the backyard as make-shift stairs. When the queen delivered the child, he would jump into the room and abduct the baby. If Jufen failed to kill the queen, he would fulfill that too.

And then he would run out the window into the storm, use his hay bale stairs to jump over the wall and run. Even if anyone was awake in the castle, it would be difficult for them to follow him on this dark and stormy night. Within an hour he would be floating downstream on the little no-name stream which merged into the Hamal river flowing in rapid currents toward the West. It brought a smile to his face when he realized that he was using exactly the same tactics these Khetans had used in King Yuda's abduction. Kunduj, under his father, had foiled these tactics but these Khetans would fail miserably in anticipating, let alone countering his.

He was certain that he was Kaidbar. As surely as a mountain would outlive a man, equally surely his fortune would outlive this night. Suvaid was proudly confident of that.

Ж

He shouldn't have been so proud; the antagonist to his plan was very much on-site and belonged to a formidable class: an ordinary woman. The extraordinary power of ordinary folks is dangerous because it is so well hidden. When Baegan realized that the king was gone and that all others in the castle were drugged, she knew it was entirely up to her to stop Jufen.

Baegan came back to Mali's labor room and told her all she found out. Mali was very worried but Baegan reassured her calmly: "I will find out what she is planning and will stop it".

Over the next hour, Jufen shuttled between the Queen's chamber and Mali's room. Since the queen seemed to be hours behind Mali, it seemed that Jufen might be able to attend both women if Seeress Groot did not get in on time. This suited Jufen's plans just fine.

But after the first hour, Queen's labor progressed with precipitate haste and it was unclear who would actually deliver first. Jufen also began to worry because Baegan was up and alert. Luckily, Baegan told her to stay with the Queen and that she can look after Mali. That worked well for Jufen as it would keep the lone alert person in the castle out of the queen's room.

As Mali's labor progressed, neither Baegan nor Mali had the time to spare a thought for the queen.

Suvaid was waiting right outside the Queen's window like a mongoose waiting to pounce on a snake. Listening to some of the chaos inside, he smiled. Both labors going on at the same time was good for him. The increased confusion gave him great cover, just as much as the dark clouds and rain. Kaidbar was mighty pleased with his luck and felt confident he could complete his plan and slink away with the prince. Such confidence is self fulfilling because it begets more luck.

As if to shake that confidence, the rain suddenly stopped. Exemplifying how fast spring clouds move, the sky started to clear rapidly. Within minutes the sky was crystal clear and a bright full moon was visible in the sky. Suvaid realized that he was now exposed and vulnerable; he would be visible to anyone looking out any window on the west-side of the castle. So, he moved away from the queen's window to hide in the bushes of a large himalayan yew. He was still within the castle's backyard and could get to the Queen's window in about a minute. So, if this setback caused him to question his luck, he did not dwell on it.

Queen Nuri's situation was getting more complicated. Apart from the precipitate speed of her labor, the baby appeared to be presenting in breech position. She had been worried ever since Mayun had come in to tell her that he was going out to personally supervise the Fire Cluster.

The relentless storm outside and the lack of personnel inside spooked Nuri further. She worried about why Seeress Groot had not yet arrived. Since her labor started with precipitate haste, the pain had been high; the lack of a significant break between contractions left her exhausted and weak.

Suddenly, Choon pointed out the window. "Look Nuri Niang! The rain has stopped, the sky has cleared up. We have glorious moonlight. It means the Gods want a clear view of the prince's birth. It is a wonderful omen".

In spite of her exhaustion Nuri smiled brightly and hoped that this meant the fortune of night was turning her way.

About ten minutes after the emergence of the moon, final contractions began for both Mali and Queen Nuri. There was still no sign of Seeress Groot. Almost everyone in the castle had long ago slipped into slumber. Jufen was midwifing the queen with a little help from an extremely drowsy Choon. And Baegan was single-handedly midwifing Mali. They say that when a baby soul decides to leave the mother's womb, it creates such a frenetic environment that all other plans, good or evil, are necessarily put on hold.

So, in Mali's labor room, there was no thought about the queen's welfare. Baegan was urging Mali to push and Mali was gritting her teeth and pushing hard.

In the queen's chamber Jufen had almost forgotten about her mission. The queen glanced to her left and wondered why Choon was dozing at this time. Jufen sternly told her to not worry about old Choon who was "just old and sleepy" due to the lateness of the night. She told the queen to focus and push. She may be the queen, but she was still a mother in labor. So, Nuri complied and pushed.

At the Fire Cluster, King Mayun stood with his commander and a contingent of about thirty men. They were pretty confident about blocking any portions of the Kundujan invasion that made it through the ambushes. However, once the clouds cleared and the moon came out, Mayun grew less and less confident that an attack was imminent. He started to suspect that this was a false alarm and worried that he had emptied the castle, leaving it vulnerable. Just then, a group of men came toward him Byram in their midst. Byram quickly confirmed the king's suspicion.

"Your Majesty! It was false alarm. We mistook a boisterous group of army men going on a pilgrimage for an invasion. There is no invasion. We just watched them float past the fern forest singing hymns for Bohamir. Why are you personally out here in the middle of the night?"

Mayun ordered them back to the castle: "Tell me more later. First, let's head back to the castle. I am afraid we left it vulnerable".

At the moment they started to run back to the castle, Mali delivered a beautiful baby boy and set her head down with exhausted laughter. Simultaneously, queen Nuri also delivered a baby boy and she fell back on her bed, too exhausted from her precipitate labor to laugh. Choon was too deep in slumber and was not awakened even by child birth.

"It's a boy!" Baegan announced excitedly and put the baby, with all its messy secretions, on Mali's breast. His cry was vigorous and it was the sweetest music to Mali's ears who held him gently like a basket of flowers. They heard another cry - equally vigorous from the other end of the castle.

Mali urged Baegan: "Your work is done here. Please go and ensure that the queen is alright".

"No, not yet", Baegan smiled at Mali's naivete. "I still need to deliver the placenta and cut the cord".

Kuni's wife, who had delivered more babies than she could count, had once told Baegan that leaving a piece the placenta undelivered was very dangerous for the mother. So, without rushing and without getting distracted about the queen, Baegan took the next several minutes to carefully deliver the placenta and cut the cord with a clean, sharp gal pihiya.

In the queen's chamber on the other hand, Jufen was eager to separate the baby from the mother. So, she quickly cut the cord and announced the arrival of the baby boy: "Khet now has a new prince, your majesty!"

She put the baby on the chest of the exhausted queen. Still conflicted about whether to kill the queen, she went back to deliver the placenta. Just after, she gathered her courage and decided it was the right time for her dastardly act because the queen was exhausted and preoccupied with the baby. But just as Jufen gripped the gal pihiya in her hand the queen cried out.

"Jufen! The baby is slipping".

In her exhaustion, the queen did not hold the baby

right and he was slipping from her hands. Jufen dropped the gal pihiya and took the baby away. She wiped the child clean, set him up in the soft basket specially made for this purpose and covered him with a soft yellow cloth.

When she went back to the queen, the gal pihiya was right there. Jufen picked it up and raised it high over her head. But before she could bring it down and stab the queen, Baegan rushed in and tackled her down to the ground yelling: "Stop it. What are you doing?"

The queen, awakened by the commotion, watched in utter shock as the two elderly ladies were wrestling and trying to get a hold of the gal pihiya which was lying on the floor.

"I have to!", Jufen was saying. "The queen is the reason that my beloved daughter Chetu is dead. Vengeance shall be mine!"

Their noisy wrestling was evenly poised. The queen, exhausted by her precipitate labor, was not able to get off the bed or join the fight.

Mali, who was gaining strength by the minute, came rushing through the door. She had seen two maids unconscious outside queen's chamber and saw that Choon was unconscious in the chamber. That made her furious at Jufen for her deplorable deceit. For a trusted midwife to plot harm during labor was beyond repugnant. She saw that Jufen had gotten the upper hand and held the gal pihiya in her hand. Mali wanted to intervene but she had a baby in her arms. She quickly set him down in the only safe place she could see: in the basket, right next to the prince.

Then she ran into the wrestling, shoving Jufen back with her shoulders while forcefully punching down on her wrist. The gal pihiya cluttered to the floor, Baegan was pushed aside and fell, face down, on the queen's soft bed while Jufen fell back on the hard floor landing rough on her bottom. Mali, her fury not yet abated, picked up the gal pihiya, and slashed Jufen's shoulder with it.

There was shock in Jufen's eyes as she looked behind Mali and stuttered in a desperate voice: "The babies! He is stealing the babies! ..."

All the women turned and saw that Suvaid had jumped in through the window, had picked up the basket with both babies and was jumping out. Mali, Baegan and Nuri desperately lunged at him but they were left holding just the window as Suvaid jumped out and ran toward the back wall.

Mali threw the gal pihiya in her hand toward him. But there was more desperation than aim in the throw. It gashed Suvaid on the back of his thigh, then bounced off the baby basket and fell to the ground. Limping, but still determined, Suvaid continued on.

Just then, as Mali and Nuri watched in horror and wailed, King Mayun dashed into the Queen's chamber along with Jenon, Minister Byram and a few guards. With no time to explain, Mali snatched the spear from one of the guards and went out through the window. Jenon grabbed another spear and jumped out after her. That is when they saw in clear moonlight that Suvaid, tired of limping with an unwieldy basket, had taken the two babies out and was carrying them toward the back wall.

Instantly, Jenon felt that he knew about this. This was the scene from his dream. His dream, which started this whole saga, had not indicated an angel bringing the two babies down to earth but this evil person taking them away.

Initially Suvaid had not known that the basket contained two babies. He had just grabbed it and run. When he was hit in the leg, he let go of the basket and went to pick up the baby. That was when he realized there was not one but two babies in there. He made a split-second decision to pick them both up in his arms and ran. It was much faster this way than with the basket.

Suvaid climbed his make-shift stairs made out of hay bales. Finding it difficult to climb on his injured leg, he set the babies on top of one and pulled himself up by his hands; then moved them up the next "stair". He made it to the top and stood up on top of the back wall. He was about to bend down to pick up the babies.

Here he was, standing on the wall, seconds away from accomplishing his mission. Even if the queen was unharmed, he would still steal the prince and have his victory!

With no hope of reaching him in time, both Mali and Jenon threw their spears at Suvaid with as much strength as they could muster. Mali's weak throw fell well short and hit the hay bale at its base. Suvaid let out a wicked laugh upon seeing this – there was no stopping him now.

He congratulated himself on being Kaidbar. His luck was impregnable like a fort made of diamond. He was proudly aware of that.

Now, there are those who believe it was at that moment that Kaidbar's luck ran out. There are others who say that he lost it, the moment the storm let up and bright moon light peacefully bathed the castle. Still others go further back and claim that Mother Amu confiscated all his luck when he defiled her temple by conspiring the wicked scheme on the sacred premises. Yet others go even farther back and think his luck was completely depleted when he was forced to pick a reluctant Jufen as his confederate. And then there are those tiresome non-believers who insist that the whole notion that Suvaid was a particularly lucky individual was non-sense and was based on just a handful of coincidental observations.

In any event, everyone does agree that his pot of luck was empty at that moment, when he stood up on the wall, his figure forming a clear silhouette in the moonlit night. With a satisfied smile, he wondered which whoop or war cry would be appropriate when he picked up the babies.

He did not have long to wonder because a moment later, Jenon's strong and unerring throw planted a spear deep in his chest. He fell to his doom on the other side of the wall with his hands empty and with shocked disbelief disfiguring his face.

He fell down from full standing height on the tall wall to the hard ground with a spear piercing his chest. Even as he died instantly, he felt confident that his luck would bring him redemption in the afterlife.

He was Kaidbar. He was supremely confident in his great fortune right up until the moment of his death. Such a mental state is a rare gift indeed.

Ж

Jenon ran to the hay bales and safely brought both babies back into the chamber. Traditionally, names are given to babies on the twenty third day after birth; until then they are referred to by the mother's name. So Mali's baby would be called Malya and Nuri's would be Nourya.

237

But there was a problem: no one had a way to tell apart Nourya from Malya. No one had marked them in any way. If the king was around or if Choon was awake, the new prince would have been gifted a bracelet or an anklet. If she was not in such a hurry to go help the queen, Baegan would have put a flower on Maalya's ear or marked his cheek with haridra.

Given the circumstances, none of that was done. There had been a yellow cloth wrapping prince Nourya which could have distinguished them, but Suvaid had discarded it for ease of carrying.

Baegan explained the glaringly obvious to a troubled Jenon: "The queen is dark skinned and the king is light skinned. You, Jenon, are dark skinned and Mali is light skinned. So, no surprise that both babies have an intermediate complexion. I don't know how to tell them apart".

Everyone gave her exasperated looks which made Baegan bite her tongue.

Nuri and Mali tried to cover up the tension. They fussed over and cooed to both babies and then passed them around to the others. The King and queen thanked Mali and Jenon for their heroic actions in preventing the abduction. Jenon thanked Baegan for acting the midwife at a moment's notice. On the surface, it all looked very civil and happy, but the tension under the surface was undeniable. Everyone hoped that the Seeress would get here soon and that she would have some resolution for the problem. But, no one knew what happened to the Seeress.

The night guards who were drugged with osilla, awakened and felt ashamed for having been hoodwinked so easily; they enthusiastically complied when Byram ordered Jufen to be locked up in the dungeon. Then Byram tried to send them home but no one wanted to leave. Guards of day duty had come and the castle was abuzz with excitement and activity. The story of the previous night was told and recapped multiple times until everyone in the castle knew what happened.

Around mid-day, just as the initial excitement was dying down, Seeress Groot arrived at the castle along with Vika and the three guards. While listening to the ordeal of the night, she examined both the babies and checked on the mothers. Baegan requested her to please find a way to tell apart Prince Nourya from Malya.

A less ethical seer might have simply lied. Knowing that it was impossible to tell the difference, she might have simply picked one at random and crowned him prince. That would have maintained her stature and authority. But Groot could never lie about things like that.

A more powerful seer might have devised some way to examine the bloods of the two babies to decide who had royal blood. Alas, she was not so powerful. So, after much thought and prayer, she gave the shocking, but expected, verdict in the presence of the entire staff of the castle.

"This is not a miracle I can perform. Rock Boha has not granted me the ability to distinguish between these two children. I know of no way to tell who is Nourya and who is Malya."

Then, Seeress Groot asked everyone to leave the queen's chamber so she could do a detailed examination of both mothers. Just then, Byram pulled King Mayun to the secret chamber.

"Your majesty," Byram began without a preamble. "We must do the difficult thing".

"And what is that?"

"Order Jenon and Mali to leave the baby and get out of the queendom" Byram replied without hesitation.

"What?!"

"Your majesty, they are a young couple" Byram replied in a reasonable voice. "They can have other children. Also, Malya would have a better life as a member of the royal household than with a lowly soldier. And finally..."

"Enough", Mayun hissed. "Did you not notice that they are the ones that rescued both babies? If it were not for them, we might have lost the prince altogether. And this is the thanks ..."

"No your majesty", Byram dared to interrupt the king. "The thanks is the enormous wealth that we'll give them so they can live in luxury anywhere they choose. They are not Khetans. They came here from deep in Ivchea; so, they can go elsewhere to set up for the rest of their life".

"I said enough!" Mayun was barely able to contain his fury.

"Are you sure, your majesty?" Byram had the impudence to persist. "Queen is older and has had trouble conceiving in the past. This could be her only chance to conceive and your only chance for an heir. Can you afford to have doubts about who is the real prince?"

"You shall not speak of this again" Mayun said but the fury was gone from his voice.

"Jenon has said several times that he is willing to give his life for you" Byram persisted speaking of it. "He can be pushed into this with the right kind of inducement. If they are not around, you can crown both the boys as princes".

"But would Jenon agree? Would Mali allow him?" King Mayun asked, even as he felt ashamed for considering the idea.

"That is irrelevant, Your Majesty", Byram advised. "This is just an exercise in wielding power responsibly. What is the point of having power, if one is unwilling to use it in critical situations. In fact, shouldn't Jenon be offering this on his own?"

"No" King Mayun said after some thought. "And you will do nothing about this".

"As you wish, your Majesty".

Even though he forbade Byram from doing anything, Mayun was seriously disturbed by the conversation. On the one hand, he found it despicable that his minister would even consider it. How could he even think of separating a new mother from her baby? Just after she heroically rescued the prince!

On the other hand, he wondered if it really was so outlandish. Weren't there many times when Royal families simply "adopted" children from lesser households? How was this any different? Wasn't it true that an undoubted prince, a clear heir, is desperately needed for the queendom? Wasn't it better to disturb one family than to subject the whole country to uncertainty?

Mayun wanted to shake the notion out of his head. But, the poisonous seed had been planted and he could not let go of it. Seeress was still examining Queen Nuri behind closed doors. So he sought the solitude of the prayer room to cleanse his mind.

He prayed to Mother Amu fervently to show him the way out of this dilemma. And to keep him away from straying on to this despicable path.

This prayer by King Mayun to Mother Amu is in the Seesam meter followed by a verse in Aaata veladi.

సీ.   రాలు రువ్విన వాని రవ్వంత కరుణించి
          మధురమౌ ఫలమిచ్చు మావి చెట్టు.
      తికమక పరిచిన తుమ్మెదలకు పూవు
          తేనియ వడ్డించు తగవు పడక.
      అదెపోల శాపనార్థములు పలుకు పౌరు
          లకు గూడ రక్షణ నొసగు వాడె
      రాజని ధర్మ మెఱింగిన వేత్తలు
          నొక్కి వక్కాణించి బోధ సేయ

ఆ. వె.   పుత్ర భిక్ష వెట్టి పరమోపకారము
          సేసి నట్టి పరమ సేవకులను
      దుష్ట బుద్ధి తోడ దండించు ఘోరము
          జరుగ నీకు నాదు జేత తల్లి.

Seesam:
>   *Raalu Ruvvina vaani ravvanta karuninchi*
>   *Madhuramou phalamiccu Maavi chettu.*
>   *Tikamaka parichina tummedalaku poovu*
>   *Teniya vaddinchu tagavu padaka.*
>   *Adepola shapanarthamulu paluku pouru*
>   *niki gooda rakshana nosagu vaade*
>   *Rajani dharmameringina vettalu*
>   *Nokki vakkaaninchi bodha seya*

Aata Veladi:
>   *Putra bhiksha vetti paramopakaramu*

Sesinatti parama sevakulanu
Dushta buddhi thoda dandinchu ghoramu
Jaruga neeku naadu jaeta talli.

Meaning:
A mango tree, with a little kindness,
       presents a fruit to the one
       pelting her with stones.
Flower serves honey to the bee
       that does nothing but disturb her.
Similarly, only the one that looks to defend
       Even citizens who criticize abusively
Is fit to be king: while philosophers learned
       In ethical politics insist and teach so,

O' Mother! Please stop me, with vile tyranny
       In my heart, from committing the atrocity
Of punishing the loyal servants who did me
       the great favor of heroically saving my son.

If Mother Amu was amused that the one with the power was praying her to stop him from misusing that power, she gave no outward indication of it. Apparently unconscious of the irony, Mayun spent some time meditating that prayer.

As often happens in the minds of royalty, he convinced himself that removing doubts about who was his heir was in the best interests of the country. So, the competing interests were not his and Jenon's. Rather he had to weigh the interests of Jenon's family against those of the entire country. If he were to banish Jenon and Mali, he would be hurting himself by punishing dear servants. But he might have to bear that sacrifice for the welfare of the country.

Just when he had convinced himself of that logic, a servant entered the room and informed him that the Seeress wanted to see him immediately in the queen's chamber.

When he got there, the Seeress gave Malya and Nourya

to Mali with some whispered instructions. Mayun whispered in Byram's ear: "Don't let Jenon and Mali leave the castle. No force. Just softly." Byram nodded and left to make arrangements.

Mali went into her labor room, followed by Jenon. She sat down on the bed and latched a baby to each of her breasts. Jenon tenderly kissed her on the cheek and said:

"You look beautiful. And I am so sorry that I did not get here sooner to stop that monster from separating us from our son".

"That's alright", Mali replied with a smile. "Isn't it just like you to come in at the last minute to save the day? I really do hope Mother Groot finds a way out of this predicament. Although..."

"What? Although ...?"

"It may be just because I am breast feeding them, but I love both these boys now. I don't want to let go of either of them".

The babies had stopped nursing. She took them off and set them on her lap. Jenon picked one of them up and said.

"Well, you are going to have to let go of at least one of them! I can't imagine that the Royals would just let us keep the prince. Just pray that they don't ask us to leave both."

"What?!"

"Oh, don't worry. That is not likely to happen. King Mayun, and especially Queen Nuri, would never do that. I was just saying you are going to have to let go of one of them."

"Really? Which one?" challenged Mali.

"You've got a point," Jenon conceded. "But however, this gets resolved, ..."

Distraught voices coming from outside stopped their conversation. They followed the loud voices and went into the queen's chamber, each carrying one baby. Queen Nuri was lying down on her bed and King Mayun, looking ashen-faced, had his hand on her forehead. Nuri smiled weakly and said.

"Don't worry, my brave soldier. Whatever Mother Amu does is acceptable to me".

Mayun appeared to be in shock and unable to speak. Byram took charge and asked in a voice filled with barely contained fury.

"Seeress, how did this happen?"

"Well, childbirth is complicated. Sometimes even experienced midwives miss these things."

"But", Byram persisted, "exactly what did Jufen miss?"

"The placenta was not fully delivered. It appears that a piece of it is still inside the queen. Her majesty is still bleeding. Jufen missed it probably because of all the excitement around that time".

"Excitement that she herself created".

Seeress was quiet.

"Why don't you remove the piece left inside".

"That is what I have been trying", the Seeress replied in an exasperated voice. "Almost since the moment I got here, and ever since I noticed that the bleeding had not stopped, this has been my sole concern".

"Forgive me Seeress", Byram conciliated. "I didn't mean to say you were not trying. But are you not able to find it?"

"That is essentially correct", Seeress replied in a deflated voice. "Or something else is causing the bleeding. I just ..."

"Don't worry, Mother Groot!" Queen Nuri said. "You have tried what you could. I am not afraid, but are you saying that if this bleeding does not stop, I will die?"

"Yes, your Majesty. But I still hope to stop it. I have not given up yet and neither should you".

Jenon and Mali looked on stunned,

"That Jufen!" hissed Byram with venom in his voice. He left in a flash, his eyes red with rage.

Nuri raised her arms toward Jenon and Mali asking for the babies. They stepped forward and put both babies on her chest.

"Now I must ask you all to leave", Seeress Groot said. "Allow me to try some things".

"Wait!", Nuri stoppped everyone. "I have to say something publicly. Call in all the senior maids and servants!"

"Nuri Niang!" old Choon interrupted. "Please let the Seeress do what she wants to".

"Yes Choon ti!" Nuri replied. "But I have to do this before I lose my energy".

Several other maids came in. Nuri called Mali to the bedside and said.

"You have fed both these babies from your breast today. So, you are my new sister. I want you to promise me that you will treat them both equally. These are both your sons. Promise me."

"Yes, Your Majesty, I promise", Mali rushed because Choon was looking impatiently on.

"No!" Queen Nuri violently jerked Mali's arm. When she had Mali's full attention, Nuri continued.

"Both these boys will be your sons. As they grow, they might ignore you, exasperate you, cause you hardship and pain. But promise me you will never give up on either one of them. Promise me, my son will not be mother-less even if I die".

Mali was touched. She felt guilty and ashamed that moments ago, she had wanted to snatch the prince away from the queen. Looking into the queen's eyes, Mali replied in an earnest voice choked with emotion.

"Your Majesty, I can't tell which of these two came from my womb. Even if wanted to, I don't know how to choose one to prefer over the other. But in the future, even if I can tell who is who, I promise you that I will never make any distinction between them. They will both be my sons. As long as I am alive, neither will lack maternal love."

Satisfied, the queen then turned to everyone assembled and made a proclamation:

"Early this morning, Bohamir sent down two souls to this castle. It appears that the souls got mixed up and we cannot say which soul was to go to whom. So, I claim both these boys as mine. Both are my heirs. I appoint Mali to look after my boys as mother, for as long as she lives. Whether Mother Groot is able to save my life or not, Mali will be mother to both. I want you all to witness that this is my wish".

Nuri looked at Mayun who was still in shock. But he nodded his assent to the queen's wish.

"Lucky are these boys. They each have two mothers and

two fathers. I consent to the queen's wish both these boys are joint heirs to this throne".

Then Mayun prayed silently, in his heart: "Oh Mother Amu! Is this your way of preventing me from administering the horrible punishment I was contemplating? I promise, I will not consider it anymore. Please allow my timid girl to live. She is the righteous one, my conscience. Please do not snatch her away in this untimely way".

Seeress Groot then spoke loudly, to sanctify the proclamation:

"The Royal Family calls on Bohamir to recognize that these boys shall forever be: *Tanithai Judwai,* twin brothers from different mothers. This may be the only example in history and there may never be another example in the future. So behold everyone, these two children shall be twin brothers forever, even though each came from a different mother".

Everyone clapped and cheered for both babies: "Victory to *Tanithai Judwai.* Victory to the twin brothers. Victory to Nourya. Victory to Malya. Victory forever to the Queendom. Victory to Queen Nuri. Victory to King Mayun". After about a minute of this the Seeress put a stop to it by raising her hand.

"Now I insist", she ordered. "Everyone get out! I need to try some things to treat the Queen".

The queen held on to Choon with one hand and Mali with the other. She said in a low voice: "I want my mother and my sister to stay with me".

An hour later, the Seeress told Mayun that she had managed to stop the bleeding for now but that the queen's condition was still precarious. The next day would be crucial, she told him.

"What can I do?" Mayun asked.

"Pray, your Majesty", the Seeress instructed. "That is the only thing to do at this time".

"Don't worry, my brave soldier", Queen Nuri spoke in a crisp voice filled with conviction. "If Mother Amu wants me back, she can have me. But I will demand that she give my curtailed lifespan to our sons. They will be fine with three parents and the kingdom will be fine with you as king. If the Gods are coming to collect on my *Niji sheng,* I am ready"

However, just a few moments later, all the conviction in her voice was gone when she gently caressed the *Tanithai Judwai* with intense longing in her eyes and muttered: "I have no regrets".

Story of the Story - 7

I was on my way to work – late one morning after having pulled a late nighter working on the book. I was feeling tired but cheerful that I had finally caught up to where Jalal was in the book. Just as I was thinking about calling him, my phone rang. It was DubDee.

"Hello DubDee!" I picked up the call in a cheerful tone. "How are you?"

"Hi there" she replied in a somber tone.

"Is everything alright?"

She sighed "Jalal passed away last night".

"Oh my God! I was on the phone with him till about eight last night. He gave me an earful about falling behind. I stayed up till nearly 3 AM to catch up. I was just thinking about calling him to tell him that I am all caught up. He sounded completely fine when I hung up with him last night".

"Yeah. His MedicAlert was activated around midnight. When the medics arrived they noted he was alive but unconscious".

"They weren't able to revive him, huh?"

"Yeah. He was still alive when I got to the hospital at 4 this morning. Died soon after".

"I am so sorry DubDee". I didn't know what else to say. "At least you were able to see him".

"His last thoughts were about the book. He again told me to remember that I was Nuri and that it was now my turn to help you complete the book". Her voice broke as she said it.

"You know", I tried to console her, "the portion of translation I just completed established beyond any doubt that Nuri is the noblest character in the book. If Jalal thinks you are Nuri, he must think very highly of you indeed!"

I could hear quiet sobbing from her side. We were quiet for a few moments each lost in our own thoughts. She cleared her throat and spoke up.

"So, may be I am inviting his cancer psychosis into my mind" there was a sad laughter in her voice. "But, I am

going to accept that I am an incarnation of Nuri and take interest in the book".

"I'll send you a copy of our work so far".

"We'll organize a celebration of life service for Jalal a week from Sunday. Can you attend?"

"Definitely!" I replied.

"I'll send you details in a few days".

"OK. For now, I'll block the date".

After I hung up, I called my wife to give her the News.

"Hey" she said cheerfully. "Are you up? You stayed up till very late last night."

"Yeah, I am up and on my way to work".

"What's wrong?" she asked detecting the sad note in my voice.

"Just got a call from DubDee. Jalal passed away early this morning".

"Oh no!"

We were both quiet for a few moments before I replied. "She said that they are organizing a memorial for a week from Sunday".

"OK, let's book plane tickets tonight".

"Right".

"Are you OK?"

"I was way behind him in the translation project. I just caught up with him last night. And now, I don't know when I will even complete."

"How much do you think is left?"

"I don't know – about forty or fifty pages".

"I think you should try and finish it before the memorial".

"What?!"

"I said, I think ..."

"I heard what you said", I interrupted. "But, are you crazy? From now on, translation will be much slower because Jalal has not touched the rest. I'll have to do it from scratch".

"I understand, but you are more ...".

"Also, I am feeling sad. This was news we have been expecting for a while now, but still ..."

"I know what you mean" she interrupted firmly. *"But I think you can channel that grief into something productive. Use the expertise you gained the past years. You said you had vacation days which will go to waste if you don't use them. Take the days off from work! And fulfill your obligation to Jalal".*

"Hmm".

"If you can put this book down at his memorial, it will be a lot more meaningful than a wreath of flowers or anything else".

I called my boss to book vacation days and turned back to head home. And then, like a student during final exams week, I devoted my next week to the book with maniacal intensity.

14. Samra Keledi

"But you are the midwife!" Baegan exclaimed. "How could you contemplate something like this, let alone complete it?"

Jufen was silent. Having just related her story she had nothing more to add. Her eyes were downcast as if she was looking at the shattered pieces of her self-image strewn on the cell floor. Baegan had come down to the dungeon to talk to Jufen while everyone was busy upstairs. She was looking at Jufen across the cell door as if at a caged animal who deserved no sympathy.

"Granted that you lost your beloved daughter, Chetu, to conspiracy by Queen Nuri. I understand that you wanted revenge. But, Jufen! Chetu was a soldier and she was killed in combat. Instead of taking that in your stride, you come here to take revenge on the queen. You call it Pannam Keledi – the third conspiracy. I can even understand that. But coming in as a midwife. Trying to kill her with the Gal Pihiya! During labor!!"

"It was actually Suvaid's idea. Don't get me wrong. I take full responsibility for my actions and I deserve to die. But I am just saying the idea was not mine".

"But you joined him knowing full well".

"No. Suvaid, the Fortunate, probably had it all worked out from the beginning when we were in Kunduj. But only revealed it to me in dribs and drabs. Each step was innocuous in itself. Like moving to Khet. Like getting the midwife job in the castle. Like relaying information from here to him".

"So, you were not to kill her?"

"Oh, I knew we would kill the queen. And the king too. But I always had the notion that it would be long after the prince was born. And they can be held responsible for their cowardly acts. It all came down to this horrible act only two days ago. Even then, I resisted to the extent I could, to not harm the queen before she delivered".

"How noble of you!"

"You don't understand, Baegan! Suvaid the fortunate, was to be my son in law. I always knew he had a slick tongue and could convince almost anybody of anything. But I never thought he would use his skill against me. He called this the

Pannam Keledi – the third conspiracy. Till two days ago it looked good. Like any ordinary conspiracy against royalty. It became this evil only two days ago. But I still went with it".

With that Jufen collapsed to the floor holding her head in her two hands repeatedly muttering to herself "What have I done?"

Baegan was about to retort angrily when Byram entered the dungeon, looking like fury incarnate. "What are *you* doing here?" he barked at Baegan.

"I was just talking to Jufen sir. Trying to tell her that what she did was unspeakably evil".

Byram ignored her response and just said "Leave!" Baegan left the dungeon with trembling steps quickened by the intensity of Byram's fury.

Ж

"Who gave you the authority to execute her?" Mayun asked furiously. "Did I ever tell you that you could punish prisoners without my orders?"

"My humble apologies, your majesty" there was no regret in Byram's voice. "When the Seeress explained how Jufen mistreated the Queen and mismanaged her labor, I was unable to control my anger. I just ..."

"I never gave you the authority to vent your fury at prisoners!"

Byram looked downcast.

"Byram, Byram" Mayun said in a deflated voice. "With this action you have ruined the trust that we developed over years. Do you understand why I cannot tolerate this?"

"I do your Majesty. I should have sought your permission before executing Jufen. But may I explain why I lost control?"

Mayun sighed and nodded. Byram was trying to encapsulate his crime with boundaries to make it seem like it was not as bad as it seemed.

"She deceived me. Personally, your majesty. I am the one that chose her to serve the Queen. She told me a sad tale about being a refugee from Kunduj. And I fell for it. That story was mostly a lie. She betrayed my trust. And she was actively part of the plot; it was not just a matter of being an

252

incompetent midwife. I could not abide that. When I questioned her, she readily admitted to everything. She said it was Pannam Keledi – the third conspiracy. She was ready for death. She almost dared me to lift my mace".

"Byram!" Mayun replied in a controlled voice. "Jufen's punishment, should have been given after an interrogation and a full confession in open court. This kind of killing, in the dead of night, is more murder than justice. And this is just the kind of headache I didn't need this morning when the Queen is still unwell".

Byram was silent. The door to the secret chamber opened noisily and a maid burst in.

"Victory to your Majesty!", she bowed. "Sire, Queen Nuri requests your urgent presence, if you are able to spare …"

"Is the queen alright?" Mayun got up and rushed toward the Queen's chamber.

"Your Majesty", the maid replied, running with the king and trying to keep up. "the fever has gotten worse. Mother Choon and the Seeress both appear very worried. But I have hope. I have vowed a prayer of a hundred and eight lychees at the Amu temple after the queen recovers".

They reached the side of the Queen's bed. Nuri lifted her hand, a signal for everyone to leave the room. While everyone left, the queen requested Seeress Groot to stay by holding her hand. The king caressed Nuri's face and smiled at her.

"Is it true?" Nuri asked in an accusative tone.

"Is what true?" Mayun countered.

"Don't play games with me, my lord. Is it true? Baegan told me that Byram has executed Jufen."

Mayun sighed and replied in a level voice.

"Yes. I just heard the news myself. Byram executed Jufen in the dungeon last night. I was in the middle of giving him a furious tongue-lashing when you called me. He said his blood got boiling when he heard about how Jufen mistreated you. I also spoke to Baegan who spent hours talking with Jufen yesterday …".

"You can't count on Byram anymore" Nuri's voice was weak but her message was blunt and vehement. "You cannot accept his excuse".

"I know", Mayun sighed and then tried to reassure her. "Don't worry, we will deal with him".

"There may not be a 'we' anymore, dear. I am reaping my Niji Sheng Saaban".

"You will be fine, my dear", the king said. "Won't she Mother Groot?"

"It is all in Mother Amu's hands now" the seeress replied with a resigned voice.

"Don't worry, my brave soldier", the queen replied in a weak but determined voice. "I am ready although on seeing my boys, I really wish God would grant me .... But anyway, if I were to die, I know my sons will be well taken care of for they will have three devoted parents. No, my worry is about our people. I can't help but wonder about the wisdom of letting Byram continue in his post. Who knows what he will do next? If he can do this with a prominent political prisoner, how can we trust him to deal fairly with ordinary people?".

"My dear, I completely agree with you" the King smiled tenderly and tried to change the subject. "You just get better and I will ensure he faces your full wrath. As we all know, you may be a timid girl, but your wrath has enough power to subdue the fiercest warrior with a single glance".

"I am serious!" Nuri was not mollified. "Promise me you will banish him".

"But, he is your cousin!" the King exclaimed.

"Which means he is far less important than my subjects!", the queen retorted and coughed due to the exertion. Wheezing, she continued on. "My dear, Promise me. You've honored me by calling this my Queendom. I don't trust him to take care of it. I would fail in my duty if I took care of my sons but left my subjects vulnerable".

"I promise", Mayun said, gently holding her shoulders. "I promise that Byram will be ejected. I also promise that people's welfare will be paramount in this Queendom as long as I live. Now, take rest my love. I want you back. Not just because you are my beloved. But also because you are my most trusted adviser and my conscience."

Queen's breathing got more labored: "Now, I am at

peace. Mother Amu, I am ready!"

As the King held her with tears in his eyes, the Queen breathed her last with the two new-borns next to her.

Ж

"Grand Laushu!" Balu bent down to touch Gramani's feet. "My Laushu, Zvuk Meza, and my shumi, Rasi, sent me to you to learn about village administration".

Gramani was sitting on a swing, which was a small bed hanging by ropes from a beam. Balu sat on the floor, facing Gramani and started gently swinging it.

"Ah yes. Glad to see you my boy", Gramani beamed at Balu. "Rasi is probably the best pupil I ever had. I was very proud of how she took my advice and defended you".

"Indeed Grand Laushu. For that advice to Shumi, I am already deep in your debt before you give me a single lesson. But still, I would be much obliged if you would impart some of your knowledge to me and putme deeper in your debt".

"Hmm. Tell me, did you pass through Khet on your way here?"

"Yes, sir. I spent a few hours there and spoke to a number of people. The whole town was abuzz with the what happened ..." Balu stopped mid-sentence because Gramani raised his palm.

"Wait", Gramani said with a smile, "Don't call me 'sir'. I have been and always will be Gramani. That is what you will call me. OK?"

"Yes, Gramani".

"Now go ahead, tell me all you learned about what happened in Khet".

"I am ashamed to admit it, but it is true. Two Kundujan citizens – that too the son of a venerable minister and the mother of a venerable warrior – were involved in a despicable act. It seems, they called it Pannam Keledi – the third conspiracy".

Balu narrated the story of how the queen was killed during child birth by her own midwife. And how both the killers met their own end. He explained that the story had become widely known in Khet. Queen Nuri, who had gained genuine affection after her Niji Sheng Saaban, had now

255

become even more venerated. Her concern for public welfare was being talked about in exaggerated tones. Public outrage around the murder was growing; some Khetans wanted their king to launch an outright war against Kunduj – though the more experienced ones called that foolish and dangerous.

Gramani was quiet throughout the narration other than an occasional 'Oh!' and 'Really?". When Balu was done, Gramani asked:

"Was there no secrecy around this high profile event? That is a bit surprising".

"No. No secrecy around it at all. Most people seemed to know not just the outlines of what happened but also a lot of details. Apparently, a woman called Baegan, a mid-wife herself, had interrogated Jufen before she was executed. And, being the gregarious kind, Baegan had spread the word far and wide. Anyway, most people in Khet seem to have an opinion about what is to be done in reaction to this act".

"Hmm" Gramani said and lapsed into silent thinking. As behooves a new student, Balu sat silently, waiting attentively for his Grand Laushu to give formal assent to teach him village management. He received it soon enough.

"When Zvuk and Rasi asked me last week, I was not sure whether I should accept you. Whether I have the energy to accept a student at this age. But now, I want to teach you".

"Thank you, Grand Laushu .. er Gramani".

"As repayment for my teaching, I want you to launch a Samra Keledi".

"What is that?"

"Well, they called it Pannam Keledi: the third conspiracy. After the first two were foiled, this third one succeeded. But let's change the story. That was not the third conspiracy. Samra Keledi – The Real Third (one) is yet to come. It is something you and I will hatch and you will execute with advice and help from me and your Shumi".

"Oh?" Balu was guarded. "Whom are we targeting in this REAL third conspiracy".

"All of them, my boy! All the royalty of this region. It has happened too often around here that rivalries between kingdoms – sometimes petty and other times serious – play out in ways that hurt the villages foremost, while all attention is focused on what happens to royalty themselves. Today, you and I are going to plan something that turns that dynamic upside down. We will establish here something that will make Queen Nuri proud. Something that will establish public welfare as a top concern – not just in pious renditions of political philosophy but in real practice. And not just in Nuri's Queendom but this whole region".

"How? Are you asking me to lead a rebellion? Then you should know, I will not betray my King".

"No" Gramani said dismissively. "A rebellion will only make lives worse for the villagers. And no. I will never ask you to betray Kunduj".

"Nor its king" Balu said pointedly.

"I am glad my boy, that you have grasped the distinction between king and country. You know that tradition here in Khiwani is to name members of the royal family after the kingdom as if there is no distinction. So, our king is called King Khiwani. His sister is Princess Khiwani. But naturally, everyone knows they are not the country. Anyway, to answer your concern: No. I will not ask you to betray Kunduj or its King Yuda. I do want you to remember though that as an orphan, you were raised by the people of Kunduj like Talu and Rasi and Chetu. Not by the Royal family. So your first loyalty should be to the people of Kunduj, not its ruling family".

"So, what is this Samra Keledi?"

"We will unite all these kingdoms together under one umbrella. We will create a political structure that will emphasize unity".

"How?" Balu seemed completely lost.

"I suspect that the legend of Queen Nuri will only grow in the near future. We will take advantage of that and will take advantage of the weaknesses of our kings here".

"I apologize Grand Laushu, but I am totally lost. First of all, which kingdoms are we targeting?"

"No apology necessary, my boy! I will lay it out for you. For starters, our goal is to unite Kunduj, Khet, Khiwani and Koka into a single nation. Then, we will try to incorporate Gandar either through diplomacy or invasion".

Balu was so stunned at that statement, he literally staggered back with mouth agape. Gramani just smiled and let him stay speechless for a few moments before asking, "Will you help me make this happen, as payment for my lessons?"

"Grand Laushu", Balu finally said with more skepticism than conviction in his voice. "If it does not involve betraying my king, I would be happy to help an endeavor to bring about such a union".

"Good! I am very happy to formally accept you as my pupil. You will turn out to be an even better student than Rasi, I feel sure".

Thus was born a conspiracy between teacher and student where neither stood to gain personally if the plan succeeded. Indeed each risked the chance of being executed if they were exposed. But the reward was high enough that they pursued it.

Over the next week, in between lessons on village management, Gramani coached Balu on what the probable weakness of each king was. And how to take advantage of that weakness to establish a Saam Raake – a council of co-equal kings. The first target was Khet.

"King Mayun's weakness", Gramani taught "is his love for dear departed Queen Nuri and his new self-image as a just ruler who keeps public interest paramount. We must use that to conscript him to our cause. But his suspicion of fellow royalty is high meaning he would suspect other kings are not joining the Saam Rake in good faith".

"But still, you think I should just go up to him and ask whether he will agree to relinquish his authority?" Balu sounded incredulous.

"Well yes. You should just go up to him and ask. But no – you do not ask him to relinquish authority. You ask him to join a Saam Raake – a council of co-equal kings. Wouldn't he like to be on a council to deal with the kings of Khiwani, Kunduj and Koka through meetings rather than constantly worry that they were going to attack him? Then later, he could even conspire with them to conquer and rule Gandar".

Ж

For twelve days after Nuri's death, King Mayun was in a daze. The whole town came to the cremation on the banks of

258

the Amu and the Seeress spoke heart-felt words about what a wonderful queen Nuri was. Mayun was unable to say anything. It was good that elaborate last rites went on for those twelve days with priests giving him very specific directions on the how to fulfill various rituals. He unthinkingly followed all such instructions like a puppet.

Byram managed day-to-day affairs but avoided face-time with Mayun. That too was good because the king did not have the emotional strength to confront Byram.

Of course, the king did not have to take care of the babies. Mali was doing that with help from Baegan, Jenon and Vika. But, upon Groot's advice, Mali and Jenon made it a point to come to the castle twice a day with Nourya and Malya.

They spent time with the King and told him boring details of what the babies did that day. Mali also gave the king simple directions to hold a baby, or to show them to the Sun. Mayun dutifully did those things too, but without any joy. His lack of a smile or a response was a dispiriting. But Seeress Groot insisted that Mali and Jenon continue with the visits.

On the thirteenth day, it was time for the water drop: ritual for bidding farewell to Queen Nuri. Nearly two thousand people from the surrounding towns and kingdoms converged at the banks of the Amu. At the appointed time, a loud gong was struck and everyone reverently picked up a handful of water from the Amu. Then, letting it slide back into the river, said out loud in unison: "Farewell O' Queen. May your soul rest in peace, even as you protect your earthly domain from the great beyond".

That simple prayer brought tears to everyone's eyes which they refused to choke back. Their tears joined the river on its journey toward the Sea.

Upon conclusion of the ritual, Mayun sat on a boulder, still in a daze. He looked intently at the river as if to see whether Nuri could be seen floating downstream. His reverie was broken when Jenon came running up to him and huffed.

"Chief! Come quickly, He is about to kill him."

King Mayun looked up blankly without any emotion on his face.

"Chief", Jenon said vehemently and with a sharp clap of his hands. "You need to enliven! Minister Byram is back to his old tricks. He is about to kill an ambassador and you are the only one that can stop him."

"What?!" Mayun snapped him out of his funk. "What ambassador? What is happening?"

Mayun stood up and was already walking toward town. Jenon kept up with him as he related the details.

"An ambassador from Kunduj arrived today to pay his respects to the Queen. I am not sure who it is, but Minister Byram arrested him at the town entrance and had him thrown in the dungeon. Just now, I saw the minister get his mace and walk toward the dungeon. I tried to stop him but was not able to. He angrily told me to shut up and leave. I asked him what he planned to do and he said that he was going to kill the Kundujan. That Kunduj was now a sworn enemy for Khet. And that he would strike the first blow by ending this man's life".

Mayun remembered back to his last promise to Queen Nuri. It may have been his imagination but Nuri whispered in his ear: "Hurry up now! He has to be stopped".

When they reached the prison, they saw a prisoner tied up to a pole. Byram's mace was sitting idly some distance away in an indication that he intended to use it in the near future. For now, Byram was punching the prisoner while a guard was pleading with Byram.

"My lord. I think he has had enough. I think you can stop now."

"You stay out of this!", Byram responded with fury as he turned back to the prisoner and punched again him in the ribs. "How dare you plot against our Queen!"

"Byram!" the King bellowed. "Who is this?"

Byram stopped and turned around.

"Your Majesty. He claims to be an ambassador from our mortal enemy, Kunduj. He says he came by this day to pay respects to our beloved Queen. Obviously it is a lie and he is looking to ..."

"That's enough!" King Mayun shouted. "I want you to leave here and go to your home and stay there until I send for you".

"But, your Majesty..." Byram started and stopped upon

seeing the king's deadly stare. He went quietly picked up his mace.

"Are there any other prisoners?" The king asked the guard.

"No sire. Just this one".

King Mayun then told the guard so everyone including Byram could hear: "Take Minister Byram to his home and stay there till I send for you".

"Yes, Your Majesty!"

Mayun made Jenon untie the prisoner who had blood on his face and bruises on his chest. Jenon helped him to a pail of water so he could wash his face. The king then spoke in a dignified voice:

"I apologize for my minister's behavior. Who are you?"

"Thank you for stopping the punishment, your majesty", the prisoner replied. "My name is Balu".

Jenon, taken aback, looked at the prisoner closely. He noticed indeed that this was the same young man he had almost killed months ago. He was wearing more refined clothes and had bruises on his face and chest. But he was the same young man that had been judged and let go from King Pascheega's court. The same young man that was appointed Praesha and Commander of Kundujan forces. What was he doing here?

Balu finished washing his face, came back and bowed to the King.

"Your Majesty, on behalf of King Yuda and the entire kingdom of Kunduj, I express our profound grief at the passing of Queen Nuri, the Righteous. We are deeply chagrined at suggestions that Kundujan citizens plotted to kill her. We assure you that we had no role in this conspiracy and extend our deepest condolences".

The king patted Balu's shoulder and turned to Jenon: "Take our guest to the castle and make him comfortable. I will join you shortly".

Jenon and Balu both bowed to the King and walked toward the castle. King Mayun sat down on the floor in the deserted jail and meditated for thirty minutes on what his duty is in the current situation. His conscience, in the form of

Nuri's voice, whispered in his ear. Mayun resolved that his mission in life now, was to live up to his last promise to Nuri. The Queendom and its people must be made safe from threats: internal threats like Minister Byram and any external threats like those from Kunduj.

Ж

For the first time in thirteen days, Mayun was sitting in his secret chamber. And just like last time, he was involved in an intense conversation with Minister Byram.

"It seems that we have drifted apart in terms of what we want for the Queendom. I find myself questioning most of your decisions. I find myself disagreeing with you on most decisions. To be terse, I think it is time for us to part ways".

"I am the queen's cousin" Byram said in a matter of fact voice. "Now that she is dead, you want to get rid of me? Do I cause you so much grief? Do I remind you so much of her?"

"You are nothing like her!" Mayun said with a hollow laugh. "No, you do not remind me of her at all. Besides, this was her idea. On her deathbed she extracted a promise from me that I would eject you. I have been remiss in doing it these past days because I was paralyzed by grief".

Byram did not believe Mayun. Nuri would not have wanted him relieved of duty. But he did not dare to question Mayun at that moment. Mayun read Byram's doubts about the veracity of his statement and felt that insisting on it would only make it worse. He let the silence extend for a few moments and said:

"We only need to look at a handful of events in the past month to see how far apart we have drifted. When we sent Jenon to observe Balu's trial, your first instinct was to kill Talu and Rasi".

"That was just politics".

"But not moral politics – which is what we will do in this Queendom from now on. And then, you sent word from Kunduj that an invasion was imminent when it was not".

"But it seemed like it was".

"Only because you were looking at it with a preconceived notion in your mind. If you evaluated it objectively, I don't think you would have reached that

262

conclusion. Next, when the two princes were born, you talked to me about banishing Mali and Jenon and snatching their baby".

"What is wrong with that? They should have done it themselves for the good of the country".

"No!" Mayun allowed some anger to seep into his voice. "These were folks that had just rescued the prince. Had just averted catastrophe. They should be rewarded, not punished. The fact that even now you feel the same way, shows that we have drifted too far apart. That we are just not thinking along the same lines. And the fact that I almost got ready to do it, shows that your counsel is going to drive me down wrong paths. Paths that I will come to regret bitterly".

Byram was quiet.

"Finally, this business today of beating up on an ambassador".

"He just claims to be an ambassador. He might be here to create havoc when we are in mourning. How can we know?"

"Not by beating him up!" Mayun replied. "We would know by asking him questions and evaluating his answers for truthfulness".

Again Byram was quiet.

"Owing to your long service, I wanted to give you a full explanation as I have just done. I want you to leave your post. I want you to tell everyone that you are heartbroken over the Queen's death and are going to the south of Ivchea to join a Jangma monastery; to search for some peace of mind. If you give me your word that you will stay east of the Sindhu, I will maintain that story and your name will be taken with reverence in this Queendom".

Byram looked up at the King with shock in his eyes and said "Your Majesty, I don't want to cause you any trouble".

"I am glad to hear it. I'd hate to have to fight you in this uncertain time. I know you are a formidable opponent".

Byram realized he was being appeased and allowed it. Somehow, he did not want to hurt this king even after this dismissal. Maybe Mayun was right. Living in this dinky little village on the edge of civilization was no longer fun. Perhaps it

263

was time to move on; time for him to get back to Ivchea. With the skills learned here on the frontier, he could potentially grab some territory. Perhaps this time he could be King himself.

Besides, if he continued here, what could he look forward to? Now that a prince, rather two princes, were born, he was condemned to a ministerial role for the rest of his life.

"Perhaps you are right, Your Majesty" Byram conceded. "Perhaps it is time for me to go back to Ivchea. I might even actually spend time at a monastery to gain some insight into the right way to govern. And who knows, we might meet again in the future".

"Anything is possible", Mayun replied. "Wish you good luck in Ivchea, Byram. Hope you find yourself a good life".

"Thank you, Your Majesty".

"On your way out, stop at Seeress Groot's cloister and seek her blessings. They will hold you in good stead".

Mayun also hoped that the Seeress might also reveal the Queen's dying wish so Byram would know that he was not lying. Byram bowed in agreement and stood up. The two men embraced before Byram departed. Mayun did wonder if Byram might be planning some subterfuge and decided to keep surveillance on him at least until he crossed the city of Gandar.

Overall, a conversation that Mayun had expected to be difficult, ended on a surprisingly amiable note.

Mayun's next conversation was expected to be a short, easy one: Balu would offer some message of condolence, Mayun would accept and move on. But, that one turned out to be a lot more contentious.

It started out mildly enough. Balu extended his personal thanks for being saved from Byram and then conveyed King Yuda's grief at the passing of "Queen Nuri, the Righteous".

It was the first time that Mayun had heard Nuri referred to as Righteous. And it pleased him. Mayun accepted the condolence and thanked Balu for coming. The meeting should have been over then. But Balu sat silently for an uncomfortably long moment. Just as Mayun was about to dismiss Balu, he spoke in a frustrated voice.

"Your Majesty! What are we doing?"

"What?"

"I mean here in the Amu Valley" Balu said, as if explaining. "What are we doing?"

"You better explain yourself, young man!"

"Yes, your majesty. It distresses me that we seem to be constantly conspiring against each other and not getting anywhere".

Mayun waited for him to continue.

"It began", Balu began "as far as I can tell, with Khet trying to abduct King Yuda and ...".

"You are wrong", Mayun interrupted in an irritated voice."It began when your King Yuda spoke in friendly terms when we arrived at his coronation. All the while, he was conspiring to stab us in the back by invading us".

"Agreed, Your Majesty", Balu readily admitted and surprised Mayun. "One might say open declaration of war and invasion is not a conspiracy but I don't want to object or argue about who started it all. So, let's agree it started when His Majesty, King Yuda, made a plot to invade Khet. You became aware of it and decided to stop it by conspiring to abduct the King himself. That first conspiracy failed.

"We, in Kunduj, thought that the attempt was from Koka. So we conspired to invade and occupy them. That second conspiracy also failed. Then the truth of your role in the abduction got revealed. So, King Yuda was furious and wanted to invade you. But, by then I was commander and my Shumi was minister. We had enough power that we were able to dissuade our King; instead we sent all our warriors on a pilgrimage to Koka".

"Am I supposed to thank you for preventing war? Just to be clear, I think you made a wise choice. Any invasion of Khet will have received a befitting response. And I assure you it would not have been good for you".

"No, your Majesty", Balu replied with a sigh. "I am not looking for gratitude from you and I agree an invasion would have been bad. My only purpose is to list the various conspiracies. Though we prevented war, a couple of individuals from Kunduj plotted a fiendish conspiracy against your queen Nuri, the Righteous. That third conspiracy also failed and those individuals reached their deserved end. But it is a matter of great grief that the great queen still passed away. Anyway, we have had three conspiracies all failures. And nothing's changed".

"It seems to me that Kunduj is the culprit", Mayun retorted angrily. "By your own count, two of those conspiracies were started either by Kundujan forces or Kundujan citizens".

Balu did not respond. He closed his eyes with both palms, looked upward to the ceiling and took a deep breath. Mayun was puzzled; he had expected Balu to defend Kunduj.

"I apologize that I am not clearly expressing the thought, Your Majesty. Perhaps it is because I lack diplomatic experience. Please forgive me".

"What are you trying to say?" Mayun asked with some puzzlement and a bit more kindness.

"I am trying to say that it does not matter who started it. In the end, the people of the kingdoms suffer".

"Perhaps you shouldn't indulge in such conspiracies, then".

"I do intend to refrain, Your Majesty", Balu replied, ignoring the sarcasm in Mayun's remark. "As long as I have power, I intend to refrain. But the recent deposing of Minister Vaid has shown that my power may have a short lifespan. I would like to bring about a change which will last much longer".

"And what is that change?"

"Nuristan, your majesty!", Balu replied in an excited voice. "I hope to persuade the kings of this region to combine their territories to form one big country called Nuristan, in honor of her majesty Queen Nuri, the Righteous".

Mayun did not know it yet, but at a sub-conscious level, he was already convinced of it. What would be a better gift for his beloved timid girl than to name a large territory after her? Especially if it was done with the express intent of improving the lives of people.

But suspicions remained. He wondered if this was Kunduj subordinating Khet to a feudatory status, doused in the honey of honor. However, Queen Nuri had once said that paying tribute to remove the Kundujan threat was worth it. So, Mayun was intrigued.

"And who all do you include in this Nuristan?" Mayun asked, relishing the sound of the new name on his tongue.

"At a minimum, Your Majesty", Balu replied, "Kunduj, Khet and Koka. I learned this idea from Gramani of Khiwani. So I am hoping that we can persuade Khiwani to join in as well. And if those four are in, perhaps Gandar would join as well".

"I hail your audacity, young man!" Mayun replied. "That is quite a tall ambition".

"I hope not, Your Majesty", Balu replied. "Because, Ivchea is ten times bigger that this combined Nuristan. Gramani said that Gandar has changed hands between Nuristan and Ivchea a few times in the past. And each time with significant hardship for the people. With this arrangement, perhaps we can finally be big enough that Ivchea would not dare to occupy our territory".

Mayun found it very easy to to flow along with an ethnic pride for Nuristan in this young man's talk. But his suspicions were not yet assuaged.

"And who would be king of this Nuristan?" he asked.

"Well, Your Majesty" Balu hemmed and hawed. "I think that is not clear. What I mean to say is that it is not up to me. No, I mean. Of course it is not for me to be king maker but ..."

"I think I understand you", Mayun replied in a surprisingly calm voice. "It would be your King Yuda".

"No, Majesty", Balu replied in a low enough voice that there was no conviction behind it.

"And what do you expect? That the rest of the kingdoms would pay a tribute?". Mayun continued in a more sarcastic voice "I do have to salute you Young Man. Within months of becoming Commander, you are looking to make your King something of an emperor".

"Your Majesty, No! It would not be His Majesty, King Yuda".

"Oh? Then who?"

"Your Majesty", Balu replied more firmly. "It would be a Saam Raake. It is a concept Gramani taught me and expressed the view that we all in Nuristan would be better off under such an arrangement".

"A council of equal kings? It is an academic concept – not very practical".

"We canmake it work, Your Majesty. All participating kings would have equal responsibility. Kings of Koka, Kunduj, Khet, Khiwani and possibly Gandar, would all jointly take decisions in a Royal Council. The implementation of those decisions would be left up to individuals that your majesties put in charge. There would be no tribute but the Royal Council may decide that each territory would contribute toward things to do together. Say, for defense against an attack by Ivchea. And ..."

"Who all have already joined in?"

"I hope to get all four, Your Majesty ..."

"You are saying no one has agreed yet?"

"Well, ..."

"Not even Kunduj? Did you not even talk to your own King?"

"Your Majesty, I wanted to ask you first."

"Before even Yuda? Why?"

"Because of Her Majesty, Queen Nuri the Righteous. When she did her Niji Sheng Saaban, she gave me the inspiration to dedicate my life to public welfare. So, it is only fitting that this Saam Raake starts out with Khet, in her honor".

"Maybe you know this. But young man, you need to always stay loyal to your king".

"No question your Majesty", Balu was vigorously nodding his head in agreement. "No one can make me turn against my king. Ever. But, it is my duty to create positive opportunities and to advise my king to take them. That is exactly what I am doing. It will be to King Yuda's great advantage to make this happen".

"So, you don't really have a Saam Raake. You can't really ask me to join it. What really do you want from me?"

"Your blessings, your Majesty" Balu said without hesitation. He knelt on the floor in front of Mayun and looked up at him, supplicant-style, with palms open, facing up and held together. "If you agree to consider this, I can take it to His Majesty King Yuda and try to convince him. If he agrees, then I will go to Koka and Khiwani. I know there will be many details to work out. But if you give your blessing for starting this, I can proceed with the strength of ten thousand elephants".

Mayun smiled and looked with admiration at the earnest young man. "You may be right that this will be good for the people of all four kingdoms. I also think that Queen Nuri would be delighted. So, with some reservations, you have my blessing. Go ahead. Make it happen. Let us create a new Nuristan!".

"Thank you, Your Majesty".

When Mali and Jenon came by with Nourya and Malya that evening they were happy to see that he was not a funk, for the first time since Nuri's passing. He played with the babies unbidden and with real joy. He also made cheerful plans for the future: "I want our kids to think they have three living parents and one guardian angel. Let's work together as a family to raise these boys. I am sure Mother Amu and my beloved Nuri will shower their blessings on them".

Ж

"That is how it happened" Balu concluded. "Other than Byram almost killing me, it was pretty good".

"Good!?" Gramani exclaimed. "That was excellent! At your very first meeting, you have gotten the first king. I really thought it would take several weeks. No, this was wonderful".

"I feel guilty though" Balu said. "I made promises on behalf of King Yuda which I had no authority to make. My own Laushu – Zvuk Meza – got into trouble in his younger days for doing that. And now I am repeating the exact same thing".

"Don't worry my boy! You are going back to Kunduj in a few days and you will tell him everything truthfully. You can tell him this was something you cooked up because of lessons from me. Just present it in the way I will teach you. It will make him think that he did he exact right thing to make you Commander since you are going to do better than Elite Minister Vaid".

"Grand Laushu?"

"Hmm?"

269

"Are you playing on my weakness just as you are teaching me to play on the weaknesses of our kings?"

"What do you mean?" Gramani asked in an innocent voice.

"Because I can feel you boosting my ego".

"Ha ha! Yes of course my boy! But it was not to manipulate you – just to show you that you are indeed on the right track and that I am confident you will be able to complete this mission. Anyway, before you go back, I want you to accompany me to the Full Moon festival at the temple. Princess Khiwani will be there and I want you you to meet her. When you meet King Yuda tell him the truth about how beautiful and politically astute she is".

"That's it?"

"As far as you are concerned, yes. Report everything to him and talk about Princess Khiwani. I am meeting with Rasi at the festival and will give her another angle on this. If we present this to King Yuda correctly, we will have the three kingdoms of Khet, Kunduj and Khiwani together with one stroke".

Ж

Balu was nervous. This was to be the first time Balu briefed King Yuda on the Saam Rake scheme. Would this one go as well as the meeting with Mayun had gone?

Rasi was pleased with him and told him not to worry about King Yuda; they would be able to get him to agree. She knew that Yuda wanted territory. And she had a strategy to convince Yuda that Saam Rake was a great way to accomplish it.

Yuda came in from outside flanked by two guards. "Let's talk in the secret chamber", he told Rasi and Balu as he took off the shawl he was wearing and tossed it to one of the guards. The guards stopped at the door while Balu, Rasi and Yuda walked in and closed the door.

"What's on your mind?" Yuda asked Balu.

"Your Majesty, I have been thinking of a plan to expand your domain. I wanted to seek your permission to proceed".

"Go ahead, let's hear it," Yuda said to Balu.

"We propose a Saam Rake, Your Majesty. We can

270

combine all the territories in the Amu valley under a single power structure".

"Did you just learn about Saam Rake?" Yuda asked with a smile as if to say not everything you learn in Kul works in the real world.

"Yes Your Majesty", Rasi smiled as if poking fun at Balu. "Zvuk sent him to Gramani last week for lessons in village management. Gramani taught him about this. Nevertheless, I think it just might work in this case".

"Well then", Yuda laughed. "How can I disagree with my Prime Minister? Go ahead Balu. How would it increase our territory?"

"Your Majesty", Balu replied "I will try to convince Khet, Koka and Khiwani to join with you in this, so all their territory would be included. We offer them a seat on the Royal Council and tell them that decisions will be made jointly there".

"Won't that dilute my authority?"

"Superficially yes, Your Majesty", Rasi explained. "But as you know, any council will go where its leader takes it. Is there any doubt that you are the strongest leader of this bunch?"

"Hmm" Yuda liked the flattery but appeared unconvinced.

"Your Majesty", Balu continued, "the Royal Council would consist of the four kings. As shumi says, you are the most vigorous of the four and it will invariably fall to you to lead the charge in everything".

"Well, maybe" Yuda countered. "But a young man like Khiwani ..."

"Is more interested in arts than politics, your majesty", Rasi explained. "I have been visiting Khiwani the past couple of months to meet with Gramani, my ailing Laushu. Everyone there thinks the new king is not adept at politics. He is happier surrounded by dancers and poets than by his council of ministers".

"So, why not just invade and capture it?"

"Your Majesty", Rasi replied "his ministers and commanders are still quite capable. Of course we can defeat them but, the idea here is that we will get the same result without the trouble of invading. And we will have the added bonus that his ministers will become our ministers. My plan is to convince King Khiwani, over time, to quietly skip the Royal Council meetings. Wouldn't take much to convince him to go on a tour of Amu Valley to gather together poets, artists, dancers and story-tellers to form a Kul or an arts academy".

"Really?"

"Indeed, Your Majesty", Rasi put in the final word. "Balu, why don't you explain to his Majesty why Gramani even thought of proposing a Samra".

"Yes Minister", Balu replied. "Gramani is worried for Khiwani. He thought if an invasion were to come, Khiwani would lose because the new king is not very capable in warcraft. So, Gramani thought Saam Raake could help Khiwani by allowing capable rulers of other kingdoms to watch over Khiwani".

"Hmm" Yuda was still not convinced.

"But Your Majesty", Rasi said with practiced ease. "Let's not even talk about Khiwani in this manner. Because I have a better way to bring them into your fold".

"What is that, Minister Rasi?"

"You should marry Princess Khiwani".

"What?"

"That is a wondeful idea!" Balu jumped in, realizing that this was why Gramani had him meet the princess. "Your Majesty, I met the princess at the Full Moon festival. She is beautiful and, to hear what everyone there said, very politically savvy. All the ministers were talking more with her than her brother, the king. She will be a wonderful queen for Your Majesty".

Yuda turned to Rasi who smiled and said "He is right, Your Majesty. She is a beautiful young woman and the right consort for a politically ambitious monarch such as yourself. And having her on the Saam Rake would naturally give you control over half of the Royal Council. It is a good idea, your majesty".

Yuda was lost in thought for a few minutes. He was impressed with the unconventional thinking of his new advisers. And they were patiently awaiting his opinion. This was far better than getting lectured to and always having to bow down to Minister Vaid. This Saam Raake idea seemed promising. But what about the other half of the Royal Council?

Balu also was finally feeling relieved. He was still running a conspiracy but he was doing it with his king's full knowledge and involvement. This was much better for his own peace of mind.

"What about Pascheega?" Yuda finally asked.

"He is old, Your Majesty", Balu replied. "It is a heartless thing to say because he is a nice man and he really is Justice Incarnate. But, he has no heirs and he is too old to beget any more. I am sure he is worried about what happens to Koka after him. Perhaps even worried about some people within his court who may be plotting their moves. This will give him a good way out. And we can sweeten the deal by asking him to expand his justice system to the entire valley. That will give enough of a boost to his ego and will be enough of an inducement to make him join".

"Hmm", Yuda said thoughfully. "And then there would be Mayun! He would be formidable. He even tried to abduct me. To topple us".

"He is not the same man any more, Your Majesty", Balu replied. "He just lost his wife. He barely knows who his son is because they got mixed up at birth. We bring him in by promising to call this whole territory Nuristan, after his Late Queen".

"And then we can easily out-maneuver him in the council, Your Majesty", Rasi jumped in. "If he becomes too difficult, we can deal with him. Just among ourselves, two of our citizens already got rid of one Khetan Royalty. I am not saying we want to repeat that but we could, if needed. And it still would be far cheaper than going to war".

Balu was shocked. Did Minister Rasi – his gentle, loving shumi – really suggest that Mayun could be killed? That too, in such a cold-blooded, matter-of-fact way? But then Balu was pleasantly surprised to see that the argument seemed to have an impact on Yuda; he seemed to be coming around to agree.

"That is true" he said looking thoughtful. "So, what would we do next?"

"With your permission, Your Majesty", Balu replied, "I will go back to Khet, then Koka and Khiwani. Let's invite them to send their representatives here to Kunduj ...".

"No", Rasi interrupted. "You go to Khet and Koka. With his majesty's permission, I will send a delegation to Khiwani to propose marriage between our king and their Princess; that would be more appropriate".

"Agreed!" Yuda ordered. "Let's Proceed".

Ж

"You did very well!", Gramani complimented. "As planned, you got Kunduj and Khiwani in one stroke".

"My teacher", Balu replied. "I was taught well. By you, by Laushu Zvuk Meza and by Minister Rasi who is also my Shumi. I am simply using your lessons. Once King Mayun gave permission it gave me enormous courage to think this might actually be possible. And once I started discussing with King Yuda, I started feeling less guilty about it. This is now my king's order – not just a scheme I cooked up with you".

"Good!" Gramani said. "I want you to have a clear conscience about this, because this is a very good thing to do. Alright let's not lose any time now. Go on and conquer Koka as well. Remember: we need Pascheega's adherence to justice. Tell him that if he joins the Saam Raake, that his legacy will continue. That his legendary justice is what people of this whole region need. Including his own people after he passes away".

"Wait" Balu said skeptically. "Is that wise? I thought old people don't like to be reminded of their impending death".

"You are right", Gramani admitted. "As an old person, I can tell you that we don't like reminders of death. But we are also not fools. We know it is coming. So, being able to ensure that something of ours stays on after, is a great comfort. In fact, as I told you before, that is what keeps me interested in this Saam Raake project. I have seen Kings come and go. And many in this region have been real rogues. Doing this could restrain future ones just a little and hopefully provide a better life for the people. Anyway, I agree that unnecessary reminders of death are annoying. But action oriented reminders about what can be done are usually welcome".

With that lesson under his belt Balu made a pilgrimage

274

to Koka. After visiting the temple, he left town to go outside and sent word that a representative from King Yuda of Kunduj requests King Pascheega's audience. In that meeting, he explained the Saam Raake structure and asked the king if he wanted to join.

"You already got the agreement from the other three?" King Pascheega asked incredulously.

"Yes, Your Majesty", Balu replied. "They have given their permission to explore this. Soon, they will come to Kunduj with their ministers to work out the details in this arrangement. On behalf of their majesties Yuda, Mayun and Khiwani, I invite you to this meeting to explore the alliance".

"I don't trust him, Your Majesty", the high priest said from his seat. "This was the same Yuda who tried to invade us in the name of a pious religious observation. This could well be an ambush to kill everyone in one fell swoop".

"No your highness", Balu protested. "This is not true. As you know, our entire army, myself included, has taken a Niji Sheng; we are honor bound to protect Koka. We would never lift a finger against you. And as Commander, I give you my personal word: there is no subterfuge here. If there were, I invite all the Gods to strike me down right now. This is a true and honest attempt to ensure that the kingdoms of Amu Valley, do not fight among themselves but stand together to share in good times and aid each other in bad times".

Balu knelt down and put his palms together and facing upward in supplication. "I implore you, Your Majesty. We can move forward from this mutual mistrust. If we stand together, your temple will be a beacon for the whole region; the legendary justice of King Pascheega will spread to the whole region. And it can continue to function even after your reign ends. We need the sagacity of statesmen like you to establish this. The future of then entire Amu valley is in your wise hands".

"You have not earned His Majesty's trust to ..." the High Priest started to object but fell quiet because King Pascheega stood up. It was clear he had heard enough and was ready to pronounce his decision.

"Young man! The high priest is right. Mistrust exists and is deep. It is not something that can simply be set aside.

We cannot trust you, just on your say so and possibly get fooled again. We know you are honor-bound to protect us, but we don't yet know how much honor you have.

"Nevertheless, your proposal is intriguing and, if it is sincere, we would be interested in joining. So, yes. We will attend this meeting.

"However, this meeting will not take place in Kunduj but right here in Koka under our auspices. All the kings will come here to the temple with their ministers and no armed forces. Our High Priest will conduct the meetings and if there is agreement, Saam Raake will be established. If there is not, everyone will go back. There will be no recriminations from our end".

"Thank you, Your Majesty", Balu happily bowed down from his kneeling position. "This is the kind of wise direction, only you could provide. This will be acceptable to the others. With your guidance, I know it will succeed".

"Don't celebrate yet, young man!" Pascheega said as he was turning away to leave the room. "The mistrust amongst these four kingdoms is very real and very deep. We can't simply turn it into trust at the snap of a finger. We have to devise ways so that any conspiracy hatched anywhere will become known to the other three and so that internal invasions can never happen. This is not an easy task, but let us take the next few months to work at it and make it happen".

Ж

Over the next two months there was furious diplomatic activity with messages going back and forth between the kingdoms. It was as if the killing of Queen Nuri had jolted the kingdoms and goodwill was somehow rising. There were specifically three happy occasions which aided in cementing the ties.

The first such occasion was the twenty ninth day after the birth of Nourya and Malya. It was Full Moon day again. Per tradition, it was the day the babies were to be given names. Mali suggested that the Naming Ceremony take place near their Deodar cedar near the temple in Koka.

Mayun sent word to the three other kingdoms to invite them to the ceremony. The invitations were accepted and it

276

provided a perfect and natural way for the kings to have a summit meeting on the sidelines without formally committing to anything.

Under Seeress Groot's direction, the naming ceremony was held next to the little Deodar, which was still barely waist high. Upon Mali's invitation, Talu attended and said she was honored to be involved. The High Priest of Koka was invited because Seeress Groot determined that it would be disrespectful to exclude him from a ritual happening in front of his temple.

The three parents, Mali, Jenon and Mayun announced the names with great pomp. One was named Heyvanser (meaning animal-lover) and the other Bilikser (meaning scholar or knowledge-lover). Everyone in attendance was invited to pass by the babies, address them by their newly given names and give them a blessing.

When it was Talu's turn, she added on a bit of baby-talk to her blessing. "I wonder what we will do if Heyvanser becomes a scholar and Bilikser a Nature-lover who goes into the forest".

Amidst laughter from the gathering, she bit her tongue wondering if she offended someone because these were King Mayun's sons. Perhaps they were supposed to become kings and warriors. But, Mali gave a full-throated reply.

"Actually, Mother Talu. We hope they both grow to love and enjoy both things: nature and knowledge".

Talu put her two palms on the baby's foreheads and blessed: "It shall indeed be thus!".

After all the blessings were done, Jenon and Mali requested the High Priest to help them name the Deodar as well.

"The tree?! What is your interest in this tree?" the High Priest demanded.

"Your Highness", Jenon replied. "This tree is one we have been observing since it was a mere sapling. It has grown strong and we hope it continues to grow into a magnificent cedar to give enjoyment to all the pilgrims to this temple. We have thought of it as our cedar, just as we think of Bohamir as our god. On this occasion of giving names to our sons, it does not seem right to leave our cedar without a name".

High Priest agreed and they named the cedar Thuloh Roo - literally, "great tree". Everyone then sang devotional songs to Thuloh Roo followed by lullabies for Heyvanser and Bilikser.

When it was Yuda's turn, he picked up both babies in his two arms and played an elaborately choreographed abduction. He returned them to Mayun after a few minutes and embraced him. Then he loudly made a public statement of rapprochement so all atendees cuold hear it.

"I have no hard feelings for when King Mayun tried to abduct me. I think about it in a sportive way, because after all, we did foil that plot. I also want to announce here that I think of King Mayun as my elder brother. So, I cannot be blamed if I wanted to abduct my adorable nephews. No, no. But I won't".

Mayun reciprocated the sentiment by embracing Yuda and again and patting him on the back while all the attendees clapped in applause. On the sidelines of all this merriment, the four kings discussed about the Saam Raake.

It got contentious quite quickly on the topic of naming the territory. Despite having been briefed by Balu, the Kundujan Praesha objected to the suggested name of Nuristan. He said it was insulting to the others to name it after the queen of one of the kingdoms. Why not Pascheegastan after the king of Koka? King Khiwani suggested Khiwa Land after Khiwa the terrible, the legendary Yeti who lives in the hills of Khiwani.

Pascheega, who was silent through much of the argument, stood up on a boulder and had the High Priest hold up his royal flag. The whole group fell silent just like they do in the Justice Hall when Pascheega is ready to proclaim his decision.

"This is a silly topic for us to quarrel about. Let's hope that all our quarrels in the future would be as trivial as this one. So here, when we named these two babies and this magnificent Deodar, let us also dispense with this question conclusively.

"I suggest that it does not matter what is the 'official name'. Most people and places have multiple names. For example Heyvanser will also be called Nourya or Malya to honor his two mothers and will also be called Maayna and Jaenya after his two fathers. Bilikser will also share those four names. So, if a little baby could have five names, is it really a problem if a country has more than one name?

"It will be called by multiple names: the Valley of Amu, Nuristan, Pascheegastan, Khiwa Land, Yudastan and Gandar Territory. It might even be called Bohamir Kingdom or even simply Earth. Let us not get held up on this. Accept all suggested names and move on to other issues".

Mayun was impressed. He stood up and bowed to the King. While everyone expected that he would make a speech himself, he simply took on the role of a congregant and led the group in slogan raising "Victory to King Pascheega". Then the group continued sloganeering victories to Mayun, Yuda, Khiwani, Nuristan, Nourya, Malya, Thuloh Roo.

Heyvanser and Bilikser, woken up by the sloganeering, started crying as if they too wanted to join in. Mali picked them up, turned away from the crowd and nursed them, one at each breast.

Ж

The next occasion for the kings to meet was just ten days later. Through successful diplomacy by Minister Rasi, Princess Khiwani wed King Yuda on the eleventh day of the waning fortnight.

When it was Mayun's turn to wish the couple, he put together an elaborate charade of kidnapping the couple. Then, to everyone's mirthful laughter, he brought them back to the center of the ceremony and said:

"King Yuda said ten days ago that he thinks of me as his elder brother. Here, I publicly reciprocate the claim and wish my younger brother and his lovely bride many years of happy married life. I also want to urge us to make real progress. Let us pledge today that by the next Full moon we will all have agreed to principles that will get Saam Raake implemented".

"Yes we should!" the whole congregation roared.

Samra Keledi! I leave it up to you, dear reader to determine if the killing of Queen Nuri or the formation of the Saam Raake was the real third conspiracy, but either way, a Saam Raake was born. Although aided by a amarriage, this

279

was the first time in history that kingdoms in a region came together other than by invasion. So many events! So improbable! Yet, that auspicious moment did happen. Hail Rock Boha! Nothing is impossible for Him.

The only blemish on this historic achievement was the absence of Gandar. And since they declined to join the alliance, some were already itching to bring it into the fold through an invasion.

Queen Nuri became legendary after her death. This was evident from the way her name started shrinking. At death, she was often referred to as Her Venerable Majesty the Late Queen Nuri, Righteous and Pure. Within a year she was referred to as just Queen Nuri. Around then the visions started. Several young women reported visions of Queen Nuri, usually just before they got pregnant. Several temples, with her as the main deity, were established in Khet. There were a few in the other three kingdoms as well. None of this was done by any of the royalty and none of the temples were really grand. It was just ordinary folks building simple structures with a small, often crudely made, statue of her.

And then her name changed again to Nuri Ma (Mother Nuri). Once that happened, the issue of naming the region was conclusively resolved. None of the other names stood a chance compared to Nuristan. Erudite scholars sometimes showed off by calling it Amu Valley or Khiwa Land but those became descriptors rather than names. The nucleus of the future empire was called Nuristan.

Ж

Jenon and Mali raised Heyvanser and Bilikser luxuriously with support from Mayun's royal house.

Vika was roped back into royal service as Chief Messenger. The number of people and messages going across all villages in the region increased manifold and he was tasked with building a robust system for ensuring secure delivery.

Baegan was happy to see her husband's stature rise dramatically. Though her plan for a long pilgrimage was discarded, she was able to take many short ones, and was happy to partake in the joy of raising the boys.

Once Nuristan was formed, Talu was offered her old job back. Yuda even sent her a message that her old mistakes

280

were all forgiven because they led to the formation of this new country. But she declined saying that she had a new position at the temple which she could not give up. In reality, all she had was a very unofficial position as the "lay priest" to lead the worship about once a week.

King Khiwani was able to indulge his passion and encourage arts throughout the domain. He recruited scholars to collect poetry and plays from all territories including Chada. Several observers claim that it was this effort was very important in bringing Chadans on board. They finally felt that they were getting their due respect, they gave up their resentment and accepted full membership in the Saam Raake, even though the so called civilized kingdoms proved their prejudice against tribals by not giving a seat on the Royal Council to any of the Chadan tribes.

Gramani was happy to see the Saam Raake established and felt his life mission fulfilled. Even though he was disappointed at Gandar not joining the alliance, he told Balu and Rasi to not give up. "Keep trying! They will join within a few years", he said. When he died two years later, the whole territory took his name in reverence and a Kul was built in his name to train diplomats and other royal servants.

It was inevitable that Yuda, the most ambitious member of the four, was outwardly happy but was inwardly chafing at the resrtictions placed on his authority. It took all of Minister Rasi's political skills to hold him back from doing something rash.

"This is the first step, Your Majesty", she would say. "Over time we will pull Gandar in and will consolidate power around you. Then this territory will be so strong, we can move eastward and even occupy Ivchea!"

That was a huge prize. Rasi was able to use that inducement to keep him playing nicely within the Saam Raake rules.

King Mayun never remarried and tried his best to live up to Nuri's high standards. As an opponent to Yuda, he also provided for a certain balance of power on the Royal Council.

When Mayun passed away, the balance of power was disturbed and it was felt by all of Nuristan. But, That is the story for another day.

For now, we can just say mere mortals like us cannot understand why Rock Boha would work in all those improbable events to set up Nuristan. But then also plant the seeds for its eventual end. His ways are always inscrutable to us.

Epilogue

"Phew! We made it!", we breathed a sigh of relief as we buckled our seat belts on the plane. On the way to the airport, I stopped at a copy shop to get a print out of the story for the memorial. As my wife tried to lean back and sleep, she said:

"Good job! Under intense time pressure, you finally finished it".

"Actually", I replied with an embarassed smile. "there is one more leaf. I have its picture on my laptop. I'll translate it once they let me use my computer".

"You and your procrastination!" she rolled her eyes and poked me in the arm.

"No", I said defensively. "I've been efficient with this since Jalal died – not procrastinating. It is just too much ...".

"I know. I am just joshing you. You really did a good job. Proud of you!" she gave me a kiss on the cheek. Then she opened her phone to call our son at college and tell him we are on the plane and were switching our phones off for the next four hours.

It had been an awfully busy week for her at work. She switched off her phone and, adjusting her neck pillow, she shut the window and slunk back in her seat to get some shut-eye.

With just one more leaf to translate, I was too close to the end and too excited to sleep. After we reached cruising altitude, they announced that we could use our electronics. My neighbor pulled out his computer to watch some super-hero movie. I took out my laptop and opened up the picture of the last leaf. It took me several switches back and forth between the image of the leaf and the dictionaries I had on file but, I was done in about thirty minutes. I was relieved that it was a conclusion of sorts and added nothing to the story. I would not have to add to the print-out that I would leave at Jalal's memorial. The last leaf said:

This concludes *Birth of an Empire: Initial Stirrings*, transcribed from an earlier copy by Bada Ravi who was born in Shalya Gotra as the youngest and dearest son of

I leaned back in my seat in exhausted relief that this was completed. However, relief was somewhat incomplete for two reasons. The first reason was that even as I was writing down the translation, the last part of the book felt rushed. I wondered if I missed something. But a double check of the original leaves showed that the rushed story telling was in the original. That last part was more in the nature of an epilogue than a continuation of the story. I could convince myself of that but I could not let go of the second reason that my relief was somewhat incomplete. I wondered where the second book was. The story itself made reference to it in the end and now this epitaph by Bada Ravi also mentioned it.

I decided not to worry about it and simply shut my computer down to get some sleep as the plane hurtled its way to Bar Harbor, Maine.

Ж

The memorial was a suitably solemn affair. A number of friends, acquaintances and former clients of Jalal were there with bouquets and wreaths. Some of the closer ones gave short speeches about their memories of Jalal. Upon advice from my wife, I left the print-out among the wreaths – its while paper sticking out prominently among the green.

We met DubDee just for a brief time during the ceremony since she was busy and also appeared distraught. Toward the end, as we were getting ready to leave, we noticed that DubDee was nowhere to be found. And my printout was also missing from among the wreaths. I tried calling DubDee but got a message that her phone was switched off. My wife tried to ask some of her colleagues – naturally it was her company managing the event – but they had no idea where DubDee had gone to.

Disappointed with the lack of connection, we went back to our hotel room to wait for our flight back which was late night next day.

Next morning we were having breakfast in the lobby and DubDee came into the hotel, spotted us and came to our table. Her eyes were red as if she had not slept.

"I am sorry to have left so suddenly yesterday" she said.

"That is OK. Won't you please join us?" My wife said pointing to a third chair at our table. DubDee set her briefcase down and sat with a nod of her head.

"When I saw your printout, I picked it up and walked out. I stayed up all night reading it".

"So, did you like the book?" I asked her.

"Yes, it is a wonderful story – I can see why Jalal was so into it. And I feel honored that he tried to equate me with Nuri".

She was fidgeting uncomfortably. I thought it was because of losing Jalal.

"Are you alright?" my wife asked her.

"Yes, I am fine. Thank you" she said and then took a deep breath and continued. "There is something I only came to know a month ago. Apparently, Jalal received a package from Haji Pir Basha's nephew last year. It seems that it is the second book – a sequel to the one you have been working on".

"Whoa! Really?"

"Yes, Jalal told me about it only last month and told me to give it you after you are done with the first book. It is yours if you want it. Jalal particularly wanted me to emphasize that he is very thankful. There is no obligation for you to do anything with it. This is simply a gift that you can do with as you please".

She opened her briefcase to show another full set of leaves – about as many as in the first book.

Naturally, I took it expressing my profound thanks to DubDee. So, here I go on my next quest to translate the second book.

I just hope it does not take me another 15 years.